# The Chronicles of Soraya Thenayu
# Darkwood Academy

Christina A. Silva



ISBN: 979-8-5448-8065-3

## DEDICATION

To my wonderful husband, son and friends.
Thank you all for your endless love and support.

# Contents

# Chapter 1: The Thenayu Family

Autumn leaves of red and gold spun in the air, carried along by the cool east wind. Slowly, they dropped into the icy river below, creating ripples that ruffled the former mirror-like surface. They turned occasionally while floating downstream towards the rolling hills and valleys below.

"Mama! Don't those look like little boats?" Soraya Thenayu exclaimed, grabbing the hem of her mother's dress and pointing earnestly at the leaves. Adonia looked down into her daughter's bright sky-blue eyes, a smile tugging at her thin lips.

"They sure do, sweetie," she said, patting Soraya's strawberry blond hair. "You have such a vivid imagination, just like your father."

Pleased with her mother's answer, the young girl skipped a few steps ahead and twirled in the breeze before shifting her gaze over the edge of the cliff. Puffs of smoke billowed up from the chimneys of the houses below.

"Soraya," Adonia said. "We've been walking for quite a few hours now. Would you like to take a break by helping me look for some spices?"

Her daughter's face lit up. "That would be fun!" she cried,

then spun around and scampered towards the fringes of the forest.

"Let's try not to go deep into the woods. We're just going to search along the path!" Adonia called after her.

Soraya nodded from ahead before stooping low to the ground, scanning the bushes in search of familiar herbs that her mother had taught her to look for.

Meanwhile, Adonia found a Willaby tree to rest beneath. Its long, drooping branches swayed in the breeze, the twilight colored leaves rustling a lullaby. Although she kept her eyes open and watched her daughter dart around, Adonia relaxed as a soft chorus of violins and cellos emanated from the tree's limbs.

After a few minutes, Soraya spotted a patch of clover shaped plants huddled together in the dirt. She carefully knelt over them and sniffed the air.

"Mama, what's the name of the plants that smell like syrup again?"

"Fenugreek, my love," Adonia replied. "Did you find some?"

"Yeah! A bunch of them!" Soraya declared proudly.

"I'll be over shortly," Adonia grunted while getting up. Her round belly sometimes made it difficult for her to balance, so she made sure to bring a cane for support. In another three weeks her child would be born, and she wanted to make sure her husband was with her for the birth.

While waiting for her mother, Soraya looked up towards the Averlore mountains that lay beyond the town. Somewhere along those peaks was her father's study. He kept his magic research well hidden from the prying eyes of other Mages from neighboring kingdoms.

"We want the leaves and the seeds," Adonia explained while digging into the soil around the fenugreek and scooping them up along with their roots. "Not only are they good for you, but they have medicinal properties as well," Adonia then placed the contents into an empty jar that was on hand for such an occasion.

Soraya nodded to her mother's wise words. Once the jar was placed into Soraya's pouch, the pair continued their way down the dirt road towards the town. The sun climbed higher and higher into the sky. Large, pillow shaped clouds lazily drifted by in the wind, casting dark shadows onto the hills and treetops.

Soraya took in the serene surroundings and wished she could somehow capture its beauty. As she turned to share her thoughts with her mother, she noticed that Adonia had stopped walking.

"Mama?"

Her mother's red eyes, partially covered by her long autumn red hair, were wide with fear, her jaws clenched tightly together. She cried and doubled over, clutching her protruding belly.

"Soraya!" she gasped. "Something's… wrong..."

The young girl was startled at her mother's panicked voice.

"W-what's the matter?" Soraya had never seen her look so scared before.

"Go… to the village…" Adonia panted, falling to her knees, her breaths turning to sharp gasps. "Ask for help… please hurry, Soraya…"

Her daughter bobbed her head and sprinted off towards the town of Averlore. She felt bad about leaving her mother behind but had to find someone who could take care of her.

For the next few minutes, all Soraya could hear was the crunching of her feet upon the dirt harmonizing with the pounding of her heart. She ran as fast as her little legs could carry her, her mother's terrified expression still fresh in her mind. That motivated her to keep going even though her muscles ached and burned.

Just as she started losing steam, she spotted an old man riding a horse-drawn carriage a few feet ahead. Soraya slowed down, inhaled sharply, and bellowed at the top of her lungs.

"*Heeeeellllp*!"

The horses whinnied as the driver pulled on their reins, slowing them to a halt. Soraya made her last few bounds towards the carriage and collapsed onto the ground. She had never run so fast for so long before, and her entire body was shaking. She closed her eyes for a moment and listened to the creaking of wood followed by heavy footsteps landing with a loud crunch beside her.

"Are you all right, child?" a soft-spoken voice of an elderly man asked. Soraya's eyes met with a worried gaze from dark blue eyes. The man's face was wrinkled from age and his white eyebrows were furrowed in concern.

"My… mom… she's having... a baby…" Soraya managed to gasp in between breaths. "She's… alone. She needs help."

The old man scooped her up and set her atop a seat before settling in beside her. "Having a baby is both a wonderful and terrifying time for a mother," he frowned, using one withered hand to clutch the reins while the other stroked his long silvery white beard in thought. "Take me to her, child, I'll see what I can do."

Soraya only needed to point straight down the path where she had come for the man to crack a whip over the horse's heads to get them galloping.

The trip back to her mother was certainly faster than Soraya had expected it to be. She was grateful, especially when she and the elderly man spotted Adonia clutching her belly and crying in pain on the side of the road.

"Mama! We have help!" Soraya yelled from the carriage seat. Adonia looked over at Soraya and the elderly man with frightened bright red eyes.

Immediately, the old man's demeanor changed. His face grew dark with apprehension as he tugged on the ropes, stopping the horses from getting closer.

"What's someone like *you* doing here?" he muttered under his breath, his hands tightened into shaking fists.

Soraya's mother, though clearly in pain, attempted to reason with the man.

"Please, sir, if you can't help me…" she inhaled sharply. "Then please find someone who can."

The old man scowled, his dark blue eyes and crooked teeth shining through his shadowed face. "If you want help, then go back to where you came from, demon eyes!"

He spat on the ground before twisting around in his seat, roughly picking up Soraya from the carriage and plopping her onto the dirt road.

"Wait! Why are you leaving?" Soraya gasped, reaching out to grab his cloak, but he swiftly swept it just beyond her grasp.

"Get away from me, demons!" he growled, then cracked his whip over the horses. They neighed and thrust themselves forward, the wooden cart jerking into motion with a loud creak.

Stunned, the young girl chased after him but couldn't keep up for long as the old man's horses sped away.

"Come back!" she cried, watching him disappear around the trees. "Come back…" Tears streamed down her face while her mother's screams filled the air.

"Why did you kill me?" Adonia wailed, pointing a finger at her daughter. Soraya shrank back in fear, watching in terror as the skin peel off of her mother's hands and face, revealing porcelain white bones. "I wouldn't have died if you had found someone else to help me!"

Soraya covered her eyes, but instead of seeing the palms of her hands, she found herself staring at a gravestone sitting atop a pile of grass and dirt. Everything else was shrouded in pitch, black darkness. Adonia's rotting skull was partially uncovered from the dirt, staring at her daughter with unseeing eyes.

"It's all your fault," her mother's voice rang inside her head.

The girl covered her ears and cried, "I'm so sorry!"

* * *

Soraya Thenayu woke up with a start. Her forehead was hot and sweaty, her breathing short and rapid. Her hands shook as she searched in the dark for her bedsheets and threw them off. Sitting up, she wiped her wet face with her long sleeves. She often had nightmares about the last time she could remember being with her mother, but this time had been different.

*Was the elderly man real or just part of the dream?*

The girl slipped out of bed and gazed out the large window overlooking the backyard. Her mother's grave was still there, and her skeleton was thankfully not clawing its way out of the ground. The tombstone was covered in a crisp pile of snow glistening in the moonlight. The still night air was calm and serene, and the cloudless night sky seemed to stretch for miles in every direction.

Regardless of how many times her father had told her she had done nothing wrong, Soraya still believed she was responsible for her mother's death. Although she couldn't remember how her mother had died, her father's explanation of it being so traumatic that her memories were suppressed didn't make any sense.

With a shiver, she grabbed for her robe draped over the bedpost and slipped it on. The bedroom was much colder than the warm blankets she had been lying beneath. She took a step forward, but held her foot in the air, using it to feel around in the dark. The girl brushed up against a small lump and carefully moved around it.

Her pandacoon, Yabo, was asleep, snoring lightly on the rug. He was a small flying squirrel with dark red fur on his back and belly, and black fur on all four limbs. His red furry face had large patches of white around his cheeks, nose, and eyes. He was curled up like a cat with his long, bushy striped tail wrapped around his legs.

Soraya knelt down and kissed her beloved pet lightly on the

head before tip toeing out of the dark room and heading for her father's study. The light from her father's lantern seeped through the cracks of his closed office door, illuminating the oil paintings lining the hallway. She crept down the carpeted floor before silently pushing the wooden door open.

Her father's office was lined with shelves filled to the brim with books of all sizes, shapes and colors. Large stacks of papers, strange trinkets from other countries, and family pictures covered his desk. Hanging on the wall was a cabinet with glass doors. Inside were thin tubes and vials filled with brightly colored liquids that glowed at night. They were potions her father had concocted from various plants, but he wouldn't tell her anything beyond that.

Tishva Thenayu was bent over his large desk, writing notes furiously onto parchment paper. Although his golden hair was tied back in a ponytail, there were loose strands sticking out every which way. Soraya knew he had to work twice as hard since her mother died, but she hardly saw him anymore. Tishva always seemed tired, the dark circles under his eyes not only lingered, but grew darker by the day.

"Papa, I miss you."

Tishva paused from writing his letter. Soraya stepped forward and wrapped her thin arms around his shoulders and gave him a small squeeze.

Her father's grayish blue eyes stared at the ink letters he had just written on the pale yellow parchment before him. A single drop trickled down his face and onto the gold whiskers above his lip.

"I miss you too, Soraya," he whispered back. Tishva put the red feathered quill down and placed a weathered hand over his daughter's arm. The two of them sat in silence, each lost in their own thoughts. The red velvet drapes rustled slightly from the cool breeze that had worked its way inside through the small cracks in the frame. Soraya shivered from the cold despite wearing her thick pink robe.

"I had… another nightmare about Mama," Soraya murmured, causing Tishva's shoulders to tense up. Despite knowing what he was going to say next, she still hoped that one of these days her father would give her a straight answer as to what had happened to her mother and why she couldn't remember all the details.

"Your mother... died while giving birth to your brother, who also didn't make it…" her father said, as though each word he uttered caused him physical pain. "It wasn't your fault, there was nothing you could do. Now, think no more of it."

Soraya frowned. *He's still not giving me the full story. I'll just have to ask again later.*

Just then, Tishva coughed. He covered his mouth with a handkerchief and spat up some blood. Soraya gasped when he tossed the red stained cloth aside and kept working as though nothing was wrong.

"Papa, please go to bed!" she pleaded while tugging at his arm. "You get no rest by staying up late every night and waking up early every morning, that's why you're getting sick!"

Her father exhaled deeply and ruffled his daughter's strawberry blonde hair. "Sorry kiddo, I have to work. Orders are orders."

Soraya stood on her tiptoes to view the various letters and books that lay scattered across her father's desk. Some of them were written in Azakuin, the common language of their country, Azakua.

Other books were written in Casmerahn, the same language her father used for his Arcanology research papers. Soraya only knew this because she had taken the time to memorize some letters, allowing her to occasionally translate words on envelops her father mailed off.

Tishva would step outside the cabin, his Casmerahn letters safely tucked into his jacket pockets, before running down the sloping hills and leaping into the air. By using Air Magic, he rode the wind and flew just above the forest until he reached their mailbox, which stood at the foot of the Averlore Mountains.

Despite her father leaving around three in the morning to do this, Soraya would hide in the shadows and watch through the windows. She had asked her father countless times to teach her how to use magic, but he instead insisted that she read books about it first.

"I need more books to read, Papa," Soraya stated in a matter of fact tone.

It wasn't the first time she had asked for more material to learn. The last time she had stated this, her father had ordered Etheria Historia, which was an encyclopedia divided into several volumes and covered all the world's major historical events.

Each book was categorized by country. The chapters covered various topics such as mythologies pertaining to how that country came to be established, how their languages were created, their unique studies in magic through Arcanology, technological advances by scientists, rulers throughout the ages, animals, geographical regions, famous foods, potions, and so on.

Soraya had spent well over two years poring through the various pages of knowledge each book contained, and had re-read her favorite sections. Mythologies and fairy tales always had intrigued her, along with learning about the different elemental magic mined for in each country.

"Can I… is it okay if I, well, read some of your books?" she continued. "Just in case I need to help you?"

Tishva's expression remained emotionless while he stared at the wall in thought.

Soraya had finished reading all the novels in the house and was starving for something new she could sink her teeth into. Although she desperately wanted to help her father in his research on magic, she knew that whatever he was unearthing had to stay under wraps. Her father had only reminded her of this fact well over a hundred times. However, it wasn't easy entertaining herself. There were no other children to play with in the Averlore Mountains.

The closest village to their cabin was Rivinsdeep, which was about an hour's trek down the winding mountain path. The town was full of elderly folk and young families with toddlers nowhere near Soraya's age, but it was her only access to having a social life.

Soraya would visit the villagers at least four times a week by herself to talk with the neighbors and earn money by doing odd jobs for them, such as farming, cooking, delivering mail, grocery shopping, mowing lawns, and helping with finding ingredients for the local restaurants. The neighbors were always kind and gave her extra supplies to take home after completing tasks in addition to payment.

"Papa?" Soraya asked again with trepidation. "Can I please read through your books?"

Tishva sat stiffly in his seat, studying the large, aging world map that took up the entire wall. It depicted all eight Kingdoms and even named and illustrated the various floating islands roaming freely across the sky.

Soraya had always loved staring at the Etherian world map, both on the wall and in her books.

Suddenly, without turning, Soraya's father said something that she had never heard him utter before. "Soraya, do you really want to learn how to harvest and use magic?"

His daughter's face lit up. "Oh yes! Absolutely!"

Tishva gave her a small smile and stood up from his chair. "I can't tell you everything," he paused to yawn and stretch his broad arms high into the air. "But I will teach you the basics tomorrow."

Soraya could barely contain her excitement. "But tomorrow is already today! Can you show me something now?"

Tishva gave his daughter a tired smile. "Not this minute,

but I'll take you out later this morning. Is that a deal?"

"Yeah!" Soraya couldn't stop grinning even after her father had tucked her back into bed and kissed her forehead goodnight. After years of asking, begging, and even praying, her wish to learn how to wield magic was about to come true.

*I wonder if I could learn to fly, or become invisible!*

Slowly but surely, as the clock ticked forward, the girl drifted off to sleep, blissfully unaware that her father's declining health had taken a turn for the worse.

## Chapter 2: Arcanology

The morning sunlight seeped into Soraya's room through the cracks of the curtains in the window, bathing everything in yellow and orange hues. The girl awoke the moment light crept onto her closed eyelids. Blinking, Soraya sprung eagerly out of bed, reached for her navy blue curtains and pulled them apart.

The walls, ceiling, and floor were all made of light wooden planks with dark brown spots and circles scattered unevenly about. Her bed frame and furniture were made from Redwood Oaks, which grew near the peaks of the Averlore Mountains.

When she was eight, Soraya had read about the two kinds of oak trees that grew in their country; Redwoods and Bloods. They looked similar, both with thick ruby colored trunks towering high and proudly displaying lush leaves resembling fire when dancing in the wind. However, where Redwood Oaks were like any other tree that remained planted firmly in the ground, Blood Oaks were known for eating Etherians and animals.

Anyone who dared come too close would be wrapped around the legs by their thick roots and dragged into the base of the tree. There, the unfortunate victim would be completely encased in roots, thorns embedding themselves into their flesh and sucking them dry of all their blood, giving the tree its color and name.

Soraya shook her head as she remembered how afraid she had been of the furniture in her room after reading about the Blood Oaks. She had been so terrified, in fact, that she insisted on sleeping downstairs near the fireplace in case she needed to burn the furniture should it come to life and try to eat her. Her father, finding her fear humorous, had taken her to the top of their mountain to explain their differences.

"Blood Oaks can't grow or survive in cold climates," Tishva said with an undercurrent of mirth while placing his gloved hand on the bark of a Redwood. "They freeze like our bodies do when exposed to low temperatures for too long. You'll never encounter one in the snow, I promise."

Her father had gone one step further, pointing out something that her book hadn't. "If you're not sure which tree it is, just stand still from a distance and watch the trunk. A Redwood Oak will stay completely still, but a Blood Oak pulsates."

Soraya snapped her thoughts back to the present and shifted her gaze out the window. Trees lined the mountainside straight ahead, and on the ground, two stories below, was her mother's grave. She often found herself talking to it, as if Adonia was actually listening.

Stuffed animals lined the top of Soraya's dresser, her favorite ones being an orange and black striped tiger with black button eyes and a white rabbit with long droopy ears, both of which her mother had sewn for her. She loved them dearly, but was too old to have them sleeping next to her on the bed, or so her father said.

Despite Tishva's wishes, she'd sometimes sneak them under the bed covers when she knew her father would be too busy working to wish her goodnight.

"I'm learning Arcanology today!" Soraya exclaimed while skipping towards her closet and flinging open the sliding door. All of her clothes were hung up and organized by category.

Yabo, her pandacoon, yawned and flashed his pearly white fangs before sitting up and stretching himself out on the bed. He cocked his head, watching Soraya rummage through her closet. Within moments, Soraya's robe and pajamas lay on the floor.

"What do you think?" she asked her pet while posing in front of the large oval shaped mirror in the corner of her bedroom. She spun so her pink dress twirled. Yabo simply flexed his claws and kneaded the thick blankets with them.

"Don't scratch up the bed!" Soraya scolded. After untangling his paws from the comforter, she placed him on her shoulder. Yabo let out a purr, which sounded like the coo of a dove, and rubbed his face into Soraya's cheek.

"You little goofball," Soraya said, kissing her pandacoon's fluffy face. After tugging red tights onto her stick-thin legs, she scampered through the long narrow hallway and flew down the spiral staircase.

Her father stood in the kitchen, chopping green apples into thick rings. The steady thuds from his knife hitting the cutting block filled the air while bacon and eggs sizzled and hissed on the heated stove top in the corner of the room.

"Morning kiddo," said Tishva as he glanced up at his daughter.

"Morning Papa!" Soraya plopped herself down onto a bar

stool and scooted closer to the countertop. Yabo hopped down from her shoulder, landed on the table, and waited for his portion of breakfast. He had his own placemat to sit on, which was white with printed patterns of red apples.

"Need help with that?" Soraya asked cheerfully.

Tishva chuckled. "Your mom taught you your manners alright," without skipping a beat, he continued. "Go fetch her for breakfast. She'll love that we're making it for her."

"Papa… she's not here anymore…"

"But she was just here five minutes ago…"

As soon as the words left his lips, Tishva frowned and furrowed his golden eyebrows together. An awkward silence fell over the room as Soraya shifted uncomfortably on her stool. For the past three years, her father would randomly ask Soraya to go fetch her mother. Despite her being dead.

"I need to show you something," Soraya said before sliding off her seat and heading for the back porch. She pointed out the window at the gravestone with her mother's name carved into it. "Mama's out there. Do you remember?"

Her father closed his eyes and placed his calloused hands onto his forehead in sorrow. "You mean… she wasn't in the kitchen just a few seconds ago?" he asked in a quivering voice. "Are you sure?"

"Yes, I'm sure."

Tishva slumped to the floor with a haunted look on his face.

Soraya's heart broke every time he did this. She ran over to him, draping her arms around his large shoulders, and squeezed him tightly. "I'm so sorry," she whispered.

Her father remained on the floor for another minute to calm himself down. "Soraya," he lowered his hands from his face, uncovering tear stains, and glanced at her with bloodshot eyes. "How often do I forget that Adonia is dead?"

Soraya's gaze fell to her feet. Although she knew the truth would upset him, she knew he needed to hear it. "You used to forget once or twice a month, but now…" she hesitated.

"But now?"

Her father's weary eyes looked so worried that it pained Soraya to continue, but she knew she had to tell him.

"Now, you forget at least once a week."

Tishva stared blankly across the room at the roaring fireplace, his golden eyebrows knit tightly together.

"Papa?"

He didn't reply, for he was lost in his own thoughts. It bothered Soraya that she didn't know how to help him. The only thing she could think to do was distract him from his woes.

"I'm going to set the table for us, so we can have breakfast. Does that sound good?"

"Yes…"

Rolling up her sleeves, Soraya got to work. Within minutes, breakfast was on the table and places for three were set out. The bacon and eggs were a little burnt from being left on the stove top too long, but that wouldn't stop them from eating it. She cut up some meat into small pieces before placing them into a small white bowl for Yabo, who was impatiently meowing for his morning meal.

"You're such a brat," she sighed, setting his bowl in front of him at the table. Yabo shoved his furry face into his food and chowed down. Soraya finished cutting the apples and placed them on their plates before checking on her father again.

"Breakfast is ready!" she called. Tishva finally snapped out of his thoughts and shuffled over to the table to join his daughter.

"Thanks kiddo," he said with a sad smile. "Sorry for worrying you so much."

Soraya shook her head. "No, don't apologize for that."

The two tucked in and ate in silence. After a few moments of chewing on the slightly burnt bacon, Tishva got up and walked over to his record player, which sat in the living room. He carefully chose a black vinyl disc and gently placed it onto the turntable. The needle slowly descended, sitting on the spinning record. After a few seconds of listening to hissing and popping static, Soraya could hear a faint female voice singing and growing louder. Her father slid back into his seat as the beautiful voice accompanied by an orchestra filled the still air with a soothing song.

"Nightshade was your mom's favorite band," he said, his eyes wandering towards the grave outside. "She was into music that was hauntingly beautiful. Any song with a cello was automatically her favorite."

"This is my favorite band too," Soraya said. His love for her Mom was beautiful and warmed her heart.

*I hope you can see how much he misses you.* The girl imagined Adonia could hear their conversation from the Heavens and smiled at the ceiling.

Soraya finished all of her food, but her father had barely eaten half of his portion. He cut up the rest of his meal and placed it into Yabo's bowl before bringing his dishes to the sink. The music made washing and putting away their dinnerware seem a lot more fun than it really was. Soraya tried to scrub the plates and place them on a rack to dry in time with the rhythm of the music.

"Don't drop them," Tishva warned as a plate nearly slipped from his daughter's hand.

"Sorry, Papa," Soraya's cheeks grew red. "I got distracted, is all."

"It's alright, but you can stop now," Tishva already had on his black boots and dark blue winter coat and was tossing on thick wool gloves. "You can finish the dishes when we get back. It's time to teach you how to harvest magic."

"Oh yay! Let's go!"

Within seconds, Soraya ran over to the living room closet and pulled on her black boots, buttoned up her pink coat, tossed her black and white plaid scarf around her neck, and thrown white fuzzy gloves on. "I'm ready!"

Tishva opened up their cabin door and stepped out into the snow. Soraya rushed out after him, but then turned around and called into the house, "be good, Yabo," before closing the door behind her.

The two traveled off into the winter wonderland surrounding their humble abode. Everything the eye could see was covered in a soft pillowy blanket of white. Soraya followed her father, hopping into the large footprints he left behind in the snow.

Tishva whistled an old tune as they trekked deeper into the woods, his sad and beautiful song filling the serene forest air. Soraya listened intently, trying to memorize the song. After her father finished holding out the last note he glanced over his shoulder at Soraya.

"Guess where I learned that from," he asked, his grayish blue eyes twinkling.

"Um…" Soraya scrunched up her face in concentration. "It reminds me of the Rivengale bird's song."

"Yes, you're correct," Tishva placed a hand on Soraya's head to mess up her long strawberry blonde hair.

"It's been a few months since we've heard any birds sing."

Tishva nodded. "Our winters here are long and harsh. The birds should be back in two more months if spring begins on time," he suddenly halted in his tracks. "Look!"

Soraya followed his hand to where he was pointing. Just ahead of them was a small circle of rocks barely peeking out of the snow, each a dull gray with light icy blue etchings spreading across each one like interlaced spiderwebs.

Tishva stooped down to clear away the snow. Soraya

watched as he waved his right hand over the rocks. Half of the web-like etchings immediately lifted into the air, circled around his hand, and disappeared into his palm. It happened so fast that Soraya thought she must have imagined it.

"What I did just there was something you need to learn how to do," Tishva said, tucking his hand back into his glove while turning around to face his daughter. His friendly blue eyes turned dark, a fiercely billowing fire behind them. "And you can't tell anyone that you know how to do this."

"Does this have to do with your job?" Soraya's sky-blue eyes widened in excitement. Her father rarely talked about his work, and whenever he did, he always told her that he'd explain more when she was older.

The edges of Tishva's eyes crinkled. "I can only teach you the basics of Arcanology right now, but I'll show you more later on," he beckoned Soraya to come over with a wave of his hand. "I harvested some Ice Magic just now. There's still more left, and I'd like to teach you how to take and use it."

Her father took hold of Soraya's right glove and tugged it off. He then guided her hand, so it barely hovered over the rocks. "I want you to concentrate and imagine the blue etchings peeling off the rocks and attaching themselves to your skin."

Soraya stared hard at the designs that were left on the rocks and tried to do as her father had instructed.

After a few minutes of gazing at the elemental magic pattern, Soraya closed her eyes and could see the spiderweb pattern clearly in her mind's eye.

"Just imagine it moving onto my hand?"

"Yes." Tishva nodded.

The girl wished with all her might that the web would move onto her hand and believed it would do so just as it had done for her father. Without warning, the Ice Magic lifted into the air and sank into the palm of her hand. She jumped as a cold kiss of ice planted itself on her skin. To her astonishment, Soraya found faded, light blue etchings had indeed formed the same web-like pattern just below her fingers.

"I actually did it!" Soraya gasped.

"Well, of course you did." Tishva beamed. "I wouldn't expect anything less, especially since you have such a vivid imagination. And that was the easy part."

She looked from her hand to her father in surprise. "The next part is harder?"

"Well, you have to learn the different ways for using the magic you took from the ground."

Tishva held up his pinky, middle, ring and pointer fingers on his right hand and placed them over his left shoulder. In a flash, he turned his torso, flinging his right arm while curving his body. Ice Magic flowed from his fingers and froze a large Red Oak.

Soraya's eyes grew wide when the tree was suddenly covered in icicles all pointing in the same direction, resembling spiked fur blowing in the wind.

Her father shuffled closer, showing Soraya the barely visible light blue etchings on his palm. "When you first absorb Ice Magic, it looks like a light blue tattoo. The more you use the magic you absorb, the more the web design fades from your skin. When the design is completely gone, it means you ran out of Ice Magic and have to find more to harvest."

Tishva pointed to a faded yellow design close to his thumb. "You can harvest and store multiple kinds of magic. There are four kinds that we know of, which are the four elements; air, water, fire, and earth. Blue is water or ice, as you now know, and yellow is air."

Tishva held up his pointer and middle fingers on his right hand, then lifted it high to feel for the wind before jumping off the ground. His feet never came back down. Soraya gaped as her father floated up into the air.

"That's incredible!" Soraya exclaimed. Flying was what she wanted to do more than anything else in the world.

Her father glided back down, landing softly in the snow next to her. The yellow etchings on the palm of his hand looked relatively the same. "I didn't use much magic for that trick," he explained.

"You have Water and Air Magic on your right hand, yet you used them separately," Soraya observed. "How did you do that?"

Tishva held out his right hand. "Remember that tractor you drove to mow Mr. Corbi's lawn down in Rivinsdeep?"

Soraya nodded. Mr. Corbi was an elderly man who owned a farm with his wife. The girl was more than happy to mow their lawn and take care of the horses and other farm animals. In exchange, the elderly neighbors would load up a large basket for her with food, usually eggs, apples, and cheese, as payment.

"That tractor is a manual, meaning you have to switch gears depending on the speed you were going. Your hand is where you release magic, and your fingers operate as different gears for shifting."

Tishva raised his left hand and only raised his pointer finger, "Earth Magic," he then raised his pointer and middle fingers together. "Air Magic," Tishva raised his ring finger with his pointer and middle fingers. "Fire magic," Lastly, he held his pinky up with the other three. "Water Magic."

"What happens if you have all five fingers raised?" asked Soraya.

"Then whatever magic you have stored on your arm would all be used at the same time. It's difficult to control two kinds of magic at once, especially from one hand, so I recommend not doing it."

Tishva took off the glove on his left hand and showed

Soraya that there were no markings on his palm. "Even though I stored both Water and Air Magic on my right hand, my left hand can still cast magic, it would just take a split second or two for the magic to transfer over to that hand. It runs through your veins like blood."

"So, you only have two kinds of magic?"

"Yes. It's not as easy to find magic in nature anymore, since most Etherians figured out where to look for it. Many royal families from neighboring kingdoms have taken it all for themselves so that common folk, like you and I, can't find or use it."

"Can we find Air Magic today?" Soraya asked giddily. She wanted more than anything to soar high above the clouds and see what the world looked like from such a high view.

Tishva frowned. "I found a stash of it in a cave around here several years ago and have used it all up since then. What I have absorbed on my skin is all there is left," he saw his daughter's face fall. "I can show you the cave, but I've already searched everywhere for more."

"Okay..." Soraya was disappointed, but she still wanted to have a look.

Her father led the way to a winding path leading higher into the Averlore mountains. Soraya followed closely behind and took in the surrounding scenery.

They walked by a clearing at the edge of a cliff and could see the town of Rivinsdeep and landscape far below. The towns folk looked as small as insects from their perch, and the buildings looked like miniature models and doll houses.

The second Tishva started his ascent up the steeper slopes of the mountain, he stopped dead in his tracks.

"Papa?" Soraya piped up. "Are you alright?"

Tishva stood still and stared off into the distance as though he had not heard her.

"Papa!"

Soraya panicked. Her father wasn't responding to her at all. She ran up and stood in front of him, so he could see her, but her father said nothing and looked past her as if she didn't exist.

"Papa, please! Look at me!" his daughter cried in exasperation. Tishva finally looked down at her, but had a blank look on his face as he studied the girl. Soraya reached out for his hand, but he shuffled awkwardly away.

"Don't you have a family to go home to?" Tishva asked with a hint of annoyance in his voice. "Your parents will be upset if they find out that you followed a stranger into the woods."

*He… he forgot who I am?*

## Chapter 3: Tishva's Failing Memory

How could Tishva, her own father, forget that she was his daughter? Soraya's eyes filled with tears as she racked through her brain to figure out what to do. Never before had her father forgotten who she was. Fear gripped her heart and made it beat faster than it ever had in her life.

"Can you… walk me back home?" the girl asked in a shaky voice. Soraya wasn't sure how long it would take for her father to snap out of this episode, but she hoped that taking him back to their house would help jog his memory faster.

"Well..." her father's voice trailed off in thought. "I suppose I can't let you walk back alone..." he looked Soraya up and down again, as if seeing her for the first time, before shrugging his broad shoulders. "Alright, I'll take you to your house. Lead the way."

"Th-thank you," Soraya stammered. She trudged through the thick snow back towards their cabin, looking over her shoulder every other minute to not lose sight of her father, who still looked confused and out of sorts.

As they made their way together through the thick snow, Tishva paused and looked up into the trees glistening in the pale sunlight.

"Little girl, do you hear that?"

Soraya stopped and cocked her head, but heard nothing at all. The stillness of the forest surrounded them both. Tishva's face softened, his grayish blue eyes coming into focus before he closed his eyes.

"It's my wife's favorite tune, the song of the Rivengale," Tishva whispered, blinking rapidly before looking over at his daughter. "I should play it for her tonight."

"Papa..." Soraya could barely take it. Her father's random spells of not remembering current events was lasting much longer than normal, and now he was hearing things that weren't there.

"I'm not your father," Tishva said firmly. "Stop calling me that."

"Sorry," his daughter sighed. "Please, just walk me home."

Soraya thought about their family portrait sitting on the mantel above the fireplace. It clearly showed Tishva and Adonia sitting on a wooden bench together, with Soraya as a toddler between them. Surely that would bring her father back to his senses.

"Is this a trick?"

The air around Soraya suddenly turned thin, and she struggled to breathe. Her father had his right hand raised, along with his pointer and middle fingers. The girl realized he was using magic to suffocate her.

"Are you a spy sent to steal my research?" Tishva hissed. "The other one poisoned himself before I could get information out of him. I'm not making that same mistake again."

"N-no!" Soraya gasped. She had never heard or seen her father act so violently. Tishva was a kind, gentle soul, either always curled up with a book in his office or exploring and taking notes on his surroundings. This side of him frightened her.

Soraya's chest burned, but she knew she needed to stay calm and choose between trying to gulp down more air or lose what little she had stored up in her lungs by trying to further convince him that she wasn't lying.

"It's me… your daughter…" Soraya managed to whisper while sinking to her knees. There was no air around her anymore. She held her breath and prayed to the Gods to have mercy on her.

Time seemed to stop as Soraya's vision blurred. She looked up at Tishva's shadow cast face before closing her eyes.

This was it. She was going to die. At least she would see her mother again.

"Soraya!"

The flame in Tishva's eyes vanished. A look of horror crossed his face as he became aware of what was happening.

"Oh Gods, what have I done?"

He put his right hand down, and air immediately surrounded his daughter once more. "Are… are you okay?" he asked, his voice trembling. He stooped down, wrapping his arms around her.

Soraya took several deep breaths in, the burning in her lungs disappearing completely. After calming down and processing what had just happened, she burst into tears. "Papa! Why?" she sobbed into her father's shoulder. "Why did you hurt me?"

"Oh kiddo, I am so sorry," he planted a kiss on his daughter's head. "Hold on tight, we're going home."

He swiftly picked up Soraya, cradling her in his arms before taking three bounds forward and leaping into the air. They flew high above the trees.

The girl's jaw dropped open as the ground fell away beneath their feet. The cool morning air blew in their faces, running its icy fingers through their hair. For a few seconds, Soraya was almost filled with bliss from soaring into the sky. Then, Tishva landed gracefully in front of their home.

"How was that?" he asked with a trembling voice. "You

finally got to fly."

"I-it was wonderful," Soraya smiled sadly.

Tishva put his daughter down onto the ground. "Hold out your left hand," he said softly. Soraya did as she was told, and Tishva placed his right hand on top of hers. "I'm going to give you the last bit of magic that I have."

The faded yellow wind tattoo on his skin disappeared, as did his faded blue web pattern. Two icy kisses planted themselves on both her palms, similar to when she had absorbed Ice Magic. When Tishva took away his hand, Soraya spotted the Air Magic pattern near the center of her left hand. When she looked at her right palm, the Ice Magic tattoo was now a brighter blue and less translucent.

"Th…Thank you, Papa!" Soraya stuttered. She sounded more excited than she actually was. Her father had forgotten who she was and had attempted to murder her just moments before. The girl wasn't sure how to react.

"I want you to have this magic since I don't trust myself with it anymore," Tishva looked down at both of his hands and shuddered. "I don't trust myself at all with anything, anymore…"

Soraya threw her arms around him and hugged tightly. "You'll get better, right Papa?"

Instead of answering, Tishva stooped down and hugged his daughter back. "I'll try. I promise, but the situation just grew more dangerous. I need to keep you safe, even if that means from myself."

Her father released her and opened the front door of their cabin. They both stepped inside and shook off the snow from their boots. Soraya looked over at the clock hanging on the wall and read the time.

*Eleven forty-seven… it feels a lot later than that.*

Soraya wanted to fall asleep, wake up, and for her father forgetting who she was and nearly suffocating her to death to have just been a bad dream. But she knew it had actually happened. What made it worse was knowing it could happen again.

She looked down at the palms of her hands. Earlier that morning, they had nothing on them. Now, before noon, she had Air Magic on her left and Water Magic on her right. So much had changed in just a few short hours.

While Soraya pondered over the morning events, Tishva was pacing the room, wiping his face with sweaty hands and staring out the window.

"Papa, what's wrong?" Soraya asked gently.

Tishva turned to face her, his grayish blue eyes filling with tears. "Soraya, I don't think you can live with me anymore… I'm too dangerous."

It was the last thing she had expected to hear her father say. "No! Papa, you're all I have left!" his daughter cried in horror. "I can go to Rivinsdeep and get a doctor back up here to help. We can figure out what's wrong with your memory, just don't send me away!"

Soraya's whole body shook like a leaf in the wind. Leaving her father alone in the woods wasn't going to fix his memory, it would only make it worse, especially since he wouldn't have her to help bring him back to his senses.

Tishva scooped his daughter up gently from the ground, nestling her in his thick arms. "No, kiddo, what I have is beyond what the village doctors can help me with. I have to figure out what's going on with my memory, but you can't come with me. I'll send you to the school I went to when I was your age. It's called Darkwood Academy. You'll like it there, you'll finally be around kids your own age."

Soraya's head was spinning. Everything was happening too fast. "I can't live with you… anymore… ever?" she managed to ask between sobs.

"No, not forever. Just for right now," Tishva's grayish blue eyes looked sad, but he forced a smile on his face. "I will get better, but that can't happen unless you help me, and you going to school means you'll be safe. Is that alright?"

"Okay..." It was far from okay, but Soraya knew she couldn't change her father's mind.

Tishva could tell Soraya was struggling, so he kissed the top of his daughter's forehead. "Kiddo," he said. "I don't want to hurt you, ever, but we both know that me forgetting who you are might happen again. I can't lose you, you're all that I have left too."

Soraya choked and sobbed even more. "I love you, Papa."

"I love you too, kiddo."

They hugged each other tightly. It didn't last long enough.

The next thing Soraya knew, her father was making phone calls left and right from his office. Soraya had always been curious about the strange device that allowed her father to talk with others from hundreds of miles away. He rarely used it and instead seemed to be content with writing letters and flying down the mountain himself to deliver them.

The phone was a wooden box that hung from the wall just above his desk. A large, white circle with smaller buttons hung in the middle, the numbers zero through nine carved into each. There was a long, black plastic piece called a receiver that hung on the left.

Soraya waited outside of Tishva's office, listening intently while he scribbled notes onto a pad of paper with his red feathered quill.

"So she can live on campus? That sounds good... Yes, she's thirteen years old... I'll be purchasing tickets for her after this phone call... yes, I'll give you the details once I have them..." Tishva paused and looked at the world map hanging on his wall in front of his desk.

Soraya leaned forward, straining to hear the faint female voice coming from the other end of the line.

"Sir, because it's the middle of the school year, she'll need to be tested upon arriving. She may qualify to be here age wise, but is she academically where she needs to be?"

"I'm sure you'll find that she is," Tishva replied confidently.

"Okay," the woman continued. "Make sure she brings two forms of identification papers. A copy of her birth certificate and her travel permit will do."

"Perfect."

"That's everything then," the female replied in a monotone voice. "We will pick up Soraya Thenayu from the Valtic Train Station, and you will call back and provide the day and time for us to come pick her up."

"Thank you again," Tishva hung up the phone and turned towards his office door. "Soraya, I know you're there."

She poked her head into her father's office. "I'm taking a train to this new school?"

"Yes, I just have to call the station and get you your tickets, then follow up with the school so they can pick you up," Tishva stood and pointed at their country, Azakua, on the Etherian world map. It was a north eastern continent that hovered almost perfectly between the equator and North Pole.

"Darkwood Academy is an upper class school located in Matumi, near the Valtic Ocean. You'll be living in one of the wealthiest parts of our country."

"How far away is this place from here?" Soraya asked. She knew what the world map looked like, she simply wasn't sure how long it would take to travel to different parts of it.

Tishva pointed at the Averlore mountains in the far north western part of their continent, then moved his finger towards the south eastern section of Azakua. "It's about a one day travel by train," he stated calmly, though his gaze shifted down at his daughter, as if he was worried that she would overreact to the news.

Soraya frowned. "That's too far away for me to come see

you whenever I want."

Tishva nodded. "That's true, but you will be able to write me letters and make phone calls."

His daughter sighed. It was better than having no communication with her father at all.

"Kiddo."

"Yes Papa?"

Tishva knelt down, taking his daughters hands into his own.

"I know this is going to be difficult on both of us, but I want you to have fun and learn as much as you can while there. You're very sociable, you're going to make lots of friends and do well because you're smart and kind."

Soraya blushed. "Thanks, Papa."

A small smile crept onto her father's lips. "I'll keep you updated on my progress too. We'll both work hard and do our best. Do you promise to do that for me?"

"I promise I will."

Tishva patted his daughter's head and messed up her strawberry blond hair before straightening up and going back to his desk. "I have some more phone calls to make, can you go to your room and start making a pile of things to bring with you?"

"Okay."

"Remember," Tishva swiveled around in his chair. "You will only have a small suitcase and backpack for space, and you have to carry everything on you for a full day. Bring practical things you'll need on a daily basis. We're going to buy your school books before you leave, so make room for them too."

Soraya nodded and left for her room. "Bring practical things…" she murmured while swiveling around in circles on the soles of her feet. Soraya pulled out different outfits she liked wearing, separating them into piles of undergarments, socks, shirts, pants, dresses, and skirts.

"I can't take these all with me, so I will only bring my absolute favorites," she said aloud. Upon hearing her, Yabo tread over to Soraya's suitcase and plopped himself inside.

"Oh yes, you are my favorite, so I have to bring you too," she laughed while stroking Yabo's ears.

Soraya settled on leaving behind the clothes that were too tight. She carefully packed around Yabo and only moved him when she had to make more room for her sketchbook, pencils and her two favorite books from the Etheria Historia encyclopedia set.

"I think those are the important things to bring," Soraya said aloud while pulling open the dresser drawers, searching around for anything else she might have forgotten about.

"Are you done packing?" Tishva's voice floated in from Soraya's doorway. "I'd like to double check your work once you are."

Soraya placed her hands on her hips and looked up at her father with confidence. "I'm finished."

Tishva unloaded the suitcase and inspected his daughter's work. Soraya stepped back and watched as he glanced through each pile, nodding in approval before carefully repacking.

"I think you'll be prepared, though if you need more clothes you could always buy them."

"What about Yabo?" Soraya asked as she cuddled her pandacoon, who was curled up in a ball and starting to doze off. "He's going to miss me a lot if I leave him… Can't I take him with me?"

Tishva smiled. "I'll see what I can do. I might have to pay extra for you to keep him with you, but I can easily afford that."

"Oh, I hope he can come too!" Soraya exclaimed. The thought of parting both with her pandacoon and her father was a little more than she could bear.

"Are you saving the backpack for your school books?" Tishva asked while plucking a grey bag with black straps from the top shelf of her closet.

"Uh, yes..." she stammered, blushing with embarrassment. She had completely forgotten about her father mentioning it.

"You didn't remember me telling you to use this, did you?" Tishva's voice was stern, but a smile played onto the edges of his lips.

Soraya hated messing up and forgetting things, even if it was over trivial matters.

"Well, it does make sense to keep it empty… I want to start reading the text books when I'm on the train, and they'll be easier to access in the backpack."

"Fair enough," Tishva grinned, holding back on teasing her further. "That's everything then?"

Soraya screwed up her face in thought. "I think so."

Tishva clapped his large hands together. "Alright, we'll leave first thing in the morning. For now, rest up." He took the suitcase, zipped it up, and placed it by the bed before closing the navy blue curtains and drowning out the sunlight. "You can look around your room again later today in case you think of anything else to bring."

Before exiting, he turned and added, "I'll be in my office if you need me. I love you."

Soraya watched her father leave, then turned her gaze to the curtains. Although the sun was still high in the sky, the girl was exhausted from all the stress she had endured earlier that morning. Resting didn't sound like such a bad idea.

She pulled down the thick comforter and joined her pandacoon in bed. Between Yabo's purring and the faint rustling of papers from her father working down the hall, Soraya relaxed enough to drift off to sleep.

## Chapter 4: Tishva's Secret Library

"You're so beautiful."

Adonia gazed lovingly down at her newborn daughter, who she was cradling in her thin, olive toned arms.

Soraya could hear her mother's sweet voice, which, to her, was the most marvelous sound in the world. She blinked her eyes open and noticed that everything looked bright and blurry around them. Her mother's ruby eyes and hair were the only features that came into focus from the white and gray background.

"Can I name her?" Adonia pleaded to what seemed to be the corner of the room. The infant noticed a figure slowly slide away from the shadows and glide closer towards them. He was tall, thin, and had seemingly long silvery hair. Soraya couldn't quite make out his eye color or facial features since they were pale and blended in with the white walls that surrounded them.

"Of course," a male voice said. "Just remember, you can't stay with her for too long."

"I understand," the red-eyed woman replied sadly. "But just look at how wonderful she is," Adonia bent down and kissed Soraya's cheek before whispering in her ear, "please, save your younger brother."

* * *

Soraya opened her eyes and gazed at the ceiling of her room. The wood patterns of the blue spruce trees flowed and ebbed in one direction, similar to the current of a winding river. Light creeped in from the cracks of the drawn curtains, but it was of bright reds and oranges from the setting sun.

All the events from earlier that day swarmed around the girl's mind. For a split second, Soraya relaxed, believing she had also dreamed about harvesting magic and her father nearly suffocating her until she gazed down at the palms of her hands. On her left, she had faded yellow swirls tattooed near the center of her palm, and on her right, she had faded blue web-like designs in the same location.

It had all happened. It was all real.

Shivers ran down Soraya's spine when she thought about her father behaving violently earlier that day. The shadows that had formed over his face. The fire behind his blue eyes. Him raising his hands, as if to strike her while using Air Magic to take away her ability to breathe…

Her pet, Yabo, noticed her discomfort and rubbed himself against her hands. "Mow?" he chirped, cocking his head sideways and looking up at her with empathetic black, beady eyes.

"Oh Yabo, thank you," Soraya whispered gratefully to him. He always knew how to cheer her up.

She turned her attention towards the hallway outside her bedroom door, which was lit from the lantern in her father's office. She needed to go check on him, but part of her was worried that he would have another spell of forgetting who she was.

Soraya climbed out of bed and tip toed down the hallway towards the light. She was tempted to grab the family portrait just in case her father needed to be reminded of who she was again. However, Soraya remembered that she had her father's Air Magic and that he wouldn't be able to suffocate her again.

*Why am I even thinking like this? Maybe it is best that I'm leaving tomorrow, I shouldn't have to worry about my father accidentally killing me.*

The girl peeked cautiously into her father's study and found him sitting at his desk. The room was growing darker as the sun outside the window fell beneath the mountain peaks. The trees outside their cabin were black silhouettes against the fiery red and orange sky.

"Kiddo," Tishva said without turning his head. "I need to talk to you."

"Okay..."

Her father moved so his daughter could sit in his red velvet chair. She timidly climbed into his seat and looked up into her father's grayish blue eyes. He wasn't smiling.

"Earlier this morning, when I did the unthinkable..." Tishva bowed his head, covering his face in shame. "You didn't defend yourself against me, even though you had Water Magic... why?"

Soraya blinked in surprise. She hadn't expected that to be brought up again.

"You're my dad, I don't want to hurt you," she stated in a matter-of-fact tone. "And, I thought... I thought that you'd remember me again…" her voice faltered as she realized how precarious their situation had been earlier that day.

"You thought I'd remember you again, even when you almost passed out from losing oxygen?" Tishva's voice was slightly raised, though he wasn't angry. He sounded more concerned than anything else.

Soraya thought back and remembered accepting her fate of dying and shuddered. "I thought about seeing Mama again..."

Tishva pushed his hand heavily into the desk and towered over his daughter. His face was dark, a storm brewing behind his grey blue eyes. "If I ever do anything like that to you again, don't hesitate to protect yourself. In fact, if anyone ever tries to hurt you, ever, do whatever it takes to be safe, even if that means hurting someone else."

He placed his left hand gently on Soraya's cheek and looked her in the eyes. "Promise me that you'll value your life."

"I promise..." she replied hesitantly. Her father wasn't acting his normal self at all. "But," Soraya continued. "I don't want to hurt anyone. I thought the Gods didn't like violence."

"You're right, they don't," Tishva sighed. "The Sacred Scrolls from, *The Path,* teach us to love our neighbors and protect them, but part of that is defending yourself from those that would hurt you."

He paused and stooped low to the ground so he was at eye level with his daughter. "You were made by your mother and I, and we've made many sacrifices to keep you safe, but we can't protect you forever. You must learn to stand up for yourself."

Tishva then glanced at the pile of books he had made, plucked off the top one, and placed it on the desk in front of his daughter. "I want you to look through and read all the pages starting from the first chapter up to where I put bookmarks in. Do not read anything past the bookmarks, you must promise me."

"I promise," Soraya vowed. Her curiosity was enticed, but she couldn't bring herself to disobey her father, especially when she wouldn't be seeing him again for a long time. The last thing she wanted was a guilty conscience in addition to worrying about his declining health.

"You can't take these with you, so make sure to study up and memorize as much as you can."

He held his hand on top of the green book and gazed down at his daughter. "I suggest making notes and studying them while on the train. It's a one day ride to Matumi, and you'll need to kill some time. Just erase your notes before arriving at school."

Soraya let out a small gasp of astonishment when her father revealed the book. It had a dark green leather cover with the words, *Arcanology: The Study of Magic Volume I,* carved into the front. Beneath the title was an alchemist cauldron with fluffy clouds of smoke billowing from the lip of the pot.

"These are your Arcanology books!" Soraya exclaimed ecstatically. A bittersweet wave washed through her as she realized her father was only allowing her to read from his secret library because she was leaving the next day.

A half smile curled onto Tishva's lips. "They certainly are. These books will cover the basics of magic and teach you how to use it, the history and myths surrounding it, and even give theories for how to further our use of it. This knowledge will give you a good foundation to build upon."

Soraya threw her arms around her father and gently squeezed him. "Papa, thank you for sharing this with me!"

"Of course," Tishva planted a kiss on the top of his daughter's head. "Now, go ahead and study up. I'll make us dinner," he said before disappearing down the hallway.

Soraya ran her thin fingers down the faded golden parchment lining the inside of the green leather cover, savoring the moment she had been waiting so long for.

The book itself was thick, tall and full of pages with small black font, including illustrated pictures depicting each Magic pattern and charts dividing up the text.

*My Water and Air Magic tattoos look just like these pictures,* Soraya mused before picking up the book, placing her nose in its spine, and inhaling deeply. The smell reminded her of vanilla and almonds.

Although she knew her father was right about saving the majority of the reading for the trip, she couldn't resist taking her time with the first page.

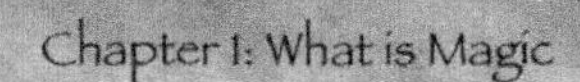

## Chapter 1: What is Magic

Magic is the fifth element found in nature that allows Etherians to fuse with the other four elements. There are a sundry of theories as to why and how Magic came to be, many of which are rooted in various religions and mythologies. The purpose of this book is to soley extract the scientific uses from their teachings and allow the reader to determine for themselves how they wish to apply Magic into their own lives.

Magic can be found in four forms:
Fire Magic, Water Magic, Earth Magic, and Air Magic.

Fire Magic is usually located near volcanoes in tropical regions and has a red pattern of swirls that look like flames. This allows Etherians to without getting burned, cast and control fire and lightening from their hands, and even summon lightening from brewing storms in the clouds.

Earth Magic is a light green pattern of triangular shapes found in forests and near the edges of volcanoes. Those who have absorbed Earth Magic into their bodies have been able to literally move mountains, create tunnels underground, and even speak with plants.

Water Magic, also known as Ice magic, is a light blue web pattern found resting on rocks in the snow, ocean, lakes, rivers, and any other allows Etherians to breath underwater, control the movement of water, calm tumultuous seas, cause flooding, turn water into ice, stay warm in colder weather, summon rain, and heal wounds.

Air Magic is a light yellow pattern of curls found in caves where air is trapped in the earth. This allows Etherians to fly, move and levitate objects by controlling the wind, control where the weather travels in the sky, and even take away air.

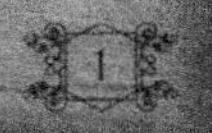


"And even take away air…" Soraya whispered while thinking about her father nearly suffocating her with Air Magic just hours earlier. She was tempted to run downstairs and ask her father about what she had just read, but being reminded of the horrors from earlier that day quelled her desire. Instead, she flipped open a small notebook and made notes within it while reading.

Once she found the bookmark, she closed the book and set it aside, refusing to disobey her father's command of not reading further than what he had marked.

After a few minutes of double checking her work, she was satisfied with the reminders she had written, and commenced with the following book on the top of the tall stack before her, which was titled, *Alchemy for Beginners: Basics and Beyond.*

She wasn't sure how much time had passed before her father called her name from downstairs, but the sky was pitch black outside the office window. Yabo was curled up in a ball and purring loudly in her lap. Four of the books were set aside in what Soraya named the "done" pile, and only one remained for her to scan through called, *The Mage's Companion.*

"I guess I can take a break…" Soraya murmured. Her stomach gnawed at her, making low gurgling sounds in protest of not having any food since that morning. "Yabo, let's go."

The pandacoon blearily blinked open his black, beady eyes, digging his tiny paws into her dress in protest as she picked him up.

"Sorry to move you, but we need to eat," she said, then untangled his claws from her clothes before carrying him towards the kitchen.

"Hey Papa!" Soraya called once she reached the bottom of the spiral staircase. "What are we having tonight?"

Tishva winked while opening the oven door. The fresh aroma of cooked meat and melted cheese wafted through the air. "Your favorite, toasted steak sandwiches."

"You know me so well!" the girl beamed as she hurried to set the table.

Yabo jumped down from his owner's shoulder and sat expectantly on his apple patterned tablecloth. Soraya placed a small bowl of minced steak in front of him that her father had prepared, and her pandacoon immediately stuffed his face into it.

Tishva grabbed two tall, thin glasses and a bottle of freshly squeezed apple cider from their neighbor's apple orchard down in

Rivinsdeep, and poured each of them a cup. He then cut the large sandwich in half and placed each overstuffed piece onto two light blue plates.

The melted white cheese laying between the layers of steak, onions and red peppers was oozing down the sides of the lightly toasted bread and dripping down onto the dishes. Soraya's mouth watered as she waited impatiently for her father to pray.

"You needn't fidget," Tishva gently chided, then sat down heavily into his seat at the head of the square table. Soraya immediately stiffened up and held still. Her father smiled at her. "Thank you. Now, let's thank the Gods for this meal."

He took his daughter's small hands into his own from across the table and they both bowed their heads and closed their eyes. "Dear Heavenly Deities, we thank you for this day, your blessings, and mercy," Tishva gently squeezed Soraya's hands. "Please be with my daughter as she travels to Matumi. Protect her, guide her, and guard her faith in you. In your names we pray, Amen."

"Amen." Soraya chimed in. They waited a few seconds before letting go of each other's hands and tucking into their meals. Soraya dug her fork and knife into her sandwich and shoved a big piece of juicy steak and cheese into her mouth.

"Kiddo."

"Yesh?" Soraya replied.

"Before you leave for Matumi tomorrow, what are the rules when talking to others?" Tishva's grayish blue eyes were staring intently into his daughter's sky blue eyes. He had hardly touched his sandwich.

"Don't tell anyone about what you do," Soraya paused and watched her father nod his head in approval. "And don't tell anyone that Mama had red eyes."

"And if anyone asks what I do for a living and what color your mother's eyes were?"

"Tell them you're a retired soldier and Adonia is my step-mother, my real mother's eyes were blue," she frowned as she finished the sentence that had been beaten into her memory since she was a child. "Papa, why do I have to lie about Mama being my real mother and her real eye color?"

There were eight kingdoms that split up the six ground continents and two major floating islands that hovered above Etheria, and she knew eye color took a major role in that division, but not much else on the topic.

Her Etheria Historia books had missing pages in them, which her father assured her had just been misprints, but somehow they all lacked information on why the differences in eye color was important. Soraya had even thought about asking their neighbors in Rivinsdeep, but had never tried lest her father find out and become disappointed in her.

Tishva sighed heavily and placed his apple cider glass down onto the table. "I can't shield you forever from the ugliness of the world," he cleared his throat. "Etherians are petty creatures that have to find flaws in others to feel better about themselves. Blue eyes are more rare due to them being a genetically recessive trait, so our country's leaders, who mind you, are most likely inbred and mentally unstable, tout that they are a superior race due to having this rare feature."

Soraya squinted her face in disgust. "That's stupid!" she exclaimed. "It doesn't even make any sense!"

"I know..." Tishva went silent. The orange flames hissing and crackling while dancing in the fireplace was the only sound that filled the still air.

"Once upon a time, Azakua was one of the most powerful nations in the world. We traveled and explored most of Etheria and made peace treaties and trade deals with many other countries, which are now divided into eight major kingdoms. Our main trading resources used to be Water and Air Magic, along with Nevertrees. These set us apart from many other nations simply due to the abundance our country has."

Soraya remembered reading about Nevertrees, which, when grown, created floating islands that roamed freely across the sky. Their country Azakua was where they originated from, and they aided early Azakuin explorers in finding other lands and nations. Although they were now mainly used in creating flying ships and prison islands, the kingdom of Golaytia was the largest man made floating island ever constructed in Etheria's history.

"Our language is still well known and taught throughout the world," Tishva continued with a hint of sadness in his voice. "But our weakness is something we didn't foresee."

He looked down at his pale hands. "Our blue eyes, which unites us native Azakuins, is genetically recessive. The more we've mingled with foreigners, the less each new generation looked like their predecessors."

"Our country's leaders took a dramatic approach to solving that problem by limiting the number of foreigners allowed to immigrate into our country. It became a double edged sword, however, as we sacrificed our position of power in the world in exchange for salvaging our traditions and heritage. Since we've attempted to shut out most of the world for the last fifty years, we're no longer the powerful and influential country we once were."

Tishva lifted his glass of cider. "Azakua is currently divided between voting for two different candidates. Starlene Inos advocates for keeping the borders open for travel and immigration. She has a lot of other policies that I agree with, which is why I voted for her."

"Who is the other one?" Soraya asked curiously.

"Stefawn Zabok, who wants to stop immigration completely."

The girl blinked. "But why?"

Tishva frowned. "Native Azakuin girls have been going missing throughout our country, and he's blaming foreigners for being the cause of it."

"That's awful!" Soraya cried.

"I know," Tishva traced a finger around the top of his glass. "This is why you have to learn to protect yourself. As far as anyone can visibly see, you are pure Azakuin, and there will be many who will envy you because of your eyes."

A strange thought popped into Soraya's head, and she couldn't help but blurt it out. "But, I'm not pure Azakuin, am I?"

Her father didn't answer immediately. Instead, he picked up his tall, thin glass of cider and took a long, slow sip before responding. "No, you're not."

The girl thought about her mother, with her ruby eyes and soft autumn red hair, and frowned. "The old man from my dream said that Mama had demon eyes..."

Tishva bowed his head and covered his eyes with his hands, as if he were in pain. "Your mother was Casmerahn, but you cannot tell another soul that. No one would believe you, and worse, if they did, you would quickly become a lab rat to scientists."

"Why would that happen?" Soraya asked while leaning forward and tightly gripped the handles of her chair. Her father had just confirmed a suspicion she had had ever since she had read about the Kingdom of Casmerahn and how its citizens naturally had red eyes. Her mother was one of them after all.

"Your eyes are blue when they should either be red or brown. It's believed to be genetically impossible that you look the way you do considering Adonia's genetics," Tishva turned and looked at her.

"Red is a dominant eye color, and blue disappears completely from the offspring of someone with red eyes. Brown eyes are created when red mixes with any other colored eyes. Brown eyed parents can create blue eyed offspring, but Red never creates blue."

"Papa..." the girl sat up and took a deep breath. She had only asked this question a thousand times, but it seemed appropriate to try again. "Please, tell me how Mama died."

Tishva shook his head. "I can't, even if I wanted to I couldn't, because…" His hands trembled as he stared at the roaring flames inside the fireplace. "I don't even remember how she died."

Soraya's stomach churned and formed into knots. "You don't?"

It was the last thing she had expected him to say. All this time she had believed he just wouldn't tell her to protect her from something unpleasant. It had never occurred to her that he didn't know either.

"Papa, you need to get better!" she cried in disbelief, jumping up from her seat. "Y-you need to remember what happened! We both need to know the truth!"

Tishva's already pale face turned white as a sheet. "You're right… So many memories are slipping away, and at an unprecedented rate. I used to remember how Adonia died, but I don't anymore…"

An unsettling thought occurred to Soraya, and she was too upset to hold it in. "Do I have what you have? Will I forget things like you are?"

"No, what you have is different." He stated firmly. "You have repressed memories from trauma. I have something entirely different…"

Tishva's shaky hands reached for his glass of cider again, but he flinched back and let them drop onto his lap. "It's as if my memories are hiding in the corners of my mind. When I try to bring them into the light, they slink down further into the shadows and cracks in the walls. I honestly don't know what to do other than seek help from old friends of mine."

Soraya ran over and hugged her father. "We'll get through this," she vowed. "You'll get your memories back, and I'll do well in school until you do."

"Okay," Tishva softly planted a kiss on his daughter's cheek and hugged her back. "Thank you kiddo. Let's both work hard."

After a few moments, Soraya went back to her seat and finished her dinner in silence. Even Yabo, who had finished his meal long before them, was keeping quiet by sitting with his paws tucked beneath him. Only his bushy red and white tail swished occasionally from side to side, along with his black eyes glancing up at his guardian, but she hardly noticed.

Soraya was lost in her own thoughts and couldn't help but wonder why she had blue eyes if it was genetically impossible for her to have them, but it seemed as though her father didn't even know how to answer to that. Her mother may have been able to tell her, but she was buried in their backyard under a snow covered tombstone.

"You said you have old friends who can help you?" the girl prodded.

"Yes, old colleagues," Tishva said while undoing his long, golden ponytail, which was looking rather haggard and unruly. "We go way back, though I highly doubt they're alive anymore. Even if they are, they might not want to talk to me. Still, they might have some answers. It's worth a try."

Soraya was about to ask more about them, but her father stood up and took his dishes to the sink. He hadn't eaten very much, and that bothered her greatly.

"You should finish your dinner," she playfully scolded. "Or you can't have dessert."

"That rule only applies to children, not adults," Tishva winked while wrapping his sandwich tightly in a tea towel before disappearing behind the pantry door.

In the back of the wooden shelves lined with various spices and ingredients was a staircase leading down into the basement. There, they kept their leftovers in a large ice box since it was built underground and always cold.

"You should finish reading those books I gave you!" her father bellowed while making his way back up the creaking basement stairs. "I'll clean up, go do your work and then go to bed!"

"Okay!"

Soraya headed up the spiral staircase and back to her father's study with Yabo hitching a ride in her hoodie.

Once she was seated again at her father's desk, she opened the book, *The Mage's Companion*. After scanning through the first three chapters, she found herself yawning and struggling to keep her eyelids from drooping down by the fourth. It didn't help that Yabo was purring loudly in the hood of her jacket, which made her want to lie down on her bed and fall asleep cuddling him.

"Still at it?" Tishva's voice called faintly from down the hall. Soraya listened to her father's heavy footsteps drawing nearer and nearer until they appeared behind her chair. The smell of freshly baked goods floated through the air.

"You made me dessert?" the girl grinned as her father placed a small plate with three round white chocolate cranberry oatmeal cookies in front of her.

"Yes. I used the ingredients I had on hand, so forgive me for having to be creative," he ruffled her hair while leaning forward and looking over her shoulder.

"If you're too tired to keep going tonight, you can finish it in the morning or when you get back from school in another few months. I made some arrangements for you for the next few days, and I'll go over the plans with you over breakfast. You can sleep in until eight, how does that sound?"

"Sounds good," Soraya managed to say while yawning and stretching. Her body was fatigued, it was time to listen to it and get ready for sleep.

"Eat your dessert, go brush your teeth, and go to bed." Tishva planted another kiss on the top of her head. "I'll see you in the morning."

Soraya ate through two and a half of the cookies and gave Yabo half of the last one before hopping down from her father's desk chair and going to the restroom. Unlike many of their neighbors in Rivinsdeep, who had outhouses, their cabin had indoor plumbing.

After washing up and changing into pajamas, Soraya put her notebook into her backpack, then collapsed onto her bed once more and closed her eyes. Little did she know it would be the very last night she'd ever spend in that bedroom.

## Chapter 5: Lesson in Air Magic

Even though she slept soundly under her thick navy blue comforter, Soraya sensed her father's presence creeping closer towards her bedroom. She awoke just as he towered over her bed.

*I'm leaving for Matumi today. This is the last time I'll see Papa for quite awhile.*

Tishva gently nudged his daughter's shoulder with his weathered hand. "Morning kiddo," he said, his voice low and firm. "It's time to get ready."

Soraya knew there was no time for dragging her heels. She sat up, being careful not to bump Yabo, who was sleeping by her feet.

Tishva drew apart the dark navy blue curtains, letting in a pale yellow stream of light from the rising sun. "Today's going to be a long day for you," he said while picking up Soraya's suitcase. "I let you sleep in as long as possible and made us breakfast. I'll explain more while you're eating at the table."

"Sounds good," Soraya yawned in reply. Before her feet hit the icy wooden floor, her father had already vanished down the hall, his heavy footsteps growing fainter as he descended down the spiral staircase.

"I wonder what today will bring," Soraya pondered while staring at the sunlight pouring in from her window. She hopped out of bed and looked down at the ground below. The pearly white snow covering the trees and ground outside sparkled and looked enchanting. "I'll miss you," she whispered to her mother's grave. "Please help Papa remember me."

The girl changed into warm black stockings and a light green dress with long sleeves and a jade ribbon around her waist. It reached down a little past her knees. Soraya loved the two deep pockets sewn into either side, which in her opinion, made it the most practical for traveling in. She then scooped up her pandacoon, who was sluggish from having just woken up, and cradled him like a baby.

"I want to take you with me so badly, Yabo," she wished longingly. "I just can't leave you behind, I love you too much."

Soraya planted several kisses on his fuzzy face and placed him on her shoulder, where he happily sat and stretched to wake himself up. She then flew towards the kitchen, where her father stood at the dining room table, waiting.

"Kiddo," Tishva said, setting a plate filled with bacon and eggs in front of her seat. "I'm worried about going into town with you today. We'll run some errands and I can drop you off at the train station, but we'll have to hurry. I wish I could take you to Matumi, but I'm afraid of straying too far from home in my condition."

"I understand…"

They were both worried that he might forget who she was out in public. Although it made sense for him to stay behind, Soraya was nervous about getting to the other side of their country on her own. The town of Rivinsdeep was a small and tight knit community made up mostly of elderly Azakuins. Everyone knew everybody and looked out for each other like a family. She wasn't sure how the bustling oceanside city life of Matumi would be in comparison.

Soraya pushed her nervousness away by sitting down and

tucking into breakfast. Yabo plopped onto her lap, sitting on hind legs while meowing for morsels. She obliged, sharing bits of egg and bacon by placing them in his outstretched paws.

"Look at how cute he is!" Soraya exclaimed in adoration, pointing at Yabo chewing his food. Her father didn't seem to pay any attention to either of them. Instead, he dug out paperwork from a large brown box.

"In case I have an episode and have to come back home early, I've written a list of chores for you to do today while in town," he explained, sliding a small piece of parchment paper next to Soraya's plate. "I need you to read this over and keep it in your pocket in case you lose this piece of paper."

Soraya glanced down at her father's neat handwriting.

**1. Visit bank:**

**- Give Soraya access to bank account.**

**2. Visit the Library and buy:**

**- Etherian Biology**

**- Etherian World History**

**- Azakuin Language and Composition**

**- Music Theory**

**- Casmerahn Volume I**

**- Algebra I**

**3. Visit Dr. Yosef Athan and get a doctor's note**

**4. Visit Train Station and pick up:**

**- Prepaid train ticket to Matumi**

**- Train leaves at 18 o'clock**

"This is it?" Soraya asked. It was a lot smaller of a list than she had anticipated.

"Yes," Tishva placed a small card in front of her. It had her father's name, address, and a twelve digit number printed on the front right. On the left was a picture of a red dragon with golden eyes towering over a pile of precious jewels.

"In case anything happens to me, you need access to my Lari. We're making you a card like this today at the bank. That way, you're not left stranded or wanting for anything," her father placed his finger on the list and pointed at number two.

"These books should all be at our local library. If there are any missing, you'll be able to purchase or rent them from Darkwood Academy's library. Also, the doctor's note is so you can keep Yabo with you at school. They will accommodate for you as long as a doctor says he's an emotional support animal."

"It all seems so simple and straightforward," Soraya commented with a hint of distrust. "Are you sure there's nothing missing?" she half joked, smiling up at her father. Although his eyes twinkled, he wasn't joining her on kidding around.

"Darkwood Academy provides school outfits so you'll be measured and fitted once you arrive," he prattled on as if Soraya hadn't said anything. "However, I need to go over some details with you about traveling."

He placed a small dark blue booklet in front of her. On the front was the pattern of the Azakuin nation's flag, which was a creature called a gremowlkin, a blend of an owl and cat. Gremowlkins were known for being great hunters, explorers and capable of adapting to any climate, which is why their government had chosen the creature for being the symbol of their country.

"This is your travel permit," Tishva said sternly. "Do not lose this or let it out of your sight. You'll need it for traveling across the country. Keep it in either your dress pocket or your jacket pocket for easy access."

Her father opened the booklet, taking out a small rectangular piece of paper from inside.

"This is a copy of your birth certificate. Keep this in here and only take it out to show adults when asked, and even then, only workers such as the train attendants and the principal at your school.

Others may try to steal this information from you, so be careful."

His daughter studied the document. She had never seen her own birth certificate before.

Province Farenwell of Azckua

Department of Public Health

Name: Soraya Thenayu

Birth Town: Rivinsdeep

Date of Birth: 6/09/3081

State Number: 86490951

Mother's Name: Adoria Litrigen

Sex: F

Father's Name: Tishva Thenayu

*This is a factual certificate of name and birth facts*

Tishva Thenayu
Witness Signature

Amrathael Ziyni
Witness Signature

"And kiddo?"

"Yes Papa?" Soraya noticed her father was holding something else in his hands.

"This is very important," Tishva placed a pair of black fingerless gloves onto the table. "You need to wear these at all times to cover the magic tattoos on the palms of your hands. You may wear them for religious reasons, and you can tell others it's because you're a follower of *The Path*."

Soraya reached for the gloves and slipped them on over her hands. They felt fuzzy and warm, decent for wearing outside and not too hot for wearing indoors. She was grateful they were fingerless, she liked touchings the textures of objects.

"That's it then. Are you finished eating your breakfast?" Tishva glanced over at the clock hanging on the wall next to their seats. It was almost nine in the morning.

"Yes, I'm done," the girl brought her dishes over to the sink and started washing them, but her father interjected.

"Don't worry about that, I can clean up when I get back home later today. Let's get ready to leave."

Soraya remembered what she had been doing the night before. "Should I finish reading through those books you gave me before we go?"

Tishva shook his head. "You'll have to do that when you come back in the next few months. We can't risk waiting too long to complete these chores, you can't miss the train."

The Azakuin Train Station was about an hour and a half away from Rivinsdeep. It would be a long day of walking outside in the snow, which was why they were leaving so early in the morning.

"Alright…" Soraya was disappointed at the thought of having to wait, but he had allowed her to read some chapters from his library, so she was grateful for that.

The duo bundled up before making their way outside into the cold snow with Soraya's suitcase and backpack. Yabo rode in the hood of Soraya's light pink coat, poking his head out every so often before diving back in to hide from the icy breeze.

Tishva closed the door behind them while his daughter took in the sight of her home one more time. The log cabin looked small on the outside, but she would never forget how spacious and cozy the interior was. No matter where she ended up, she would always love her humble abode hidden deep in the Averlore Mountains.

"Let's go, kiddo. We have a long day ahead of us," Tishva said, hoisting the suitcase up, carrying it under his right arm while Soraya wore her backpack.

A cold, strong gust of wind blew by them, rustling through the naked branches of trees and whatever leaves remained on others.

Tishva shivered while Soraya remained warm and cozy despite her clothes being a bit thin for such weather. She remembered reading the night before in the book, *Arcanology: The Study of Magic Volume I*, that Water Magic helped with staying warm in colder weather. She was impressed that it seemed to be holding up as a fact.

"Papa?" Soraya piped up. "Can I try gliding down the mountain for a little bit? I don't want to leave you behind, I just want to try flying."

"Of course," Tishva grinned. "It'll be awhile before I can teach you anything else about magic."

He pointed at the path leading down to Rivinsdeep. "Run forward, jump into the air, and believe you can fly. Mind over matter plays a huge role in using magic. You are fusing with the elements and becoming one with it, you have to believe you can use it."

His daughter studied the obstacles she'd be encountering if she did indeed manage to fly. The looming trees were tall and obscured most of the blue sky above. Even if she hovered five feet above the ground, she wouldn't hit their limbs.

"Yabo, stay with Papa for a few minutes," Soraya lightly prodded at her pandacoon to move. Instead of obliging, Yabo dug his claws into her coat and clung on tightly.

"Okay, don't say I didn't warn you."

Tishva held his hand out for the backpack, which Soraya took off and handed to him. The girl then inhaled deeply and glanced down the path one more time.

This was the moment she had been dreaming about ever since she could remember. She had always longed to fly, and now it was finally becoming a reality. Poised and ready for action, she sprinted forward. All she could hear was the snow crunching beneath her boots with each step.

*Three... two... one...*

Soraya leapt away from the earth and into the air with all

her might. For a split second, she thought she was being carried up by the wind and became excited, but then realized she was coming back down.

*Thud!*

She fell on her face in the soft snow beneath her. Yabo clambered out of her hoodie, meowing in concern as he placed his black paws on Soraya's forehead and tried pushing her up and out of the snow.

Tishva's roaring laughter echoed around them. "Oh, I forgot to tell you to hold up your pointer and middle fingers on either hand to use Air Magic!" he calmed himself rather ungracefully as he ran forward and plucked his daughter up from the snow. "Are you okay?"

Soraya lifted her head and glared up at her father. "You forgot to tell me the most important detail for flying?"

"Sorry, kiddo," Tishva chuckled while hoisting his daughter back up onto her feet. "You have to admit that was funny."

His daughter's sour face broke into a grin and she laughed with him. "Yeah, you're right," Soraya placed her hands on her hips, attempting to hide her smile. "Was there anything else I needed to know before I try again?"

"No, that's everything," Tishva smirked. "You should fly this time."

Yabo, who was getting cold from standing in the snow, leapt onto Soraya's dress and clambered his way back up into her hoodie where it was warm. He chirped loudly once he was safely inside.

"That didn't scare you?" Soraya asked, reaching over her shoulder to pat his furry head. "You're a lot braver than I thought. Hold on tight, I'm actually going to fly this time."

The girl brushed off the snow from her dress and coat and held her pointer and middle finger out on her right hand. Even though Air Magic was tattooed on her left hand, she wanted to see how fast it would take for the magic to transfer to her right. She took in another deep breath before sprinting forward and jumping into the air. This time, she stayed afloat and hovered a few feet above the snow, just as she had hoped to do.

"There you go!" shouted Tishva from behind her. "That's exactly right!"

"I'm doing it! I'm flying!" the girl gasped in delight. She looked down, seeing her legs suspended above the ground. Even though Soraya was barely hovering over the earth, being in the air gave her an amazing sense of freedom. She was suddenly aware of every small change in the wind around her and found it interesting that flying felt a lot like swimming, except her movements were not slowed by water, nor did she have to worry about holding her breath.

"Now, lean your body the way you want to go and bend the wind to propel you in that direction," instructed her father from below.

Soraya did as he commanded. "It feels a lot like I'm asking the air to help me," she said in wonder as the current changed and pushed her further down the mountain.

"That's exactly what you're doing," Tishva explained. "The elements are like immortal beings. Magic allows you to become one with them, and they can hear you and give you what you need."

The girl loved the sensation of weightlessness. She spun around a few times in the air before rising up higher to touch the tallest branches of the trees towering overhead.

"See? I told you I'd do it," she told her pandacoon, who was clinging tightly to her clothing from inside the hoodie with his little velvet black paws. "Are you alright?"

Yabo meowed in reply.

"I'll take that as a yes."

"Hey kiddo," her father called from below. "I gave you all I had left for Air Magic, and it's not a lot. Try not to fly too high for too long, or you'll fall from a great height and could get seriously injured, if not killed."

Soraya heard him but didn't respond immediately. Instead, she touched a red leaf hanging on a thin branch high above before focusing on coming back down. The wind pushed up gently from beneath, allowing her to float down gracefully until her feet planted themselves firmly in the snow.

"I did it!" she beamed proudly up at her father.

"You certainly did," Tishva smiled and patted her head with his gloved hand. "You're a natural."

"Thank you," she curtsied. "I can take my backpack now," Soraya held out her right hand and waited patiently for her father to hand it to her.

"For future reference, whenever you fly, whatever you're carrying with you also becomes lighter. You can fly with your backpack on, or even with another person, like we did the other day."

Soraya thought back to her father holding her while flying and sadness enveloped her heart. She didn't ever want to think about being choked by her father again, but the memory was still fresh and tied in with Air Magic even though she wished it wasn't.

Her father noticed his daughter's change of mood and switched subjects. "I haven't been to Rivinsdeep in years. You're the one whose been visiting and doing chores for our neighbors to earn food and new clothes."

"I think it'll be good for you to see them again," Soraya thought about how concerned and sad the townsfolk looked every time they asked her about her father. They seemed to always give her extra supplies to take home whenever she told them how busy he always was.

"Yes, I think you're right. It's about time I visited."

They trudged down the mountain path in silence for a little

while after that. It was an hour long walk from their home to the little village at the foot of the Averlore Mountains, and both wanted to save their energy for the trip down.

"Careful," Tishva called out to his daughter as she found herself suddenly sliding down a steeper part of the road. "You can use magic if you need to, just be mindful of how much you have left."

"I got it, thanks Papa," his daughter called back. She was determined to save her magic for when she really needed it. There was no telling when she'd ever find more again. Soraya found her balance and skated down, managing to stay upright until she came to a halt at a small plateau at the bottom. Her father slowly stepped sideways down the small slope until he met his daughter at the leveled ground.

"I forgot how dangerous this part of the road can be," Tishva looked down at his daughter with admiration. "You do this trek all the time, and without magic. I usually just fly down to our mailbox at the foot of the mountain to deliver and pick up mail and only walk on the road when I feel like getting more exercise in. I'm impressed with you."

"Thanks," Soraya blushed. "I don't mind walking up and down the path. It's peaceful and beautiful, especially during the spring and summer."

As the duo made their way down the winding mountain path towards Rivinsdeep, a white, spindly skeleton tree that Soraya used as a landmark for the halfway point came into view. It stood alone off the path, tall and erect with long thin branches twisting and winding away from all directions.

If lightning could be frozen in place, Soraya imagined that's what it would look like. She had always found herself both terrified and fascinated by the tree's presence. There didn't seem to be anything like it anywhere else on the Averlore Mountains, which made her appreciate its uniqueness, though its ominous presence kept her from wanting to venture any closer than she had to.

"Papa, what kind of tree is that?" she asked as it came closer into view. She turned her head and gazed up at her father.

"I believe that's…" Tishva brought his gloved hand to his chin and stroked his golden beard in thought. "That's a Syraple Tree."

"Oh?"

Soraya never would have guessed that such a scary looking plant could have such a cute name.

"Yup. Those are common in snowy areas, just not on this side of the mountain. That one looks very old and frail. If you dig into the trunk near the bottom, you can drain out syrup that's sweet and edible, though I doubt this one has any left in it."

"That's neat," Soraya commented, studying the foliage before closing her eyes. The tree was clear as day behind her eyelids. "We have about thirty more minutes to go," Soraya stated once they had passed by the skeletal tree.

"We're making good time," her father pulled out his pocket watch. "Wherever we're at on our list of chores, we'll stop to eat around three o'clock. How does that sound?"

"Wonderful," Soraya grinned. "Could we have lunch at Delphi's Diner today?"

Their neighbors, the Delphi's, had turned the first floor of their home into a restaurant where they served breakfast, lunch and dinner all day. Their menu was small, but everything tasted wonderful and flavorful.

"Yes, we can eat there."

"Yes!" Soraya exclaimed. "You've never been there before, it'll be new for you."

Tishva smiled down at his daughter. "Going into town with you will be new for me too."

"That's true!" Soraya gasped. She couldn't remember the last time she and Tishva had gone to Rivinsdeep together, or if that had ever even happened.

"Might as well check the mail before we continue on."

They had reached their mailbox, which looked like a small, windowless dollhouse on a stick. Above the latch was their address written in large pearly white letters: 1408 Averlore Mountain Way, Rivinsdeep, Farenwell Province 100.

Tishva pulled the small door down, and it squeaked as it opened. Inside was a small, rectangular yellow parchment envelope.

"That should be for me," her father said nonchalantly while taking the letter out and examining the front. The envelope wasaddressed to Tishva in their language, Azakuin, but the letter was handwritten in Casmerahn.

*Salutem Tishva…* Soraya interpreted the first line quickly in her head, but the rest of the words weren't familiar to her. Despite this, she did manage to memorize the letters before her father tucked it away into his coat.

"How much further until we get to Rivinsdeep?" Tishva asked while looking down into his daughter's bright blue eyes.

Soraya knew he was asking to draw her attention away from the letter. She wanted more than anything to know what it said and who it was from, but her father wouldn't willingly divulge that information to her. Instead, she went along with the change of topic.

"It's about a two minute walk from here to the front gate," Soraya said, pointing ahead at the stone paved path which curved to the right and disappeared behind a small grove of bushy green and yellow trees. "We're practically there."

She looked back up at her father and noticed his creased forehead and furrowed brows. Out of nowhere, he coughed.

"Are you alright?" she asked, concerned about his health and him having another spell of forgetting who she was.

Tishva procured a handkerchief and wiped his mouth. When he pulled it away, Soraya saw bloodstains covering the insides.

"I'll be fine, I just haven't stopped by to talk to anyone for quite a few years. I wonder how they'll all react when they see me."

"Don't worry, Papa. It'll be fine," Soraya gave a reassuring smile and reached out for his gloved hand. "I'll be here with you."

"Thanks, kiddo." He gently grasped onto her palm. "Let's go into town.

# Chapter 6: Rivinsdeep

As the duo exited the grove of trees, Soraya spotted the front gate. It was a bright red brick wall with three arched entrances, the center being the tallest and widest. Above the central archway was the word *Rivinsdeep* carved into a porcelain plaque and painted in golden letters.

Sitting before the entryway was a golden statue of a tiger, sitting on its hind legs with two paws resting atop a blue ball with white wavy clouds curling around it. The statue's head faced outward; its open half-grinning, half-growling mouth and staring dark golden eyes gave it an eerie quality. It was as if it were assessing them for signs of hostility.

"Zodia Tigris," Tishva observed. He stopped and bowed respectfully to the statue. Soraya copied her father.

"One of the twelve animals given speech by the Gods to prophesy to men during the The Age of Darkness," he continued, his voice solemn. "Their message was for us to repent of our wickedness so we could be saved."

Soraya already knew the historical event, which was recorded in every religion and culture from around the world, but listened anyway.

"When Etherians refused to listen to their message and instead murdered each Zodia one by one, plagues ensued, each more devastating than the last," he looked down at his daughter, his grayish blue eyes cloudy like a fog covering the sea. "The death of the last Zodia, Dragonai, resulted in a plague that wiped out one third of the world's population. Nothing so devastating has ever occurred in the history of Etheria since then."

It had always been difficult for Soraya to imagine such wickedness on a global magnitude. From the perspective of their religion's writings, *The Path,* made it sound as if all Etherians had lost their reasoning and compassion. The Gods were forced to use animals as vessels for turning Etherians back to loving and serving them and each other.

"Legend has it that the souls of all twelve Zodia are tied with different gems," her father mused. "These gems go by two names: Zodia Relics and Spirit Stones. Supposedly, they choose an Etherian to wield their power, which allows them access to an infinite amount of magic."

Tishva turned and looked down at his daughter with excitement in his eyes. "Imagine never running out of magic, never again having to search in nature for the power to fuse with the elements."

"That would be really amazing," Soraya agreed. Although different countries around their world acknowledged the existence of the Zodia Relics, no one truly knew where they were located. "Do you know where they are?"

Tishva shook his head. "No, though some royal families and religious figures claim to have them."

"Do you think they do?"

"Definitely not."

Soraya's smile faded. "Why would anyone lie about something like that?"

"It's a scare tactic to remain in power."

The girl sighed. "That's terrible."

"I agree, kiddo. I agree," Tishva stared past the statue, as though he were in a trance, which bothered Soraya. She didn't want him to forget what they were doing or who she was while they were in town.

"Papa, we'd best get going," Soraya said, leading her father by the hand to the first stop on their list of chores.

Dragulji Bank was located a few buildings away, sandwiched between the Bakery and Post Office. The building itself was made of dark green bricks with ornately decorated balconies of brown and white.

The delicious smell of hot and freshly baked cinnamon rolls wafted through the cold morning air. Soraya's mouth watered despite her having had breakfast just a little over an hour before. She decided to ask Tishva about a potential second breakfast later as she grabbed one of the golden handles of the bank's huge oaken doors and pushed her way in, causing a little silver bell near the ceiling on the inside to jingle merrily.

Both father and daughter entered onto a large black mat, which they stomped on thoroughly to rid their boots of snow. Soraya gazed around at the large open room in awe. She had walked past the Rivinsdeep bank many times but had never actually ventured into it by herself.

The walls were painted in jade green while the furniture was deep and rich like the leaves covering the Averlore Mountains during the summer months. The wooden floor was so polished and clean that they could see their reflections in it like a mirror. Soraya found it all extremely fancy, like the inside of a palace.

Black stone counters with steel bars across the tops separated customers from the bankers. Large paintings decorating each wall were of precious jewels, some in treasure chests with pearls, amethysts, and diamonds, while others had gold measured in scales. The largest and grandest picture hung over the front entryway. It depicted a large red dragon with bright golden eyes protecting a huge sparkling mound of riches deep within an underground chamber.

The bank was named after the dragon in the painting, Dragulji, who had become famous for accumulating the most loot of all the dragons that had ever lived. It was said he would raid ships and castles in search of treasure and hide his wealth in the depths of the volcano Cauldra, in Zilval. Few survived the beast's scorching flames or his razor-sharp teeth and claws whenever he attacked.

According to legends, royal families and high priests were willing to share their monopoly on magic with those who vowed to slay the beast and promised them a share in the dragon's wealth. Etherians eventually overpowered and slew Dragulji, but then they murdered others until dragons were almost extinct.

"Papa, do you think the last plague wiped out so many Etherians because we murdered so many dragons?" Soraya wondered while examining the painting. "There's only a few left, and they hide from us because of the dragon... um, killings, but there's a better way of saying it…" she frowned while floundering for the right word.

"Genocide?" Tishva offered gently, his grayish blue eyes sparkling with amusement at his daughter's observation.

"Yes…"

"Your theory does seem valid, but the Gods themselves would have to come down and confirm it in order for it to be true."

"Oh, okay," Soraya looked in disappointment at her reflection in the polished floor. "I just thought it made sense, is all."

Her father placed his hand on her shoulder. "I think you're right though, and a lot of Azakuin historians have made that observation too and would agree with you."

Soraya's face lit up. Before she could reply, they both heard the clacking of heavy footsteps coming towards them.

"Upon my word! Tishva!"

They were met by a tall, heavy set man. His bushy brown beard lined the border of his round face, and he wore a white collared shirt with black pants and suspenders over each round shoulder. The man's bright blue eyes were wide with surprise as he gaped at Tishva through thinly framed crescent moon spectacles.

"It's been ages since the last time you set foot in here!" the man gasped. "If I'm recalling correctly, your last visit was about seven years ago."

"I believe you're correct, Mr. Winston," Tishva held out his hand and the other man shook it enthusiastically. Soraya watched in fascination as the large man pulled her father in for a quick hug. Tishva stiffened up, but the banker pulled away fast.

"I know we've spoken over the phone and mailed letters back and forth to make deposits and pay bills and whatnot, but you rarely come down from that mountain top of yours. It must be awful lonesome up there without any neighbors nearby."

Tishva shrugged his shoulders. "Oh no, not at all. My daughter and work keeps me plenty busy."

Mr. Winston's face fell. "You didn't miss any of us… at all?"

Soraya's father saw how hurt the banker looked and realized he had misspoken. "I have missed you, all of you, in fact," he said, then quickly added, "I just can't believe how fast the years have flown by because of how busy I've been with work. That's all."

The banker's smile returned, though it wasn't as vibrant as before. "How busy can you be as a retired soldier?" he wondered aloud with a hint of suspicion in his voice.

"I've been commissioned for writing and illustrating books for different countries, so very busy," Tishva replied without missing a beat. "The work never ends and takes many hours to do, but it has helped distract me from my problems, and for that, I'm grateful."

Winston frowned. "Well, at least your daughter visits regularly. You'll be pleased to know that she's just like you," he gestured proudly at Soraya. "I always hear compliments about her, always helping everyone with chores around their farms. She picked up right where you left off."

"Yes, that was before the incident," Tishva grimaced.

Mr. Winston's ocean blue eyes shifted uncomfortably down at the floor. "I'm still sorry for your loss. I can only imagine how difficult it was for you to suddenly become a single parent, with your wife being murdered and all."

Soraya's eyebrows raised in surprise. *Mama was murdered? So she didn't die during childbirth?*

Tishva studied Soraya's shocked expression and let out a deep sigh before speaking in as calm a tone as he could muster. "I've tried not to think about that day in years, but, please, remind me of what you saw."

The banker closed his eyes. "I remember the day you came into town. You were carrying Soraya, who was unconscious, both of you were covered in blood stains," Winston glanced at Tishva with furrowed brows.

"Your eyes.... they were haunted with unimaginable horrors. We all gathered around and offered to help in any way we could. You said Adonia had been murdered, and you had lost both her and your unborn son. That was the last time any of us saw you in person, until now…"

Winston hung his head. "The only way any of us have known you're alive is because of our business communications, and Soraya coming into town to do chores and earn food and supplies here in Rivinsdeep. Many of us have thought of visiting you in your solitude, but you had insisted on being left alone."

"And I greatly appreciate it, I really do," Tishva dug his hand into his pockets and pulled out his identification papers. "We came in here today to add Soraya to my account. She needs the ability to withdraw Lari."

Soraya sensed her father was purposefully changing the topic and the banker went along with it.

"That's a sensible thing to do, especially with her growing older," Winston's demeanor shifted as he went from grimacing to thrusting on a grin before making his way behind the barred counters.

"Since she's still a minor, her account will be connected with yours," the banker stated. "We will mail you updates whenever she deposits or withdraws Lari from your account."

"Understood," Tishva nodded, then turned to his daughter. "Take out your paperwork."

Soraya reached into her dress pockets, grabbed both her birth certificate and passport, and handed them over.

Mr. Winston took and examined her paperwork carefully, pushing his thin framed crescent moon spectacles up higher onto his tomato shaped nose. "You'll be receiving your own card today. They work with all Dragulji branches from around the world," he said, then slid the paperwork back.

"Thank you, sir." Soraya replied politely before placing her identification papers back into her dress pockets.

"You're welcome, miss." The banker strutted over to a series of metal cabinets lining the wall behind him and took a rather large wad of skeleton keys out from his pants pocket. After fumbling around, he found a small silver key and unlocked a small square door.

"Here we are," Winston stated while sliding a paper and quill towards them from under the gate. "Mr. Thenayu, just fill out this page and return it to me. Then both of you can leave and swing back by in another hour. Her card will be ready for pick up by then."

Tishva immediately got to work. The scribbling sound of the pen meeting the parchment paper filled the still air with small scraping and scratching noises.

"Um, sir?" Soraya asked timidly while looking up at the banker through the steel bars.

"Yes?" Mr. Winston replied, peering down at her through his crescent moon glasses.

"Do you know anything else about my Mama?" Soraya quickly glanced at her father, who had momentarily paused in filling out the paperwork to listen.

The banker frowned. "Unfortunately, I do not. Neither of you have lived in town for quite a few years. I just remember being told that she had wanted to be with your father when she had your younger brother…" his voice trailed off for a moment.

"I'm sorry, I don't have anything else to tell you about her. I'm just glad she adopted you and brought you up as her own. She had a good heart for being a Casmerahn."

"Casmerahn's are Etherians too, just like us," Soraya reminded him gently.

"O-of course, I'm sorry," the banker stuttered, clearly caught off guard from being corrected by a child. "I didn't mean to sound demeaning towards your mother, or anyone for that matter."

His face had turned beet red and he had to dig into his pocket for a handkerchief to wipe the sweat building up on his forehead. Tishva had already slipped the signed document back and was waiting, his arms folded across his chest.

"Alrighty then," Winston said while picking up the paperwork with his large hands, which were now shaking from embarrassment. "I'd best get to work on your card, little miss. I'll s-see you both back, er, in an hour."

Tishva placed his hands and fingertips together and bowed slightly. "Thank you for your help, Mr. Winston."

Soraya copied him and bowed even though her respect for the banker had gone down a little due to his remark about her mother.

"Not a problem," Winston smiled sheepishly before laughing awkwardly and shuffling off once again to the wall behind him. He quickly disappeared behind a doorway.

"Ready to go to the library?" Tishva asked Soraya as he extended his right arm out to her.

"Yes, Papa," she smiled and wrapped her left arm around his. Together, they walked out of the bank, arm in arm.

"You did a good job standing up for your mother," Tishva whispered to his daughter. "I'm proud of you. Most everyone in this town have blue eyes and aren't used to seeing foreigners, so sometimes they come across as demeaning without meaning to. It's good to be kind and patient," he kissed the top of Soraya's head. "Shall we go to the library now?"

Soraya nodded, turning to walk further down the street in the opposite direction of the front gate when her pandacoon fidgeted from within her hoodie.

"Mow?" Yabo's muffled meow came from behind her head. He clawed his way out of Soraya's pink jacket and perched himself firmly on her right shoulder. "Mrow!" he said adamantly, glancing at the Bunion Bakery, where the delicious smell of cinnamon rolls was coming from, then glanced back at his owner with pleading black beady eyes.

"Papa, do you suppose we could get a little something from

the bakery?" Soraya asked on behalf of Yabo. "It smells delicious, and he really wants food."

Tishva pulled out his pocket watch. "It's ten forty-seven in the morning. We're doing well on time, so that sounds fine," he put it away and stroked their pet. "He's been really good today, I don't see why we can't give him a treat."

The pandacoon rubbed his fuzzy face against Tishva's hand and purred in gratitude. He then leapt onto Tishva's arm and clambered up onto his right shoulder. Soraya and her father waltzed over to the Bunion Bakery together, arm in arm.

"Perhaps I can have a little something as well?" Soraya asked, tilting her head slightly and batted her long eyelashes innocently up at her father.

Her father rolled his eyes. "How can I say no to that?" he sighed, holding open the door of the bakery and motioned with his other hand for his daughter to enter first. "After you, m'lady."

Vanilla, sugar, and chocolate fragrances greeted their noses. Tall shelves and racks lined every wall, all filled with baked breads, pastries and cookies of different sizes. A large glass case full of colorfully frosted cakes and desserts sat next to the counter where customers paid.

A plump older woman with curly black hair that was tied up in a white bandana, and dark navy blue eyes stood behind the cash register. She had a pink and white striped dress on with a white apron covering most of the front. Her skin was dark and beautiful with light pink spots of skin on her face, arms and legs. It reminded Soraya of cats with unique patterned patches of fur and made her smile every time she saw the elderly woman. Mrs. Bunion's blue eyes lit up when she saw them enter the bakery.

"Hello dearie!" she exclaimed while hobbling around the counter and hugging the girl. Soraya gave her a small squeeze back, but was careful not to hug her too tightly.

"And hello there!" the baker said while letting go of the child and gazing up at the man towering over her. "You must be her father. It's been so long since I've last seen your handsome face."

"Yes, I am," Tishva bowed. "I remember you, Mrs. Bunion. How have you been after all these years?"

The older woman's smile faded slightly. "Life has been good," she replied. "But I worry very much about our lovely little community. Us elderly folk outnumber our youth, and I fear if that doesn't change soon, that Rivinsdeep will become a ghost town."

Tishva nodded. "Your fears are valid. It can't continue to thrive if fresh blood doesn't take it over and keep it going," he glanced down at his daughter and grimaced. "You might not want to hear this news then, but Soraya is leaving for school today."

"Oh?" Mrs. Bunion raised a dark eyebrow. "And which school would that be?"

"Darkwood Academy…" Soraya said, unsure of how the baker would take the news. To the girl's relief, the elderly woman broke into a smile, showing a row of crooked yellowing teeth.

"That is a fine school, and in such a beautiful place too," she sighed fondly. "All five of my children went there when they were around your age. My oldest daughter especially loved being in warmer weather and living near the ocean."

She pointed a short, stubby finger at Soraya and poked her shoulder. "You need to find a good young man to marry while you're there. Bring him back here and start a family. Make this town full of young children again. The Potter children are still toddlers, if you hurry, there won't be much of an age gap between them."

"I-I don't want to get married and have kids yet!" Soraya stuttered, blushing a crimson red. Starting a family was the last thing on her mind.

"Remember, Mrs. Bunion, my daughter is only thirteen years old," interrupted Tishva, whose face was also flushed. "Maybe when she's thirty I'll let her date someone."

"Papa!" Soraya laughed, "I don't need to wait that long to be with someone… do I?"

The concept of dating wasn't something she was familiar with other than in the romance novels she had read. She just assumed it meant kissing and holding hands a lot.

"I had my first child when I was eighteen, before I got married," Mrs. Bunion winked at Soraya. "My husband and I have been together for forty years now, and three of our five children are married with grandkids. I just wish they all hadn't moved away…" she gazed out of the large front window of the shop. "I'm just grateful for whenever they visit."

Before Mrs. Bunion could continue on, Yabo, who had been patiently waiting for food, leapt onto the countertop and meowed while staring at the cakes and pastries in the glass case.

"Poor Yabo," Soraya cooed. "We came in here to give him a treat and we totally forgot."

Mrs. Bunion disappeared through an open door in the back. After a minute, she reappeared with a small jar of berries tied with a red ribbon and three hard boiled eggs. "These will do," she said.

Tishva glanced down at his daughter and noticed her eyeing the cinnamon rolls. "We'll have one of those as well," he said while pointing at the largest piece behind the glass case.

"Oh, thank you Papa!" Soraya beamed and spun around

ecstatically in a circle on the soles of her feet.

"That'll be ten Lari," Mrs. Bunion said, smiling at the sight of the young girl's excitement. While placing the cinnamon roll in a brown bag and handing it to Soraya, she turned to Tishva. "Is she always this full of energy?"

"Why do you think I send her down here so often?" he chuckled, handing her his Dragulji credit card. "I'm sure she could power a whole city if I could just figure out how to plug her into a wall socket."

Soraya had stopped paying attention to their conversation. She was too busy enjoying the first bite and tasting the sweetness of the cream cheese frosting and cinnamon bread as it melted in her mouth.

"Take care, Mrs. Bunion," Mr. Thenayu said, putting the tips of his fingers together and bowing. It was only after he nudged Soraya and snapped her out of her cinnamon roll heaven that she noticed they were about to leave and did the same.

"Thank you again," Soraya said with a mouthful of food.

"Of course," smiled Mrs. Bunion. "Soraya, my dear, have a wonderful time in Matumi, and Tishva, don't be a stranger. With your daughter leaving, you won't have anyone going into town to do chores for you. Promise me you'll visit us more often than once in a blue moon. We all want to be there for you."

"Thank you, I promise I will," Tishva bent down and hugged her gently before taking a step back. He extended his arm to Yabo, who leapt onto him from the glass case and clambered up to his shoulder. He then opened the bakery door for his daughter. "After you."

Soraya stepped outside back into the cold winter air. Although the wind was picking up and kicking about snow from the ground, it wasn't as harsh as the winds that blew through the tops of the Averlore Mountains. The colorful buildings of Rivinsdeep were built tightly together and kept a lot of it out.

"For being so good, Yabo should have an egg first," she exclaimed. Tishva gave her one and placed the other two into Soraya's backpack along with the jar of berries.

Soraya cracked the egg by thwacking it onto the brick wall of the bakery and carefully peeling off the shell before tossing it into the snow. Her pandacoon spun in circles on Tishva's shoulder, then sat on his hind legs in anticipation.

"Here you go, you goofball," Soraya held out Yabo's second breakfast. He hungrily took it into his tiny black paws and nibbled on the top.

"Alright," Tishva's eyes twinkled merrily. "Save the rest in your backpack. Yabo will need snacks for when you're both on the train," he said, holding out his hand for his daughter to take. "Let's go finish our errands."

## Chapter 7: All Saint's Church

The Rivinsdeep library was located inside the All Saints Church at the other end of town. It was a beautiful blue building with stained glass windows, a tall bell tower, and large, spacious rooms. Phases of the moon circling Etheria were engraved in stone above the entrance.

Most of the books inside were donations made by locals, and even Tishva had given some of his novels to them over the years. Soraya knew this because she had been the one to carry them down the mountain every time he cleaned out his office. She would, of course, read through the books before giving them to the library just in case there was something new for her to learn, but none of them had ever been from his personal collection on Arcanology.

"Mrowr!" Yabo chirped, leaping from Tishva's shoulder onto Soraya's. She knew he wanted some of her cinnamon roll since he had finished his egg, so she tore off a small piece of the bread to give to her pet. She loved the glaze too much to want to share it with him.

"Soraya, I'm sure Yabo would love to try more than just the bread," her father scolded, noticing her small selfish act.

"Oh, okay," his daughter sighed, blushing at being caught. She tore off another piece, this time with cream cheese frosting on it, and placed it into Yabo's outstretched paws. Her pandacoon sniffed at it, licking the morsel with his small pink tongue before shoving the whole piece into his mouth.

"See? He can eat most anything you can," Tishva said, his frown deepening. "Yabo's the only sibling you have, treat him nicely."

"Sorry," Soraya kissed her pet's fuzzy face. He returned the favor by licking her cheek.

Finally, they arrived at All Saint's Church. The girl gave her pandacoon one more piece of her second breakfast and inhaled the rest.

Tishva opened one of the beautifully decorated iron doors. Above the entryway was a crescent shaped stained glass window with a white squared cross in the center.

Soraya entered into the narthex of the church, the main hall where churchgoers socialized before and after services. It was a wide open space with a large blue carpet with golden flowers and vines decorating the frayed edges covering the white marble ground.

Mannequins stood proudly in the four corners of the room, clothed in traditional Azakuin garments. Long blue robes with white fur on the collars and ends masked their royal blue porcelain bodies. Colorful beaded necklaces embedded with fangs and claws shrouded their necks, and their heads were crowned with feathered headdresses of all colors from Rivingales and Gremowlkins, the two best hunters of Azakua's native birds.

Colorful tapestries, traditional Azakuin tribal masks and flags from different clans covered the stone walls. All of the masks were a combination of human and animal features and represented the twelve Zodia that had lived over a thousand years ago.

Through another set of large oaken doors was the nave, the largest room in the church, where the congregation would sit on giant multicolored pillows and listen to Priests interpret passages of *The Path.* Although worship services were held on Solis Diem, the first day of the week, everyone was allowed to enter and pray to the

Gods or have private confession and absolution at anytime. Since everyone in Rivinsdeep respected the Church, no one ever stolen or vandalized anything inside despite it remaining open to the public.

"Which way do we go?" Tishva whispered, his question echoing off the walls.

"This way," his daughter pointed at a plaque above a closed white door that read, *Library*.

They tiptoed over, gently pushing their way inside another spacious room, but this one had tall, full bookshelves lining all of the blue stone walls. To their right was a large dark brown desk with a black cash register on top. Behind that, pacing in circles while reading, was the librarian, Ms. Veda.

"Hello!" Soraya whispered excitedly, waving at the older woman.

The librarian stopped what she was doing and looked up at them. She had dark skin, long blond curly hair tied in a bun, and bright blue eyes that shined brightly behind her large glasses. She was dressed in traditional Azakuin church attire since she was working inside a holy place.

"Well, hello there, little bookworm," she nodded curtly at the girl. "And hello, Mr. Thenayu. I've been expecting you both."

Tishva bowed. "Yes ma'am. Did you find all the school books?"

"I did, and I have them all prepared here for you," she bent down behind her desk and came back up with a large stack of novels. "Our library only owned one of the six school books that were needed, so I pulled three from my personal shelves at home and received the other two from a neighbor in town."

"Thank you so much, Ms. Veda," Soraya grinned. "Did you go to Darkwood Academy?"

"Yes, many moons ago," laughed the librarian, her bright blue eyes sparkling. "It's a wonderful and beautiful place. I think you'll love it."

The positivity about the school from both Mrs. Bunion and Ms. Veda helped ease the girl's mind about leaving. Excitement welled up inside as she thought about seeing and experiencing living in Matumi for herself.

"How much for all of the books?" Tishva asked while digging around in his pocket for his Dragulji credit card.

"It's ten for each book, so sixty Lari, please," Ms. Veda replied. "I'll make sure to give our neighbor twenty for contributing two of his books."

Soraya's father was about to hand her his card, but hesitated for a moment. "You know what? Go ahead and tack on an extra two hundred Lari," he thought aloud. "Yes, please make it two hundred and fifty Lari for the total. It's been too long since I've last donated money to the community."

The librarian's bright blue eyes widened in surprise. "That is awfully generous of you," she said, then slid the card through the slot in the machine and handed it back. "Would you like the receipt?"

"Yes, thank you ma'am," Tishva smiled as he took it. "Well, we'd best be off. We only have a few hours left together before she leaves, and we have a few more errands to run around town."

A hint of sadness glowed in his grayish blue eyes. "Kiddo, make sure to put the books into your backpack."

Soraya put all of her new school belongings away.

Ms. Veda nodded. "Enjoy Darkwood Academy. Tell me all about it when you come back."

"I will!" Soraya promised.

"Thank you again, and take care, Ms. Veda," Tishva bowed respectfully. His daughter followed suit before they turned to leave. However, before they could exit through the front doors of the church, they ran into a large group of elderly folk in the main foyer of the building.

"Tishva!" a man's voice called from the other end of the large room.

"You're still alive, eh?" teased another.

"Welcome back!"

Tishva was surrounded and given affection by many of their different neighbors. Several women gave him hugs, some men gave him pats on the back, while others clasped their gloved hands around his. One of the men who did this was Dr. Yosef Athan, the man they needed to see next on their list of errands.

"You don't have to hide from us, you know," winked the doctor as he let go of Tishva's hand. "After everything you've done to help this town, you should know that we're all grateful for you."

Tishva looked embarrassed, yet pleased at all the unexpected care and concern he was receiving. "I'm… I'm really sorry for not visiting with any of you sooner, Yosef. I didn't know how to deal with my wife and son's death other than drowning my sorrows in work."

Dr. Athan was a tall, thin, dark skinned man with bright blue eyes. He had long, midnight black hair tied into braids flowing past his broad shoulders. He also had a nicely kept black beard and goatee. Yosef wore a long white coat that went down to his knees and a multicolored scarf. The doctor pulled Soraya's father into a gentle side hug.

"We're here for you, don't forget that," he whispered in a comforting voice. "When you told me on the phone you were coming down today, I could hardly believe it, but Mr. Winston and Mrs. Bunion confirmed you were here when I went to visit them both this morning. I had to come see you for myself, as did these kind folk here."

Yosef dug into his coat pocket, pulling out a sealed envelope with melted blue wax in the center. "I brought that note for your daughter so she can take her pet with her to school. Give this to the principal, and Yabo can reside with you," he said while handing the parchment envelope to Soraya.

"Thank you, sir," the girl bowed to the kind man. "Yabo, you can come with me!" she rubbed her face into his furry chest, and he licked her forehead with his small pink tongue. She made sure to tuck the envelope safely into her backpack so it wouldn't get lost.

"While we're here, let's all pray for you both, for Ms. Thenayu to have safe travels, and for Mr. Thenayu to be given comfort and peace by the Gods," Dr. Athan smiled, showing his straight, pearly white teeth. "Would you have time for that today?

Tishva checked his pocket watch. "It's eleven fifty-six in the morning, so yes, we have time."

"Excellent!" Dr. Athan held open the inner church doors for everyone to enter inside. Each member sat on large, beaded pillows that lay scattered evenly across the room.

Soraya joined her father at the back of the room. She liked being near the multicolored, stained glass-windows, each depicting a different story from *The Path.* A large mural at the front of the church depicted the three Deities in the Azakuin Triune God: El, the

Father of all, Nevaeh, the Spirit of wisdom, and Emmanuel, the son of El. As a fusion, they become Kyrios, who likes to be called They, Gods, and God.

Although no one knew what each deity looked like, Azakuin artwork always depicted El as having dark skin with one silver eye and one golden eye, Nevaeh as having pale skin with one pink eye and one purple eye, and Emmanuel as having dark skin with pale spots and one red eye and one green eye. Their fusion, Kyrios, had ivory skin and blue eyes.

Between all three deities and their fusion came all features, from skin color to eye color, which is why *The Path* writes that all men and women are created as equals in the image of the Gods.

Yosef stood at the front of the Church with his back turned towards the congregation. His head was bowed to the stained glass mosaic covering the majority of the front wall. The large wooden table before him had a chalice full of wine, a silver plate full of bread, a folded white cloth, and a small glass bottle filled with golden oil.

Once the murmuring faded, the Doctor spoke in a loud, bold voice. "It is said that Etherians are created in the image of our three deities and their fusion, Kyrios. Our task, as their creations, is to take care of Etheria and all it's inhabitants, from plants and animals, to our fellow kin," he faced the assembly, beckoning for Tishva and Soraya to come forward. "May Mr. and Ms. Thenayu please rise and join me?"

Both father and daughter blushed from being called out. Soraya and Tishva rose from their pillows and walked towards the front, making sure not to trip on anyone along the way.

"Please bow your heads in prayer," Yosef commanded, the congregation obeying. "Thank our Lords for these two wonderful, Gods fearing members of our community. Guide and protect Soraya as she travels today, may you all watch over and protect her along her journey."

Dr. Athan gently squeezed Soraya's hand before moving on. "Please help Tishva heal from his past tragedies and find peace and mercy in your unfailing love," the doctor let go of them, then reached for the small glass bottle of oil. After uncorking and pouring a small amount onto a white cloth, he wiped some of the oil onto the foreheads of both Tishva and Soraya.

"Mew!" Yabo called from Soraya's shoulder. The congregation chuckled as Yosef also anointed the pandacoon with a small dab of oil on his forehead.

"May the Gods also aid this beautiful creation of theirs in his travels," he added with a serious tone, though the edges of his lips were curled in amusement. "The Gods will hear our prayers and remember all three of you," he beamed at them before facing the congregation with outstretched arms. "The Gods be with you all."

"And also with you. Thanks be to the Gods," the multitude said in unison. With that, they rose and came forward to give Tishva and Soraya support.

"Darling, we'll miss seeing you every week," said their neighbor, Mrs. Fern, one of the gardeners who had taught Soraya how to grow tomatoes and other vegetables.

"We'll miss seeing your cheerful smile. Hopefully your new community will enjoy seeing it as much as we have," said Mr. Gale, an elderly man who thought of Soraya as his own granddaughter.

"Th-thank you all," stammered Soraya, the realization of her not seeing any of them for a long time finally dawning upon her.

After many hugs and several long goodbyes, the number of neighbors dwindled down as each turned to hobble slowly out of the church. As the girl sadly watched them leave, a few tears escaped her blue eyes and rolled down her face. Yabo noticed and leaned over to lick them off.

"What would I do without you?" she asked while patting her pandacoon.

"Are you alright, Ms. Thenayu?" Yosef noticed her crying and brought her a white tissue. He knelt down, holding it out with his gloved hand.

"I'm okay, thank you," Soraya replied, taking the small cloth and dabbing at her eyes with them. Everyone else had left them but the doctor. The air, which had been buzzing with several simultaneous conversations just a few moments before, was completely still once more.

"May I take all three of you out to eat?" Dr. Athan asked her father politely. "Delphi's Diner is close by, and it's really good food. I'll pay for you all, my treat."

"We would be honored to join you for lunch, my brother," her father replied, bowing out of gratitude. "However, you don't need to pay for us."

The Doctor grinned mischievously and winked at Tishva. "If I happen to give them my card first, you'll just have to accept lunch as my treat."

Tishva smirked. "The same applies to you. I might just beat you to it."

Soraya watched in fascination through tear stained eyes as both men stared each other down, each reaching for their jacket pockets as they were speaking. In a flash, they simultaneously whipped out their bank cards. They both stood still for a brief moment afterwards before Tishva sighed and lowered his card.

"It's a draw, as usual."

Yosef's booming laughs echoing around them. "After all of these years, we're still at a tie?" He came over to Tishva and pat his back. "Man, it's good to see you again."

"Likewise," Tishva chuckled. "I need to visit you more, I've missed our little duels."

"Is that all that you've missed about me?" the doctor placed his right gloved hand over his heart and dramatically turned his head away. "I am *so* hurt right now," he gasped and fake pouted.

Soraya's sadness was losing its grip on her. She giggled from behind them, causing Dr. Athan to burst out laughing again. Tishva joined in, their merriment filling the narthex.

"Could you please keep it down?"

All three turned and spotted Ms. Veda standing in front of the library entrance, her arms folded across her chest, her foot tapping impatiently on the marble ground.

Tishva and Yosef froze in place, like two children caught stealing treats from a cookie jar. Ms. Veda was trying to look serious, but the edges of her lips were curved in amusement at the guilty expressions of the two grown men.

"Go be loud somewhere else," she commanded while pointing at the front doors. "I can't focus with all this racket."

"Sorry, Ms. Veda," Dr. Athan bowed respectfully to her. "We're on our way out… right now."

As he slunk out the church doors, Ms. Veda looked down at Soraya. "Keep an eye on these two, will you? They're nothing but trouble when they're together."

Soraya straightened up and saluted before rejoining her father and the doctor, who were cackling with glee and giving each other soft punches on the shoulder.

"This is why they tried so hard to split us up at school," Tishva chuckled. "We're just terrible when we're together."

"True, but we also turned in the best projects and were at the tops of our classes. That made us nearly untouchable," Yosef bragged. "I miss those carefree days..." his expression was replaced with a long look of sorrow. "I'm sorry that we didn't keep in touch these past few years. I should've been there for you, and I wasn't. I'm truly sorry."

Mr. Thenayu shook his head. "No, I'm sorry, I shouldn't have shut you and everyone else out. It's my fault and my fault completely."

The two men continued their conversation as they all walked towards Delphi's Diner. Soraya stayed a few steps behind and kept silent so as not to interrupt them reconnecting with one another. She enjoyed seeing her father's playful side shining through despite the grim reality he was facing, and knowing that the doctor was a close friend of his made her feel more relaxed about leaving.

*Papa has someone he can talk to. Yosef will help him. He just needs to open up to him about what's going on with him. I really hope he does.*

## Chapter 8: Delphi's Diner

The restaurant was just a few buildings down on the right side of the street. It was a beautiful, three story jade green house with flower and vine designs spiraling and encircling the balcony overhanging the porch. The third floor had a smaller balcony where the banner, *Delphi's Diner*, hung from. Multi-colored shingles were embedded into the roof, making the house stand out from the other buildings on the street.

"I remember this place," breathed Tishva while gazing at the front in admiration. "It's really cute, like a dollhouse."

"Yes, and it's also one of the oldest homes here," Yosef said proudly. "Just wait until you see the inside, the Delphi family renovated it four years ago and turned the entire downstairs portion into a diner. They live in the second and third story levels."

As they all walked up the front steps, Soraya's father added, "I keep forgetting that some things have changed during my seven year hiatus. I don't recall the Delphi's owning this property. I just thought they had an entirely new restaurant built here in town, not that they refurbished this place for that purpose."

The doctor nodded. "You're right, they didn't own this seven years ago, the Creeds family did," Dr. Athan stopped and shook off the snow from his black boots. A navy blue mat lay before the entrance that he stomped on to get the last pieces off.

"After you," Yosef said while holding the door open.

"Thank you, brother," Tishva said while summoning his daughter to enter first.

The large, rectangular room had booths and dark blue cushioned seats set up alongside walls decorated with painted pictures by local artists. Wooden barrels covered in blue and white checkered cloths were spread out across the middle to accommodate for more customers.

Even though it had barely turned noon, there were already several families seated and enjoying their meals together.

"Table for three?" a tall, slender woman asked as she approached them while carrying a menu in her hands. She had skin that was dark, like the trunk of a willaby tree, long, light pink hair, and icy, bright blue eyes.

"Hello Kalisha!" Soraya grinned up at her. She had always thought the youngest sibling of the Delphi family was the most beautiful person in town. She also secretly wished her hair could be pink like hers.

The waitress waved cheerfully. "Hi Soraya! Are you here to help in the restaurant today, or to have lunch?"

Although there was a nineteen year age difference between the two, Kalisha was the closest person to act like an older sister towards Soraya.

"I'm having lunch today. It'll be a few months before I can

come back and work here…" the girl frowned as she finished her sentence. It suddenly dawned on her that she wouldn't be seeing the restaurant and all her friends who worked there for quite some time.

Kalisha noticed Soraya's expression change. "Is something wrong?"

"She's going to Darkwood Academy," Dr. Athan stepped forward and joined in on their conversation. "She's leaving this afternoon, actually, in a couple of hours."

"Soraya, congratulations!" the waitress gasped. "I went there when I was younger, but had to come back and help my family with the farm and business when Ma got sick…" she let out a small sigh and looked longingly out the window.

"I haven't been able to go back yet, but I plan to finish my education in the future," Kalisha pulled the girl into a gentle embrace. "You'll do great. Fill me in on how it was when you get back."

The waitress turned her attention towards the two men. "Doctor Athan, I hope you're well!" she exclaimed eagerly before realizing how loudly she had spoken and lowering her voice. "It's lovely to see you again."

"It's lovely to see you again as well, Ms. Delphi. I hope you're doing well."

The waitress couldn't help but show off her straight pearly white teeth. "I am, I hope that you are too," she was so entranced with the doctor that she almost forgot that Tishva was there.

"We'll take a table or a booth, please," Mr. Thenayu gently interrupted.

Kalisha finally turned her full attention to Tishva and froze. It was a like a light bulb went on in her head. "Mr. Thenayu!" she blurted. "I remember you, it's been years since you've come into town, hasn't it?"

Tishva, now embarrassed, simply nodded. "Just enjoying

my last few hours with my daughter until she leaves for a few months."

"Oh yes, of course," Kalisha swiveled her head around, searching for an empty place to seat them at. "Is the booth in the corner alright?

"That'll be perfect," Yosef beamed.

Kalisha picked up two more menus before leading the group to the back of the restaurant. Soraya, Yosef and Tishva followed after her and took their seats, which were covered in soft, pillowy cushions. The waitress placed the menus on the table before going back to the front of the restaurant. The second she was out of ear shot, Dr. Athan's expression changed from being jovial to concerned.

"Tishva, I have some serious news to go over with you."

Mr. Thenayu grimaced. "Alright, but is it something that's appropriate to talk about given my daughter's age?"

Dr. Athan nodded. "It concerns her too."

Tishva glanced at Soraya. "Nothing we discuss here today leaves this table. Is that understood?"

"Got it."

"I'm not sure how aware you are of everything that's been happening in our country, but we're on the cusp of a large disaster," Yosef began in a hushed tone. He looked around the restaurant to make sure no one was close enough to eavesdrop, then continued. "The government is pushing the public to ostracize non Azakuin descendants, even going so far as demanding they be deported despite them being legal citizens. Their reasoning for this is that blue eyes will apparently go extinct if we don't keep to our own."

Tishva's expression immediately turned sour. "I am aware of the anti immigration campaign, and I did give Soraya a brief explanation for it, but calling for the deportation of legal citizens is news to me," he shook his head. "What a typical move, creating chaos and fear to further divide our country in the midst of an election year."

"Yes, it's odd that now, all of a sudden, they claim to care about our Azakuin eye color being recessive," the doctor agreed. "Casmerahns, Voreans, Rosinkins, Golaytians, Zilvalians, Oransjch, and even Calgreneze have been here since we opened up our borders to foreigners over two hundred years ago. While it's true that we're a small country and their presence has decreased the number of blue eyes, their cultures and religions have become so intertwined with our own that it's impossible to separate them now. Pushing for division is just evil."

The doctor sadly gazed past Mr. Thenayu towards the other corner end of the restaurant, where the Potter family was eating lunch with their twin toddlers who both had honey colored eyes. Mr. Potter was an Azakuin descendant, while his wife was an immigrant from the kingdom of Golaytia.

"Our community thankfully hasn't really been affected by the poison the government is spreading. We are both blessed and cursed for being so far removed from more majorly populated cities. As far as I know, everyone here in Rivinsdeep is kind and accommodating to immigrants," Yosef's shoulders tightened. "Correct me if I'm wrong, but I don't remember anyone here mistreating your wife while she was still among the living."

Tishva stared down at his hands. "Adonia loved Rivinsdeep. She only stayed away because of what I was researching for the government and didn't want to lead any unwanted visitors to me. Sometimes…" he choked. "I wish I had quit. I believe she still would be here if I had just focused on being a father and worked a simple job here in town rather than having to constantly be apart from her and working on secret missions…"

Dr. Athan leaned across the table and placed a hand on Tishva's shoulder. "Brother, don't blame yourself. I know how difficult it can be working for the government."

Soraya gave her father a side hug from her seat, when she noticed something on the doctor's skin poking out from under his gloved hand. It was a faded blue design and looked similar to her Water Magic tattoo.

*Are you an Arcanologist too?* she almost blurted out her thought, but decided it was best to act naive on the matter. Although both men seemed to understand each other extremely well, the girl wondered just how close of friends they actually were.

"Father Vic and I constantly remind everyone here that we are all descendants of the first two Etherians the Gods created," the doctor resumed. "We are all equals in our world of Etheria, and it seems so simple and straightforward. And yet, despite our best efforts, I fear for the future of our citizens, especially if the government continues to paint our fellow immigrant Azakuins in such an ill manner."

Mr. Thenayu looked into Dr. Athan's sky blue eyes. "As much as I love our country, Azakua is a living contradiction. Although we've become more inclusive over the past hundred years by allowing foreigners to immigrate here, we're still exclusive with some of our traditions. Even my Casmerahn wife, who converted to our religion and adopted our practices, wasn't allowed to participate in certain public ceremonies due to her red eyes."

Tishva paused when he noticed Kalisha walking briskly toward them. In one hand were three bundles of utensils wrapped in white napkins, and in the other was a pad of white paper and a black pen.

"What would you all like to drink?" she asked politely while placing silverware on the table.

"I'll take a cream soda," Dr. Athan ordered with a wink.

"Me too!" pipped up Soraya. "And water for Yabo, please."

"Mow!" Yabo agreed as he hopped up onto the table from

the girl's hoodie and sat next to her.

"I'll take a tarragon soda," Tishva pointed at the drink portion of the menu with his gloved hands.

"Perfect." Kalisha nodded while jotting down their orders, "I'll bring those right over." The waitress flew to the other side of the restaurant where she disappeared behind double swinging brown oaken doors.

Tishva waited for her to be out of earshot before continuing with his musings. "Our country has gone from being isolated to intermingling with others and becoming one of the major superpowers in all of Etheria. Now, it seems as though we're taking steps backwards and are going back to being isolated again."

Soraya's father laughed. "If our major weakness is our recessive eye color, then we don't have anything real to complain about. We should adopt the mindset of teaching our fellow immigrant Azakuins our traditions so they too can participate and keep it alive instead of closing it off to a dying breed of purebreds."

Dr. Athan furrowed his black eyebrows together and put his lips to his hands in thought. "Absolutely. The lives of others should outweigh the importance of keeping traditions alive. Though we're pure Azakuins, that doesn't mean we should force families to leave, especially when they've been living by our side and helping us build up our communities for generations. They are just as much Azakuin as us three."

"Amen, brother," Tishva concurred. Soraya tapped the table in agreement.

"Here are your drinks."

Kalisha was back, carrying a round black tray in her right hand. On it were their four ordered beverages. Three of them were in tall, thin open bottles, while Yabo's water was in a shallow glass bowl. She placed the three fizzy drinks on the table and passed the bowl of water to Soraya, who put it in front of Yabo.

The two cream sodas were a golden color, while the tarragon soda was a bright glowing green resembling an elixir. Kalisha watched the two grown men tap their glasses together with a loud clink and down them whole.

"I didn't realize you were both that thirsty," she laughed while scooping up the empty bottles. "I'll get you both more, but only after I take your orders."

"I'll have..." Yosef stalled to briefly glance at the lunch menu. "A spicy chicken sandwich."

"You always get that," winked Kalisha. "You should try something new."

"Next time," Dr. Athan grinned wryly.

"Come on, you said that last time," giggled Kalisha while placing her hands on her hips. "And the time before that."

"Okay, I promise I'll get something different next time."

"Uh huh, sure, I'll believe it when I see it," Kalisha rolled her bright blue eyes in jest before writing down his order on a small pad of paper. She then turned her attention to Mr. Thenayu. "And what about you, sir?"

"What's the best dish here?"

"Well..." Kalisha thought about her answer for a moment. "I really love the breakfast wrap. It has steak, eggs, tomatoes, cilantro, red onions, and is covered in melted white cheese."

"You sold me, that sounds delicious."

"Excellent," the waitress said, jotting down his choice before finally turning to Soraya, who was acting unusually quiet in the corner of the booth.

"Soraya?"

"Oh, sorry," the girl turned her attention to the waitress. "I'll have the steak sandwich."

"Man, you and Yosef both..." Kalisha sighed, shaking her head in dismay. "You have to try something new from the menu when you come back from school."

"Okay, I promise I will," Soraya vowed.

After the waitress left once more, Tishva turned towards his daughter. "Hey, kiddo?"

"Yes, Papa?" Soraya straightened up in her seat.

"Promise me that you'll make sure to marry whoever makes you happy. Don't let others pressure you into only marrying a blue eyed man, you got that?"

"Okay…" Soraya frowned. "You think I'll be told I have to marry a blue eyed man?"

"No question about it," Tishva drummed his fingers on the top of the table. "I was given disapproving looks from neighboring Azakuin towns when I brought Adonia home from Casmerah…"

He stopped talking, his eyes hazing over, as if he were tuned out from everything around him. His fingers paused mid air and hovered over the table.

"Papa?" Soraya asked.

He didn't reply.

*No, not again! Not here!*

"Brother, what's wrong?" Yosef leaned forward, placing his right hand on top of Tishva's. Mr. Thenayu didn't respond to either of them and kept still, as if he were frozen in place. The doctor met Soraya's horrified gaze and clasped his left hand gently around hers.

"Soraya, does this happen often?"

"Y-yes…" she stammered. "H-he forgets that mama died, and that I'm his d-daughter…"

The doctor studied his friend's behavior, waiting to see what he would do next. Soraya held her breath and prayed for the Gods to have mercy. After a minute, Tishva blinked and looked across the table at the doctor, then slowly turned his head and looked at his child with blank eyes.

"Athan, I didn't know you had a daughter," he held out his

hand towards Soraya to shake it. "What's your name?"

"I'm *your* daughter, remember, Papa?" Soraya took her father's hand into her own, firmly grasping it. "I'm Soraya Thenayu."

Tishva chuckled. "That can't be, my wife and I have an infant, you're too old to be my daughter."

Soraya wanted to cry, but she stayed strong and pushed back her tears. "I'm thirteen, you're taking me to the train station today so I can travel to Matumi."

Mr. Thenayu's face faltered as he whipped his head around in confusion. "Where are we? I don't recognize this place…" he said in a panicked tone while rising from his seat.

"Brother, we're having lunch altogether. It's a new restaurant for you," the doctor reminded him in a soothing tone. "Our food is about to arrive. Relax, everything is alright."

Tishva paused and settled back down. "Okay, but after this, I need to go call my wife and check on her and our daughter."

Before Dr. Athan could reply, he spotted Kalisha coming towards them with a round, black tray full of piping hot food.

"Here you are," the waitress said cheerfully while setting pearly white oval shaped plates in front of the three of them.

Soraya held her breath and exchanged a worried glance with Yosef.

"Enjoy your food and let me know if you need anything else from me," Kalisha added hastily before speeding off to take care of the other customers in the diner. Soraya and Yosef both let out small sighs of relief.

It was more packed and noisy at the restaurant, meaning the youngest Delphi sibling had enough work to keep her distracted from them. The constant background chatter also helped drown out their conversation with Tishva.

"I don't remember ordering this…" Tishva commented while studying his food. "And I don't remember how we got here…"

He stared suspiciously at the doctor through squinted eyelids and raised his pointer finger at him. "Are we being sent on another mission to look for magic in forbidden territory?"

"No, brother, those days are over for us," Yosef smiled sadly. "You're safe and among your kin."

Mr. Thenayu stared thoughtfully at his friend and relaxed slightly. "If I'm done with that line of work, that means Adonia and Soraya can come back and live with me. I won't endanger their lives anymore."

Tishva's broad shoulders drooped slightly. "Our contract promises us extra protection for our line of work, so I can finally work a normal job and live a peaceful, simple life with my family."

Some of the things her father was going on about was new information for Soraya. *Where's that extra help then?* the girl thought angrily. *Papa shouldn't be suffering alone… was he lied to?*

# Chapter 9: Missing Memories

"Brother, before you do anything, I have some questions for you," Yosef began, then put down his silverware and folded his hands together, as if he were about to pray. "I want you to know it's safe to answer them here."

Tishva smirked. "Are you acting like this because you became both a physician and a priest?"

His friend's lips curved into a half smile. "Yes, that's exactly why. And I need to look out for you, my friend."

He bowed his head, closing his eyes for a moment before gazing back up into Mr. Thenayu's grayish blue eyes. "Do you remember when we went to school together at Darkwood Academy?"

"Of course. Those were some of the best years of my life."

Yosef's blue eyes sparkled. "I feel the same way," his expression hardened as he lead with another question. "Do you remember those expeditions we were sent on to search for magic during the first two years after we graduated?"

Tishva stroked his beard. "Yes, I remember them. We were young, reckless, and eager to use magic. I believe the government had sent scouts to observe us in class and had hired us the moment after we graduated."

"Good, good," the doctor reached for his utensils and sliced the halves of his sandwich into smaller pieces. "Do you remember when you disappeared for thirty years after the government separated us and placed us into different job positions?" he paused, watching his friend carefully.

Tishva stared hard at the table. To Soraya, it looked as if he were hoping the answer would be written somewhere in the white and blue checkered cloth.

"No, I don't recall any of that," Mr. Thenayu faltered.

"You don't remember what you were doing for those thirty years?" Dr. Athan skewered the lightly toasted bread of his sandwich with his fork and let it slowly sink in.

"Was I really gone for that long?"

"Yes, brother. I couldn't find any trace of you. It was as if you had never existed," Yosef stared at his friend with unblinking icy blue eyes. "And after all that time, you suddenly reappeared in Rivinsdeep with Adonia, who you say was pregnant with Soraya despite her having red eyes… How did you meet her?"

Tishva looked even more confused. "I really don't remember. It's as if I've always known her. I have a strong desire to protect her and my daughter, but I don't remember how we met. I just know that after we moved to the most remote town that existed at that time, and my daughter was born."

"I only had a short window of time to talk to you again before you disappeared back into your work," Dr. Athan's sharp blue eyes narrowed. "Strangely enough, you gave me the same answer then of not remembering those thirty years of being gone. I thought you had been joking, and I figured you'd tell me someday, but now, I think you're being serious."

Mr. Thenayu sighed. "I remember that Adonia, Soraya and I had been living altogether up until our daughter turned one. I had been given a year off from work, so I helped out around the town to earn food and supplies."

"Shortly after our daughter's first birthday was when the government required me to travel and work undercover once more. Adonia left with our daughter to live with colleagues until my contract was up…"

He frowned, then glanced over at Soraya, who was quietly listening. "Then you and your mother were gone up until Adonia became pregnant with your younger brother…"

"Tishva, how could that be Soraya's younger brother if you didn't see your wife again until she-" Dr. Athan paused, looked down at Soraya, and hesitated. "She left shortly after Soraya turned one, and she came back pregnant when Soraya was almost six," he rephrased. "That couldn't have been your son unless you're talking about a half brother."

Mr. Thenayu shook his head. "It was Soraya's younger brother," he stated adamantly while reaching out to hold his daughter's hand, his grayish eyes coming back into focus. "I am so sorry that my memories keep getting jumbled around and I keep forgetting what's actually going on."

Soraya threw her arms around her father. "It's okay, Papa." As she hugged him, Soraya couldn't help but wonder what her father had been doing for those thirty years that he didn't remember. It didn't make any sense that he would have forgotten such a huge part of his life.

*Someone must have done something to make him forget. But who did that, and how?*

"Hey, Soraya," Kalisha's soft voice came from the head of the table.

The girl pulled away from embracing her father and looked up to find the waitress holding a small pink bowl of vanilla ice cream with strawberries covering the sides. There were two small wooden spoons sticking out from the top; one was for her, and the other for

Tishva.

"We figured that you and your father could share," she said while placing it onto the table between them.

"Thanks Kalisha," Soraya sniffed. "That's so nice of you."

Tishva nodded and blinked back tears.

"No problem, enjoy," the waitress bowed and walked away to check on the other customers.

"Where's Yosef?" Soraya asked when she noticed he was no longer sitting across from them. She swiveled her head and spotted him whispering into Kalisha's ear. Both he and the waitress gazed at her and Tishva with empathy in their eyes.

"I think the doctor is a lovely person," Soraya stated. "You should trust him, he really wants to help you."

"I know he does," Mr. Thenayu agreed. "I guess I've just been so used to dealing with my own problems by myself for so long that I've forgotten how to let others in," He ruffled Soraya's strawberry blond hair. "I'll confide in him more about my problems while you're at school, I promise."

"Thank you, Papa," Soraya tucked into her sandwich, her appetite finally kicking in. Yabo sat on the table next to her, sniffing at her plate. The girl took off the top bun, which had pieces of melted cheese and steak stuck onto it, and handed it to her pet.

"Mow!" Yabo cooed gratefully, taking the bread into his paws and munching on it. Soraya finished the rest of her sandwich before diving into the dessert. As delicious as the strawberries tasted with the vanilla ice cream, she made sure to only eat half of the bowl's contents so her father could enjoy the rest of it.

"You alright, brother?" Dr. Athan slid back into his seat and held out his black gloved hand to Tishva.

"Much better now. Thank you," Tishva placed his hand into his friend's and they held onto each other. "You're the best. I don't think I deserve you."

Yosef shook his head. "Nah, I haven't done enough. I'm not leaving you alone this time. No more disappearing for thirty years for you."

Tishva chuckled. "Okay, I won't do it again."

The two men continued their playful banter and soon had each other roaring in laughter. Soraya found herself giggling, the knots that had formed in her stomach from worry had loosened, and she had her father's friend to thank for that.

*That man is magical. He really cares about us.*

"Oh!" Tishva exclaimed, causing Yosef, Soraya and Yabo to jump in their seats. "Soraya needs her credit card!"

He pulled out his golden pocket watch and glanced at the time, his teeth biting his lower lip. "We were supposed to go back and grab your card around twelve thirty," he said, sliding out of the booth so Soraya could leave. "Can you run to the bank and grab it?"

"Yes, Papa!" Soraya saluted. "Come on, Yabo," she placed her hand on the table next to him. Her pandacoon stuffed the remaining piece of bread into his mouth before clambering up her sleeved arm and sliding inside his guardian's hoodie. Soraya hurried to the entrance of the diner, where she flung open the front doors and ran out onto the cold street outside.

Small white flecks of snow were falling gracefully from the dull, gray sky. A few pieces fell onto Soraya's face, giving her small icy kisses before melting and sliding down to the ground below. The girl and her pandacoon carefully made their way to the front of the town towards Dragulji Bank.

"We'll be there shortly," Soraya said to her shivering pet.

Upon arriving at the entrance, she thrust open the heavy door on the right and heard the jingling of the silver bell inside.

"Hello again, Ms. Thenayu," the banker called from the other end of the room."Your credit card is ready."

Soraya kicked off the snow from her black boots before

walking over to Winston.

"Here you are, miss," he said jovially while handing the card to her. Soraya gazed at the designs and inscriptions in Azakuin on the front and slid her slender fingers over the smooth, glossy surface.

"This looks really nice," she breathed. "Thank you."

"You're welcome," Winston beamed. "Just be mindful of how much Lari you have in your account. You'll receive updates in the mail while at school once a month. I wish you safe travels."

Soraya bowed and headed back to the snowy streets outside with her brand new credit card safely stowed within her dress pocket.

"Yabo, just think, this time tomorrow we'll see the Valtic Ocean for the first time," she mused to her pet, who was shivering again within the hood of her jacket. With each passing second, the wind picked up, blowing the snow diagonally. Although her Water Magic kept her from being cold, it didn't help her poor pandacoon, who was shaking uncontrollably.

Soraya picked up the pace, trudging through the ever growing mounds of soft snow. Seconds later, she shook off the snow from her boots and entered the restaurant. Her father and the doctor were both laughing together in the corner.

"Papa, it's snowing outside. We need to leave soon so we're not late."

The two men stifled their chuckling and turned their attention towards Soraya.

"You're right, we should go now," Mr. Thenayu reached for his credit card, but Dr. Athan pulled his out first.

"This is my treat, let me pay," he insisted, beckoning Kalisha to come over from the other end of the restaurant.

Tishva heaved a large sigh. "Alright, I don't have time to fight you on this. Next time we go out together for lunch, I'll pay."

"Deal," Yosef turned his head, watching the waitress waltz towards them. Kalisha noticed and blushed at the man's gaze. "I'm paying for all our meals toady," he stated in a loud voice while handing his card to her. "Thank you for your wonderful service."

"You're welcome," she turned an even darker shade when her thin fingers brushed the doctor's upon taking the card.

Mr. Thenayu got up and stretched his limbs. "Thanks again for everything," he said, shuffling out of his seat to give Yosef a big hug. "If you have time tomorrow to talk, let me know."

"I'll check my schedule and make time for you," Dr. Athan replied, patting Mr. Thenayu's back. Tishva picked up the girl's suitcase while Soraya scooped up her backpack, carefully putting it on without squishing Yabo.

"How are you both going to travel to the train station from here?" Dr. Athan asked curiously.

Mr. Thenayu shrugged his broad shoulders. "We'll probably just walk there."

"Walk? In this weather?" the doctor pointed out the restaurant window, where they could see large clusters of snow falling from the sky. "You wouldn't make it on foot in time."

Soraya grimaced. "I don't think Yabo would do well if we stay outside for too long. Couldn't we take a horse drawn carriage? That would be much faster."

"Yes, and I do own horses and a carriage," added Yosef

thoughtfully. "I could drive you both there for free if you'd like."

Tishva shook his head. "You've done enough for us, I couldn't possibly ask you to go out of your way to drive us to the train station."

"Brother," Dr. Athan stared straight into Tishva's grayish blue eyes. "Please, let me do this for you both. I want to help."

Soraya glanced between her father and their friend and noticed how the doctor's expression was full of sadness and concern.

"Papa, please let him take us there," she interjected. "We don't want to miss the train, and he offered to take us."

Tishva's shoulders drooped in defeat. "Alright Yosef, lead the way," he placed his fingertips together and bowed lowly to his friend. "Thanks for your generosity. I won't forget your kindness."

The doctor bowed back. "It's an honor to help my best friend and his family."

"I hope you enjoyed the food," Kalisha called to them as they passed by the front desk.

"It was perfect, as were you," Yosef replied, his blue eyes sparkling as he nodded to Kalisha before opening the white oaken door so the Thenayus could exit.

The waitress's face flushed and she floundered for a response before settling on bowing back. "Take care!" she blurted before the door swung shut.

Soraya followed closely behind Yosef and Tishva, watching the surrounding buildings turn into silhouettes before disappearing into the thick gray fog.

## Chapter 10: The Azakuin Station

Soraya loved watching the sunrise with her mother.

When the warm rays of light rose from the east, they breathed life into Etheria. Birds burst into songs, the rainbow colored mountains towering over them danced before their eyes, the flowers and trees stretching out for miles around them bloomed, and the babbling brook near their home gently flowed downstream. Rivingale Falls was a remote, backwater part of Azakua, and it happened to be the most beautiful place the young girl had ever seen.

"Isn't it so peaceful?" Adonia murmured, as if she were afraid speaking too loudly would disturb the enchanting orchestration around them.

"Yes, mama," Soraya replied, equally quiet. They sat together on the stoop of their front porch, taking in the scenery around them. A light breeze rustled through the grass, kicking up loose leaves from the ground so they spun around slowly in the air.

The young girl watched them land next to two dandelions rocking back and forth in the wind. She hopped up and skipped over to the two tiny plants, where she knelt down to pluck them.

*"No!"*

Adonia's voice cut through the air like a sharp knife. Soraya paused, turning to see her mother covering her ears. She stared at her daughter with large, ruby eyes filled with horror and dread.

"Don't hurt them!"

"I'm sorry!" Soraya's sky-blue eyes filled with tears as she backed away from the dandelions. The young girl didn't like seeing her mother upset, especially at her. "Don't be mad, I'm sorry!" she cried, then ran to her mother and threw her arms around her. Adonia froze in her daughter's embrace, as if she didn't want to be touched.

"Plants have feelings too," Adonia stated in a serious tone. "We only take a life for survival, not for fun or pleasure," she pointed at the dandelions. "They're defenseless. We can't eat or use them, so let them be."

"Okay…" her daughter sniffled. "I-I just wanna make a wish with you," Soraya sobbed, burying her face into the hem of her mother's blue dress.

Adonia patted her daughter's back. "We can still do that, just in a different way."

The young girl observed her mother blow away the seeds on one without touching it. They watched in silence as the white fuzz at the tops caught the wind and were carried further into the forest surrounding their cabin.

"See? We can still help them without taking away their lives. Spreading their seeds allows new plants to grow in other places. And we get to make our wishes. Everybody wins."

"Everybody wins…" Soraya echoed. Before she blew on the other tiny plant, she paused and looked up at her mother curiously. "What did you wish for?"

"My wish has already come true," her mother pat Soraya's shoulder. "I'm finally free to live how I want to, and that's all thanks to your father and all of his friends. They saved me."

"Did Uncle Atohi and Aunt Che save you too?" asked Soraya. She had only ever seen them once, and even then, from a distance, when they dropped supplies off for Adonia. They seemed more like ghosts or spirits from a story than actual Etherians.

"Yes, they did. That's why they let us stay in their home. They watch over us and protect us," Adonia smiled. "That's also why we take care of their farm."

She placed one of her delicate hands onto her daughter's head and ruffled her strawberry blond hair. "I didn't make a wish, I thanked the Gods that I have you as a daughter."

Soraya blushed, showing off some missing baby teeth, then took a deep breath and blew on her dandelion. The seeds flew away into the breeze and disappeared into the forest.

"What did you wish for, little love?" Adonia asked playfully.

"For Papa to be here with us."

"Yes, I agree. That would make everything perfect."

In the distance, they could hear the rooster from Uncle Atohi and Aunt Chenoa's farm crow as the sun climbed higher into the sky. Adonia and Soraya both got up from the grass, shaking off the morning dew from their blue dresses.

"It's time to get to work," Adonia yawned while stretching her arms. "Go get the eggs from the hen house so I can make us breakfast."

"Okay," Soraya replied, skipping over to the farm next door when she stopped and spun around. "Can we have pancakes?"

"Yes," her mother chuckled. "Of course we can."

* * *

"Papa, have you tried reaching out to Uncle Atohi and Aunt Che?" Soraya asked her father. "Mama told me that they watched over us when we lived in Rivingale Falls. Maybe they can help you."

Living in the cottage with her mother and looking after farm animals already seemed like a lifetime ago. Even Soraya's memory of seeing her aunt and uncle from a distance felt fabricated, like a dream she woke up from.

Tishva stared out the window at the pale, gray sky while stroking his beard. Yosef's caravan rocked back and forth as they traveled through the thick piles of snow covering the gravel road leading to the train station. The Thenayu family sat inside of the red covered wagon while Dr. Athan stayed at the front and lead the horses with sturdy reins.

Soraya had never seen such a beautifully intricate, ornate and decorated piece of handiwork before. The inside of the wagon was like a small bedroom and kitchen all in one, packed to the brim with built in furniture and trinkets. She sat on a small blue velvet couch with Yabo, who was curled up on her lap.

Tishva sat opposite of her next to a small fireplace. Both cushioned seats were covered in large, multicolored beaded pillows and lay atop dark wooden drawers.

"I have, actually," her father said after a brief pause. "And I never heard back from them," Tishva turned his attention towards his daughter. "Though they kept to themselves, they did help with keeping others away from harassing you and your mother while you both lived at their residence."

Soraya took in a deep breath and decided to pry into her father's memory about something that was bothering her. "I remembered Mama talking about being freed," she paused, glancing up to see if her father would have a spell of not remembering who she was or not. "She said you saved her, and they helped. What did she mean by that?"

Mr. Thenayu looked into his daughter's sky blue eyes curiously before replying. "What do you remember reading about the Kingdom of Casmerah?"

"Well, it's very…" his daughter hesitated and mentally searched for the proper word. "Unfair."

"How so?"

Soraya hadn't expected her father to quiz her. "Women

don't have the same amount of rights as men."

"It's sad, but true," her father shook his head. "Although more districts within Casmerah have been championing for change and equality, there are still Etherians in power who hold onto an unfair view of order and control."

"Why?" Soraya queried.

"Casmerahn politics are heavily tied together with their religion, and the pontiffs in power have grown more extreme with their interpretations these past few years," he pushed up his glasses, which were dropping down to the edge of his nose, with one gloved hand.

"It's evil how many crimes against women go unreported. The Casmerahn religion is peaceful, like ours, but some use their beliefs to beat others down, and unfortunately, these extremists are currently the ones running their country."

Soraya contorted her mouth into a mix of fright and disgust.

"You being able to go to school with boys, for instance, is something that's forbidden for Casmerahn girls to do," Tishva continued in a grave voice. "They can only go to school with other girls, and they are not taught how to read and write. Their skills only extend to cooking, sewing, mending wounds, and anything related to child rearing."

"I feel awful for them," Soraya stated solemnly.

"Your mother was mistreated while living there," Tishva folded his hands together onto his lap and looked down at the golden rug covering the wooden floor of the wagon. "Though I don't remember all the circumstances surrounding her upbringing, she exhibited many signs of being abused."

Soraya thought back to all the times she wanted to hug her mother, and how Adonia would either stiffen up and looked terrified or shy away from her affection, and realized that must be what her father was referring to.

"Adonia was so grateful to be released from Casmerah, she thanked me all the time," her father's voice quivered. "I know it was difficult for her to be away from me, but at the same time, being in control of her own schedule helped her heal. You being an easy going kid helped her tremendously as well," he reached his hand out for his daughter's, and she clasped firmly onto his.

"Thanks, Papa."

The carriage ground to a halt, and Dr. Athan poked his head inside. "We're here, and we've made it with time to spare."

The on and off heavy downpour of snow had made traveling to the train station take even longer than usual, but despite the worsening weather, they had still managed to arrive early.

"Yosef, you've done so much for us, truly, thank you," Mr. Thenayu said with the utmost sincerity before picking up Soraya's suitcase. He had to hunch over slightly as the roof of the wagon was too short for him to fully stand erect.

"Yes, thank you so much," Soraya chimed in. She was grateful her father didn't have to walk all the way back to Rivinsdeep, and then tread all the way up the Averlore Mountain path by himself in such harsh weather.

"The pleasure is all mine," Yosef placed a hand over his heart. "I'm making sure your father gets home so you don't have to worry about a thing." He then stepped off of the wagon to allow both father and daughter to exit through the small wooden door at the front of the caravan.

The girl placed Yabo onto her shoulder once more, scooped up her backpack, and left with her father by making a small leap onto the snow covered ground below.

"Yosef, I really love your caravan," Soraya commented while staring at it one last time. From the outside it looked like a small red house on wheels. "Where did you get it from?"

"I made this," the Doctor said proudly. "It took me quite a bit of time to do, but it was well worth it. I based it off of Calgreneze circus carts. They have such gorgeous designs, and I really wanted to capture that."

"I think you did a superb job," Tishva commented. "It really feels like a comfortable portable home in there."

"Thanks, brother," said Yosef. "That means a lot to me."

Before them stood a quaint building towering over a pair of steel train tracks running east and disappeared into the horizon. A large colorful clock sat in the center above the arched entryway. Beneath it was a faded green plaque with golden letters that read, *Azakuin Station.* Three stained-glass windows rested above the station's clock, each with floral designs.

"We need to get your ticket, and then wait for the train to arrive," Tishva extended his right arm to his daughter, who gladly placed her arm around his. "I'll be back in awhile, Yosef."

"I'll be here," the Doctor turned and tended to the midnight furred horses, which were pawing their black hooves into the snow.

Upon entering the station, Soraya noticed how empty the giant room was. Rows of unoccupied benches stretched out evenly to accommodate for passengers waiting to board their train. A large clock tower stood at the front of the room with a small balcony carved just above the clock's face, which made Soraya think a small doll dressed like a princess should be placed onto it to complete the fairy tale look.

There were only a few others occupying the space, an elderly couple and two men dressed in what appeared to be business coats. To their left was a wooden office carved into the wall, which had many windows available for Etherians to line up at for purchasing tickets. Mr. Thenayu and his daughter made their way over and waited at Window One.

"Where to?" asked the Booking Clerk gruffly while shuffling over from inside the ticket booth. The man was dressed in a heavy dark blue coat with golden buttons.

"Matumi," Mr. Thenayu promptly replied. "I pre-paid for a ticket on the ninth of Yule of this year. It's for the eighteen o'clock train that leaves today. It should be under the name, Soraya Thenayu."

"One moment, sir," the man moved away from the window and disappeared from view for a few seconds before reappearing with a ticket in his hand. "Yes, we have her prepaid ticket here. May I see some identification papers and the card used for the purchase?"

Soraya and her father both dug into their pockets and provided the man with the appropriate documentation. After a few seconds of listening to the Booking Clerk mumble to himself, he gave it all back and handed the girl her train ticket.

"You'll be sitting in Row Thirty-four in Seat G. The Rivingale Express is arriving slightly early, so you won't be waiting long. Have a good trip," he nodded curtly.

"Thank you, sir," Soraya bowed respectfully, but the man had already moved away from the window again to sort through paperwork in the back of the ticket office.

"Kiddo, I have something to give to you," Tishva pulled out a small pouch from his inside coat pocket and handed it to her. "I wanted to wait until we were here because I figured it would be a good distraction for you during your train ride."

His daughter eagerly took it, drawing the string to take a peek inside. "You made me cookies!" she laughed as the smell of white chocolate, oatmeal and cranberries wafted through the air.

"Yes I did," Tishva laughed. "I figured having extra rations for you and Yabo on a long train ride would help."

"Thank you, Papa!" Soraya could barely contain her excitement as she wondered what her first day at Darkwood

Academy was going to be like.

Tishva's grayish blue eyes sparkled with amusement as he watched her spin in place. "Careful, you need to pay attention to what you're doing," he warned, though his voice was on the verge of laughing.

Soraya came to a halt, suddenly remembering what her attending school was going to mean for them. "When will I see you again?"

"Next year, on the last day of school."

"That's several months away…" she chagrined. "Are you sure you can't visit sooner?"

Tishva sighed. "I can't, but I will come back for you. I promise."

Soraya threw herself at her father, wrapping her thin arms around him. "I love you, Papa."

"Love you too, kiddo."

They hugged for several moments before letting go of each other. Soraya held back her tears. She wanted to be brave for her father and knew he was only doing this so he could figure out why he was losing his memories. Her doing well in school would mean he wouldn't have to stress and worry about her as much.

"I'll write to you every day," she promised. "Please let me know how you're doing."

"I will."

The walls and windows rattled and shook as the Rivingale Express rumbled its way towards the station. Light poured in through the glass frames as the mighty steam engine rapidly approached towards them.

"Let's go!" Soraya yelled, sprinting towards the door leading to the tracks outside and gazed at the oncoming train. A large gust of icy wind whipped through her long hair as the locomotive passed by, slowing to a stop. A shrill whistle blasted from the navy blue steam engine, the golden rims around the front circular frame and sides glinting in the pale light.

The many box cars in its wake were of different sizes and colors, which reminded the girl of the buildings in Rivinsdeep, but the caboose was a dark ruby red. All the windows were ablaze with a pale yellow light, and she could see silhouettes of other passengers sitting and walking about inside. The girl was impressed with how beautifully sleek and shiny it all looked, like a life sized toy.

"There's your ride," a single tear trickled down Tishva's face. "Now, you'd best be off. I expect you to do well in your studies and make lots of friends, but most importantly, stay safe."

He bent down and kissed her head before taking her small gloved hands into his own. "Only protect yourself if you absolutely have to."

"Okay," Soraya replied with a slight quiver in her voice as her father gently ruffled her strawberry blond hair.

The train whistle gave another shrill blast that pierced through the cold evening air. A small line of passengers formed outside of the multi colored train carts.

"You'll see me again before you know it," Tishva waved. "Don't forget to show the conductor your boarding pass."

"Right," Soraya said, placing her hand inside her coat pocket. The train ticket was safely stashed inside, so she took it out to show her father.

Tishva nodded in approval and backed away before heading back into the train station, his blond hair glinting in the last rays of the setting sun and his pony tail blowing faintly in the icy breeze. He disappeared through the doorway, and Soraya caught one last glimpse of him walking away through the window before he completely vanished from view.

## Chapter 11: The Rivingale Express

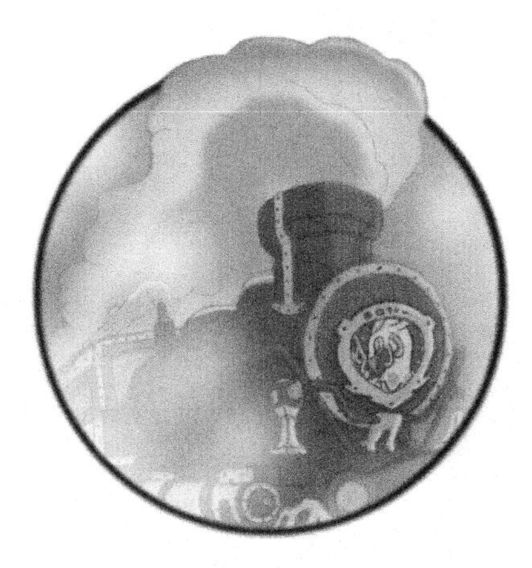

Soraya took in a deep breath and stepped forward, joining the short line of Etherians heading towards Matumi. Within a few short seconds, she would be boarding the train, leaving her home of Rivinsdeep and the Averlore Mountains behind and heading off to live in a town she had never seen before on the other side of her country. Her thin fingers nervously clutched both straps of her backpack as she watched the Etherians ahead of her climb aboard the train.

"Ticket, please."

The girl flung it forward, and the conductor gave it a dark blue stamp. Soraya hastily stuffed it back into her coat pocket before hoisting herself up into the train along with her suitcase. Only after she was in the hallway did she take her ticket back out to look at it.

The stamp was a silhouetted outline of their country's crest of a gremowlkin in flight. The girl was impressed with how sleek and professional the design looked. Near the top of the ticket was the train's name: The Rivingale Express.

"Did you need help finding your seat, miss?"

One of the train attendants studied her with bright blue eyes. The woman was wearing a long, dark navy blue coat with golden buttons, similar to the Booking Clerk's inside the train station.

She had light skin, with even lighter patches spotting on her face and hands, reminding Soraya of Mrs. Bunion at the bakery back in Rivinsdeep. The train attendant's golden hair was tied into a long braid on the back of her head, and she had a name tag pinned to her coat that read, Olivia.

"Yes, please," Soraya held up the ticket towards her.

"Row Thirty-four, Seat G," Olivia read. "Follow me."

Together, they walked down the long, narrow corridor of the passenger train. A row of three navy blue cushioned seats faced the back of the train, followed by a decent amount of dark blue carpeted floor, before another row of three seats were placed pointing towards the front. Each section had a large, rounded, rectangular window for all the passengers to look out of.

Some Etherians they passed by stared out their windows, while others read magazines and novels. Some had even reclined their seats and were snoozing away under blankets. The majority of the Azakuin passengers had blue eyes, though some of them had green and brown eyes. There were a lot of empty seats that they passed by, and the girl wondered why that was.

Soraya was disappointed that there were no other passengers aboard the train that looked close to her age, but then reminded herself that she would soon be at a huge school with lots of other children, and became excited again.

"Here we are."

Olivia gestured towards a seat on their left. It was one facing the back of the train rather than the front, and was closest to a window. There was only one other person seated in her section, and she was sitting across from Soraya. The upper half of the body was hiding behind a large black and white newspaper. The girl assumed it was a woman simply because of their long black dress that went all the way down to their feet.

The mysterious Etherian across from her shyly peeked their

head above the paper to catch a quick glimpse of the girl and train attendant. Soraya noticed the woman had pale skin and ruby colored eyes, the same color as her mother's. However, this woman had long braided hair that was black like the midnight sky, and she looked much older and more weathered in her facial features.

They made eye contact. Then, the older woman shifted her gaze down and hid back behind the newspaper.

"If you need anything, just press the train attendant button," Olivia said, pointing at two white squared buttons with golden symbols protruded from the wall. One was of an Etherian, and the other was of an oval looking shape, similar to an upside down vase, with lines forming what looked to be a halo around it.

"What does that one do?" Soraya asked, pointing at the strange oval shaped symbol.

"It turns on a light overhead in case you want to read while it's dark," Olivia directed her hand towards a small light bulb in the ceiling above the girl. "There are also restrooms in the back and the front of the train, and there will be a food cart that comes around every three hours."

"Thank you, ma'am," Soraya placed her fingertips together and bowed politely to the train attendant.

"You're welcome," Olivia nodded curtly. "Make sure to stay seated. We're leaving shortly."

The train attendant pointed at a gray, plastic lever on the right side of her seat. "You can push that down to lean your seat back if you want to sleep more comfortably," Olivia explained, then turned and walked towards the back of the train cart.

Soraya placed her suitcase under her seat and put her backpack in between her legs before sitting down. She was grateful for having so many books to read during the ride, and not just the physical ones she had brought with her. Soraya wanted to close her eyes and read through the ones she had been memorizing the day before in her father's study. There would be useful information about magic in those, and she hoped that by reading through her father's collection that she would feel closer to him and maybe even understand him better.

The girl looked across at the newspaper the red-eyed Azakuin was reading. The front page had several black and white photos of different children around her age, and was titled in large and bolded font, *Missing and Murdered Azakuin Girls.*

Soraya's stomach churned at the thought of being held hostage, but she couldn't help but wondered if her father could even come to her rescue should anything happen to her.

*No wonder Papa wanted me to learn how to defend myself,* Soraya drummed her fingers against the armrest. *He might not get better, he might not be able to save me if I need help.* Thinking about being alone in the world without both of her parents was too much for her to bear, so she instead focused on praying to the Gods.

*Surely you can heal him,* Soraya insisted internally to her Heavenly deities. *Please heal him, have mercy on us.*

The girl remembered the letter that had arrived in the mail for her father from Casmerah and wondered if she could decipher it. She wanted to know who Tishva had been corresponding with and if he was making any progress in figuring out what was wrong with him. She bent down in her seat and searched her backpack for the book, *Casmerahn Volume 1*, along with her notepad, ink bottle and blue feathered quill.

When she pulled out the textbook, she couldn't help but admire the artwork on the cover.

It depicted an ancient Casmerahn Rune Stone carving of two dragons facing each other, as if to duel.

Soraya knew to read the letters from left to right since that was how Azakuins also read, but apart from that, she didn't know much about the Casmerahn language or its grammatical rules. Many

of the letters on the textbook cover were new to her, but she did know that the symbol of the bleeding moon stood for Cas, which meant red. She was excited to take a class that would teach her how to read and speak in a different language, especially one that both her parents knew so well. She hoped to become as fluent in it as her father was, and her mother had been.

"Mow?" Chirped Yabo from inside her hoodie.

Soraya smiled. "How are you feeling?"

Yabo purred, rubbing his fuzzy face into her hand. The girl

pet him for a minute before setting her notepad upon her lap to create a makeshift desk. Soraya then dipped her quill into the black ink bottle and closed her eyes to see her father's letter in her mind's eye. After focusing on seeing the symbols from her memory, she jotted down the Casmerahn letters and looked back over what she had written, hoping it was correct.

"This is Demothi Komorebi, your driver, speaking. The train is now leaving the station. Make sure to stay seated until it is safe to move about the boxcar."

Soraya jolted in her seat, almost dropping her quill while wincing in fright as a booming voice blasted from the ceiling above her. She didn't understand why she could hear the driver speaking but not see him. Yabo, who was also spooked, dug his tiny claws into the hood of her jacket and puffed up his fur in fear.

"Our first destination is the town of Batilde, which we will reach in twelve hours," the voice continued pleasantly over the intercom. "We hope you have a great trip aboard the Rivingale Express."

Soraya searched frantically around to see the reactions of the other passengers. No one else looked concerned about hearing a voice coming from the ceiling, which bothered her greatly. She hovered her hand over a button, hem and hawed for a few seconds, and pressed it to speak with the train attendant. After a few seconds of waiting, she pressed it again, and then several times more just to be sure that it worked.

"You don't need to press it a million times, I heard you."

Olivia had appeared next to her, her lips frowning, her eyes ablaze. Several of the other train attendants were standing a few feet away in the narrow aisle, all of them studying her. Most of them looked annoyed and were staring through narrowed eyelids, but some seemed to be amused by her terrified expression and were holding back their laughter.

"How did he do that?" Soraya asked in awe, completely perplexed by what she thought was a new kind of magic. "Why could we hear him if he wasn't in here?"

"We have speakers built into every boxcar…" Olivia now stared oddly down at the girl, almost as if she were looking at something that confused her, like pieces to an unsolved puzzle. "It's completely normal to hear the driver from everywhere aboard the train."

"Normal?"

"Yes."

"Oh… okay…" Soraya laughed nervously and slumped down into her seat. She felt ill-prepared for that surprise. "Thank you, sorry to bother you."

Olivia's face remained stern as she stared at the girl. "Was there anything else you needed?"

"No, I'm good, thanks," Soraya averted her gaze to the floor and waited for Olivia to leave before allowing her eyes to wander again. The other train attendants had scattered, attempting to look busy, but kept glancing her way.

After giving it some thought, Soraya wondered if the speakers on the train were at all related to the technology used for the telephone that her father had in his office back at home. Although she had read about machines in her books and had used tractors and ran registers in Rivinsdeep, she hadn't seen much else from that realm growing up. It unsettled her to think that she might have to encounter such contraptions on a regular basis, but she was determined to learn and adjust to her new surroundings.

The train's shrill whistle pierced the air, interrupting her thoughts, and their boxcar lurched forward. Soraya clung tightly to the armrests, digging her nails into them as the locomotive picked up speed. She turned her attention towards the window and watched as the world outside sped by. It was akin to being on a horse-drawn carriage, but the speed was much faster and the ride smoother.

After a few minutes of the steam engine traveling at it's top speed, Soraya relaxed, loosening her grip on the armrests. It was strange to know she wasn't moving at all while the world outside her window rapidly whipped by, so she decided to distract herself by reading her Casmerahn textbook.

# Casmerahn Volume 1

Salutem Scholasticus! - Greetings student!
In this book, you will learn the basics to reading and writing in Casmerahn. There are three alphabets in this language:

Cursivus: The main alphabet, which has lines above each letter that connect to make words

Confragus: The second alphabet used only for foreign names and words.

Symbolus: Symbols that represent roots, suffixes, prefixes, words, and ideas. We will cover a small portion of them in this book.

You will also be learning Casmerahn Numbers (Numerals) and Particles (Particula). By the end of these lessons, you will have a foundational understanding of the language that will help you tour throughout the Casmerahn Kingdom with ease.

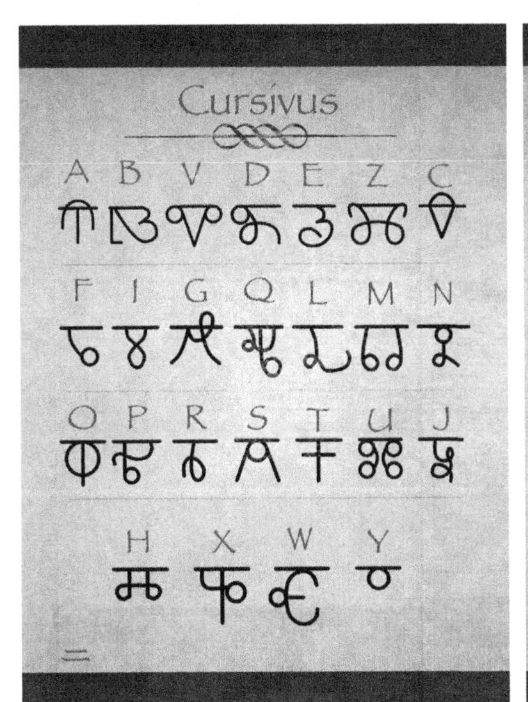
Cursivus
A B V D E Z C
F I G Q L M N
O P R S T U J
H X W Y

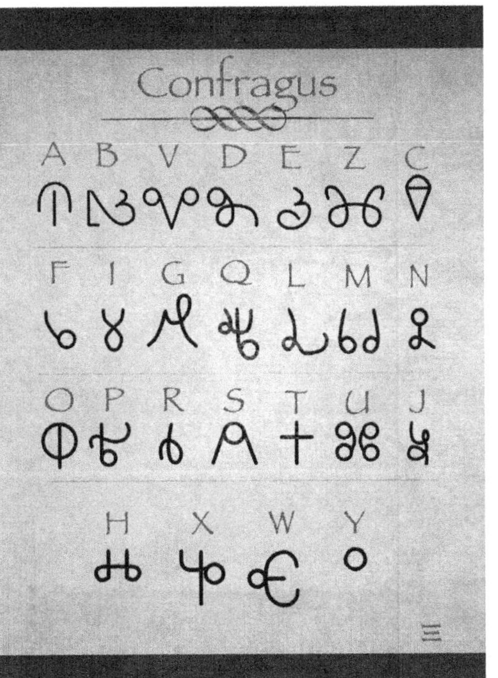
Confragus
A B V D E Z C
F I G Q L M N
O P R S T U J
H X W Y

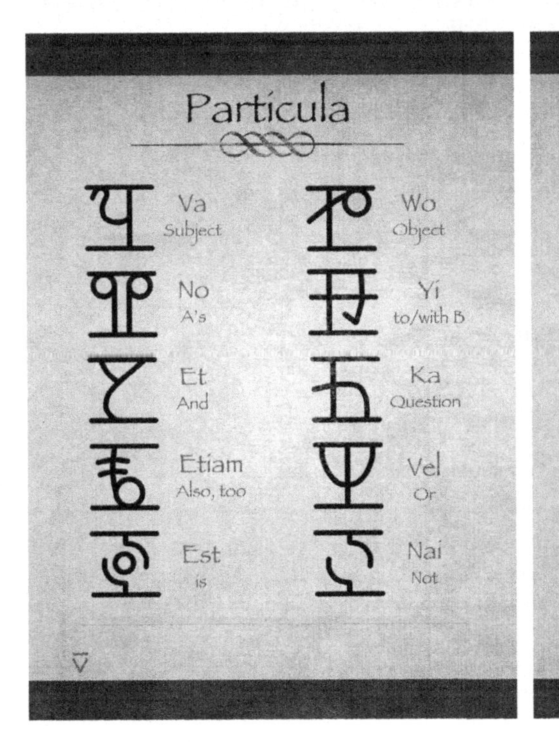
Particula
Va
Subject
Wo
Object
No
A's
Yi
to/with B
Et
And
Ka
Question
Etiam
Also, too
Vel
Or
Est
is
Nai
Not

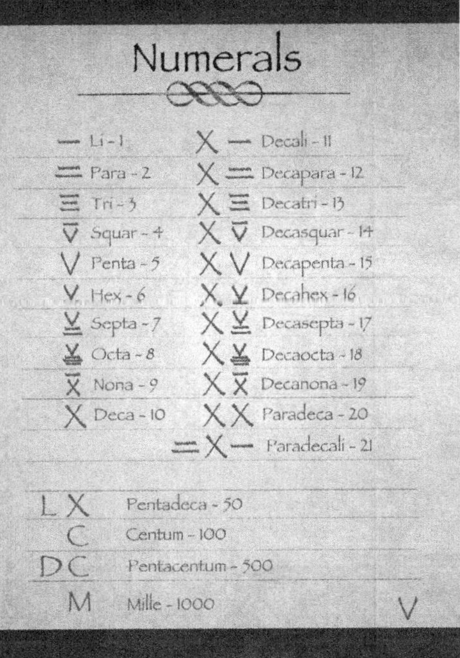
Numerals
Li - 1
Decali - 11
Para - 2
Decapara - 12
Tri - 3
Decatri - 13
Squar - 4
Decasquar - 14
Penta - 5
Decapenta - 15
Hex - 6
Decahex - 16
Septa - 7
Decasepta - 17
Octa - 8
Decaocta - 18
Nona - 9
Decanona - 19
Deca - 10
Paradeca - 20
Paradecali - 21
Pentadeca - 50
Centum - 100
Pentacentum - 500
Mille - 1000

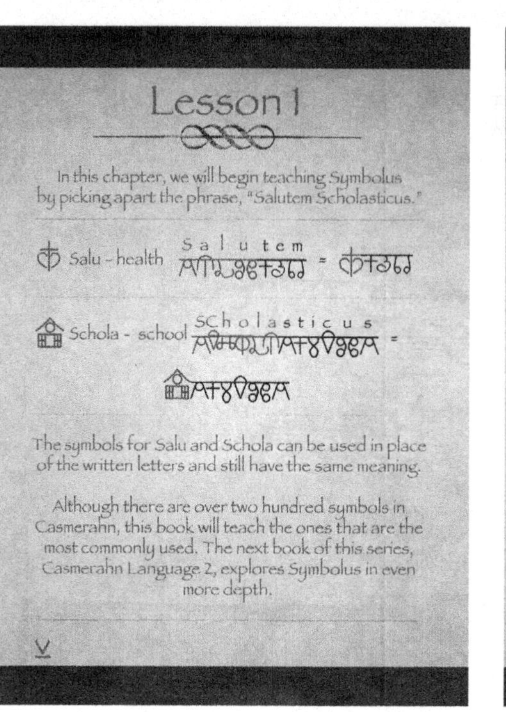

Lesson 1

In this chapter, we will begin teaching Symbolus by picking apart the phrase, "Salutem Scholasticus."

Salu - health  S a l u t e m =

Schola - school  SCh o l a s t i c u s =

The symbols for Salu and Schola can be used in place of the written letters and still have the same meaning.

Although there are over two hundred symbols in Casmerahn, this book will teach the ones that are the most commonly used. The next book of this series, Casmerahn Language 2, explores Symbolus in even more depth.

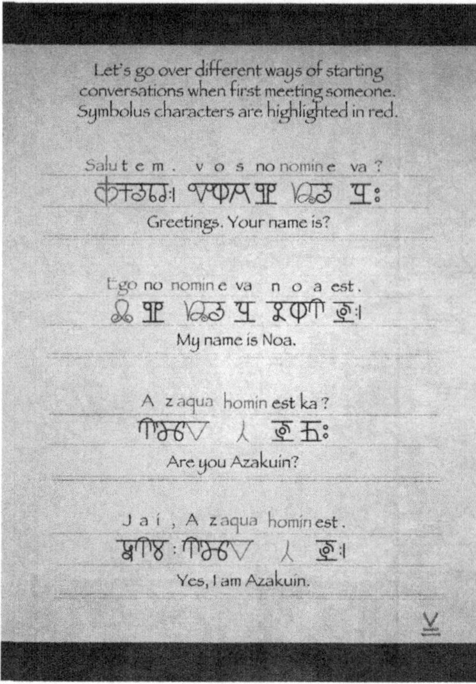

Let's go over different ways of starting conversations when first meeting someone. Symbolus characters are highlighted in red.

Salu t e m .  v o s  no nomin e  va ?

Greetings. Your name is?

Ego no nomin e va  n o a est.

My name is Noa.

A zaqua homin est ka ?

Are you Azakuin?

J a i , A zaqua homin est.

Yes, I am Azakuin.

Soraya stopped reading her textbook and looked up at the stranger sitting across from her. The newspaper the red-eyed Azakuin had been reading was now folded and lying in her lap. She had pulled out crochet needles and was knitting gloves. Although the older woman's outfit was a long black dress flowing down to her ankles, she also wore a white scarf pattered with dark red silhouettes of flowers.

"Salutem," Soraya spoke without warning. The older woman stopped knitting and glanced over at her suspiciously with her dark wine colored eyes.

"Salutem, puella," she replied, her black eyebrows raised.

Soraya wasn't sure what the older woman had called her, but her tone sounded nice enough. She glanced down at her textbook and read aloud, "vos no nomine va?"

"Ego no nomine va Stellaiya est," the woman replied, the edges of her eyes crinkling. "Vos va quam ka?"

"Uh…" Soraya quickly searched throughout her textbook

to decipher what the woman was asking her. After a few seconds of turning pages and unsuccessfully finding the phrase, she shrugged her shoulders in defeat. "I don't know what that means."

"You, how?" the woman translated literally. "Azakuins say, how about you?"

"Ego no nomine va, Soraya Thenayu est," the girl grinned sheepishly. "I'm just now learning Casmerahn, so I don't know that much."

Stellaiya set down her sewing project and folded her weathered hands together onto her lap. "You, Casmerahn, why study?" she asked in a more serious tone.

"Well, my parents know it, so I want to know it too," Soraya answered while holding up her notepad with the copy of her father's letter written on it. "I also want to know what this means."

Stellaiya took the paper, studying the message through narrowed eyelids. "Don't look for your history," she translated slowly. "If we talk, you will get hurt. Be happy you don't remember."

*What does that mean?* Soraya grimaced and took the notepad back. *Papa, did you do something horrible in the past? What happened?*

She thought back to when her father had almost killed her when he didn't remember who she was. During his spell, he had mentioned a spy getting away from him by poisoning himself, and how he wouldn't allow that to happen again.

Soraya shuddered at her memories and put them out of her mind for the moment. She was in public and didn't want others to think that there was something wrong. Instead, she put on a smile.

"Thank you for translating that for me."

"You can say, mille gratias, which is a thousand thanks," Stellaiya nodded. "And nihil est means, you're welcome."

"Mille gratias," Soraya repeated. When she looked back down at the copy of her father's letter again, she realized she didn't remember seeing the signature of whoever had sent it.

*Papa, who were you talking with?*

The girl closed her eyes, thinking back to the letter her father had taken out of the envelope. Soraya trusted her ability to recall details and was confident she hadn't missed anything.

"You alright?" the elderly Casmerahn woman asked, her black eyebrows raised in concern.

"Jai," Soraya replied while snapping her eyes back open. "Just a little tired."

She wasn't lying. Not only had it been a long day, but her emotions had been whipped back and forth like the limbs of a tree in a violent storm. She was leaving everyone and everything she knew behind, traveling into the unknown to live in a new place with new Etherians. On top of that, she had to hide her illegal possession of magic and her father's condition was worsening. Having Yosef care for Tishva helped with putting her mind at ease, but even so, she wanted answers to her father's mysterious illness and past.

"Sleep," Stellaiya said, flashing the girl a weathered smile.

Soraya nodded and placed her book and writing supplies away into her backpack. Although the gray, thick clouds and falling snow had hidden the sun from view, the snow covered horizon grew darker with blood-red hues highlighting the sky. She gazed out the window and watched as a thick fog rolled in, engulfing and hiding everything from sight.

The girl turned her head, spotting Olivia, along with several other train attendants, walking up the aisle from the back of the boxcar. They were handing out small white pillows and navy blue blankets to everyone, and were making their way towards them.

"Come on out," Soraya lifted Yabo from the hood of her pink jacket and set him onto her lap, where he curled up into a ball.

"That, what is it?" The elderly Casmerahn woman asked, pointing at the furry mammal resting comfortably on her.

"My pandacoon, Yabo," Soraya stroked his back. "Do you

want to pet him?"

"Well…" Stellaiya hesitated for a moment before standing up and walking towards her with slow, frail steps. "He is cute," she murmured, bending down while trailing her pale, wrinkly fingers across Yabo's red furry back. She smiled, showing off yellowing teeth, when Yabo purred from her touch.

"He's very friendly," Soraya assured the older woman.

"Yes, he is."

"Would you both like a blanket and pillow?" Olivia's voice rang out from behind Stellaiya.

"Yes, please," Soraya replied jovially.

As the elderly woman moved back to her seat, Olivia caught sight of the pandacoon and immediately froze up.

"W...why do you have a rodent on your lap?" she gasped, taking a step backwards. Yabo, startled by the sudden shriek from the train attendant, scrambled to sit up and stared at her with confused black, beady eyes.

"Who gave you permission to bring an animal aboard?" Olivia demanded, her hands on her hips.

"My doctor…"

The thought of anyone being afraid of Yabo had never occurred to Soraya. She searched her backpack for the note Yosef Athan had given to her and handed it to the train attendant, whose face had turned pale from fright.

"He's my support animal," Soraya explained. Part of her wanted to laugh at Olivia being so terrified of a creature that was so small and adorable, but she held it in out of respect for the woman. "I'm allowed to take him with me to school."

"That certainly seems to be the case…" the train attendant flung the letter back at Soraya, being careful not to get too close to Yabo as she did. "How many more surprises are you going to pull on me before this trip is over?"

"I'm not sure, but we have at least twenty-three hours left to find out."

Soraya smiled innocently at the train attendant and hoped she would do the same, but instead, Olivia glared daggers at her.

"Just make sure that *thing* doesn't roam about the cabin," Olivia commanded, pointing a thin finger at Yabo, who cowered and lowered his ears at the sight of the tall woman's fiery blue gaze. The train attendant tossed blankets and pillows towards Stellaiya and Soraya, so she wouldn't have to get close to either of them. "If I see it hop down onto the floor, I'm having it thrown into a cage."

Once the clacking of the train attendant's shoes faded, the Casmerahn woman chuckled. "Making friends already?"

"I guess so," Soraya sighed. "Yabo, you can't leave my lap, or we'll both be in trouble."

"Mow?" her pāndacoon tilted his head and looked up in confusion.

"Yes, not even for a second."

Soraya pat Yabo until he was calm enough to curl back into a ball on her lap.

Stellaiya had already tilted her seat back, her head lying on the soft white pillow, the thick navy blue blanket touching the floor and hiding her feet. The cabin was so dark that Soraya could barely see where the restroom sign was at the back of their boxcar. It looked as though everyone else was either already asleep or was getting ready to go to bed.

The girl searched for the plastic lever on the side of her seat, the tips of her fingers brushing over it, and she created her makeshift bed.

"Sleep tight, Yabo," she whispered, covering them both with the warm, thick blanket. After staring out the window, she closed her eyes and slowly drifted off to sleep.

## Chapter 12: A Grave Situation

"Papa, can you play with me?"

Tishva paused while cleaning the dishes. His daughter stared up at him with large, innocent sky blue eyes. The novel he had given to her hours ago was tucked under her arm, looking huge in comparison to her small stature.

"Did you finish reading it already?" he asked, amused by her eagerness.

Soraya bobbed her head up and down, her long, unkempt strawberry blond hair bouncing as she did.

"We can play after you clean that rat's nest of yours, and after you tell me what you learned from your readings."

"Okay!"

Soraya struggled with placing the book onto the kitchen table above her before sprinting up the spiral staircase with her scrawny stick legs.

Tishva looked around their home with pride as he thought back to the many months it took him to build everything by hand. It had taken him a shorter amount of time back then because he had used Earth Magic to aid him. Some Redwood trees had been kind enough to lend their bodies for making their cabin in exchange for Tishva spreading their seeds. Tishva had not only done so, but he even paid some townsfolk in Rivinsdeep to spread the seeds far and wide on their travels.

Mr. Thenayu sighed as his thoughts came back to their present situation. It had been three months since he had brought his daughter back to his cabin, and he had buried her mother and younger brother's corpses in the backyard. He noticed Soraya hadn't been eating much, and that she often had nightmares about her mother's death. She felt responsible despite him reassuring her that there was nothing she could have done.

He wrinkled his forehead as he thought back to bursting through a small hut door and seeing his wife bleeding and dying on the ground. His friend, who had been tending to Adonia, had said that neither she nor their son were going to make it because they had been so badly attacked by strangers who hated Casmerahns. Soraya had been sobbing in the corner of the hut, feeling helpless and not knowing what to do for her mother or younger brother…

*What happened afterwards?*

No matter how hard he tried to remember the details of how he suddenly appeared in Rivinsdeep with his daughter, it never made any sense. The lapse in his memory scared him. The only rough idea that he had of time changing was knowing that he had shaved his golden beard before seeing his wife, and that small scruff had already grown in around his jawline and chin when he suddenly appeared in town. It took him about three days to go from a clean shave to growing that same amount of hair on his face.

*What transpired during that time?*

He tried picturing his friend's face and voice, but those, too, were out of focus and disjointed. *Who had been there helping Adonia?*

He couldn't even remember how he had brought Adonia's lifeless body up to their house, all he could recall was digging in the cold, hard ground, and placing her corpse, along with their son's, in the pit before burying her in the dirt.

Another concept occurred to him, one that was even more frightening than the latter. *What if there are more memories that I'm forgetting? How do I figure out what's missing from my mind?*

"Got the knots out!" Soraya shouted while descending the spiral staircase. Tishva snapped out of his thoughts. His daughter needed him, now more than ever. He was all she had left, and he had to make sure she didn't feel alone.

After inspecting her now brushed hair, he smiled. "Good job. Now, what did you learn about today?"

"I learned about the Kingdom of Golaytia," she smiled proudly. "It's one of the most techno… logic… ally…" she scrunched up her face as she floundered her way through the word. "Advanced kingdoms in all the world."

"How so?"

Tishva always found it cute when his daughter struggled to pronounce larger words. Her determination to never give up was both adorable and inspiring to him.

"They have computers and robots, moving pictures on screens, and other strange things that seem alive, but they are all powered by electricity…" she looked up inquisitively at her father. "Why don't we have those things here?"

Tishva thought for a moment about how to simplify the complicated political reasons for why such technology was banned from their country.

"Well, Azakua wants to remain balanced in all things as much as possible. We are afraid of straying too far from our roots and would rather rely more on magic than machinery. Although magic is illegal to possess without a license, it is still attainable after years of rigorous training and through having job occupations such as being a farmer, or even a soldier in the military."

"But, we have farmers in town," Soraya interjected. "I've seen them drive tractors."

"That is true," Tishva nodded. "Our country allows some technology to be created and used here, but we don't have computers, robots or moving pictures, only simpler machines, the ones that can't think or act on their own."

"Could we go see Golaytia someday?" Soraya pleaded, batting her long eyelashes. "I wanna see techno... logy."

"Technology," Tishva corrected her gently. "Someday, we'll travel the world together."

"Oh yay!" she exclaimed, spinning in a circle on the sole of her foot. "That'll be so fun! I wanna see other lands!"

"You will," her father assured her. "But first, you have to get me."

Before Soraya could respond, Tishva tapped her shoulder and whispered, "you're it," before sprinting away as fast as he could.

"Hey!" she whined. "Come back here!"

"Nope," he chuckled, stopping to look at her before making a mad dash towards the staircase. Their laughter filled their home as they sprinted throughout the house chasing each other.

* * *

"Tishva?"

Yosef rapped the back of his knuckles gently on the dark red office door. "Are you alright in there?"

"Yes, I'm fine, come in," came Tishva's muffled reply. Yosef exhaled sharply before twisting the round golden doorknob to the right and pushing the door in.

Mr. Thenayu had his back facing towards him and was staring at a small, round picture of his daughter that hung on the left corner above his wooden desk.

"There's something I need to do," Tishva murmured. "I know it would be frowned upon for doing this, but something is bothering me, and it would put my mind at ease if I knew the answer to my question."

"What's the problem?" Dr. Athan asked, carefully placing a mug of cloudberry tea onto Tishva's desk. The sweet aroma from the freshly brewed drink filled the air as small wisps of steam rose from the lip of the cup, curling and twisting while floating towards the ceiling before slowly fading into oblivion.

Tishva swiveled around in his desk chair to face his friend. "Are my wife and son's bodies actually buried in my backyard?"

Yosef bit his lower lip. "You want to dig up the grave site?" he asked, his voice full of unease.

Tishva picked up the mug, blew on the top and took a sip. "I know it sounds crazy that they wouldn't be in there, but there are so many details that are missing from my mind, that I have to make sure I know what's real and what's not."

"I'll help you," Yosef placed a hand on his chin. "But we probably shouldn't tell Soraya about this, or anyone for that matter. Digging up corpses is already a taboo topic, and I'm sure your daughter would be even more concerned about you if we told her what you were doing."

"Agreed. This stays between us."

Both men bundled up for the cold weather, and Tishva grabbed a shovel before they walked outside. The snowfall from earlier that day had added another few inches to the already covered ground. Tishva knelt down and dusted off Adonia's gravestone before looking up at Yosef.

"This is going to take a while. I understand if you want to wait inside where it's warm."

His friend chuckled while stepping forward. "Do you honestly think I'm going to let you do all the hard work alone?"

Yosef swiveled his head around warily to make sure they were completely alone before taking off his gloves, revealing a blue Water Magic tattoo on his right wrist. After placing both hands in front of him, he shifted the thumb of his right hand to lay underneath so only four fingers remained up before sweeping both hands apart. The snow on the ground immediately parted into two huge piles on either side, leaving the ground exposed.

"Thank you, that definitely helped a lot."

"Not a problem," Dr. Athan smiled. "I haven't used magic in a while. That was fun to do, just like the good old days."

Tishva read the engravings on the tombstone: *Here lies Adonia Thenayu. A loving wife and mother.* Adonia's ruby red eyes and autumn red hair flashed through his mind. He remembered her radiant smile, her laughter sounding like silver bells, and her incredible ability to understand, even seemingly communicate with, plants and animals within nature.

His unborn son came to mind. Tishva had never named him. He couldn't bring himself to do it, his loss would be even more real and painful. Instead, Soraya had thought of one. Tishva often overheard his daughter praying at night to their Heavenly Deities for both Adonia and Malik, though she tried not to bring up her younger brother as often as possible since Tishva didn't like talking about him.

"Ready?" Yosef asked with bated breath.

Tishva's grayish blue eyes met with Yosef's icy gaze. "Let's do it."

Even with Dr. Athan clearing off the snow and thawing the ground, it took them several hours to exhume the coffin. Tishva had to take several breaks since he started coughing up blood again, but despite this and Yosef insisting that he rest, Tishva continued digging down into the cold ground below.

Sweating, panting, and exhausted, both men paused once the lid of the coffin was more visible under the thin layer of dirt that covered it. They had dug deep into the earth and had just enough room to stand on either side. The coffin was decomposing, the center collapsing in on itself. Tishva kicked into the lid to save time.

With a loud crack, the wood gave way.

"No…" Tishva whispered, his skin paling. "That can't be!"

Both men stared at the empty casket, chills running down their spines. Tishva backed away and leaned against the wall of dirt inside the pit they had dug, his breathing short and erratic as his mind spun out of control.

*Where is my wife? Why can't I remember everything that happened? Is she… alive?*

"Breathe!" Yosef commanded as he rushed to his friend's side, holding his hands firmly in his own. "Look at me, don't hyperventilate, that's the last thing you need to do right now."

Tishva's voice quivered as his whole body shook in fear. "Wh-where is she?" he cried in exasperation. "What's going on?"

He slid down the wall to the ground and curled up into a ball. Yosef turned his head and looked back at the coffin, then at his panicking friend, and shook his head angrily.

"This is evil," he breathed. "Someone is messing with you, and they've gone too far. We have to find out who is behind this, and what their motives are."

Yosef lent his hand and helped Tishva get back up onto his feet. "We need to find out what happened to you during those thirty years you went missing," he continued, his blue eyes aflame with fury. "They're not getting away with this."

"Brother," Tishva uttered weakly. "Is it possible to take out one's memories and replace them with false ones?"

"I'm not sure…" Yosef went silent, folded his arms in front of him, and stared at the empty coffin. "The Kingdom of Golaytia has many impressive inventions. I suppose it's possible that their government has created something that could achieve such a feat, but I've never heard it being possible outside of make believe stories."

Tishva closed his eyes and focused on breathing and

exhaling more slowly. As his pounding heart calmed down, his senses and mind sharpened.

"I remember my arms getting sore and the soil sinking beneath my boots, the pungent smell of damp grass and dirt clogging my nose, making it difficult to breathe at times…" Tishva took another deep breath in. "I placed her into this coffin, and I put all the dirt back over her, so why is her body gone? Who would have had time to dig her up while I was working? I'm always here, always on alert, never gone for more than an hour…"

He paused in the middle of his rant and looked up into Yosef's eyes. "Until today."

"Do you think someone stole her body while you were out?" Yosef whispered. Both men suddenly wondered if they were being watched, and the thought unsettled them greatly.

"It's possible," Tishva said, tracing his fingertips along the cold wall of dirt surrounding them. "Earth Magic would make digging up Adonia's body much faster, and it would be difficult to detect if the person wielding it was talented enough."

"I haven't seen Earth Magic within nature in a long time," Yosef frowned. "We both know that only a selected few have access to its power, and that would be between government officials, the elite, and MagiCorp."

With that in mind, both men climbed out of the grave. Yosef filled in the site with snow using magic to make the gravesite appear untouched before heading inside Tishva's cabin, where they could talk in private. They remained silent until they had both searched every inch of the cabin to make sure it hadn't been infiltrated in their absence. Only when they knew they were completely alone did they begin speaking again, but not with their voices. They instead spoke using sign language, an old habit they had used back when they went on secret missions together.

"MagiCorp…" Tishva spelled with his hands. "I keep in

communication with the presidents of their company since I report my findings of magic to them…"

"And?" Yosef prodded his friend's shoulder, his black eyebrows raised.

"Well, I asked them if they knew anything about my memory loss and what could have potentially caused it. I received a letter from them earlier this morning that told me not to search for my past, or I would get hurt. That I'm better off not knowing."

Yosef's icy blue eyes widened with intrigue. "That sounds incredibly suspicious." He stretched his hands out in front of him and cracked his knuckles. "Who are all the presidents of MagiCorp?"

"They write under pseudonyms and purposefully keep that information outdated, so the public doesn't know," Tishva pulled out a paper from his desk with a list of names. "All of these Etherians are dead, and those are the current names of the owners of the organization."

Yosef's icy blue eyes sprang to life. He seemed excited about the mystery afoot, giddy even, as he paced in circles. Tishva missed seeing him look so intensely interested in solving problems. He knew this was, in part, why Yosef became a priest and psychologist. His friend couldn't help but get involved in problems, he loved improving the lives of others.

"These Etherians obviously know something about what happened to you," his friend pondered with his hands while glancing between Tishva and the window of his office. "They're probably the ones who caused it. And with them being in such a high position they are nearly untouchable, they'll most likely disregard all polite requests for information…"

He grinned, shaking his head. "You must have been involved in something huge for them to go through such great lengths of keeping it this secret. You are one of the most loyal workers they've ever had, and even you don't know what transpired."

Tishva blushed at his friend's compliment. "Part of me wonders if I should just stop looking for answers. I can't take on this organization alone, they would kill me if I rebel, and I can't knowingly endanger my life, for Soraya's sake."

"True, but I can do my own research. I still have friends in the government, finding out something is better than nothing," Yosef suggested. "If you haven't already, ask them if they know of anything that would help with your mind staying more stable. They have an obligation to take care of your well-being, it's in your contract with them."

"I'll write to them and bring them up to speed on more recent events," Tishva explained with his hands. "I have to tell you what happened between Soraya and I…" His face fell when his eyes rested on the small round picture of his beloved daughter. "Perhaps, if they knew, they would give me something to ensure I don't have another violent episode."

"Violent episode?" signed Yosef, his eyes widening in concern. "With your daughter?"

Tishva nodded grimly. "I thought she was a spy, and forgot who she was…"

Yosef furrowed his eyebrows. "This is very serious, brother. MagiCorp owes you their protection. They can't abandon you, especially if your condition means you pose a threat to yourself and others. What are they thinking?"

"Honestly, I don't know," Tishva shook his head. "I don't know."

## Chapter 13: The Never Tree Islands

It was still dark in the cabin when Soraya awoke to find Yabo chirping in her ear. Whenever he made shorter and higher pitched yowls, it meant that he either wanted food or needed to use the bathroom. Since the sun hadn't risen yet, and it felt incredibly early in the morning, the girl was sure it was the latter reason.

"Shhhh…" she hushed, stroking her pandacoon's ears. "I heard you, hold on."

Soraya readjusted her chair, so it was no longer a bed, then rose to her feet while carrying Yabo on her shoulder. The girl thought about taking her backpack and suitcase with her to prevent others from stealing her belongings, but then decided on covering them both up with the blanket and pillow she had been sleeping with instead. Finally, she tiptoed down the train corridor towards the glowing bathroom signs.

Soraya glanced at the sleeping passengers on either side of their train cart, hoping no one else had been woken up by her pet's cries. Even though the train rattled as it chugged down the tracks, the humming noise it produced was muffled in comparison to her pandacoon's meowing.

"Almost there, just wait a little longer," she murmured, knowing he didn't understand how rude it was to be loud that early in the morning.

The bathroom was thankfully unoccupied. Yabo danced impatiently on her shoulder as she pushed the door into the wall before entering and sliding it shut.

The space was tight and compact, with just enough room to spin around in a circle and take a half step forward. At that moment, Soraya was grateful to be tiny. It was already uncomfortable being in there, and she couldn't imagine being any taller or larger and attempting to use the train bathroom.

"Okay, do your business. I won't look," Soraya promised, placing Yabo on the edge of the toilet seat before turning around and closing her eyes.

Her father had potty-trained Yabo, which she thought had been incredibly clever of him to do. Soraya wasn't sure what she would've done if she had to clean up after her pet every day.

"Mow!" chirped Yabo from behind her. Soraya turned back around and flushed the toilet while her pandacoon hopped down onto the blue carpeted floor and pawed at the door to be let out.

*I might as well use this while I'm here.*

There was no telling how long the lines would be once everyone aboard the train woke up. She did her business, washed and dried her hands thoroughly, and scooped up Yabo from the floor, much to his chagrin, and placed him back upon her shoulder.

"Sorry, I can't let Olivia see you on the ground," Soraya sighed. She didn't want to cause any more problems for the crabby train attendant and was sure that the woman wanted to throw her in a cage along with her pet at this point. "I'll find somewhere for us both to walk around."

Soraya slipped back into the dark hallway. She wasn't tired anymore and wanted to stretch her legs, so she wandered towards the back of the train to see if she could reach the end of it. All the passengers snoozed away in their reclined seats, hidden by the blankets they had received from the train attendants the night before.

"Where are you heading off to at this ungodsly hour?"

Soraya froze in her steps. A rather tall and bulky figure stood up from a seat on her left and stepped into the hallway. His voice sounded familiar, though she couldn't quite see what the man looked like since the cabin was still pitch black.

"I just wanted to walk around a bit…" she squeaked. "Is that… alright for me to do?"

"Yes it is, but you shouldn't be unsupervised, young lady."

With a small click, a tiny lightbulb in the ceiling lit up, allowing her to see him properly. The man had beautifully dark skin, like the bark of an oak tree, with midnight black hair and bright orange eyes. He was wearing an outfit similar to the train attendant's, but he had a lot more golden badges to display on his navy blue coat. His glowing name tag read, *Engineer Komorebi.*

"Oh! You're the driver!" Soraya blurted in surprise. "Aren't you supposed to be driving the train?"

The large man flashed her a pearly white smile. "Technically yes, but there are two drivers on this shift, and it's my turn to rest. We switch off every six hours."

A woman dressed in train attendant garb was lying down in the seat across from his. Her short, curly brown hair framed her pretty pale face. She groaned as the light shone in her closed eyelids.

"It can't be time to get up already," she murmured, slowly peeling her sea green eyes open and staring irritably at the child standing before her.

The train driver glanced down at his golden wristwatch and chuckled. "Hate to break it to you, but you slept in a little. It's five and nine minutes in the morning, and we'll be reaching Batilde in a little over an hour."

"Oh no!" the woman exclaimed, hastily springing up. "You said you'd set an alarm!" she huffed while struggling to pull her shoes on.

"I did, we were going to sleep in until…" the driver paused, and his golden wristwatch beeped loudly. "Right now."

"I said I wanted to wake up ten minutes *before* five, not ten minutes after!" she growled through gritted teeth.

"Sorry, Dinah, I must have misheard you," he replied sweetly. "I knew you needed that extra rest, you always work hard."

The woman exhaled, her irritated expression transforming into a small smile. "Thank you," she said in a defeated tone. "But don't do that again."

Dinah picked up her bag and playfully grazed her shoulder against the driver's before heading towards the bathroom.

"She needs time to put on her makeup," Komorebi explained to Soraya while rolling his beautifully bright orange eyes to the ceiling, his large, thick lips curling into a smug looking smirk. "She doesn't realize how gorgeous she is without it, but she won't believe me for some reason."

Soraya stifled a giggle. She could tell they had a close relationship, and it warmed her heart. From what little she could tell in the dim light, the woman indeed looked beautiful and petite, like the Calgreneze dolls she had seen in the toy store back in Rivinsdeep.

The driver decided to switch topics and cleared his throat in an attempt to act more serious. "I'm not sure if you're aware of this, but you're the only child aboard this train without a guardian traveling with you. We were all given specific instructions to make sure you were under adult supervision at all times," Komorebi pointed a white gloved finger at her. "We always keep extra eyes on child passengers to ensure their safety."

"That makes sense," Soraya shrugged her shoulders. "I just want to know if there's somewhere Yabo and I can walk around without disturbing anyone."

"I'm assuming you're referring to your pet?" Komorebi

extended a large hand towards the girl's pandacoon. Yabo sniffed at his thick fingers and licked them, which told Soraya that he was comfortable and liked the man.

"Yes, do you have any suggestions?"

"The caboose is currently empty."

Both the driver and Soraya heard Dinah chime in as she made her way back towards them. Soraya could now see the woman more clearly and found herself agreeing with the driver about her natural beauty. She was short, petite, and slim, with a pretty pale face and jade green eyes, which were now highlighted by the dark mascara she wore on her eyelashes. "You and your adorable little pet can pace around in there without disturbing others," she winked.

"Perfect. I can escort you there," Komorebi suggested.

"Okay!" Soraya exclaimed, then paused and looked around before adding more quietly, "that sounds great."

Before walking away, she couldn't help but say something to the Calgreneze woman. "He's right, you know, you are very pretty."

"Aww, thank you!" Dinah's eyes lit up at the unexpected compliment. "You are so sweet," she bowed. "I'll look after your belongings and make sure they aren't stolen while you're getting some exercise in."

"I appreciate that greatly," Soraya waved and followed in the wake of the tall, muscular driver. Komorebi made sure to stop at the end of each train cart and speak with the train attendants, letting them all know where he was going with Soraya. Olivia stood at the entrance of their destination.

"You can't let them run around in the last train cart!" she hissed while pointing angrily at Yabo. "What if it makes a mess on the carpet or claws at the seats?"

The train attendant's piercing, icy gaze bore through the child's skull with pure contempt, causing Soraya to feel scared and avoid looking at her altogether.

"H-he is potty-trained, and he won't destroy anything," Soraya stuttered meekly. She was beginning to dislike this woman more and more with each passing second.

"You're being completely unreasonable," Komorebi said with a hint of irritation in his voice. "Now, if you'll excuse us, these two would like space to roam about freely and will both be in the caboose since it's unoccupied."

Before the train attendant could retaliate, the loudspeakers on the ceilings blasted the voice of the other driver.

"Good morning passengers, it is currently five twenty in the morning. We will be reaching Batilde in about an hour. Breakfast will be served shortly. We hope you all had a good night's rest aboard the Rivingale Express."

"Did you two want breakfast?" Komorebi asked cordially to Soraya and Yabo.

"Yeah, that sounds great!"

"Mew!" her pandacoon agreed.

"Fetch them fresh food, please," the train driver commanded. "And don't spit in their meals," he added as Olivia's cheeks and ears flushed a crimson red.

"Why would you even insinuate that I would ever do something that immature?" Olivia snapped before turning on her heels and strutting away.

"Is she usually like this?" Soraya whispered once she was out of ear shot.

"No, she's not," Komorebi replied. "I know it's not easy to do at the moment, but try not to let her actions get you down. You haven't done anything wrong, and she shouldn't be taking her frustrations out on you. It's extremely unprofessional of her to act like this."

He opened the door leading into the caboose and beckoned Soraya to enter through first. Yabo, who had been anticipating this moment for far too long, immediately hopped down from his owner's shoulder and proceeded to roam about the cabin freely, sniffing and crawling under the seats as he went.

The driver held his hand up, as if he was about to say something else, when his honey colored eyes caught the light of the rising sun as it seeped in through the large windows. He paused to gaze outside at the grassy valley stretching out before them. The snow covered Averlore mountains were just barely visible over the horizon, meaning they were now crossing over into the warmer areas of their country.

"Look at that," Komorebi breathed.

High in the sky above them were floating islands, each containing chains linking them all together. Each hovering rock was tied to tall towers that lay beneath them, reminding Soraya of balloons attached to weights to keep them from floating away. The large, thick Never Trees keeping the islands afloat swayed back and forth, their leaves rustling in the invisible, cold breeze.

"They're so beautiful," gaped the girl in awe. She was finally, for the first time in her young life, seeing sky islands in person rather than drawings on a map or photos in her books. It excited and inspired her down to her very core.

"Yes, yes they are," Komorebi's bright, fiery eyes twinkled in amusement at her wonder filled expression. "Did you know there's an old legend about one that was so large that it floated away into space and became its own tiny planet?"

"I think I've read about that before somewhere..." Soraya closed her eyes, mentally flipping through pages of a book which she believed contained that legend. "There were ancient Azakuins who wanted to find the heavens, so they created the largest sky island in Etheria's history. They say the location of that planet is on the right of two brightly glowing stars," she read aloud from memory. "Never Tree Island is what it's called."

"Good, you know your Azakuin mythology," Komorebi beamed, clearly impressed with her knowledge on what he thought to be an obscure piece of trivia.

"Do you know any Oransjch mythologies?" Soraya asked the man curiously while gazing into his beautiful orange eyes. "I've read a handful of them, but there are many more that weren't covered in my encyclopedia collection."

The driver's demeanor changed, his expression cold and hardened, the light in his orange eyes snuffed out like a blown out candle. "I don't really know anything about my ancestral history. I was born and raised here in Azakua, and have never seen any other country in my life."

"Oh…"

Soraya heard the stiffness in his voice and realized that she had offended him, but didn't understand why or how. Her cheeks reddened with shame, and his expression softened.

"You're simply young and curious, I can see that you didn't mean to be rude."

Soraya bowed to him out of respect. "I'm really sorry, I didn't mean to make you upset in any way."

The driver's smile returned, though it wasn't as broad as before. "I accept your apology," he crouched down to Soraya's level, so they met eye to eye.

"It's not kind or respectful to assume that someone knows about their ancestry simply because their features are different. I know that I am Azakuin through and through, but when others think I'm knowledgeable about my great-grandparent's main homeland, that I speak that language or immigrated here from overseas simply because I don't look Azakuin, it makes me feel like an outcast in my own country. Does that make sense?"

The girl had never thought about it like that before. "Yes, it does."

"I saw you look at my eyes the way you looked at the sky islands, and I know that you are very open-minded and accepting of others with different features," he resumed, his tone more lax than before. "Not everyone looks at me that way, however. Some wear sneers of disgust simply because my eyes are not blue like theirs."

He turned and looked out the window once more and watched as the beautifully bright sun continued to climb into the sky and cast its warmth upon everything beneath it. "I used to struggle with my self worth for a long time, wishing I could rid myself of my orange eyes. I even thought about poking them out and being blind so no one could comment on them anymore. I almost convinced myself that not having them at all would make me happier."

*He never should have been made to feel that way.*

Tears welled up inside Soraya as she thought about her mother being called a demon and spat at simply for having red eyes.

*All colors are beautiful. Why can't everyone see that?*

"Here..." Komorebi dug into his coat pocket, procuring a small white handkerchief for the girl to use. "Maybe I gave you too many details, and I'm sorry for that. The real world can sometimes be a cruel and terrible place, but there are also plenty of wonderful things in it too," he stood up and bowed. "You're a good kid."

"Thank you..." Soraya wiped her eyes with the soft white cloth.

"Mow?" Yabo cooed as he ran up towards Soraya and rubbed himself against her legs.

"I'm fine, thanks though," she scratched his furry back lovingly with her long, slender fingers.

"Great, now you're helping it shed its hair everywhere!" Olivia groaned from behind them. She was holding two black trays, each filled with an assortment of food. Before Soraya or Komorebi could reply, she set them both atop two of the closest seats to her before bolting out the door.

The train driver chuckled and rolled his eyes to the ceiling at her over the top behavior. "To be honest, I didn't even expect her to come back at all."

"I was thinking that too," Soraya agreed. They both looked at each other for a moment, their lips growing into wide, tooth filled grins, before they burst out laughing together.

"Okay, okay," the driver breathed, regaining his poised and professional composure. "Go ahead and enjoy your food."

The trays contained one khachapuri, a small bread boat with a sunny side egg sitting in the middle, two steaming sausages, sliced oranges, and a bottle of unopened apple cider. The smell wafting off the food was incredible, and it took a lot of self-restraint for Soraya to think of feeding her pet first.

She sliced one of the sausages into smaller, bite-sized pieces and held out a piece to Yabo, who held his front paws out, ready to receive his portion. She watched as he plucked it from her fingers and downed it in seconds before reaching out for more.

"Maybe I should buy myself a pandacoon," Komorebi mused, his voice full of mirth. "I think Olivia would absolutely *love* it if I brought it to work all the time, don't you?"

"Oh yes, she would be *thrilled*," Soraya replied sarcastically, attempting to stifle her giggles, but failed as they came tumbling out of her mouth anyway.

"I'm here to switch off with you," Dinah's voice rang from the front doors of the caboose. The train attendant had brought Soraya's backpack and rolling suitcase with her.

"Perfect," Komorebi stood up while taking his breakfast tray with him. "Soraya, it was lovely meeting you. I hope we meet again someday."

"I hope so, too. Take care!" Soraya waved, watching as he walked out the door and disappeared into the next train cart over.

# Chapter 14: Matumi

At six twenty, the Rivengale Express stopped to drop off passengers in the town of Batilde, then resumed its course at six forty-five towards Matumi. As the clock ticked forward along with the progression of the train towards its destination, Soraya grew more and more anxious about seeing the other side of her country for the first time.

*I miss you, Papa.*

The snowy Averlore Mountains were long gone from view like a faded memory. Instead, the landscape outside was replaced with a lush green countryside. Floating islands were scattered across the bright blue sky, all tied down to tall stone pillars. As beautiful as everything looked, it didn't feel like home anymore.

Around seven, the girl took out a pencil and sketched the Syraple Tree into her journal. After many repeated attempts of drawing lines, closing her eyes, sighing, scrubbing an eraser back and forth over her newly made marks, and attempting again, she had finally completed her picture and was satisfied with the final outcome. She then added a bullet list of facts about the tree next to her sketch before asking the train attendant, Dinah, for the time. Much to her dismay, all of that work had only taken one hour to complete.

*Today is going to be a very long day…*

Around eight in the morning, both Soraya and Yabo walked several laps up and down the caboose hallway together.

At eight twenty, Soraya read through all the pages she had memorized from her father's personal library two nights prior. She learned that Earth Magic was deemed the most powerful and influential of all four Elements. The reason for this was because it gave Etherians the ability to connect with and understand nature.

"Plants that are hundreds of years old have the potential of passing along information of what they have seen in the past," she read aloud. "Many murder cases, for example, have been solved because the trees, bushes, and sometimes even flowers, were witnesses of the event."

"It is said that once the blood of the victim is spilled on the ground, it's swallowed up by the soil and absorbed into the roots of all the plants in that surrounding area. If a Mage were to use Earth Magic to connect with those plants, they could then replay the whole scene of what had taken place within the person's mind."

*I wonder if Papa ever tried using Earth Magic to find out who murdered Mama.*

Soraya then supposed it was possible that there hadn't been any plants around the location of where her mother died, but promised herself to investigate in the future.

Around twelve, Soraya and Yabo ate lunch together. Soraya was given a fresh batch of boiled khinkali filled with lamb, mushrooms, white cheese and broth, along with slices of apples and bottled cloudberry cider. Each dumpling looked like a tiny white bag, twisted counterclockwise and bunched up at the top. The proper way of devouring them was biting off the tip, drinking the inside contents, and eating the remaining portion.

Soraya turned one of the dumplings into a bowl and blew

gently on the rising steam. She then set it on the edge of the tray so her pandacoon could lap up the innards, even though he had already eaten his hard-boiled eggs and fruit from Mrs. Bunion's bakery.

"Careful, it's hot," she warned Yabo with a stern voice.

Her pet ignored her and tucked in anyway. Ironically enough, Soraya was the one who burned her tongue. She also spilled broth on her tray, despite doing her best to keep her dumpling from falling apart in her hands. Her pet dove in, lapping up the extra morsels she had dropped.

"Drat…" she muttered under her breath before laughing at herself. "Papa would be shaking his head and rolling his eyes at me if he were here."

After Soraya cleaned off her hands with a small white napkin, she turned her attention to the train windows once more.

"Look!" she exclaimed to her pet. Yabo hopped onto the windowsill, stood up on his hind legs, and pressed his black button nose into the glass to get a better view.

On their right were tall, scaling mountains covered in bright blue flowers. To their left, Soraya could just make out the dark blue Valtic Ocean sparkling and dancing under the blazing sun. Even the air smelled and tasted different. It now had a strong salty flavor, unlike back in Rivinsdeep, where a subtle hint of oranges and cloudberries always lingered in the breeze.

"Yabo, while we're in Matumi, we're going to visit the beach," Soraya promised. During the summer months, when the lakes surrounding Rivinsdeep were thawed, she had perfected her swimming. Ever since Soraya could remember, she had been obsessed with feeling weightless in the water. To her, it had been the closest feeling to flying that existed. Now that she actually had Air Magic in her possession, Soraya planned to practice using it in secret whenever she could.

*I can breathe underwater now too.*

The thought of exploring the deep, dark depths of the sea was simultaneously exhilarating and frightening. Soraya fidgeted with her black fingerless gloves and snuck a quick peek at both magic tattoos. They were still slightly faded, which meant that she didn't have a lot to use.

*As long as I pay attention to what I have left, I'll be fine.*

At fourteen o'clock, Soraya read her Casmerahn textbook. She was determined to learn more phrases and have the ability to carry on a conversation. The only problem was, she wasn't sure how to pronounce the words that she was reading. She had watched Stellaiya, the elderly Casmerahn woman, get off the train earlier that morning, so she no longer had the ability to ask her for help.

*I'll just focus on memorizing spellings and vocabulary.*

Around fifteen o'clock, Soraya's eyelids grew heavy. She put away her book and took a nap with Yabo, who had settled down onto her lap to join her.

* * *

"Good evening passengers," Komorebi's voice filled the still cabin air, waking the girl with a start. "We are reaching Matumi in ten minutes. Thank you for riding the Rivingale Express. We hope you all had a pleasant trip."

Soraya stretched her stiff limbs and turned her gaze outside the train window. She gaped in awe at the colorful buildings surrounding them on all sides.

Everything she could see was warm and inviting, not a snowflake in sight. Each multicolored building that flew by was unique in its design and shape. Regardless of whether they were tall or short, the majority of them had balconies, pillars, and even stone statues. Beyond the shops lay rolling hills scattered about with tall green trees. Soraya could see a large church sitting atop of one, and it made her think of a castle from a fairy tale land.

"Miss Thenayu," Dinah poked her head in through the

glass door at the front of the cabin. "Once we stop at the train station, I'll take you to Ms. Faye. She's one of the groundskeepers of Darkwood Academy, and she'll escort you the rest of the way."

"Alright, thank you."

"I'll be right back. Stay put for now," Dinah added before disappearing behind the doorway.

Nervousness settled inside Soraya's stomach. She was about to attend school for the first time in her life and didn't know what to expect. There would also be children close to her age, and that was also going to be a new experience for her. As the Rivingale Express slowed its pace down to a crawl, the girl's heart rate sped up.

*Will I make any friends? Will I do well in my studies? I wonder what my new room will look like. I hope the teachers are nice.*

Yabo rubbed his fluffy face into her hands, momentarily distracting her from the thoughts racing through her head.

"Are you ready?" Soraya scratched the backsides of his black, fuzzy ears. The train had finally stopped, and she could see that they had parked inside a huge dome shaped building with paintings of angels and a cloudy, sunny sky in the circular center of the ceiling.

"We have now reached Matumi," Komorebi's pleasant voice showered down from the ceiling of the train. "Please make sure to take all of your belongings with you and exit safely in an organized fashion. Take care and safe travels."

"Here we go," Soraya inhaled sharply, stood up, threw on her backpack, and picked up the handle of her rolling suitcase with quivering hands. Yabo clambered up her arm and slid into the hood of her pink jacket. They both waited patiently at the glass door for Dinah to fetch them.

"This way," the train attendant beckoned with a gloved hand.

They joined a short line of Etherians standing together in the aisle. After shuffling towards the exit, everyone stepped off onto the cold, stone marble ground. Their shoes clacked and echoed around the huge room with each step they took. The polished floor beneath their feet was a mixture of navy blue and twilight purples swirling around together and peppered with white and golden specks.

"This is the most beautiful design I've ever seen," Soraya stated as she took in the gorgeous art filling the Matumi Train Station floor. "It's like I'm walking across stars and planets!"

"You'll see even grander sights than this," laughed Dinah.

Milky white marble walls surrounded them, each with statues depicting spirits from various Azakuin mythologies carved into them. Stained-glass windows similar to All Saint's Church back in Rivinsdeep filled every wall, and their country's flag proudly hung from a golden pillar. Silver bells on red ribbons hung from tall lamp posts, reminding Soraya it was the Yuletide Season.

"This looks like the inside of a palace," Soraya murmured.

Dinah halted, causing the girl to bump into her from behind.

"Sorry!" Soraya gasped, but Dinah simply smiled back.

"It's alright," she pointed at a set of revolving doors ahead of them. "Have you ever seen that before?"

"No..."

Soraya watched with fascination as several Etherians from outside the station jumped into the small wedges of space, walked clockwise along with the glass in front of them, and entered into the building the second they could escape the circular moving doors.

"I heard about you being scared of the voice from the ceiling," Dinah's emerald green eyes sparkled. "I think that a lot of what you're about to see in Matumi will be new to you."

"Oh..." Soraya blushed a dark crimson red. "Reading about things is a lot different from actually experiencing them in person."

"This happens more often than you'd think," the train attendant assured her. "Most Azakuins live in smaller towns and take pride in keeping older traditions and ways of living alive. Matumi is one of the few big cities that actually utilizes technology as much as possible."

Dinah offered Soraya her hand. "Are you ready to try and go through them?"

Soraya curled her fingers around the woman's glove. "Okay, let's go."

Together, they entered into one of the thin moving spaces.

The doors never stopped sliding forward, so the girl shuffled her feet at a medium pace without touching the glass before or behind her. Within a few seconds, they made it to the other side of the station.

"Good job," Dinah beamed proudly. "Did you like that?"

"Yeah, it was neat! Let's do it again!"

However, before Soraya could run towards the revolving doors, she heard a slight cough from her right.

"Ahem."

She paused and spotted a tall, thin, older woman wearing a white collared shirt and long, black pants that went down to her ankles. She had piercing blue eyes, light colored skin that looked weathered and tanned, and dark freckles scattered across her face. Her long, brown hair was tied up neatly into a bun that sat on the top of her head. Her thin, pink lips were curled into a slight frown as she towered over the girl.

"You must be Soraya Thenayu, correct?"

"Yes, I am," the girl bowed to the woman she assumed was Ms. Faye. "Pleased to meet you, ma'am."

Yabo poked his head out of Soraya's hood and chirped.

"Are you aware of the pandacoon hitching a ride on your back?" the older woman asked with a hint of curiosity in her voice.

"Yes, this is my pet," Soraya explained as she dug out Dr. Athan's letter from her backpack and handed it to the groundskeeper. The woman took it into her thin fingers, skimmed through it quickly, glanced at the tiny mammal, and nodded.

"Everything seems to be in order," she handed the letter back to Soraya. "I'll be making a copy of that once we arrive at the school, but it's best that you hold onto it for now."

Ms. Faye gave a curt bow to Dinah. "You take care now, dear," she added in a softer tone, "it's good to see you again."

"Same with you," Dinah smiled before turning to the girl. "I bid you farewell. Hopefully I'll see you again at the end of the school year."

"Thank you for everything!"

Once the train attendant disappeared back into the Matumi Train Station, Ms. Faye spoke again, but in a stricter tone.

"This way," she ordered.

"Y-yes ma'am!"

They walked from the curb onto a grassy knoll overlooking more of the city streets below. Soraya could hardly believe how enchanting and colorful everything around her was and couldn't stop swiveling her head to take in the scenery.

"Have you ever ridden in a car before?" Ms. Faye's question cut through Soraya's concentration.

"No, but I've read about them…"

"It's like being on a train, except there are more stops and turns involved," the older woman continued thoughtfully. "It's not too scary, you'll be fine."

They headed towards another sidewalk, except this one had a dark blue car parked alongside it. Soraya had never seen an automobile before and was perplexed by its strange and sleek design. In her opinion, it wasn't nearly as impressive looking as Dr. Athan's hand built Calgreneze wagon.

"Hop in," Ms. Faye ordered while popping open one of the rear side doors. Soraya pushed her suitcase and backpack into the leather seats next to her before sitting down by the open door. Yabo hopped out of her hood and settled himself onto her lap.

"Seat belt," Ms. Faye leaned over Soraya and buckled her and Yabo in. Soraya felt the sturdy strap in her hands and wondered why it was necessary to wear it when the train didn't even have them.

"Now sit there and wait until we arrive at the school."

The woman slid into the driver's seat and closed the door with a mighty slam. The girl watched in fascination as Ms. Faye pulled out a set of keys and placed one into a small slot next to the wheel. The vehicle roared to life, causing everything within it to shake and rattle fiercely. Soraya dug her fingers into the seat directly in front of her and didn't let go for the remainder of the ride.

The groundskeeper thrust the automobile forward, and it jerked forward with a terrible lurching noise.

"What the…" Ms. Faye growled while gazing down at the pedals beneath her feet, then stared at the strange gray sticks between her and the passenger seat on her right.

"Oh, it's in park, hold on."

The woman pressed a button on the edge of one of the wands with a loud click and thrust it down forcefully.

"Now it'll work."

Ms. Faye straightened up in her gray leather seat and floored her foot down onto the clutch and gas pedals. The car leapt forward freely this time and headed straight down the hill. Colorful blurred buildings flew past the windows on either side of the vehicle.

The groundskeeper's driving terrified Soraya. The girl closed her eyes several times because she was sure the older woman was going to hit someone or something. The driver also liked to curse aloud, mutter under her breath, and yell at other drivers as they made their way towards the school.

"For heaven's sake! That was a blue light! Just go!"

"No! Don't go five miles under the speed limit! What is wrong with them?"

"I have the right of way! *Move it!*"

Needless to say, both Soraya and Yabo could hardly wait to be out of the car. Their stomachs churned from the sudden halts and tight turns.

*Maybe I should have just walked to school…*

The automobile finally slowed down upon turning onto a gravel driveway. Soraya could hear the crunching of leaves and rocks under the turning wheels as they made their way through a hall of tall green, leafy trees with looming branches overhead. At the end of the tunnel was a large steel gate, and it had already started swinging open, so they could enter. Only after they had passed by the entrance did the car stop completely.

"We're here. Out!"

Soraya struggled with unlocking the seat belt and gratefully jumped out of the car. For a split second she didn't know where Yabo was, but then looked down. He had been so terrified that his claws were buried deep into the girl's dress, and he was still hanging onto her.

"You're okay," she laughed while freeing her pandacoon.

"Here are your things," the groundskeeper continued as if she hadn't mentally scarred them for life. She grabbed Soraya's belongings from the back seat and thrust them at the girl with such force that it nearly knocked her off her feet. "Now follow me."

Before them was a large water fountain. It had a large, round bottom layer with a medium middle and smaller top, like a three tier cake. Water gushed down in thick waterfalls from all sides.

Just beyond that was a huge building with balconies, archways and towers, similar to the shops they had seen in the city. There were two golden lion heads carved into both of the front two pillars, and a beautiful, round stained-glass window of two unicorns holding up a red heart was in the center of the entrance.

A grand staircase sat before the school, leading up to the large, oak front doors of the building. To the left of the entryway was a statue of a gremowlkin, along with the insignia of the school framed beneath it in stone.

Ms. Faye gestured towards the grand architectural feat. "Welcome to Darkwood Academy, your new home."

## Chapter 15: Darkwood Academy

"We actually get to live here!"

Soraya gazed up at the school in awe, noticing that the twelve Zodia, along with the four Elemental Magic symbols, decorated the stained-glass windows.

"That, up there, is one of the many dormitories we have," Ms. Faye pointed at the tall spire with a large statue of a dragon sitting atop one of its many balconies. "You'll be tested in the morning to determine which house you'll be a part of and what uniform you'll be wearing."

"Wait… tested?" Soraya asked. "What does that mean, exactly?"

"Every new student is given a series of rigorous evaluations in order to determine how they best learn," the groundskeeper explained while opening one of the large, oaken doors.

The foyer was huge and grand, with portraits of what Soraya assumed were faculty staff members and other Etherians in prestigious positions at the school. The polished, wooden floor was a mix of navy blues and purples and stretched out into the tall, long hallway before her. Giant, curving staircases leading to balconies were on both sides of the room. Beyond the stairways were long corridors leading to various classrooms.

"There are three houses here; Red, Blue and Green," Ms. Faye said while ascending the staircase, her voice bouncing off of the cold stone walls. "Red is for audible learners, Blue is for visual, and Green for kinesthetic."

The groundskeeper gestured towards three giant banners overhanging the middle hallway, each coinciding with the different houses. The red tapestry had a bat stitched into it, its giant wings spread out on either side, and its claws outstretched before it, as if it were about to latch onto something. The blue banner had a large tiger embroidered in its center. Elegant and sleek, its face centered right in the middle and staring straight at them. To the right hung the green banner depicting a wolf howling towards the heavens.

"That sounds very organized," Soraya managed to say in between breaths while scampering after the tall woman leading the way before her. Ms. Faye took great leaps in skipping over steps, while Soraya struggled to keep up despite being quick on her feet.

*I'll probably be placed into the Blue House because of my photographic memory.*

"For now, you and your pet will be put up in one of the dorms for tonight and be given dinner."

They wandered down another grand hallway towards one of the spires. Lanterns built into the walls lit the way as they passed by many elegant paintings and closed oaken classroom doors leading to what Soraya assumed were more classrooms.

"I suggest you go to bed early. You will be awoken around eight in the morning tomorrow, and I promise that it will be a long day full of tests and tours."

When they reached the end of the hall, they were greeted by a large blue door that read, *Blue Female Dormitory* in silver script.

"Your father told us you're a visual learner, so you'll stay here for tonight, though after your evaluations are graded tomorrow you may change houses, so be prepared for that," Ms. Faye prattled on while placing her slim hand on the silver doorknob and turning it. "Your fellow students will show you to your dorm from here."

Mixed voices of girls chatting away filled the air, greeting Soraya's ears. They all quieted down when the door creaked open.

"Thank you for everything," Soraya said before timidly entering the large room. There was a huge, roaring fireplace under a stone wall. Surrounding it were dark blue velvet couches. White frilled curtains covered every window within the circular room while wooden chairs, tables and bookshelves stood against every wall.

Soraya was immediately greeted by a million multicolored eyes staring at her from all directions.

"H…hello," she stuttered, her body stiffening up, her heartbeat quickening within her chest. She had never been a fan of being the center of attention.

"Hey, Soraya Thenayu's here!" exclaimed a feminine voice on her right. Soraya was met with a pair of brown eyes on a pale face surrounded by chocolate colored curls.

"Hi, my name is Emrose Savis," the student boldly stepped forward, bowing politely. It both surprised and worried Soraya that a complete stranger already knew her name. Before she had time to ponder over this, the girl on Emrose's left spoke up.

"I'm Vamera Barden," she introduced herself with an air of

grace.

Soraya almost gasped when she stared at the girl's gorgeous violet eyes and hair. Her mahogany skin complimented the purple perfectly, in the girl's opinion, and she had to rip her gaze away, so she wouldn't come across as being rude.

"It's nice to meet you both," Soraya grinned shyly, digging her fingers into the thick backpack straps on her shoulders and tightening her grip on her rolling suitcase.

Yabo meowed from within the girl's hood and poked his head out to greet everyone. The air was immediately filled with "oohs" and "awes" as everyone came closer to get a better look at the pandacoon.

"Oh my gosh! You brought an animal? Lucky!"

"That is the cutest thing I've ever seen!"

Yabo soaked in the attention, loving every second of it, while Soraya grew more and more uncomfortable and wanted to melt and disappear into the floor. She looked over at Emrose and Vamera and noticed how they looked unamused. Although she had just met them, Soraya could tell they were already judging her.

"So… where can I put my stuff?" Soraya interrupted while untangling herself from all the outstretched arms petting her pandacoon.

"The bedrooms are upstairs," said one of the girls in front of her. She had emerald green eyes, similar to Dinah's back on the Rivingale Express, and long blackish blue hair tied into two ponytails. "I can show you, if you'd like," she smiled sweetly. "My name's Moiya by the way."

Moiya stepped away from the crowd of girls and gestured towards the back right of the room, where there was an open wall leading to a stairwell hidden in the shadows.

Yabo, still wanting affection, hopped down from Soraya's shoulders and proceeded to sprawl himself out onto the navy blue and silver carpeted floor. He looked mischievously up at his owner with his black beady eyes before slowly and dramatically rolling himself onto his side, so his fluffy stomach faced the students.

"Can I… can I put my face in his belly?" asked one of the girls after squealing at the pandacoon's cuteness.

"Yes, definitely," Soraya rolled her sky blue eyes at her pet's attention seeking behavior. "He loves cuddling."

While Yabo received the most pats, belly rubs, ear stroking and kisses he'd ever had in his life, Soraya followed Moiya upstairs to see where they'd be sleeping.

"I hope you get high marks in your visual scoring tomorrow," the green-eyed Azakuin stated. "I don't want that cutie to leave us."

"We'll definitely be staying here," Soraya vowed with confidence. "I'm not the greatest at remembering what I hear, and although I do learn alright by copying what I see others do, I'm best with visual learning."

Moiya seemed pleased at her response and skipped into the room at the top of the stairs, twirling around, so her dress spun along with her. Soraya followed her into the bedroom and took in her new surroundings.

The ceiling was a crescent dome with realistic paintings of the sky and clouds covering every inch of the bowl shaped interior. Every wall was light blue, and ornately decorated wood carvings of flowers and vines lined the bottom frames. Rich brown, wooden bunk beds were pushed up against the walls on all sides, each covered with navy blue blankets and white pillows.

"I do hope we can be friends," Moiya said meekly. "It can be quite lonely here sometimes."

"I would love to be friends with you!" Soraya replied, completely missing the hint of sorrow in her new acquaintance's voice. "I've always wanted to be close to someone around my age…" She hesitated, thought back to Komorebi, and realized she was assuming things about Moiya. "How old are you? I'm thirteen."

"I'm thirteen as well," Moiya beamed.

"Where are you from originally?" Soraya asked.

"I was born in Batilde, but moved here a few years ago. Even though Matumi is beautiful, I actually like my hometown a bit better, to be honest…" she eyed the stairs warily. "Some Etherians around here can be a bit stuck up and snobby."

"Oh…" Soraya wasn't sure what to make of this new information, but she tucked it into the back of her head.

"Don't get on Emrose and Vamera's bad sides, or Jacquelle's…" Moiya whispered, a hint of fear in her voice. "They run our house because they're the rich kids, and will make life difficult for you really fast if you don't do what they say."

Her voice lowered even more, and Soraya had to lean in to hear the rest of what her new friend was saying. "They like spreading rumors about others. I heard one about me just yesterday… I really wish I knew why they were upset at me…"

"Hey!"

Both girls snapped their heads towards the stairs. A different student was standing there, one that Soraya hadn't met yet. She was tall, thin, and smiling at them from the dark. Her long, curly blond hair fell gracefully around her pale face, and her dark blue eyes were gorgeous like the night sky. Despite her innocent appearance, the air immediately turned colder with her presence.

"Aren't you both going to join us for dinner?"

The girl's grin grew wider, showing more glistening white

teeth. The hairs on Soraya's arms stood straight up as her heart skipped a beat within her chest.

"Yes, Jacquelle, we'll be down in a minute," Moiya said as calmly as she could, though Soraya could see her legs shaking.

The girl by the stairway didn't budge. Instead, she stared into the girl's emerald eyes with such intensity, that Moiya cowered back and lowered her gaze to the floor in silent defeat.

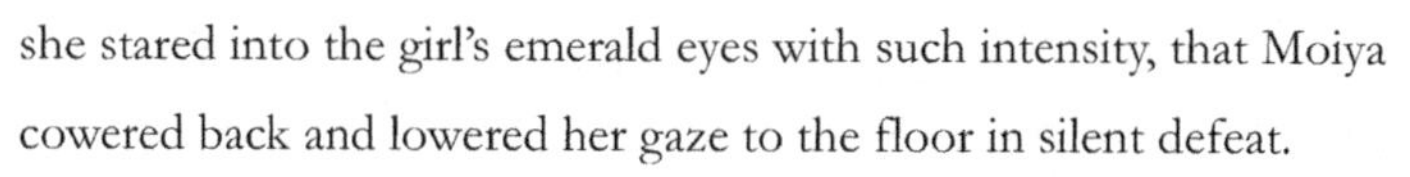

*What was that about?* Soraya pondered as adrenaline kicked into her system.

"Let's go," Jacquelle commanded, swiftly turning on her heel and walking gracefully down the marble steps like a princess out of a fairy tale would.

Both girls followed after her but kept their distance, as if that would somehow protect them. Soraya was grateful she had magic in her possession. Jacquelle frightened her, though she didn't understand why. The girl stared at Jacquelle's beautiful golden locks as they bounced with each step the girl took.

*I'm on to you.*

* * *

All the students in the Blue House made their way towards the center of the school, where the Dining Hall was located. Three long, rectangular wooden tables stretched out across the room, accompanied by long, log-like benches for students to use as chairs. The walls were lined with lit lanterns, paintings of different landscapes throughout Azakua, and multicolored stained-glass windows.

"Let's sit here," Moiya suggested while leading Soraya and Yabo through the sea of students towards a pair of empty seats near the middle of the far right table. "No one likes sitting in the center, which means we don't have to fight anyone for a spot."

When Soraya sat down, Yabo leapt onto the table and danced impatiently in circles.

"Food will be arriving shortly, just wait a little longer," Moiya assured the pandacoon.

"Mow!" Yabo complained. Some other students chuckled at him, but this time, it was from a group of male students dressed in blue.

"How did you get that in here?" asked a boy while placing his amber colored hand on Yabo's ears and gently scratching them. "You'll get into so much trouble if the teachers see him."

"I have a doctor's note, but thanks for your concern-" Soraya explained, but gasped as she stared at the boy's features. He looked Etherian in every way except for the two, velvety cat-like ears that stood on either side of his head.

"Are you a Shadelkin?" she blurted while thinking back to her Encyclopedia Historia. According to mythologies, when the Nomadic Shadelkin Tribe turned from their wicked ways, they had been blessed by the Zodia and granted a fast evolution, allowing them to survive differing harsher climates through a higher degree of strength and agility.

Although a minority of Shadelkins occupied every country, their language and customs were sadly dying out. Soraya remembered reading that one of their three dialects was already extinct, and the other two were almost completely gone from the lack of usage. Soraya thought it was tragic that the remaining two languages could be completely dead in less than a hundred years.

"Yes, and proud to be," the boy grinned, his candy apple eyes sparkling when he showed off his sharp fangs.

"I'm Soraya Thenayu. What's your name?" Soraya asked and bowed.

"Ujuu Leyo," he bowed back. "And this grumpy guy…" Ujuu grabbed another boy who was standing next to him and pulled him closer. "Is my twin brother, Rhys."

"Uh… hi," Rhys said awkwardly before blushing and looking away. Although they looked incredibly similar in appearance, Soraya noticed Rhys' hair was in a long black braided ponytail, whereas Ujuu's was short and spiky around his head.

"Hello, Rhys!" Soraya exclaimed. The boy's face grew even more red as he struggled to escape his brother's grasp.

"Oh, stop being so shy around every cute girl you happen to see," Ujuu chuckled before winking at Soraya.

"Yeah, Moiya is pretty cute," Soraya glanced over at her new friend, completely overlooking the fact that Ujuu was referring to her.

"What! Me?" Moiya jumped in her seat, her cheeks flushed.

Ujuu howled with laughter, causing some neighboring students to look up and see what all the ruckus was about. "Can we sit with you both?" the Shadelkin asked, his lips grinning from ear to ear. "I haven't had this much fun in a while."

"Yes! Please join us!" Soraya shuffled over on the bench so Ujuu could squeeze in next to her on her right. Rhys quietly slid into the seat next to his brother and used him as a meat shield, so he wouldn't have to talk to either of the girls.

"Soraya, please come sit over with me and my friends."

Jacquelle stood at the opposite side of the table. The cold, eerie change in the air was back. This time, Soraya knew for sure that she wasn't imagining it. Moiya, Ujuu and Rhys all shrank back in their seats away from her. Even Yabo stiffened up, his fur raised as his ears lowered.

"Hey, we are her friends," growled Ujuu from next to her.

"Friends let friends make their own decisions about things," Jacquelle said in a sickeningly sweet voice. "And you just met her, you're hardly an acquaintance."

"Well, I'm happy sitting here with them," Soraya stated with confidence.

"Alright, I'll just join you then," Jacquelle sighed before glaring at another student who was occupying the seat across from Soraya. The terrified kid stood up and scampered to another table.

*What is her deal?* Soraya wondered as the most powerful and intimidating student in the entire school daintily sat down across from her.

*What does she want from me?*

## Chapter 16: The Calling

The second Jacquelle placed her slender, pale elbows onto the table and folded her hands under her chin, several students pushing carts full of various food platters entered through a pair of swinging doors. They were dressed in red and white gowns, similar to the school uniforms, but were designed to resemble waiter and waitress outfits.

"Oh, Soraya, you wouldn't know this since you just arrived here this evening, but all the students cook meals for each other," purred Jacquelle with a hint of pride. "Our school values the importance of passing on Azakuin traditions, and recipes are no exception to that."

Usually, the thought of cooking and baking excited Soraya, but she kept her focus on the blond, who was inspecting her over with dark, mysterious blue eyes. Although Soraya knew something was afoot, she decided to be polite and hear the girl out.

They were interrupted when students from the Red House placed huge plates full of delicious looking meals and empty white bowls and silverware in front of each student. Dumplings, flour based wraps filled with various cooked meats and vegetables, sliced fruit and vegetables alongside various dips, pasta noodles, sauces, and so much more filled the tables, that Soraya could hardly decide what she wanted to have. Yabo, on the other hand, eyed the bacon and chirped, so Soraya grabbed two slices and gave them to him.

"So, where are you from?" Jacquelle asked while filling her bowl with cooked noodles and drizzling a white cheese sauce over it.

"I'm from the Averlore Mountains," Soraya replied, purposefully keeping her answer vague.

Jacquelle's eyes narrowed in displeasure, but in the blink of an eye her expression was blank, like a white porcelain mask.

"How about you?" Soraya added, hoping to steer the conversation away from revealing more details about herself.

"I was born and raised here in Matumi," Jacquelle sounded bored. "Nothing of interest ever happens in this city…" She lazily spun her fork into the spaghetti noodles and watched the individual strands curl around her silverware.

Yabo, who had inhaled his meal, was distracted by the delicious smell of meat and cheese wafting through the air. His black beady eyes grew huge as he scrunched up his body, readying himself to pounce upon a platter full of fried wings.

"You have to share with everyone, silly," Soraya chided Yabo, scooping him up into her arms before he could leap. Her pandacoon meowed in protest and struggled to break free.

"Here you are, sweetie," Moiya giggled, plucking a wing off the plate and handing it to Yabo's tiny outstretched paws. Her emerald eyes switched between looking at the pandacoon with adoration and warily at Jacquelle.

"Mew!" Yabo cried before tucking into his meal.

Jacquelle observed Soraya and her pet before speaking up. "You're lucky you could bring that thing, you know. It's only because your mother died when you were young that he even counts as a support animal."

Soraya blinked in surprise and froze in her seat. *How did she know about that?*

As if she were reading her mind, the blond laughed. "My father owns this school, and I have access to everyone's records," she looked around the room, and everyone's eyes lowered as they tried not to look directly into her gaze.

Dread rose to Soraya's throat. *No wonder everyone fears her, she can blackmail anyone she wants.*

"Jacquelle," Ujuu spoke up, his black hair riling up while his velvety black ears lowering on either side of his head. "Leave her alone, she hasn't done anything wrong."

The blond ignored him. "Soraya, you're too good to be hanging out with these demon eyed freaks. Come over to my table, and you can sit next to me."

Although Ujuu and Soraya's eyes simultaneously flared up with fury, the boy stayed seated and remained calm, while the girl made tight fists with shaking hands.

"Don't call him that!" Soraya snapped, much to everyone's surprise. Flashbacks of her mother being called the same slur reeled through the girl's mind, making her blood boil.

*I couldn't save Mama, but I can at least stand up for my new friends.*

"What?" Jacquelle gaped at Soraya in surprise. "You're one of the few Azakuins here who has blue eyes like me, yet you're defending the foreigners?" she laughed, shaking her head in disbelief. "What's wrong with you?"

Tears formed in Soraya's eyes when she thought about her mother being abandoned simply for having red eyes when she needed help with giving birth. *How could anyone be that heartless and cruel to someone else?*

"Jacquelle, those words are hurtful and demeaning!" Soraya yelled. "Apologize to Ujuu!"

Her new friends and everyone within earshot stared at her in shock, as if they couldn't believe that someone was standing up to

Jacquelle. The blond sat in her seat, completely stunned. It was obvious she wasn't used to being talked to like that, because her expression hardened.

"Me? Apologize? They should be apologizing for invading our country!" she spat while jumping to her feet, pointing a thin finger back at Soraya. "If you really believe that I have to say sorry for anything, then you're a traitor! You don't even deserve to have blue eyes!"

Before Soraya could think of a response, Jacquelle turned on her heels and sauntered away to rejoin her group of friends, who were huddled together at the end of another table and whispering among themselves.

"Wow!" Ujuu gasped. "That was awesome! Maybe you were more polite to her than she deserved, but still, dang!"

"Thank you," Rhys chimed in. His voice was as soft and relaxing as the breeze rustling through the Averlore Mountains at night.

Although Soraya was glaring at the back of Jacquelle's swishing blond hair, the compliments from the boys helped calm her racing heart. She sank into her seat, staring down at her empty plate. The growling within her stomach had disappeared, thanks to all the knots of nervousness that had built up within it, but she had to eat something since the next day was going to be long and arduous.

Moiya, who had been silent for a while, suddenly piped up. "That was really cool, and brave too, but," she sighed. "You do know that she resides in our dormitory, right? We're going to have to see her on a regular basis."

"Oh yeah…" Soraya hadn't taken that detail into account. "Well, I don't really have anything to hide in my records, so I'm not worried if she's mad at me or not…"

Even as she spoke, Soraya knew she did indeed have a lot to keep hidden. Her father's declining health in addition to his

Arcanology research for their government, the magic she illegally had absorbed into her skin, and even Adonia being Casmerahn were all secrets that she couldn't risk being known to the public for various reasons.

"Trust me," Moiya whispered. "If she doesn't have anything on you, she'll make something up. Jacquelle is quite creative with her rumors."

"Creative?" snorted Ujuu. "You're just being nice, that's giving her way too much credit. Just a month ago, I remember hearing that Rhys and I eat mice that are still alive," he laughed as he helped himself to another portion of chicken wraps. "That was the dumbest one I've heard yet. I think she's starting to run out of ideas, to be honest."

Soraya shook her head at the insensitivity of Jacquelle. "Shadelkin are a nomadic tribe that follow dracaribou and their migration patterns. Your traditional diet consists of reindeer, fish, and cloudberries. She should know that."

"That's correct," smiled Rhys. He leaned forward, so he could see Soraya from across the table, his face glowing from the girl's knowledge of his and Ujuu's cultural practices. "Although we do have cat-like features," he continued, sounding a little more confident in himself. "That doesn't mean we necessarily act just like them in all scenarios. We take regular showers and like to swim, for example."

"Yeah, try bathing a normal cat and see what happens," Ujuu rolled his ruby red eyes towards the ceiling. "Because Jacquelle can't seem to tell the difference between us and them for some reason," he laughed and faced Moiya, but noticed how her green eyes were rooted to the floor.

"Hey, are you okay?" he asked, his jovial voice brimming with concern.

Moiya shook her head, her beautiful, bluish black braids

swishing around her freckled face as she did.

"You can tell us if you want to, and if you don't, then that's okay too," Soraya's eyebrows furrowed in empathy for her new friend.

Both Ujuu and Rhys nodded their heads in agreement.

"Okay…" Moiya inhaled, exhaled, and closed her eyes. "So, Jacquelle started spreading a rumor about me…" the girl faltered and went silent.

Her friends waited patiently for her to calm herself down.

"Remember, only say if you really want to," Rhys reminded her. "No pressure, okay?"

"I'll tell you guys another time… sorry," tears welled up in her emerald green eyes.

"Nah, don't be." Ujuu smiled at her.

"Mew!" Yabo cooed, waltzing over to the Calgreneze girl. He hopped down, plopped himself into her lap, and purred while butting his face into her hand.

"Aww! He is the sweetest thing ever!" Moiya swooned.

"Good job," Soraya whispered to her pandacoon.

"Hey, Soraya…" Rhys spoke up from the other side of Ujuu. "Maybe keep your personal belongings close to you, in case Jacquelle tries to steal them. She'll probably be desperate to use anything she can against you now."

"Good point," Moiya glanced over at the blond and her posse of friends. They were huddled altogether at the end of the neighboring table, as if they were plotting an attack. "You can keep your stuff in my locker tonight."

"Thanks, Moiya," Soraya smiled gratefully. Despite already making an enemy at her new school, Soraya had also made three new friends and felt fortunate enough to have them in her life.

*I hope we can all be lifelong friends, like Dr. Athan is for my father…*

* * *

*Dear Papa,*

*I know I've only been gone for two days, but I miss you terribly. How are you? I hope you're feeling better.*

*Today has been both fun and stressful. Fun because I was given a haircut, and I now have my school uniform, which I think is adorable. Stressful, because I have never been asked so many questions about what I know before, nor have I ever taken so many tests back to back in my life. Speaking of tests, I learned a new word today: plagiarism.*

*Mr. Thuron, my history teacher, couldn't believe that I'm able to rewrite word for word from any book I've read. He tested me by allowing me to read one page from a book I've never even heard of and wanted to see if I could completely replicate all the text within it. He was astonished and gave me, what he called, "incredibly high scores." He just told me to not do that on tests, and to instead rewrite the main ideas of what I read into my own words. I promised I would.*

*I'm definitely staying in the Blue House, which is geared towards visual learners, as you knew I would be. I was told today by the Azakuin teacher, Mrs. Sworvski, that you were a student of her mothers, and you were also in the Blue House. They have portraits of you and Dr. Athan on the walls here, since you were both at the top of your classes and made it into their hall of fame for the highest scoring students. It's nice that I get to see your face, even if you do look much younger than you are now.*

Soraya paused and tapped the red feather on the top of her quill lightly on her face in thought. She then dipped it into her midnight colored ink bottle and held it against the glass to get the excess off, and continued writing.

*There's a girl named Jacquelle Demarko who makes fun of Casmerahns and other foreigners. I got mad at her last night and told her to apologize for using slurs, and she called me a traitor to our country since I have blue eyes. She's the daughter of the owner of Darkwood Academy, and boasts about being able to see everyone's school records. Almost everyone here is afraid of her spilling information about them that they don't want others knowing. What should I do? Is there anything I can do?*

*On a more positive note, I've made some lovely friends. Moiya Marlune, Rhys Leyo, and Ujuu Leyo are all very lovely Etherians. I adore them already, and I hope you get to meet them at the end of the school year.*

*I love and miss you dearly,*

*Soraya Thenayu*

After re-reading her letter for the third time in a row, Soraya was satisfied with it. She folded the parchment paper into thirds before slipping it into a faded yellow envelope, which she had previously labeled with her home address.

She glanced down at her school schedule. The black, glossy ink shone from the lighted lamps around the dormitory, and the girl lightly traced her fingers over the words while putting it all to memory.

**Lunas, Ignis, Aquas, Terras and Auras Diem:**

**Cooking Class 5 am, Mr. Trog, Room 50 (Lunas and Ignis)**

**1. Azakuin: 8 - 8:45 am, Mrs. Sworvski, Room 203**

**2. History: 9 - 9:45 am, Mr. Thuron, Room 300**

**Break: 10 - 10:45 am.**

**3. Biology: 11 - 11:45 am, Mr. Yung, 320**

**4. Casmerahn: 12 - 12:45 pm, Ms. Evi, 104**

**Lunch: 13 - 13:45 pm,**

**Cooking: Aquas and Terras Diem, Mr. Trog, Room 50**

**5. Gym: 14 - 14:45 pm, Mr. Levi, 101**

**6. Orchestra: 15 - 15:45 pm, Ms. Katia, 130**

**7. Math: 16 - 16:45 pm, Mr. McLee 230**

**Dinner: 18 - 18:45 pm**

**Cooking: Aquas Diem, Mr. Trog, Room 50**

**Astros and Solis Diem: Weekend.**

*I'm so glad Moiya is in most of my classes.*

Soraya looked up at her friend, who was sitting across the

table from her. Yabo slept next to Moiya's stack of school books, his gentle snores filling the air. Light from the setting sun seeped in through the windows surrounding them.

Darkwood Academy sat atop one of the many rolling hills spread across Matumi, and Soraya could see the city buildings beyond the tall, yellow brick wall surrounding their campus. Encircling them was the bright blue Valtic Ocean with its many white sand beaches.

Nothing outside suggested it was still winter except some Yuletide decor such as leafy, circular wreaths with red ribbons and ornaments hanging from various lampposts. Matumi was warm and inviting, with green grass and sunny blue skies beckoning one to come outside and enjoy its beauty. She thought back to the Averlore mountains surrounding her home, which were still covered in thick blankets of snow and ice. The difference was baffling.

"Hey Moiya?" Soraya broke the silence between them.

Moiya stared intently at one of the pages of her Biology book, her eyebrows furrowed together as she mouthed the text quietly under her breath. "What's up?" her friend replied after finishing the paragraph she was reading.

"How do I mail letters?"

Moiya blinked and looked up. "I... don't know, actually," she frowned. "I've never done that before. I usually just make phone calls to my parents."

"Who should I ask then?"

"Maybe Rhys or Ujuu would know," Moiya suggested. "I'd go with you, but I really need to study for my exam," the girl pointed towards the entrance door. "Go left when you exit and follow the hallway all the way down. The boy's dorm for Blue is at the end."

"Thank you!" Soraya leapt down from her chair and studied her sleeping pandacoon for a moment.

"I'll keep him with me," Moiya rubbed Yabo's furry belly.

"Okay," Soraya agreed before slipping out the door and heading towards the boy's dorm, the sealed letter to her father in hand. As she passed by the huge, stained-glass windows and looked out at the gorgeous artwork depicting the different Zodia from Azakuin mythology, she heard a voice faintly calling to her.

"*Soraya!*"

The girl stopped and turned her head. There was no one nearby, only an empty room. She could hear some students chatting together as they rounded the corner of the hallway, but they didn't sound like the wispy voice that had called to her.

"*Tempus wo nai. Igo va invenio sodse. Adiuva sodse!*"

The voice was back and stronger than before. It was coming from the back of her head, as if someone were whispering to her from inside her mind.

*Is that… Casmerahn?* Soraya wondered. *Casmerahn est ka?* she thought as loudly as she could towards the mysterious voice.

"*Jai! Casmerahn est!*"

Soraya swallowed. The voice, though cool and calm, had a strange effect over her. She was compelled to listen, to obey, despite not completely understanding what it was saying to her.

*Vos va qui est ka?* Soraya asked. Studying her Casmerahn textbook while on the train was suddenly paying off. Although she wasn't sure about pronunciations, she had learned to ask some important questions, such as, "who are you?"

"*Igo va vos no-*"

The voice went silent.

*Hello? Yohai?*

There was no answer. Shivers ran down Soraya's spine as she wondered what had happened to whoever was on the other end of their conversation.

*My what? Who are you?*

She was only met with silence.

## Chapter 17: The Duet

Despite being greatly troubled by the voice she had heard inside her head, Soraya decided it was best to not tell her new friends about it. She wasn't sure how they would respond to such outlandish news, and was scared of finding out.

*I've already lost Mama, and Papa isn't doing well. I don't want to lose anyone else. Maybe, after I get to know them better, I can start confiding in them about what's happening to me…*

Soraya's hand hovered over the wooden door before she knocked on the entrance to the Blue House for boys. She watched through one of the wide windows in the hallway as the sun sank into the Valtic Ocean. The surrounding sky turned into vibrant candy pinks and oranges before being swallowed up by twilight purples and blues.

After a few moments of being distracted by the gorgeous sundry of hues outside, she knocked again. Louder this time.

A boy with light skin, golden hair and eyes opened the door and stared in confusion at the girl.

"You do know that you can just enter if you wanted to, right?" he said. "This is where we study, it's technically open for all students."

"Oh!" Soraya exclaimed. "I'm sorry, I didn't know that."

The boy moved out of the way and beckoned her inside. The first thing Soraya noticed was that the common room looked identical to theirs. It was also circular, had a fireplace, tables and chairs alongside the walls, and the same color schemes of blue, silver and white. The major difference was the view from their windows showed more of the Valtic Ocean than the town of Matumi.

Several other boys were also in the room. Some were studying and reading books, while others were chatting together. However, upon Soraya's entry, all of them looked up and seemed to be surprised that one of the girls had come over to their area.

"Are you looking for someone?" the golden eyed boy asked. "I'm Olive Wilder, by the way."

"I'm Soraya Thenayu," the girl replied. "Do you know where Ujuu and Rhys Leyo are? I wanted to ask them how to mail letters."

"Hey, Soraya!"

Ujuu, who had been sitting at one of the tables, leapt down from his seat. "Did you say, mail letters, and how to?"

"Yes I did," Soraya held up her sealed envelope. "I want to deliver this to my father."

"Oh sweet! I'm also writing a letter. Check this out!" He picked up a parchment envelope and pointed at who it was addressed to with one of his sharp claws.

"Zaruna Markies? Who is that?" Soraya asked while studying his Azakuin handwriting. His letters were drawn beautifully, as if it had been done by a professional calligrapher.

"My absolute best friend aside from my dear brother," his candy apple eyes sparkled like rubies while he sighed longingly and looked out towards the sea.

"Oh no, there he goes about Zaruna again," Olive shook his head. "She has no idea how lucky she is. He never shuts up about how great she is."

"You wouldn't either if you ever had the chance to meet her," Ujuu winked before heading towards the entrance door and beckoning for Soraya to follow him. "I was about to mail a letter myself. I'll show you where to go."

He paused and looked up at the ceiling in thought. "We'll also stop by my locker on the way, so I can give you some stamps. I have a lot saved up, so I don't mind sharing."

"Thank you so much, Ujuu!" Soraya exclaimed. "Do you need me to pay you back?"

"Nope. Thank you for offering, but don't worry about that," Ujuu held the door open and insisted that she exit first. "I want to be a proper gent, let me spoil you, please, if that's okay."

"You're too kind."

As the two of them made their way down the hallway together, Soraya couldn't help but wonder who Zaruna was.

"Can I hear more about your best friend?"

"Well, we used to be next door neighbors for four wonderful years," Ujuu's face turned red. "She is such a beautiful soul. So sweet, intelligent, kind, and beautiful, like you," he winked. "But I already swore to marry her someday, so sorry, you're out of luck."

He held up his right hand, showing a piece of red string tied to his ring finger. "She wears the other half of the string. I know it sounds silly to make vows at such a young age, but I swear to Gods, I will be with her one day."

"You're so romantic," Soraya gasped in adoration. "That's the cutest thing I've ever seen! Zaruna is so lucky to have you."

"Thank you," Ujuu beamed. "I'll be traveling to go see her at the end of this school year. I've saved up enough Lari to ride a sky ship over to the Kingdom of Rosinka. Her family is going to let me stay with them. I can hardly wait!"

He skipped in his steps, causing Soraya's heart to swell with happiness at how over the moon he was for Zaruna.

*I hope everything works out for them. He deserves to be happy, and she must be amazing for him to act like this.*

They flew down several flights of stone staircases and stopped at a hallway full of tall, rectangular shaped metal lockers covering both sides of the wall. Ujuu hummed to himself and made a beeline towards one near the top. He turned a black dial knob with numbers on it, and with a small click, he pried open the door.

"I keep pictures of my family and Zaruna in here. Take a look."

Soraya peeked her head in and spotted several photos lining the inside of his locker. One was of his parents. His father had beautiful red eyes, black hair, and black ears, like his sons. Their mother, on the other hand, had bright blue eyes and light dirty blond hair. They were both smiling, as if they were in the middle of laughing, while holding each other.

"They look lovely," Soraya commented, before turning her attention to a picture of her friends as children. Both of the twins looked like smaller and cuter versions of themselves, while Ujuu's crush was similar to Kalisha. Zaruna had dark skin, like the bark of a chestnut tree, light pink hair, and dark magenta eyes.

"She's so adorable!" Soraya gasped. "I've never seen someone with that color of eyes before, they're stunning!"

"Aren't they?" Ujuu sighed wistfully. "In just six more months, I'll be on my way to see her again."

The boy picked up a small sheet of stamps and ripped off two before closing his locker shut. "One for you, and one for me."

"You're so sweet, Ujuu. Thanks again," Soraya looked up at the boy, half expecting his brother to be behind him. "Where's Rhys, if you don't mind me asking?"

"He's practicing the violalin," Ujuu explained. "He does that every day. I'll show you after we mail these letters. Vadamus!"

"What does that mean?" Soraya asked.

"That's how we say, let's go, in Casmerahn," Ujuu grinned. "My brother and I are fluent in our father's language. We're basically taking Casmerahn class for an easy grade."

He laughed, twirling his letter between nimble fingers. "Sometimes, we feel like we're cheating, but at the same time, we do take extra time to help the other students study outside of class, me more so than my brother since he's always busy practicing his instrument."

Soraya thought about the mysterious Casmerahn voice that had spoken with her. *Should I ask him what those phrases meant? Can I even remember what it said?*

She followed Ujuu down the corridor and found that they were already near the foyer of Darkwood Academy. "I'm taking Casmerahn too," Soraya managed to blurt out. "Papa knows it, so I want to learn too."

"Mirificoi!" Ujuu exclaimed. "Magnificent!" he added after seeing the confused look on the girl's face. "We can help you learn."

"Do you know what adio, no, wait, um…" Soraya mentally sounded out what the voice had been saying to her. "Adiuva sodse, means?"

"Help me," Ujuu translated. "That's a good one to know, actually. There are several ways of saying the word, please, in Casmerahn. Sodse is the command form. Think of someone in authority over you, like a parent, or teacher, telling you to do something."

*So, it was a cry for help?*

Ujuu noticed her puzzled expression, but assumed it was because she didn't understand what he was saying.

"I can give you more examples if you'd like," the Shadelkin offered.

"How about…" Soraya screwed up her face in

concentration. "Invenio sodse, what does that mean?"

"Find me. Again, that's in the commanding please form, like they're ordering you to do it," Ujuu furrowed his brows together. "Do you mind if I ask how you heard those words?"

Soraya's heart skipped a beat. *It's way too early to tell him that.*

"I was remembering a book my father was reading," she lied. "I forgot to ask him what those phrases meant, is all."

"Oh, okay," a toothy grin reappeared on Ujuu's face.

Although Soraya was worried about whom the voice belonged to, the clarity of the Casmerahn words brought some peace to her mind.

The two students found the mailing box hanging from the wall by the entrance of the school, just as Ujuu had said it would be. It was completely black and rectangular, and had a long thin slit running across it for putting mail inside.

Soraya eagerly placed her envelope into the open slot and watched it fall down into the dark box, where it disappeared from view. Ujuu did the same with his letter before opening up the main entrance door and beckoning Soraya to go through.

"Rhys is currently in the orchestra room, where students are allowed to practice after hours. It's in a separate building nearby on campus. Once you see it, you'll understand why."

A small gust of cold air blew through their hair upon exiting the front doors of the school. The night sky above was filled with bright stars and planets, the half moon shedding enough light to guide their way down a gravel road towards another set of buildings hiding behind a small forest of looming trees.

"Everyone here is required to learn at least one instrument regardless of which house they're in," Ujuu explained while they headed towards Room 130. "Music is considered an essential part of promoting mental health, and I agree, it really is. I just don't practice nearly as much as Rhys because I'm not competitive enough."

Upon entering, they faintly heard the sound of strings ahead. After pushing through yet another set of doors, she found herself entering into a gigantic circular shaped room. Surrounding them were empty blue velvet seats going all the way up towards the ceiling. In the middle before her stood Rhys, his dark wooden bow bouncing up and down on his electric blue, five stringed instrument.

Soraya had never heard anything so beautiful in her life. The violalin sang and groaned underneath Rhys' flying fingers. He did quick runs and slides, playing double strings, even triple strings, before suddenly pausing and holding perfectly still. The girl's sky-blue eyes widened, and she held her breath as he held the final note, the lowest c string he had, before turning and bowing to them.

"That was incredible!" Soraya clapped her hands together, the sound echoing around the amphitheater.

"You're getting lazy, bro," Ujuu yawned. "Come on, pick up your game." He laughed and narrowly dodged the piece of rosin Rhys chucked at him.

"You're one to talk," Rhys retorted, his lips curling into a big grin. "Why don't you ever practice?"

"I do, you just don't pay attention," Ujuu tried lying with a straight face, but was already bursting into laughter.

Soraya could tell the siblings weren't even upset at each other. They were taunting one another, like two brothers would. It reminded her of Tishva and Dr. Athan joking around together back in Rivinsdeep, and the girl stood back and simply enjoyed the silly insults they hurled back and forth at each other.

*Bang!*

They all jumped at the same time when the door behind them flew open and crashed into the wall. Jacquelle was standing in the hall, a cello in one hand, and a bow in the other. The whites of her eyes were red, as if she had been crying, and she was glaring with pure hatred up at Rhys.

"You and your stupid playing!" she yelled, pointing her bow, like a sword, in the boy's direction.

Rhys' black velvety ears lowered as he stared in surprise at Jacquelle's sudden fiery presence.

"What?" Rhys asked, clearly confused. "What are you talking about?"

"Didn't you see? How could you not have?" Jacquelle spat. "The beach concert coming up in four months! Don't you know who has that solo part?"

"N-no…" Rhys stuttered.

"Hey!" Ujuu butted in. "Rhys has been here practicing for the past three hours!" He stood between Jacquelle and his brother, glaring ferociously at the blond with disgust. "How would he have possibly seen that announcement?"

Jacquelle ignored Ujuu as she shoved her way past him, still staring angrily into Rhys' wide ruby red eyes.

"You and I are doing a duet! A flipping duet together!" she screamed, pure, venomous hatred dripping from her tongue. "How could the teacher do this to me?"

Soraya had never seen someone so angry before. She was at a loss for what to do, but she felt like she had to try something to extinguish the flames.

"If you're as good as he is, then you'll sound lovely together."

"*If?*' Jacquelle turned on Soraya, her eyes ablaze while she stormed up towards her. "*If?* Are you crazy? I *am* better than him!" she roared, spit flying from her lips. "He doesn't deserve to play with me! I practice every day! I've been on radio several times! Everyone around Azakua has heard my cello playing! I'm famous!"

The blond thrust her bow in Rhys' direction again, but her eyes were locked onto Soraya's. "He's a Casmerahn demon eyed freak! A nobody! How dare the teacher force me to do a duet with him!"

Jacquelle turned and glared at the boy. "I will *never* play a duet with you, do you hear me? That solo spot belongs to me and me alone!"

"Okay," Rhys said, his voice calm. "That's fine."

"What?" the girl blinked in surprise.

"I don't want to play with you anyway."

"Excuse me?" Jacquelle's face faltered. She looked as if she had been slapped. "You… not want to play with… me?" she snorted, but her lips trembled. "You've got that all wrong. I don't want to play with you because you're beneath me."

"No, Jacquelle, you can't keep up with my playing. You'll mess it up for us," Rhys bore his crimson eyes into hers. "I don't want to play a duet with you because your timing is off. You always rush by half a millisecond. I can hear the imperfection in your playing, and it throws me off."

Jacquelle went silent. She looked as if she were about to cry. "Am I… really off by that much?"

Soraya watched in fascination as Jacquelle's hand moved to the lower center of her back and caressed it in thought. Within seconds, Jacquelle's face hardened. "You're wrong, because Casmerahns aren't as good as Azakuins."

"If you don't want to make our orchestra look bad, start practicing with a metronome," Rhys stated coldly. "Now stop wasting my time. I'm not done practicing."

The Shadelkin boy turned his back on Jacquelle and played his instrument even faster than before. Soraya and Ujuu exchanged nervous glances as Jacquelle huffed loudly, as if to make her leaving known to Rhys, and waltzed off with her head held high.

"I'll be back in an hour, and you had better be done and out of here when I'm ready to practice!" she yelled before slamming the door behind her.

Rhys continued playing as if he hadn't heard her. He didn't stop creating his song even after Jacquelle was long gone from the premises.

"Rhys…" Soraya's nervous voice cut through the beautiful sound of the violalin's strings. "Are you alright?"

The boy paused, but said nothing. An uncomfortable silence settled in the air.

"Brother…" Ujuu chimed in. "It's okay, she's just a jerk."

"I know," Rhys looked down at his feet and sighed. "I didn't mean to be mean back though."

"She deserves to be put into her place," Ujuu said with a hint of anger in his voice. "Jacquelle is always demeaning towards us, you only stood up for yourself."

"Still…" Rhys finally turned his head towards his brother and Soraya. "I'm sorry you both had to see that. I didn't realize how much anger I had built up towards her until that moment…" He closed his eyes. "Playing music brings me joy, and for her to try and take that one simple thing away was too much."

"It's alright," Soraya assured him. "I am curious though, were you being serious about her speeding on songs?"

Rhys nodded. "Despite that small flaw, she really is a great cellist. The problem is, if I compliment her, she'll either say something snotty back like duh, of course," Rhys threw his voice to sound higher pitched like Jacquelle's, which made both Soraya and Ujuu giggle. "Or she'll dismiss everything I say because of my red eyes."

"Well, it's probably best not to inflate her already huge ego," Ujuu sighed. "Anyway, I hope the teacher reconsiders your duet."

Soraya thought back to her father nearly choking her by taking away the air around her and shivered at the bad memory. "I didn't think it was possible for anyone to get that angry…"

*Jacquelle's fit throwing was almost as scary as that-*

"That was the worst she's ever been," Rhys replied, cutting into Soraya's thoughts. The boy kneeled down and placed his instrument back into its black velvet case. "As for the duet, we'll see if that even happens. For now, let's just enjoy the rest of our weekend."

The three friends walked out of the Orchestra room altogether and headed back towards the main building. Soraya split off from the twins after wishing them both a good night.

*Poor Rhys and Ujuu... They're so lovely, they don't deserve to be treated like that... And poor Jacquelle. Why is she like this? Who made her this way?*

## Chapter 18: The Demon

Soraya slept comfortably on the top bunk above Moiya's bed. Yabo lay curled around her head, purring loudly in her ears, his furry face resting next to hers. The wide, open room around them was pitch black, and the faint rustling of sheets could be heard as other students tossed and turned in their beds.

"*Wake up.*"

Another voice called to her from the back of her mind, waking her with a start. She could tell it was different from what she had heard the day before. This one sounded like seven voices speaking simultaneously. All were deep, low and menacing, like how she imagined demons from the depths of Sheol would sound.

*Who are you? What do you want?* Soraya replied in her head, her heart rate increasing as fear gripped her body, leaving her paralyzed.

"*Where are you currently residing?*" the multiple voices asked with a hint of curiosity, completely ignoring her questions. "*Tell me!*"

Soraya's blood turned cold in terror. The overwhelming sense to obey the voice was back. Half of her felt compelled to answer the demon's question, but the other half knew she shouldn't.

*N…no,* Soraya thought loudly and kept her eyes shut. She recalled pictures of the stars and planets. *I live somewhere in the galaxy.*

The demonic voices erupted into monstrous cackling. "*You are quite entertaining and intelligent, my child, but I will find you.*"

A world map of Etheria flashed into Soraya's mind. "*There are only so many places you can hide from me. Eventually, you'll slip up and give me a hint of where you're living, and I'll pinpoint exactly where you are…*"

As Soraya tried with all her might to shove the demonic voices out of her head, she became aware, once again, of Yabo's loud purrs in her ears. Despite having a small, quick thought about her beloved pandacoon that lasted less than a second, the demonic voices picked up on it.

"*Yabo…*" they mused. "*Such a sweet little thing…*

*"Kill it.*"

Much to the girl's surprise and dismay, her right arm moved on its own, reaching up towards Yabo's face. Her fingers widened, like the jaws of a predator before clamping down on its prey.

*No!*

Soraya smacked down her right arm with her left and tackled it, holding it down with all her might to keep her pet safe. She was horrified that her right arm wriggled around like a snake, desperately twisting and writhing under her grasp while it hungrily reached for her pandacoon.

*Not Yabo! You're evil!* Soraya mentally screamed towards the otherworldly foe while focusing all of her energy on holding her right arm down. The second she got it to lie flat, she rolled onto her right side, pinning her arm between her body and the bed.

"*It's good to test you occasionally…*" the layered voices taunted while fading from her mind. "*You have too much Etherian blood in you. I will have to fix that…*"

The voices vanished completely, leaving Soraya panting and

shaking violently. She stayed on her side and didn't move for a few minutes, just in case her right arm tried attacking her pet again.

*Did that really just happen?*

Soraya cautiously rolled herself off of her right arm and flexed her fingers. She was in complete control of herself again.

*Too much Etherian blood in me…*

She thought back to her father telling her that Adonia was Casmerahn, and shook her head. *He's forgetting thirty years of his life, and it's genetically impossible for me to have blue eyes when mama's were red. Mama must have been something else, which means I'm half of whatever she was…*

The girl sat up in bed and folded her hands together, as if she were about to pray.

*What am I?*

* * *

Soraya awoke to the sound of an alarm clock going off. The high-pitched noises blared across the room, causing other students to groan and mumble sleepily as their dreams came to an abrupt end. Even Yabo lifted his small, fluffy head and stared in annoyance.

"Oh, did I wake you all?" Jacquelle's prissy voice filled the air before she ceased the alarm's incessant wailing with a small click of a button.

"What time is it?" yawned Moiya from beneath Soraya's bunk bed. The other students in the room stretched their limbs, rubbing the sleep away from their drooping eyes before glaring at Jacquelle. The room was still dark and absent of the sun's rays.

"It's six in the morning," replied the blond in a condescending tone. "Unlike you losers who like to sleep in, I'm getting a good start on my weekend."

Jacquelle turned her attention to Emrose and Vamera. "Come on, get up already," she commanded. Both girls sighed before pushing the warm blankets covering them aside.

A twinge of pity built up within Soraya while she watched the tired and disheveled looking pair slide out of their beds and follow their leader out of the room. Upstairs was where their lockers, showers and bathrooms were located.

*Was that all a dream, or did it actually happen?*

Soraya mulled over the night's events as she rolled up the long sleeves of her pajamas and looked down at her right arm. Dark purple bruises spotted her wrist and forearm. She moved it and winced slightly when a small sting flared up her muscles.

*It must have been real. Why else would it look and feel so beaten up?*

"Hey, Soraya!" Moiya called from beneath her. "I'm not able to fall back asleep, did you want to start the day with me?"

"Yes, that sounds good," Soraya replied. She was grateful for the distraction from the demonic entity that had attempted to possess her the night before.

"I'll show you where all of your classes are," Moiya continued. "We're together for most of them, but I still want to make sure you're ready for next week."

"Thank you, I really appreciate your help."

Moiya rolled out of bed, while Soraya leapt nimbly to the floor from her top bunk. Yabo got up from the pillow, stretched his little legs and paws, jumped down onto the ladder perched next to the bunk bed, and landed gracefully onto the wooden floor with a light thud.

"Mow?" he cooed up at the girls.

"Yes, you can come too," Soraya said, lowering her left arm for Yabo to rub his face into her gloved hand. The thought of anyone or anything wanting to hurt such a precious and innocent life chilled her to the bone.

*I won't let you control me.* Soraya stared intently at one of the windows covered by dark navy blue drapes. *I'll never hurt him. Never.*

"Hey, are you okay?" Moiya asked, snapping Soraya back to

the present.

"Yeah, I'm fine, it's just annoying that Jacquelle robbed us of our sleep."

"True," Moiya nodded. "She's just trying to get back at you by making us all suffer. That's just how she is, unfortunately."

Yabo climbed up Soraya's blue pajamas and perched himself on top of her shoulder. She kissed his small black nose and followed Moiya upstairs, so she could also get ready for the day.

Soraya wasn't comfortable with the idea of changing in front of Moiya or anyone else, so she grabbed her school uniform from her locker and made her way to one of the empty bathroom stalls. She made sure to take a long sleeved white shirt in order to hide her bruises.

*Now both my arms and hands are covered…*

The girl frowned, gazing at the soft black gloves she hadn't taken off since leaving home. As she passed by the shower room, she could hear Vamera and Emrose chatting away to each other. Soraya shielded her eyes, so she wouldn't have to see anyone without clothes on, and happened to enter the bathroom just as Jacquelle was putting her shirt on over her head. The girl caught a quick glimpse of what appeared to be long and thin scars across the blond's lower back.

"How did you get those wounds?" Soraya asked. "What happened?"

Jacquelle spun around, pulling her shirt all the way down. "That's none of your business!" she huffed. "I don't have to tell you anything."

*Someone did that to you…*

"Are you okay?" Soraya asked, her voice brimming with pity.

Jacquelle was thrown off guard by Soraya's concern for her. For a moment, it looked as if she were about to say something, but stopped herself.

"I'm fine," she replied with fake happiness in her voice. "Perfectly perfect."

"Okay, if you say so," Soraya dipped her chin in acknowledgement and headed towards an empty stall to change. She placed Yabo on the floor and took off her pajamas. As she tucked her long sleeved white shirt into her navy blue skirt and placed the straps over her shoulders, she heard a small sniffle come from the blond's direction behind the closed door separating them.

"Soraya?" Jacquelle spoke hesitantly.

"Yes?"

"I'm…" she stopped, as if she were catching herself. "I'm fine," the blond repeated. To Soraya, it sounded like she was trying to convince herself that it was true.

"If you want to be friends with me, let me know," Soraya replied. "I'd like to be your friend too."

Jacquelle didn't respond. Instead, she walked out of the bathroom in silence.

*She's so stubborn*, Soraya sighed. *At least I tried reaching out to her.*

After getting dressed, Soraya rejoined with Moiya downstairs and watched with fascination as her friend wove her long, beautiful blueish black hair into two long, thick braids. Moiya finished by adding white ribbons at the bottoms of each, tying them into thick bows.

"Do you want me to braid your hair, too?" Moiya flashed Soraya a smile when she noticed the girl gazing in admiration at her.

"I would love that!" she exclaimed. "I've never had my hair braided before!" Adonia had never learned, and Tishva had never bothered tackling her rat's nest.

Moiya sat Soraya down on the bed and settled in behind her. She slid her slender fingers down Soraya's thick strawberry blond hair, weaving and tugging gently at the three thick strands she had

created as she went. After twisting it altogether, Moiya tied a long white ribbon to secure the braid.

"And… we're done," Moiya smiled. "Now you match Rhys and I."

Soraya twirled on her heel, so she could watch her braided hair fly alongside her. "Do you think we could put a bow in Rhys' braid?"

"We can ask him at breakfast," Moiya laughed while stuffing her pocket with another white ribbon just in case.

The two girls, along with Yabo, exited their dorm and walked up and down the empty hallways together. Soraya carried her school schedule in one hand and held it up so Moiya could guide her to her classes.

"And this, to your right, is Room 203 with Mrs. Sworvski," Moiya pointed. "An easy way to remember where the rooms are located is by looking at the first number. If it's 100, it's on the first floor. 200 is on the second floor, and so on. The only exception is Room 50 because that's the kitchen, which is located on the main floor in the middle of the school."

"Good to know," Soraya commented while following her friend up to the third floor. She smiled at Yabo, who was perched on Moiya's shoulder. He was batting playfully at one of her braids with his little black paws.

"You have history class there," Moiya gestured towards Room 300 before untangling Yabo from her hair. "Biology is just around the corner, right there," she gestured towards Room 320.

"After your first two classes, you get a forty-five minute break. Elementary schools usually give out homework for students to do, but not high schools. We only study for exams. Any assignments the teachers give us are either for extra credit or practice tests."

Soraya had never been given homework before, so she simply shrugged her shoulders at Moiya's explanations.

"Breaks are usually when students gather with their study groups to practice for upcoming tests," Moiya continued. "It's also when we can ask teachers questions about topics we're struggling with. Some kids even manage to squeeze in quick naps, but I've never done that."

"Say…" Soraya spoke up. "Is there a library here?"

Moiya's emerald green eyes sparkled with amusement at the question. "Of course there is, silly," she laughed, her voice sounding like wind chimes dancing in a delicate breeze. "I'll show you, come on."

The girls flew down some more stone stairways and ran down the main floor hallway together. The pitter-patter of their steps echoed around the wide room.

"Oh, that's it," Moiya halted before a huge set of swinging wooden doors. Above them, in golden letters was Library Room 10.

"We have to keep our voices down when we go in," Moiya cautioned Soraya while holding a finger to her lips. "It's still early in the morning, so we're probably going to be the first ones in here, but the librarian will still scold us if we're too loud."

They slowly pushed the oaken doors in, and Soraya glanced around in awe at the large open room before her. Tall, magnificent shelves painted in white with golden rims lined every curved wall, reaching up towards the dome shaped ceiling painted in bright blues like the sky outside. Soraya spotted two golden staircases leading up to railed balconies that circled the entirety of the room.

"This library looks like something out of a fairy tale," Soraya breathed.

The two students walked up towards a large oval shaped desk, where a librarian sat in a red velvet chair. Her purple hair was done up in a bun, and her dark skin glowed in the bright light streaming from the overhanging lamps. She paused and looked up with bright violet eyes towards the girls.

"Can I help you two with something?" she asked, closing her novel shut.

"Yes, actually," Soraya replied. "Do you have any books about demons, by chance?"

Moiya's eyebrows raised inquisitively, but she remained silent.

"We do…" the librarian's eyes widened. "Are you studying mythologies, by chance?"

"Yes."

*I'm not really lying. Demons are in various religions and fairy tales.*

"You'll want to look under Z, for Zinvi," the librarian pointed towards the second story balcony on the far right corner of the room. "His book is all we have on that topic, unfortunately, and, if I'm remembering correctly, it's written in Casmerahn."

"That'll work. Thank you," Soraya bowed politely before heading towards the nearest staircase.

"Demons?" Moiya couldn't help but blurt out once they walked away from the desk. "Why would you want to read up on those?"

"I'm just curious, that's all."

"Okay…" Moiya stared at her friend, but didn't press for further information. Instead, she followed Soraya up the wooden staircase to the section labeled "Z."

The girls searched high and low throughout the entire section before, at last, finding the name, Amraphael Zinvi. There was indeed only one book on the shelf with that author's last name, and it was titled, *Altera No Mundus Ex No Amicusi.*

*I've seen this name somewhere before,* Soraya thought as the hairs on her arms stood on end.

"Hey, are you alright?" Moiya asked, concern showing in her voice.

*Where have I seen that name?*

Soraya closed her eyes, scanning through several pages and letters in her mind, but couldn't match it with any of those obscure documents.

*I saw this more recently…*

Soraya pulled up the image of her birth certificate in her memory and let out a small gasp. The witness signature was the same name as the author.

"You look like you've seen a ghost!" Moiya commented while leaning in to catch Soraya's attention.

"I'm sorry," the girl whispered, then took a sharp breath in. "I think my Dad might have known this author."

Her hands shook as she flipped the cover open and scanned through the names of the previous Etherians who had checked out the book, and nearly dropped it in shock. Tishva Thenayu was written, clear as day, as the last check out, from the year 3048.

## Chapter 19: Searching for Answers

"That's my dad's name and handwriting!" Soraya exclaimed in surprise.

"Shhhh!" the librarian hushed at the girl from below.

"Oh!"

Soraya peeked her head over the railing and looked down into the woman's stern, purple gaze. "Sorry," she whispered before turning towards Moiya, who looked puzzled and stood awkwardly on uneven footing.

"See? My Dad read this before. I think I should too," Soraya explained, lifting the book so her friend could see her father's signature within it. Even Yabo, who was still perched on top of Moiya's shoulder, leaned forward to look.

"I know you're taking Casmerahn…" Moiya placed her hands on her hips. "But, won't that be a bit too difficult for you to interpret by yourself? Even with your textbook, I doubt it'll cover all the vocabulary you'll need."

"You're right, I'll check out an Azakuin to Casmerahn dictionary too."

"Yes, that's a good idea, but…" Moiya paused and stared into Soraya's sky blue eyes with her emerald gems. "I really think you should ask Ujuu and Rhys for help. That's a lot of work for you to do by yourself, and it could take ages without someone who's fluent in Casmerahn."

Soraya paused and held Moiya's gaze. Her friend was right. She did need help.

"Okay, I will," Soraya promised. "You're really great."

Moiya blushed at her friend's compliment. "You are too," she grinned while glancing down at the checkered tile floor.

"Speaking of help, could you show me where the phones are?" A bundle of nervousness and excitement built up inside of Soraya, like a closed, shaken carbonated drink ready to explode. "I can't wait to write a letter to Papa about Zinvi, I have to call and ask him about this. It's important."

"Absolutely, I'll also call my folks while we're there. I haven't contacted them in two days since I've been studying for upcoming tests, so I really should check in."

The girls descended the spiral staircase and headed back towards the front desk. They noticed other students pouring into the library.

"Do you have an Azakuin to Casmerahn dictionary?" Soraya asked the librarian, her voice filled to the brim with passion, as she held up *Altera No Mundus Ex No Amicusi.*

"Yes, I'll fetch that for you," The elderly woman's stern face softened at the girl's determination to translate the novel. "Go ahead and fill in your name on the cover of that book. I'll be right back."

*Papa, who is Amraphael Zinvi?* Soraya added her name below her father's within the cover. *I hope the author's name will jog his memory somehow…*

The girl sighed while comparing her handwriting to Tishva's. His was so neat and proper looking, while hers looked cartoonish and exaggerated. As good of an artist as she was for being thirteen years old, Soraya couldn't figure out how to draw her letters as nicely as her father did.

The approaching sound of heels clacking against the tile floor made Soraya look up. The librarian had returned, clutching a dictionary in her long fingers.

"Here you are," she said while placing the book down on the polished wooden counter with a light thud. The librarian slid open a drawer from the desk before her and withdrew two slips of paper, along with a small black box and a strange looking wooden piece. The librarian then stamped both receipts with bright red ink and pushed them, along with the dictionary, towards the girl's eager outstretched hands.

"Thank you, ma'am," Soraya bowed before she and Moiya exited the library and turned down the hall towards the front office, which was located near the main entrance of the school.

"Do you know your Dad's phone number?" Moiya asked while they walked together side by side.

"What's a phone number?"

Moiya's green eyes grew wide with shock, and her mouth fell open as she gaped at the girl in surprise. "How are you going to call him if you don't know what to dial?"

Soraya wasn't entirely sure what her friend was talking about and grimaced in confusion. "I just thought I was supposed to speak into it, and it would get a hold of him."

A few small giggles escaped from Moiya's lips, her blueish black eyebrows lowering in sympathy. "Alright, we'll ask the receptionist for your Dad's contact information, and I'll show you what to do."

There was a man sitting behind a tall and wide desk within the office. He was tall, thin, pale, and wore a pair of rectangular, black thick rimmed glasses over his piercing blue eyes. His short, spiky red hair stood on end, similar to Yabo's fur rising up when he was scared. To the right of him was an open door leading to a long line of telephones jutting out from the wall.

"Excuse me, sir?" Soraya called while approaching the man. "Can I have my father's phone number? I want to call him."

"And, what's his name, miss?" the man replied, a red eyebrow raised.

"Tishva Thenayu."

"I will be back with that information. Is there anything else you need?"

"No, thank you."

* * *

Soraya had never called anyone before. She had only watched her father talk and listen through the phone in his office. Now, she found herself standing in front of one and was unsure of what to do first. The note that the receptionist had given her was clutched tightly in her wavering left hand, while her right hovered over the circular face of the rich brown telephone hanging from the wall. The golden glossy, circular buttons glistened under the lamp lights hanging from above.

"Um…"

Soraya reached for the handset and lifted the receiver to her ear. There was a low humming noise on the other end, like a steady droning from a hive full of bees.

"You have to dial in your dad's number," Moiya stood next to her, holding her library books. Yabo sat on the ground, grooming himself by their feet.

"Er, right."

Soraya looked down at the note again before tucking the handle between her ear and shoulder, and carefully punched the numbers in. She held her breath. The noise on the other end rang, paused, then rang again. It made her think of when she worked on the farm back in Rivingale Falls. The bells tied to the cows necks in the pasture would ring every time the large, gentle beasts walked or turned their massive heads.

"Hello?"

The girl jumped when she heard Tishva's gruff voice answer on the other end.

"Papa? Is that you?"

"Soraya?" her father's voice immediately softened. "Hey, kiddo. How are you?"

*I wish I could tell you everything,* the girl thought as she glanced over at her friend, who had walked further down the row of phones to give her space and was now out of ear shot. *But I probably shouldn't say anything about the demon from this morning right now.*

"I'm good!" Soraya beamed. "Darkwood Academy is amazing."

Tishva laughed heartily. "That is wonderful news, I knew you were going to love it there."

"How are you, Papa?"

There was a slight pause.

"I'm doing the best I can, kiddo," Tishva sighed. "Yosef practically moved in with me, and I'm grateful for his company. He's asleep right now, and I'll be making breakfast for us soon."

Soraya's tense shoulders relaxed. *At least he's not alone.*

"That's really great news. Did you get my letter yet?"

"When did you send it?" Tishva asked jovially. Soraya could picture her father's face and how his grayish blue eyes were probably sparkling in amusement.

"Yesterday."

"Oh," Tishva chuckled. "It'll take another day or two before it arrives. I'm looking forward to reading it."

Their conversation drifted off into silence. Soraya contemplated on how to ask her father about the author.

"Papa?"

"Yes, kiddo?"

"I found a book in the school library that you had read a long time ago…" she took a deep breath in before exhaling sharply.

"Who is Amraphael Zinvi?"

Her father did not answer immediately.

"I haven't heard that name in a long time."

"He's the witness who signed my birth certificate," Soraya reminded him. "Do you think he was there when Malik, I mean, my younger brother, was born?" Soraya waited with bated breath as her father remained silent for a moment on the other line.

"No…" he replied, his voice sounding far away in thought. "Amraphael has been dead for years. He passed away when you turned three, actually. I attended his funeral while you and your mother lived in Rivingale Falls."

Soraya's face fell.

*Dang it. I was hoping he would have some answers.*

"How did you meet him?" the girl pressed further. "You read his book in the year 3048, would that help you remember?"

"That was my graduation year from Darkwood Academy," Tishva clarified. "The author had donated his novel to our library, and I had the privilege of speaking with him while he was on campus. His theories on demons, or friends from the other side, were quite fascinating."

"Friends from the other side?"

"That's the title of his book," Tishva explained. "He believed that what we call demons are actually intelligent creatures from another dimension. They are attracted to our blood, like a shark, which is why we only ever seem to interact with them in places we consider haunted. Places where Etherians have died."

Shivers ran up the girl's spine as she thought about the demon who had visited her that morning, and she hugged herself.

Yabo, who was sitting by her feet, immediately noticed his owner's change in attitude, and rubbed himself against her leg while meowing up at her. She bent down and scratched his fuzzy, red back, and his purrs filled the room.

"Their dimension is supposedly right next to ours," her father continued, like a teacher lecturing a student. "Despite the membrane separating our worlds being thin, they cannot cut their way through. That is why Etherians have claimed to see objects move, or even feel hands push and claw at them. They can still touch things in our world, but that's about it in regard to physical actions."

"Hey, Papa…" Soraya whispered. "Do you know if anyone has passed away here on the school grounds?"

She turned her head to steal a glance at Moiya, who was now talking on the phone at the other end of the room. Her free hand was waving about while she laughed and was blissfully unaware of Soraya's conversation with her father.

"Many years ago, there was a great battle in Matumi," Tishva replied, his voice solemn. "A fleet from Golaytia tried invading our country and failed miserably. Azakuins weren't nearly as accepting of outsiders as we are today, and sadly, there were no survivors. Our country, for the most part, is peaceful, but some horrendous acts have taken place in our history, and that was one of the worst we know of."

*Once blood is spilled on the ground, the plants soak it up, and they remember our sins…* Soraya thought back to reading about Earth magic while on the train and shivered.

"Are demons able to travel into our world?" she breathed.

Tishva went silent.

One second went by. Then two… then three…

All Soraya could hear was the pounding of her heart in her ears as she anxiously awaited his response.

Four… Five… Six…

The passing time between her question and him answering unnerved her. Soraya's knuckles tightly gripped the phone in fear as she paced the floor. The receiver was hooked to a curly extension cord, which gave her some room to roam about.

Seven… Eight… Nine…

"Papa?"

Ten… Eleven… Twelve…

*Is he… having another spell of forgetting everything?*

The girl stopped walking in circles and held her breath.

"I don't know," Tishva finally responded.

Soraya sighed with relief and avoided looking at Moiya, who appeared to be done with calling her parents and was now making her way back towards her.

"Amraphael would probably have known, but he's gone now. That book and its copies are all that remains of his research…" Tishva's voice lowered as he muttered something Soraya couldn't understand. "Ignis yi id wo incendeoumvi."

"Papa? Are you okay?"

Her father sounded distant, as if he had turned his head away and was speaking to someone else in the room.

"Adonia, I know that you know… Igo no amatrix, dico queaso. Adiuva queaso."

"Papa…?"

Her father was still talking, but it wasn't to her anymore. Soraya listened closely as her father's voice faded away. She was sure he was walking away from his office.

"I love you," she whispered, hanging her head while placing the receiver back into its holster. Tears formed behind her eyes, but she closed them to hold her sadness in. Her mind wandered back to her memories of their home in the Averlore Mountains. She felt a twinge in her chest as she longed to go back and be with her father.

"Are you alright?" Moiya asked. "Is something wrong?"

Soraya didn't move or answer.

"You don't have to say anything, but I'm here for you.

That's what friends are for," Moiya stepped forward and placed a hand gently onto Soraya's shoulder.

*Should I tell her about Papa's condition?*

"You know," Moiya broke the silence between them. "Jacquelle was spreading a rumor about me…" She stiffened, but pressed on. "She told everyone that I come from a poor family, and that I'm only here because her father helped pay for my schooling…"

Soraya's friend lowered her head. "It's a partial lie. I got here because of my good grades, but my family does owe her father, which is why she likes to act as if she owns me."

Crimson red crept into Moiya's face when she glared at the floor. "I hate that she reminds me of that constantly. I don't want to be in debt, especially to someone like her."

*Why is she telling me this?* Soraya looked over at Moiya, noticed how full of anger her green eyes were, and something clicked in her brain. *That took a lot for her to say to me… She trusts me.*

*I trust her too.*

"I'm really sorry Jacquelle's treating you like that," Soraya shook her head in disgust. "She doesn't have the right to do that."

*I can tell her.*

"My father isn't well."

The second those words came tumbling out of her mouth, she felt a great weight fall away from her chest. "He's losing his memories, and sometimes can't even remember who I am."

"Oh no!" Moiya gasped. "That's awful! I am so sorry for both of you."

Soraya blinked, the tears welling up behind her eyes escaped. They cascaded down her face, and she couldn't stop them. They flowed freely, like water pouring through a floodgate that had just been raised.

"Mow?" Yabo leapt up onto his owner's shoulder and licked

away at her face.

*He's the best pet.* Love for her pandacoon swelled within her as she shook like a leaf.

"Can I hug you?" Moiya asked, her voice sounding somber. Soraya looked at her friend and saw tears were also streaming down her face.

"Yeah…"

Moiya wrapped her arms around her friend and held Soraya tight. They cried together.

*This must be what it's like to have a close friend…* Soraya and Moiya rested their heads on each other's shoulders. *Being able to confide in someone else makes such a difference.*

"Hey," Moiya peeled herself away and looked into her friend's tear stained eyes. "Do you want to go get breakfast? It'll be ready soon, and we can go see Ujuu and Rhys."

"Yes, that sounds good," Soraya unwrapped her arms from around Moiya and pointed at the library books she was still holding for her. "I'll carry those again, thanks for helping me."

"Of course," another tear escaped from Moiya's emerald eyes.

The two friends exited the office and walked down the hallway, side by side, with Yabo trailing after them. Soraya felt such an overwhelming sense of adoration for Moiya boiling over within her, that she couldn't hold in her feelings.

"I'm really grateful for you!" she blurted. "You're one of the greatest friends I've ever had!"

"Really?"

"It's true."

Moiya skipped in her steps as they finished their trek towards the Dining Hall.

## Chapter 20: Darkwood Radio

The overpowering smell of greasy, sizzling bacon mixed with freshly cut fruit, fermented cheeses, and sweet sparkling cider greeted Soraya's nose before she even had a chance to look at the various breakfast portions within the Dining Hall. Her ears were filled with the buzz of students chatting away with one another.

The girls spotted Rhys sitting in the center of one of the large tables and excitedly waved at him. His wine colored eyes lit up and sparkled like rubies when he saw them heading towards him.

"Morning," he said softly when the girls slid into the wooden chairs on the opposite side of the table from him. "How are you both?"

"Well, we would have slept in a little longer, but Jacquelle decided to wake everyone up at six," Moiya explained while rolling her emerald eyes to the ceiling. "Solis is the one day breakfast starts later in the morning, and she ruined it," she sighed. "At least tomorrow is a holiday and we have no classes."

"Mow!" Yabo cooed from beneath the table before hopping up into Moiya's lap.

"You really know how to lighten the mood, don't you?" Moiya laughed, then stabbed a thick, juicy piece of meat with her fork. She held it out towards the pandacoon's fuzzy black paws.

"How are you, Rhys?" Soraya asked the boy, her large, sky-blue eyes filled with curiosity.

"I'm well," he replied with a voice as soft as a feather floating in the wind. "I like your hair, by the way. It looks great."

Soraya's face grew hot while she stroked her braid. "Thanks, Moiya did it for me."

When her fingers reached the bottom and slid across the silky smooth ribbon at the end, Soraya suddenly remembered the spare one in her friend's pocket. "Do you want a bow in your hair, too?"

"Sure," Rhys smiled. "That sounds nice."

Moiya handed the white ribbon over to the Casmerahn boy, and he tied it around the navy blue band holding his braid together.

"Now I match you two," Rhys smiled playfully at both of his friends. "I appreciate this a lot, thank you."

"Of course," Soraya beamed. Just as she was about to ask where Ujuu was, she spotted the other twin emerging from a large crowd of chattering students surrounding the tables.

"Hello, ladies," he bobbed his head politely towards Soraya and Moiya. "Hey, bro," Ujuu slid into the empty seat beside Rhys. They bumped their fists together before piling bacon and eggs onto their plates.

"I have a question for you two," Ujuu said from behind the tall, mountainous stack of protein before him. "Would you both have time to hang with us after breakfast?"

"Oh yes!" Soraya exclaimed giddily.

"Absolutely," Moiya agreed.

The taller Shadelkin grinned mischievously while elbowing his twin's shoulder. "Do you want to tell them what we have planned for today?"

Rhys' face blushed as he looked down at the table. "My brother wants me to perform with my instrument live on the school's radio station."

"Oh wow!" Soraya gasped, startling several students nearby. "Everyone's going to love hearing you play!"

"That's right!" Ujuu declared. "And it was technically Jacquelle's idea. While she was being a total brat last night, she mentioned her cello playing being heard around our country. I work for the school radio, so I figured there was no reason why my brother couldn't also play on the air."

"That's very clever!" Soraya exclaimed before turning towards Rhys. "You should be famous for how well you sound."

The boy's face glowed like the fading embers of a campfire as he smiled sheepishly down at his plate.

"The best part is, our school broadcasts to several news stations across Azakua," Ujuu added, his candy apple eyes growing ever larger while he chattered away. "It's not just Matumi who'll be listening in, but Batilde, Umberlu, and even as far as the towns of Pinakua and Makina in the neighboring Province of Paleo!"

Moiya and Soraya noticed Rhys' black, cat-like ears lower. He twisted his long braid around his thin fingers and stared at the table in thought.

"Just do what you did last night," Soraya encouraged him. "You were so amazing. I know you can do it again."

"I've heard you play many times, and it's always a treat. Everyone else will enjoy it too," Moiya added.

"Thank you both," Rhys' face was almost as red as his crimson colored eyes. "Let's just finish breakfast and get going before I change my mind."

"Bro, you got this," laughed Ujuu while firmly patting his twin on the back. "There's literally nothing for you to worry about. I'm the one who has to figure out how to capture your crisp and clean sound."

As the four friends downed their food, Moiya cleared her

throat, catching Soraya's attention, then eyed the Casmerahn book, *Altera No Mundus Ex No Amicusi.*

*She's serious about me asking them for help.*

Soraya spoke up. "Say, guys?"

"What's up?" Rhys' cat ears perked up, and he put his fork down next to his plate. Although Ujuu was in the middle of chewing his last piece of bacon, he turned his full attention towards her.

"I was wondering if you would both like to help me translate this," Soraya pulled the red book out from her blue bag.

"Cool!" Ujuu managed to say in between bites. He swallowed and added, "Heck yeah!"

Meanwhile, Rhys glanced curiously between the novel and the girl. "Demons. Friends from the other side," he murmured thoughtfully. "Can I see it?"

Soraya handed the book over, and the boy flipped open the hard cover to read who had checked it out prior to her. "Is Tishva Thenayu a relative of yours?"

"Yeah, my father."

"Ah."

"He graduated from here," Soraya explained. "There's actually a painting of him hanging in one of the hallways along with his best friend, Yosef Athan."

"Alright, good to know," Rhys' eyebrows knit together in thought as he turned the page and read through the prologue. "Do you mind if I borrow this?" he asked without looking up. "I can translate a couple of pages for you tonight, if you'd like."

"I can help too!" Ujuu offered. "I didn't even know the library carried something like this."

He pointed at the book cover, where a drawing of a demon lay in the center. It had four slits for eyes on it's shadowed face, and there were several stretched out and grotesque human faces bursting from its right arm like boils that had popped open. "That thing looks super creepy. Is this a horror story?"

"No..." Rhys said under his breath. "This is written like a diary, and it's about a man's search for answers about demons, which he believes can be contacted and reasoned with..." He snapped the book shut and looked across the table at the girls. "I'll give you some translations tomorrow, I promise."

"Thank you both so much," Soraya said sincerely.

Rhys' serious expression softened when he looked up at her. "Of course," he flashed her a smile. "Anything for you," the boy's glimmering red eyes were filled with pure adoration.

For the first time in Soraya's life, her heart leapt within her chest. It was as if she had been struck by lightning and electricity was coursing through her veins. Every part of her body felt awake, alert, and in awe of the Casmerahn boy before her.

*Is this... what falling in love feels like?*

"Alright, is everyone done with breakfast?" Ujuu asked, attempting to break up the awkward silence that had settled over their group.

"It looks like it," Moiya replied while eyeing Rhys and Soraya, who were still lost in each other's eyes, and winked at Ujuu before turning her attention to the pandacoon sitting on her lap. "Are you done eating?"

"Merow," Yabo cried, then rubbed his face into Moiya's hands. She lovingly kissed the top of his fuzzy head and scratched his ears.

"Take Soraya on a date after the radio show," the taller twin teased his brother. "We need to go get ready."

Rhys blinked and looked back down at the table.

*A date? With Rhys? What would Papa say?* Soraya's chest clenched up while wondering if her father had really meant she couldn't date anyone until she was thirty years old, or if he had been joking.

The four friends left the Dining Hall and followed Ujuu up the first flight of stairs near the front of their school. Soraya walked next to Rhys and couldn't help but look up at his gorgeous, dark reddish brown face.

*He's so kind, and smart… and cute. I'm sure Papa would approve.*

The boy noticed her gawking at him and flashed her a timid smile. Soraya blushed from being caught staring and lowered her gaze to the floor.

"Darkwood Radio is at the top of the Spire in the West Wing," Ujuu said while leading the way. "We already moved Rhys' violalin up there this morning, so everything is ready to go."

"Can we listen in on you recording him?" Soraya asked Ujuu. "Please?"

"Of course!" grinned the taller twin. "It would be even better if you two sat in on the show with us. Rhys doesn't say much unless I really tease him."

Neither Soraya nor Moiya had ever been on a radio show before.

"What do we need to do?" Moiya asked nervously.

"Just be yourself, make comments, and sound as natural with talking as you already do in normal conversations," Ujuu explained. "Radio is all about listening and imagining the rest with your mind. Us being silent or hardly talking at all makes it boring to listen to."

"We'll do our best." Soraya vowed.

After climbing several long flights of stone stairways, all four children were panting heavily by the time they reached the radio room.

"And…" Ujuu took a deep breath in. "We're here."

With a loud creak, he pushed open the dark red door and motioned for his friends to enter. Soraya found herself looking around a large, open room with padded walls. There was a long desk built into the wall that had large and small rectangular boxes with dials, buttons, knobs and other strange devices decorating the outsides. She also spotted microphones attached to the ends of long black tubes.

"We're going to sound test before going live," Ujuu said, pointing at several chairs tucked away in the corner of the room. "Ladies, go ahead and pull up four seats for all of us and make yourselves comfortable."

Rhys pulled out his instrument, tuned, and stood next to the raised microphones.

"I have to position these around my brother and make sure he can play without hitting anything…" Ujuu explained while methodically placing the recording device, so it hovered above his brother's instrument. He paused and placed both of his hands on his hips. "That'll probably work."

The taller twin pulled a pair of thick, black headphones over his cat ears before pressing some buttons and turning up some dials. The clicks and clatter rising from his moving fingers made Soraya think of spacecrafts described within the science fiction novels she had read as a child. Ujuu finally looked at his twin and gave his brother a thumbs up.

Rhys played a sound test song. The vibrations from the violalin filled every corner of the padded room. Satisfied, the boy transitioned into a beautiful melody that Soraya had never heard before. She, Moiya and Yabo stayed silent as the violalin's warm strings sang from under Rhys' fingers.

"That sounds really great!" Ujuu laughed. "Okay, we're going live in five minutes," he added, beckoning the girls to come closer. He then gave them each a pair of headphones along with their own microphone. "Put these on, and start speaking into those."

"What do I say?" Soraya asked nervously.

"Anything," Ujuu grinned.

"Anything?" Soraya said into her black microphone.

"Perfect, yes, keep going…" Ujuu slid some buttons up on a board jutting out from the wall. "I want to make sure the levels are right."

"Hello! I'm glad Rhys is playing on the radio today, and I'm happy to be here w-with my friends," she said shakily.

"Excellent, just be more confident when you talk," Ujuu encouraged. "Moiya, you're next."

"Testing, one, two, three," she spoke steadily into the microphone. Yabo sat eagerly on her shoulder and batted at the strange device with his tiny paws. Moiya took a piece of her braid and distracted him, so he'd chew on it instead.

"Alright! Are you all ready?" Ujuu pressed more buttons and grabbed a microphone for himself before settling into the empty seat Moiya had set up for him. The blue pillow laying atop of the wooden chair sank, like a candle being snuffed out, as it deflated under his weight. Ujuu then held up his left hand and silently counted down by tucking each finger into his fist. When he reached zero, he spoke into his mic.

"Good morning Azakua, it is currently nine o'clock, and you are listening to Darkwood Station. My name is Ujuu Leyo, and joining me today are fellow students from Darkwood Academy. Would you all like to introduce yourselves?"

"I'm Rhys Leyo," the boy said in a quiet voice barely above a whisper.

"I'm Moiya Marlune," the green-eyed Azakuin said with confidence.

"Mow!" cooed Yabo.

"I-I'm Soraya Thenayu."

*Dang it, I stuttered!*

Rhys flashed her an empathetic look, causing Soraya's stomach to perform somersaults.

"We'll be kicking things off with Rhys playing a classical music piece," Ujuu continued without missing a beat. "He sits in the first chair of the violalin section, which means he's the leader of that group. In a few seconds, you will hear why," he nodded his head towards his brother, and Rhys played his instrument.

Soraya could tell her friend was more tense in his performance as his bow bounced and slid across the strings. His shoulders were stiff and his stance more rigid than the other night, but the song that emitted from his instrument was gorgeous and serene nonetheless. Once Rhys held the final note, he nodded his head towards his brother to indicate he was finished.

"That was Rhys Leyo on his violalin," Ujuu began again with gusto. "If you liked what you heard, make sure to attend the Beach Concert on Azula 9th of next year, 3095. It will start at thirteen o'clock in the afternoon on the Pier of Matumi Beach. Don't forget to mark your calendars, the next four months will fly by fast."

In the back of her head, Soraya could still hear Jacquelle complaining about having to play a duet at the beach concert with Rhys, and shook her head.

*He's such a good musician, why are you so hateful and demeaning towards him?*

Without warning, Ujuu turned his attention towards her. "Soraya Thenayu is a new student here at Darkwood Academy. What are your thoughts on what you've seen and experienced here so far?"

"Well…" Soraya hated being put on the spot, but she knew her friend was counting on her being interactive with him. "It's a very beautiful school that feels a lot like a castle," she said while looking at each of her new friends. "I'm grateful to have met each of you while being here, you've all made me feel so welcome."

"Well, we're happy you can join us," Ujuu beamed. "You grew up somewhere in the northern part of Azakua. Would you like to talk about that?"

*I shouldn't reveal too much about myself.*

"I've moved around throughout our country a bit," Soraya answered vaguely. "I worked on farms a lot as a kid and have lived around snow all my life. Matumi is the warmest place I've ever been to, actually."

"Is there anything you really want to see while you're here?" Ujuu inquired in the most professional sounding voice he could muster. Rhys, who was already hanging on her every word, leaned forward even more in his seat.

"Yeah, the beach!" Soraya exclaimed. "I've always wanted to see the sun set along the shore. I don't even know what sand feels like."

"It's itchy if it gets into your bathing suit, but other than that, it's pretty nice," Ujuu turned his attention towards his brother. "We should probably take Soraya down to the water sometime and show her around. I'm sure she'd love it."

"I will make that happen," Rhys vowed passionately.

"The sunsets at Matumi Beach are gorgeous and worth seeing at least once in your lifetime…" Moiya spoke up. Ujuu beckoned for her to keep going. "There are also some really nice restaurants along the coast," she continued while glancing at Rhys. "So make sure to check those out too."

"That all sounds so lovely," Soraya chimed in. "One of these weekends, all four of us have to go altogether."

Ujuu spoke once more into his microphone. "Just as a reminder, the Beach Concert is on Azula 9th, at Matumi Beach, at 13 o'clock. Thanks again for tuning in to Darkwood Radio, we hope you had a lovely time meeting Rhys, Moiya, Yabo, and Soraya. I'm your host, Ujuu Leyo, and I wish you all a wonderful rest of your day."

The Casmerahn boy flipped some switches on one of the many large boxes near him and pressed another few buttons before taking off his headphones and facing his friends.

"Good job everyone," he said, then glanced at Soraya. "Just so you know, I won't be able to join in taking you to the beach for a few weeks. I have a lot of work and studying to do," Ujuu winked at Moiya, who was covering her mouth with her hands, as if she were holding back on laughing.

"Yeah, I'm sorry, Soraya," Moiya said in a muffled voice. "I'm going to be busy for a while too. Is it okay if Rhys takes you without us?"

"Yes, of course," Soraya grinned. "Rhys, I'm so excited to see the beach with you! When will you be available for that?"

Rhys froze in his seat and glared daggers at his brother, who laughed even harder.

"What's so funny?" Soraya asked Ujuu innocently.

"Nothing," he replied, shooting Rhys a smirk before exiting the room. "I have to get going. Moiya, did you want to join me?"

"Yeah, of course," she said, jumping up from her seat and hastily followed him outside the room. "Have fun, you two."

Rhys slowly rose to his feet, his black ears lowering as he silently watched the door close behind them.

"Are you okay?" Soraya wasn't sure why her friend's demeanor had changed.

"Yes… just contemplating on how to kill my brother."

"Oh…"

Soraya wasn't entirely sure if he was being serious or not. "You're not actually going to do that, right?"

"I'm kidding!" Rhys added quickly and chuckled after watching her face fall. "Did you even notice what happened just now?"

Soraya's forehead scrunched up in thought. "No…"

"They set us up, so I'd take you on a date," he turned his head towards the door and spoke louder. "Even though I told Ujuu that I *didn't* want to rush anything!"

Soraya heard silence, then the squeaky scuffling of feet pitter-pattering down the stone steps outside the radio room.

"They were eavesdropping, weren't they?" the girl giggled.

"Of course they were."

Rhys stepped forward. "I think you're pretty cool."

The girl blushed. "I think you're cool too."

The boy's face lit up like the decorated trees back in Rivinsdeep during the Yuletide season.

"I will take you to the beach, if you're okay with that, and a restaurant afterwards, but it'll have to be next weekend."

The boy glanced up at the ceiling and counted off on his fingers the number of chores he still had left for the day. "I have to study, tutor some other students in Casmerahn, and translate some pages from that book for you tonight."

Rhys glanced at Soraya. "Tomorrow, the orchestra is getting together for extra practice since there are no classes. Would you like to go with me?"

"Oh yes! I would love that so much!" Soraya almost spun around in excitement, but held herself in place, so she wouldn't appear overly childish in front of her friend.

"Excellent."

Rhys stooped down to pick up his violalin case from the corner of the room and slung it over his shoulder. "Vadamus," he grinned.

"Let's go, indeed," Soraya agreed wholeheartedly. Together, they walked down the stone stairway, unaware that the school's scanner had picked up on a foreign radio signal filled with garbled, screaming voices drowning in static.

## Chapter 21: Rhys' Translations

"Morning Moiya!"

Soraya hung upside down from the top bunk, her long hair flowing down to the ground like the drooping, leafy branches of a willaby tree.

Moiya opened her bleary eyes and stared into her friend's cheerful face through half closed eyelids. Her blueish black hair lay strewn all over her pillow and off the edges, similar to waterfalls flowing over a cliff.

"Please tell me I got to sleep in," she groaned.

"Well…" Soraya glanced over at the clock sitting on the top of the dresser closest to Jacquelle's bed. "The alarm will go off in two minutes, so yes, you technically did."

Moiya blinked and sank a little further into her pillow. "It's better than yesterday. I'll take it."

Soraya sprang from her bed and leapt lightly to the floor, while Moiya slowly dragged herself out of hers. Yabo hopped down and eagerly followed after his guardian, who was already flying up the stairs to get dressed and ready for the day.

"You seem happy this morning," Moiya yawned while joining her friend in the locker room.

"I am!" Soraya exclaimed while smoothing out her dress. "I'm going to the orchestra room with Rhys today! I want to hear him play again."

Moiya smirked and rolled her emerald eyes to the ceiling. "I'm sure that's not the only reason why you're excited."

Without warning, she stretched out her limbs, so they touched both frames of the doorway, trapping her friend inside. "I want every juicy detail from yesterday," Moiya's voice lowered, the rims of her pupils glowing like a roaring fireplace as her expression was cast in long, dark shadows. "Did he ask you out?"

"Y-yes!" squeaked Soraya. Never had she imagined that sweet, innocent looking Moiya could appear so intimidating. "We're going to the beach together next weekend, and we'll have dinner afterwards too."

"Yes!" Moiya beamed triumphantly, the darkness surrounding her immediately evaporating into thin air. "I knew it! I just *had* to know, but I didn't get a chance to ask sooner," she laughed and clapped her hands together. "Sorry I had to run off after the radio show, I'm part of a study group that meets together in the library every Solis."

"No worries…" Soraya's eyelid twitched. "I had a lot of studying to do yesterday anyway. Hopefully, I won't be too far behind when I start classes tomorrow."

Soraya had skimmed through her text books for nine hours straight the day before. She could barely believe her brain ached and turned to mush from reading so much.

As the girls and Yabo made their way to the Dining Hall for breakfast, Moiya noticed how Soraya kept fidgeting with her dress and glancing occasionally towards a group of chattering boys that were steadily approaching. The Shadelkin twins were among them.

"You look fine," Moiya assured her.

"Morning!" Ujuu called, waving at them. Rhys was carrying

a small bundle of papers under one arm and flashed both girls a smile. The boy's long, beautiful braid bounced behind him with each step he took. The white ribbon she had given him yesterday was still tied at the end, like a bow on a kite string.

"Omane, igo no amicusi," Soraya stated once the twins caught up. "Belle dormiatemvi erat ka ne?"

"Good morning to you as well, my friend," Ujuu smiled in approval. "We slept well, thank you."

"Your Casmerahn is coming along nicely," Rhys chimed in, his crimson eyes sparkling. "Speaking of, I have something for you." The boy handed her a small stack of bamboo paper tied together with red string.

"That's a weird bouquet," Moiya teased.

"We translated the prologue and first chapter last night," Rhys said, ignoring his brother who was cackling with glee at Moiya's comment. "We'll try to translate one chapter per week, but it depends on what our schedules allow."

"Thank you both so very much!" Soraya accepted the bundle and gazed over Rhys' Azakuin handwriting on the front page. Although it was smaller and more rigid looking than Ujuu's professional quality script, Soraya could still read it just fine. The girl was lit with a burning curiosity and wanted more than anything to start reading through it all, but she knew it would come across as behaving rudely if she ignored her friends.

"No problem." Rhys grinned.

"Alright, let's go have breakfast," Ujuu joined in. "Vadamus!"

* * *

Soraya's insides were bursting with excitement when she and Rhys entered into the noisy amphitheater. She clutched the bamboo paper, determined to read through it while listening to her friend play his violalin. She was grateful that her desire to read was rekindled and stronger than ever.

Her shoulder felt empty without Yabo's presence, but Moiya had begged for permission to babysit him, so Soraya could spend more alone time with Rhys, and she of course consented.

There were several students spread throughout the orchestra room practicing different parts with various instruments, including Vamera and Emrose, who were both playing upright basses side by side. However, the cacophony of sound was drowned out by one song that stood above the rest. A haunting, powerful melody with dark tones resonated all around the large, circular room.

The hairs on Soraya's arm stood on end as she gaped in awe at the invisible art that filled every inch with its beauty. *That must be Jacquelle playing the cello. No wonder the teacher wants her and Rhys to play a duet together.*

The song ceased the second the two friends stepped foot onto the raised stage. The blond sat in the center of the platform, facing the entrance, watching for them, waiting to strike.

"Hey, it's Rhys and the plagiarist," Jacquelle laughed, pointing her bow in their direction.

*What is she talking about?*

It took the girl a minute to remember the history teacher, Mr. Thuron, commenting on her incredible memory and explaining how she can't copy down word for word from the books she's read when taking tests.

"I'm not a plagiarist!" Soraya gasped in surprise. "Why would you accuse me of that?"

"Because the history teacher caught you cheating on your history test," Jacquelle sneered. "Or are you calling Mr. Thuron a liar?"

"Jacquelle, you're the one who always lies," Rhys stated with an undercurrent of anger in his voice. "Leave Soraya alone."

"No. I want to know how she got higher test scores than

me," Jacquelle snapped, then rose from her seat. "What did you do?" she spat while approaching, each heavy step causing the wooden stage beneath her to creak and groan.

Soraya stood her ground and remained outwardly calm despite her heart rate rapidly increasing. She happened to glance at a pile of books sitting underneath a student's seat and had an idea.

"Jacquelle, pick one of those books and open it up to a random page."

The blond stopped her procession and stood dumbfounded. "What?"

"I'll show you what I can do."

"I don't understand what you're playing at, but whatever," Jacquelle snorted before snatching up one of the textbooks, which was titled, *Modern Day Magic*, and turning it to chapter three.

"Let me see what page you chose," Soraya asked with as little emotion in her voice as she could muster. Jacquelle thrust the book at the girl with such force that it partially smacked her face. The harsh sting from the sharp edges of the hardcover caused Soraya to stumble backwards and fall to the ground.

"*Jacquelle!*" Rhys bellowed furiously from beside Soraya, his crimson eyes shining with wrath as he glared daggers at the blond. He raised his hand and unsheathed his long, thin claws, but caught himself.

"Oh, I'm sorry," Jacquelle's shrill voice dripped with sarcasm while she stood triumphantly over Soraya, whose cheek was now throbbing in pain from being hit. The blond glanced casually at Rhys, who was struggling to retract his nails, and laughed at him. "You wouldn't hit a girl now, would you?"

"You're a monster, that shouldn't count!" he hissed through clenched teeth.

Silence filled the air when the students stopped practicing their instruments and stared at the three of them in surprise. Rhys, still scowling at Jacquelle, partially stooped down to help Soraya get back on her feet.

"Are you okay?" he asked softly, his wine-colored eyes flicking to her before returning to the blond before him.

"Yeah, I'm sorry," Soraya felt tears welling up behind her eyes, but she kept them in. Now was not the time to show any more weakness.

"Not your fault," Rhys assured her.

"So, what were you going to do?" asked Jacquelle in a bored tone. "What was the point of all that again?"

Soraya tentatively touched her face. The sharp pain in her cheek was already fading into a dull roar.

*I'm okay. I'll be fine…* She closed her eyes, pulled up the page in her mind's eye, and recited from it word for word.

"When magic is harvested, it can only be attached to an inanimate object. It will remain tied to that object either until an Etherian uses it, or the object decomposes. There are countless stories of Mages harvesting magic and storing it on their bodies, but these are all myths, all make believe."

Even as the words tumbled out of her mouth, Soraya was unsettled by the blatant lies within the book.

*This isn't right at all. I have magic tied to both of my hands right now.* The girl reminded herself not to say anything about the misinformation, lest it affect her father's work or health in any way, and continued reading from the page she had memorized.

"MagiCorp is the largest known manufacturer and distributor of magic in the form of inanimate objects such as swords, shields, staffs, and other weaponry. They are purposefully expensive in order to keep the use of magic down in everyday living, and can only be obtained by those who earn a license."

The color drained from Jacquelle's face. She stared in disbelief between Soraya and the page from the book.

"You memorized all of that in a few seconds?"

"Yes, I did."

"No way!" Jacquelle opened *Modern Day Magic* to another random page and shoved it close to Soraya's face. "How about these paragraphs?"

Soraya skimmed through the section, memorized it, closed her eyes, and recited the passage aloud. All the students stared in amazement at the girl.

"Impressive," murmured Vamera from behind her. Jacquelle shot her a glance, and the purple eyed girl stopped speaking.

"I'm not a plagiarist," Soraya repeated. "I can memorize anything I see. I was simply unaware of the rules before. I have to rewrite everything in my own words for tests, and I know that now."

Jacquelle's face turned a dark beet red when she realized the girl had proved her wrong in front of everyone. She stood quietly for a moment with her head hung low in defeat, her long golden locks blocking her face from view.

*She looks so sad and embarrassed…*

A twinge of pity vibrated within Soraya's chest. "What was that song you were playing when we came in? It was lovely. I'd like to hear more of that, if that's okay with you."

Jacquelle snorted, the air from her mouth and nose ruffling the bangs draped around her eyes, but she stayed in place. Her frown deepened with each passing second.

Soraya knew she couldn't help the blond, so she turned her attention towards Rhys instead, who was looking at her with admiration.

"I want to hear the song that's planned for the Matumi beach concert," Soraya smiled up at him. "I've been looking forward to it since yesterday."

"Absolutely."

Soraya stepped off the stage and settled herself into a cushioned front row seat while the orchestra students formed a half circle with their chairs and stands and seated themselves into their proper spots.

Rhys was at the front of the violalin section, his instrument resting atop his left shoulder, bow poised and ready in his right hand. He glanced over at Jacquelle, who was still standing off to the side and hiding her face under her hair.

"We're waiting for you," he exhaled with a hint of impatience.

Slowly, the blond shuffled over to her spot at the very front of the cello section, dragging her feet across the floor boards with each step. Her instrument and bow had been placed onto their sides next to her seat, and she gruffly scooped them up.

"Ready," she mumbled bitterly.

Rhys counted aloud for two measures before playing his instrument. His violalin sounded high-pitched, sweet and sorrowful, like the song of the Rivingale bird. The rest of the orchestra waited a few beats before adding long, lower resonating notes as a soft background.

Soraya basked in the glorious sound from all the stringed instruments before delving into the small booklet Rhys had put together for her. Her insides were itching with curiosity. She could finally read *Demons: Friends from the Other Side,* and satisfy her craving.

*My Dearest Reader,*

*If you have picked up this book, then I'm assuming you're as into the occult and demonic as I am. This was written while I was having a personal crisis of faith in the Gods. I've spent all of my life attending church, memorizing verses from The Path, praying to our Heavenly deities, singing hymns, partaking in holy communion, and yet, it did nothing for me.*

*Because I never once felt the presence of the Gods or their supposed love and mercy, I decided to work hard and earn a license to harvest magic. This was in the hopes that connecting with the elements would bring me closer to our heavenly deities, but something unexpected happened. All my life, I've felt alone in this world. Until now.*

Soraya's skin prickled with goosebumps when she turned the page. The low rumblings from the cello and bass section trembled like an ominous, oncoming storm.

*Before I delve into what I've learned about demons, you must understand, dear reader, that Earth Magic is the most powerful of all four magic elements. I have harvested and used each one, so I am more than qualified to state such a claim. The other three are indeed powerful in their own right, but connecting with and becoming one with the earth is truly a humbling and terrifying experience. It's akin to looking up at the stars and spinning galaxies and realizing how small and insignificant you are in the grand scheme of the cosmos.*

*Each and every time I've used Earth Magic, my perspective on Etheria, and its inhabitants has altered. I can hear every scream flowers make as they're plucked from the ground by greedy and curious hands. I can feel the fear of the forest as they watch their brethren be torn limb from limb and thrown into the raging fires used to power machines. I can see animals recoil and turn tail in terror whenever Etherians approach them. All creation knows that our kind are the only creatures in existence that kill for fun and pleasure.*

*I have learned the language of nature. The plants pray every day to the Gods to destroy us, so they may live freely without suffering from our hands. The Gods sometimes answer their pleas by allowing nature to consume Etherians through natural disasters such as floods, earthquakes, hurricanes, and tornadoes, but nature is never allowed to kill off all Etherians. Our Heavenly Deities, for whatever reason, insist on showing mercy over giving us the judgement we truly deserve.*

*The ground remembers our sins. The soil swallows our bodies and blood and remembers our stories. Ghosts and ghouls do not exist. Souls are not trapped in limbo. Every haunting is nothing more than the very earth itself crying out to the Gods to put to death the predators residing in our ranks. They forever replay the atrocities committed to remind the Gods of our sins, so they will punish us and give justice to countless unknown victims.*

*It was through connecting with the plants using Earth Magic that I suddenly became a Gods fearing man. And the more I let go of my Etherian self and embraced forests and animals as my true kin, the more secrets were told to me by our land. I now understand why governments from around the world keep Earth Magic to themselves and limit the common folk from being able to reach it, for it realigns the thinking of the user to become loyal with nature rather than their own rulers.*

*Many years ago, the grass and trees beckoned me to explore where blood was spilt, and they helped me come into contact with demons, who I lovingly call our friends from the other side. The more I tried to communicate with demons, the more we learned each other's language. It took me approximately three years to finally understand the basics of their tongue, which they call Apollryük, and for them to learn enough Azakuin for us to effectively understand one another.*

*It took so long because these creatures, though incredibly intelligent, were cautious with revealing too much with me at first. I had to earn their trust. They also have a very limited amount of time for engaging with me. This is because, I believe, they are from another dimension, but more on that later.*

*They told me of a mine that runs deep within the Moriuntur Mountains. There, in the very heart of that raised rock, is a closed door, standing tall and wide, waiting to be opened.*

Soraya carefully traced her fingers over the last page and re-read some phrases to herself under her breath. "The ground remembers our sins… this is similar to the books my father allowed me to read from his library, but Amraphael Zinvi's interpretation is much darker."

Loud stomping from the stage snapped Soraya's attention back to the orchestra. Rhys was pounding his foot into the ground in time with the beat and glaring over at Jacquelle.

*She must be speeding in her playing again.*

They had reached the duet section in the song, and the blond was completely ignoring Rhys despite his best attempts at reeling her back into the proper tempo. Only when the song sounded too disjointed did the Casmerahn boy abandon the rhythm completely and instead caught up to match the girl's playing.

The rest of the orchestra faded in the background as Rhys and Jacquelle's fingers flew, their bows bounced rapidly between strings. The sound resonating from both instruments was both beautiful and frightening.

"Stop… rushing!" Rhys yelled, though his voice was barely heard above the rolling waves emanating from their strings.

"Shut up, demon eyed freak!" Jacquelle screamed back, her voice drowning under Rhys' high-pitched violalin.

A few more seconds passed before their duet came to a grinding halt. Rhys didn't hesitate to turn his back on the blond, hurl his instrument into its case, sling it over his back, and hop off the stage the second their part was done.

"Let's go," he managed to say calmly, though his ruby eyes crackled with fury.

Soraya rushed to join his side. As they walked briskly out of the amphitheater together, she could see her friend's body trembling, so she placed a hand on his shoulder. "You're really amazing, and I'm sorry she's such a jerk."

Rhys shook his head. "Naw, you're amazing. She purposefully smacked you in the face with that book, and you still tried being nice to her anyway," he clenched his fist.

"I really wanted to hit her when she did that to you, and I almost did. If any of us physically harm another student, and it can be proven, we could be kicked out. Jacquelle used a book on you, so she could always claim that she tripped, and it was an accident. Me punching her in the face would mean being immediately expelled."

"Jacquelle is so manipulative," Soraya sighed.

"I know," Rhys agreed. "I admire your kindness, I really do, but don't forget to protect yourself. You don't deserve to be treated like that, and you don't have to put up with it, either. Walking away is okay, don't forget that."

"Thank you," Soraya moved her gloved hand from the boy's shoulder down to meet his fist. She nudged it, and he uncurled his fingers and timidly wrapped them around hers. "I read the translations you gave me," the girl added to change the subject. "It's incredibly dark and interesting."

"I was thinking that too. I also want to know more."

He looked down into Soraya's eyes. "There's a map at the back of the book. It shows all the major haunted areas throughout each Kingdom, and I noticed that Matumi has an X over it."

Soraya's heart skipped a beat. *Should I tell him about the demon?*

"I can't help but wonder what it would be like to use magic," the boy continued thoughtfully. "I know the courses for becoming a mage and having a degree in Arcanology are rigorous and expensive, but maybe someday, I could earn enough Lari to pursue obtaining a license."

Soraya glanced down at her and Rhys' intertwined fingers. He had no idea how close he was to actual Air and Water Magic. Two thin pieces of black fabric on both her hands was all she had to cover up her secrets.

"Having magic would be neat," the girl agreed.

The two of them walked towards the main campus together, hand in hand.

*Maybe, I can tell him about the demon while we're at the beach together... Maybe, I can tell him about the magic I have as well... Or maybe, telling Rhys would make him scared of me... Gods, what do I do?*

## Chapter 22: The Symbol

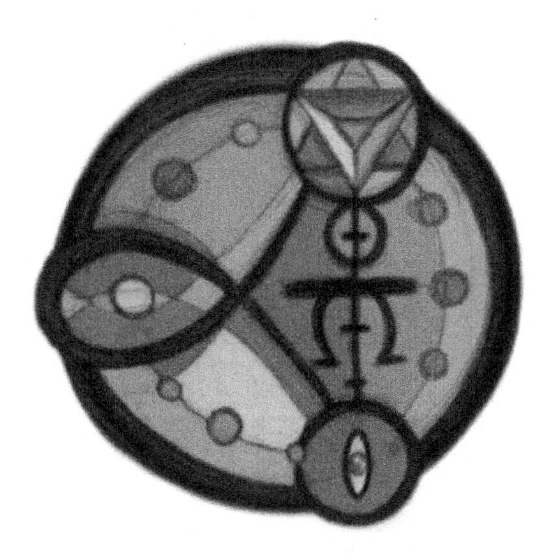

On Ignis Diem, everyone within the girl and boy's blue dormitories had to wake up at five in the morning. Cooking class started at five forty-five, and the students in the Blue House had to have breakfast prepared by seven for the whole school. Since pets weren't allowed in the kitchen, Yabo had to stay behind.

"Sorry," Soraya apologized. "The teacher thinks you'll shed everywhere. I'll see you soon," she assured her pandacoon and kissed the top of his furry head. "Don't get into too much mischief."

Yabo yawned, flashing his pearly fangs, and lay back down on Soraya's white pillow. He was asleep again within seconds.

"He's the sweetest thing," Moiya cooed while glancing at the small ball of fuzz snoring away on her friend's bed.

"Yabo really is," Soraya agreed.

The two girls waited in the hallway for the boys, as it was now part of their daily morning routine, and the four of them made their way to the kitchen on the main floor of Darkwood Academy.

Soraya was fueled with the excitement and anxiousness one would have for their very first day of school. Moiya, who wasn't a morning person, was already struggling to stay awake. Ujuu loved cooking, but he did not like having sleep being stolen from him, and Rhys was less than thrilled both at being awake at an unGodsly hour and having to make meals.

"If I start coughing a lot, do you think the teacher will let me go back to bed?" Rhys queried.

"I've already tried that before," bemoaned Moiya. "He just forces you to put on a mask. There is no escaping Mr. Trog's class."

"Oh come on, it's not that bad," interjected Ujuu.

"Yeah, but you actually like cooking," retorted Rhys. "Meals that take over thirty minutes to make aren't worth the trouble."

"You're just saying that because you're tired," grinned Ujuu. "You couldn't survive without butter rolls. Remember, they're only pillowy soft and melt in your mouth because the dough needs two hours to rise."

"That's what you're for, igo no fratello," Rhys lightly patted his younger brother's back. "You make food, and I clean the dishes."

Soraya couldn't help but smile at their bantering. She was content and grateful for sharing most of her classes with them.

All the exhausted students formed a line, each grabbing a hanging navy blue apron from the stone wall and tying it around themselves. Jacquelle, Vamera, and Emrose were at the very front, all three of them ignoring their group.

*I wonder if she's still embarrassed about the other day.*

Soraya observed each student wash their hands at a small sink before putting on gloves and entering the kitchen through a wide set of swinging doors.

*Here we go…* Soraya took a deep breath and pushed her way into the room.

The kitchen was massive and had a shining white tiled floor. Every wall was lined with hanging dark red wooden cupboards, and beneath them lay marble countertops with sliding drawers and a stove beside it with four wrapped metal coils. Far off in the corner was a large, walk-in refrigerator closed off by large, plastic drapes.

Within the center of the room stood their teacher, Mr. Trog. He was tall, clean-shaven, muscular, dark skinned, and bald. He wore a black apron over a collared white shirt, black bow tie, and black pants. His honey colored eyes shone brightly under the overhanging lamps above.

"Good morning, Blue House," he said in a gruff voice.

"Good morning, Mr. Trog," all the students replied.

"Before I say anything else, Miss Soraya Thenayu, please raise your hand."

The girl's face flushed as she slowly raised her now shaky arm into the air.

"She is a new student here at Darkwood Academy. Please make her feel welcome," the teacher said, then turned to Ujuu. "Would you like to help her today?"

"Absolutely," Ujuu's candy red apple eyes sparkled. "Our work station is over in that corner." The younger twin pointed a clawed hand at a countertop and stove combination.

Soraya and her friends shuffled over to their spot, and the rest of the students went to their respective areas. Soraya and Rhys agreed to chop vegetables, fruit and cheeses, Moiya volunteered to measure ingredients and wash the dishes, and Ujuu was happy with cooking and sautéing the meat.

"I know most of you already know this, but I will be repeating myself for the sake of filling Miss Thenayu in," Mr. Trog spoke while pacing around the room and looking each student over.

"During the week, we make as simple of breakfast recipes as possible. Cooked bacon, fruit salads, sliced cheeses, vegetables and dip, hard-boiled eggs, scrambled, sunny side up, and you get the picture. We do this because I know most of you aren't coherent enough to make anything more complex this early in the morning."

Mr. Trog glanced at Rhys, who was yawning and struggling to keep his wine colored eyes open. "For dinner, however, we'll create more complicated recipes."

He pointed at the overhanging wooden cupboards. "Spices, measuring cups, and dishes are above. Mixing bowls, frying pans, utensils, wooden spatulas, and whatever else you'll need are below."

Mr. Trog waved an arm towards the walk-in fridge. "All food items are in there," he said, then glanced up at a large golden clock on the wall. "Breakfast starts at seven. Get cooking!"

Ujuu, along with one other student per workstation, headed over to the walk-in fridge and disappeared behind large plastic drapes. He returned with two large baskets. One had bacon and eggs, while the other contained fruits, vegetables, sticks of butter, a jar of milk, another jar with oil, and cheese wedges.

"Rhys, Soraya, here you are," Ujuu placed one of the baskets in front of them. "Chop everything," he ordered before turning on the stove. Moiya had already taken out two large saucepans and placed them on the front two burners. The Casmerahn boy carefully laid out each thick, juicy piece of bacon in the saucepan on his right.

"Kindly add some oil, if you would, Moiya," Ujuu asked before humming to himself. His friend obliged and added a tablespoon of oil to the empty pan. "Eggs stick easily when they cook, so always grease up the saucepan," the boy explained.

"We're really cutting everything?" Soraya asked Rhys. They both stood side by side at the marble counter, chopping away at the food before them.

"Yup," he murmured, his voice heavy with sleep.

"So, the Blue House wakes up early to make breakfast for the first two days of the week, right?" Soraya asked.

"Yup."

"We also cook dinners on the fourth day of the week?"

"You got it."

"Who makes lunch?"

"No one," Rhys' tired eyes twinkled. "We have leftovers from the previous day. That way, no food goes to waste."

"That's smart."

Within an hour, the kitchen smelled strongly of juicy bacon and cooked eggs mixed with the sweet fragrances of fruit, crisp vegetables, and nutty cheeses. Soraya's mouth watered as she and Rhys lay out their sliced pieces onto different platters.

"Alright, start wrapping it up, folks," Mr. Trog announced heartily. "Bring your trays out to the tables in the Dining Hall, clean your stations, put away your aprons, wash hands, and go eat. Have a great rest of your day, everyone."

After Soraya and her friends ate breakfast altogether, she and Moiya headed back up to the girls' dormitory to feed Yabo table scraps and to retrieve books from their lockers.

"We're currently reading through *The Taming of the Tempest*," Moiya reminded her.

"Alright," Soraya said while digging out her books. "I couldn't help but finish it. I found the play very interesting."

"Wait, you read through it all?" Moiya's mouth dropped open in surprise.

"Yeah, that's what we were supposed to do… right?"

Moiya chuckled and shook her head. "We read through it altogether, and Mrs. Sworvski calls on some students to read aloud each part. We just finished Act One, so don't talk about anything past that. No spoilers."

*I'll have to be mindful of that,* Soraya grit her teeth together. *I've read through so many books this past weekend.*

The Azakuin Literature classroom was spacious, with twenty-five desks and chairs spread out into even rows and columns of five. The walls were covered in posters containing poems and inspirational quotes. While Soraya took in her surroundings, she noticed several students wearing red and green outfits.

"Mrs. Sworvski's teaching style encompasses all three methods, which is why it's a mixed class," Moiya explained while they sat down next to each other. Rhys and Ujuu were settled into the desks behind them, and Soraya turned to flash them both a smile.

"Good morning students!" Mrs. Sworvski sang in an eccentric, high-pitched voice. She was short and slightly plump with frizzy bubblegum colored hair, bright pink eyes, and copper colored skin. "We have a new student joining us today. Miss Soraya Thenayu, please raise your hand."

Soraya frowned as she timidly put her arm up. *This is going to get old fast.*

"Alright everyone, take out *The Taming of the Tempest* and turn to Act Two, Scene One. Who would like to read the part of Annabelle?"

Jacquelle's hand shot up faster than a lightning strike.

"Well, Ms. Demarko, since you're always Annabelle," the teacher hesitated. "Could you, maybe, be Babella today?"

"But, I don't want to be an evil witch!" Jacquelle complained.

"Too late."

Soraya bit down on her lower lip and covered her mouth, so she wouldn't burst out laughing at Ujuu's comment. She glanced over her shoulder and spotted the twins giving each other a fist bump and grinning from ear to ear. Soraya also turned her head enough to see Moiya in her peripheral vision and noticed that she, too, was stifling her giggles. Thankfully, the teacher was too busy arguing with Jacquelle to notice.

"Just be Babella today, alright? Let's give another student a chance at speaking Annabelle's part…" Mrs. Sworvski swiveled her head around the room and looked directly at Soraya. "Ms. Thenayu, could you do that today?"

Jacquelle turned in her seat and drilled her dark blue gaze into Soraya through narrowed slits.

"Yes," the girl agreed, ignoring the blond's hateful stare.

Although Soraya had already memorized the pages, she wasn't used to public speaking. After a few minutes of stuttering and stumbling over words, she stopped being self-conscious and decided to have fun with the text.

"Babella, prepareth thyself," Soraya spoke with fervor in her voice, every word dripped with sincerity as she stared back into Jacquelle's seething face. "For thou art a fiend, a vile demon Beelzebub himself hath sent from the depths of Sheol to torment the living!"

"Excellent!" Mrs. Sworvski exclaimed. "Soraya, good job for keeping your eyes open more. Jacquelle, continue!"

"Ha! Doth take one to knoweth one, Annabelle."

Soraya smirked. *That sounds like something Jacquelle would actually say.* "Come, Babella, have at thee, wench!"

"Perchance thou doth prevail, I shall curseth thee and thy children forevermore!"

"And, we'll pick that up tomorrow," Mrs. Sworvski cut in. "Impressive, girls, you were both really getting into it, especially towards the end of the chapter."

She turned to the rest of the students. "Class dismissed," she managed to say seconds before the bell rang over the speakers.

History was next on Soraya's schedule. Mr. Thuron was a tall, thin man with short white hair, grayish blue eyes, and pale, ghost-like skin. Despite having a frail appearance, his voice was unusually smooth, rich, and captivating. When he read excerpts from the text, every student had their eyes transfixed onto him, and they all hung on his every word.

"I could listen to him talk all day," Soraya stated once she and her friends were out of class.

"I know! Me too!" Moiya agreed. "He sings in a church choir outside of school, and everyone comments on how angelic his voice is."

"Moiya, Rhys, are you both ready for the Biology test?" Ujuu asked while pulling out his textbook and tapping on the hard cover with a long nail. "We have forty-five minutes of extra study time, we might as well review the chapters."

Soraya brought her printed schedule up in her mind and saw that she also had Biology as her next class. "Do you think I'll be tested too?"

Ujuu frowned. "That would be incredibly unfair if so. It's your first day of school, I'm sure the teacher will give you a some extra time to catch up."

"Well, I'll still study with you all just in case, if that's okay."

Rhys, Moiya and Ujuu smiled at her. "Of course."

Mr. Yung did not give Soraya extra time to catch up on studying. Instead, he handed her a piece of paper with fifty questions, just like every other student. She noticed how his skin was speckled with both dark and light spots, like Mrs. Bunion back in Rivinsdeep.

"I want to see how you do," he said in a stern, deep voice, his piercing orange eyes peering down at her through a pair of thick round glasses. "If you don't get a high enough score, I will test you again next week. Just do your best."

Soraya gulped and started reading through the test. She only knew the answers because of her photographic memory and not because she actually understood the content.

*Am I cheating for being able to look up the pages in my mind?*

Soraya purposefully stalled and waited for several other students to turn their tests in before she did. Her chest tightened as she rose from her desk and walked towards the front of the classroom on wobbly legs. The teacher's fiery eyes followed her every move, which unnerved the girl even more. After slipping the sheet into a wooden box on the teacher's desk, she scurried back to her seat. Relief flooded through her veins the second she heard the bell ring.

"I can't believe he made you take that," Ujuu growled. "We've been studying for weeks, and you've barely had enough time to catch up on all that reading for every single class."

"How are you feeling?" Rhys asked her, his voice filled with concern.

"Oh, I'm alright," Soraya exhaled sharply. "Just hoping that I did well."

"Same." Rhys timidly pat her shoulder. "Our next class will hopefully make up for that. Casmerahn will be much more fun."

"Shame I can't join you all," Moiya said, swinging her backpack over her shoulder. "I'll catch up with you three later," she added, waved, then darted off in the opposite direction.

"What is she taking right now?" Soraya whispered to Rhys.

"Rosinkin."

"Oh, cool!" Soraya exclaimed. A sudden thought hit her like a ton of bricks. "Say, why aren't you learning that? Doesn't Zaruna live in Rosinka?"

"She does," Ujuu blushed like a giddy child. "Rhys and I help tutor Casmerahn, and that means we have to attend the class. Moiya helps me study Rosinkin on the side. I then write to Zaruna with what little I know, and she corrects me all the time."

Soraya's heart swelled when she saw how bashful Ujuu looked.

Room 104 was also a large and open classroom with student desks spread out evenly across the floor. The walls were decorated with the three Casmerahn alphabets, along with different quotes that Soraya was having a difficult time translating.

*There's so much to learn, but I'll do my best.*

Ms. Evi was a small and petite woman with bright red eyes, long black braided hair, and tanned skin. She taught the class as if they were a bunch of toddlers rather than young adults. She held flashcards up and had the students repeat the letter and sound it made after her, and they played childish games such as guessing what the word she wrote on the board was and what it meant. The winner would receive candy from her seemingly bottomless basket.

"Soraya, what does, non erat, mean?" the teacher asked sweetly, her strawberry red eyes staring at her as if she were a baby.

"Was not," the girl replied with confidence. Rhys clapped quietly into the palm of his hand and nodded in approval.

"Very good," Ms. Evi swiftly walked down the aisle towards her desk, her basket of goodies in hand, and offered for the girl to take one.

"Mille gratias," Soraya said, plucking out a caramel apple lollipop.

"Nihil est," Ms. Evi winked.

When it was time for lunch, Soraya melted into her seat and enjoyed the aroma of food surrounding her. Just as the older twin had said earlier that morning, there were leftovers from breakfast and the previous night's dinner set on the table.

"How's your first day of school so far?" Rhys asked, his ruby eyes sparkling.

"Very good, and very exhausting," Soraya admitted. "Three more classes to go, and then I think I'll take a nap before dinner."

"Completely understandable," laughed Rhys.

"Isn't it nice that we don't have any homework?" Ujuu chimed in. "It would be even more stressful if we did.

"Yeah, I don't miss it at all," added Moiya. "I heard that college students don't have to do it either."

"They also live in elderly folk homes and take care of their roommates in exchange for free room and board," Rhys spoke up. "I think that's a wonderful system. If a college student fails out of their classes, they are simultaneously earning credits for becoming a nurse or caregiver, so they'll have a job no matter what happens."

Soraya's eyes glazed over as her friends chatted away with one another. Her entire body was fatigued, and she found herself falling forward in her seat. The table before her looked comfortable enough to rest her head on…

"Aww, look," Moiya said softly.

There was a moment of silence as they all observed Soraya snoozing away.

"Let's let her rest for a few minutes," Rhys suggested. "We all have gym next, maybe the nap will help her."

* * *

From Soraya's perspective, only a few seconds had gone by before she was lightly shaken awake on the shoulders by Rhys.

"Hey, are you ready for your last three classes?"

"Yeah," Soraya yawned and stretched her limbs. "Let's go!"

Everyone had to change into shorts that matched their house color, and white t-shirts before meeting outside in the back of the school for gym class. Soraya took her new uniform and hid in a restroom stall to inspect her bruised right arm. It was still healing and had some light discolored patches.

*Hopefully, no one will notice.*

The back of Darkwood Academy had a large, open field surrounded by a bright blue sky and tall trees casting long shadows across the short, cut grass. Several other students were already outside chatting together in small groups. Soraya joined back up with her three friends and grinned excitedly at them.

"Are we going to play a game altogether?" she asked, her voice brimming with enthusiasm as she bounced in her steps.

"No, not today," Ujuu winked. "We're running a mile to see

how fast we can go," he said, then nudged his older brother. "I don't care about beating anyone else but this guy. He keeps me on my toes."

Rhys flashed him a toothy grin. "I should stop letting you think you have a chance against me."

Ujuu spread his legs and arms apart to appear larger than he really was. "I've beaten you plenty of times, no amount of pretending you were just being nice is going to change that."

Their red eyes locked onto each other's as they paced the grass slowly in a clockwise circle, both of them attempting to look serious as they held in their laughter.

A piercing blast from the whistle made everyone whip their heads around.

"Let's go, kids!" Mr. Levi called, his dark purple eyes glowing in the sunlight. He was short with black hair, pale skin, and had a small build despite being muscular. One could have easily mistaken him for a student if it weren't for his cleanly cut black beard. "We're going to stretch first, then run a timed mile. You all know the drill, let's move!"

Soraya loved running, but had never done it competitively. She was curious to know how well she would do in comparison to everyone else. The girl was careful to copy the stretch techniques the teacher and other students surrounding her were doing.

"Alright, all of you line up."

There was a long, white line spray-painted across a dirt road. All the kids stood behind it. Rhys and Ujuu were crouching down, ready to sprint forward at a moment's notice. Moiya was also staring ahead with determination sparkling in her emerald eyes. Soraya mimicked them all and gazed at the track. Before them was a trail that led into the shady, leafy woods ahead.

"Are you all ready?" Mr. Levi asked while holding up a whistle to his lips.

"Yes!" shouted the students, each poised and ready to sprint.

The teacher simultaneously blew into a silver whistle and started a timer. The students lurched forward the second they heard the shrill blare ring in their ears. The twins were off and in the lead, Soraya was somewhere in the middle, while poor Moiya was slowly and steadily falling behind.

Soraya knew to conserve energy by not sprinting the entire time, but she couldn't help but notice how Jacquelle was slightly ahead by a few feet.

*I don't want to lose to her.*

The girl sped up her pace to match the blond's rhythm. When Jacquelle saw Soraya closing in on her left, she narrowed her eyes and forced herself to pick up her speed.

They continued their race, neck and neck, for the entirety of the mile run through the twisting, turning road interweaving throughout the tall trees. Soraya's heart pounded loudly in her ears, her legs were engulfed in flames, and her mouth and throat were parched, but she pushed herself to keep up with her rival.

*I gotta beat her.*

A vein in Jacquelle's neck ticked in irritation when Soraya kept up next to her. The blond inched over, closing the gap between them. Before Soraya could figure out what was going on, Jacquelle rammed her body into hers, sending Soraya flying off the dirt path and onto the grass.

As the girl stumbled and fell to the ground, a sickening pop and sharp pain shot up her leg when her knee buckled and dislocated. A surge of anger and hatred for Jacquelle twisted and snaked throughout Soraya's body, igniting a wrathful flame and stirring something deep inside the depths of her soul. The tips of her fingers tingled like lightning dancing between black brewing clouds, and an alien looking symbol crossed through her mind, quick as a flash of light expanding throughout a dark room.

*What was that?*

Soraya hardly noticed Jacquelle laugh and disappear around another cluster of trees and bushes. Her hands were vibrating, alive, hungry. The girl sucked in air through clenched teeth as she pulled the symbol back into her mind and stared at it through closed eyes.

It was new, something Soraya had never seen before, and yet, it had been pulled up from the deepest, darkest forgotten corner of her memories. Despite the roaring pain her knee and leg was in, she focused on studying the strange symbol. The longer she stared at the pattern, the more it unraveled before her eyes and translated itself into her native tongue of Azakuin.

"Chistyrke…"

The grass touching the exposed skin on her legs and hands drooped over and wilted, turning from a lush green to a dull gray, as if on command. Soraya watched in horror as the nearest two trees decomposed before her very eyes. The dark red bark hardened, turning brittle, before cracks formed around the tree's limbs. Soraya jumped when several large, thick branches snapped off, falling to the ground with loud thuds.

Before she had time to comprehend what was happening, a rush of adrenaline coursed through every inch of her body, the stolen souls of the plants pumping through her veins. Another loud snap came from her knee, but the raging pain subsided like flames being doused with water. All of the aches in her sore muscles disappeared, as if she hadn't been running at all. Even the dryness in her mouth and throat was quenched. Every part of her was rejuvenated and alive.

A terrible thought struck her. *Did I just… take the lives of the grass and trees?*

An equally terrifying thought plagued her mind. *What if I had touched someone else and had taken their life… Oh Gods, am I a demon?*

Several other students rounded the curve and ran by her, staring as they passed. One of them was a panting, sweaty Olive Wilder. He slowed down in his jogging and swung by her.

"You're gonna fail… if you… don't get… a good time," he breathed heavily between words. "Do you… need… help up?"

"*No!*" Soraya exhaled sharply, sounding more terrified than she had intended to. "I got it, thank you," she said in a calmer voice.

Olive nodded and continued down the path, blissfully unaware of Soraya's new dilemma.

The girl got up, dusted herself off, noticed that the bruises from her arm had completely healed, and started running. The sensation from her fingers was gone, but she was scared at the thought of anyone touching her and losing their lives. She tried not to imagine Rhys' face shriveling up and decaying into a skeleton from touching her hand, or Ujuu, Moiya, or Yabo…

*Gods! Why is this happening? What was that? Please answer me!*

Soraya had never felt more terrified than at this moment.

*Maybe, Mama must have been a demon, or part demon...* She easily caught up to Jacquelle and sped by her, much to the blond's shock and dismay.

*Why else would that demon contact me?* Soraya spotted the Leyo twins in the distance, both tied at the very front of the pack of huffing, puffing students.

*Someone messed with Papa's memory and made him forget... possibly Amraphael Zinvi...* She flew past kids on both sides, being careful not to bump or touch anyone.

*And Zinvi must have opened that door and connected our worlds...* Soraya was closing in on the twins, practically on their heels.

*I could a hybrid of an Etherian and Demon...* Soraya leapt into the air, flying a few feet forward, causing the jaws of Rhys and Ujuu to drop in awe. *Why else would I have this sort of power?*

"Seven minutes and two seconds for all three of you!' Mr.

Levi yelled when they all crossed the finish line.

"No way!" Ujuu shouted and cackled with glee. "Soraya is amazing! Are you part Shadelkin? You must be to have pulled off that stunt!"

Soraya hardly heard her friend. She was still running. All she wanted to do was get away and hide, melt into the floor, and disappear forever.

*I love my friends. I don't want to hurt them by accident!* Huge, hot tears welled up in her eyes and dripped down her face.

"Hey! Come back! You don't have to run anymore!" Rhys called from far off in the distance.

The girl slowed her pace, despite not being tired. She came up to another cluster of trees and stopped just in front of them, timidly placing her hand on the bark of one and waited. Thankfully, nothing happened.

"Soraya!" Rhys called, sprinting towards her. "What's wrong?"

*Where do I even begin?*

"I'll tell you when we're at the beach…" Soraya said meekly.

"Okay…" Rhys frowned. "If you want to wait until the weekend, that's alright," he reached out to touch Soraya's shoulder. She winced when the weight of his hand came down, but then relaxed when nothing happened to her friend.

"You did so well, by the way," he said, his crimson eyes sparkling. "Everyone's impressed."

Soraya peeked past Rhys' shoulder and saw Mr. Levi eyeing her over, his purple gems wide with amazement.

"Ms. Thenayu," he said, his voice boiling over with enthusiasm. "That was… wow, unexpected. I don't think I've ever seen anybody catch up to the Leyo twins."

Soraya looked down and said nothing.

"She's just tired, sir," Rhys spoke up. "Come on," he said,

gently guiding her towards the entrance of the girl's locker room. "Two more classes, then you can take your nap. How does that sound?"

"Lovely," Soraya smiled up at him despite the fear clawing and gnawing away at her heart. "Thank you, Rhys."

"Of course."

Orchestra and Math went by without any problems. Soraya picked out a violalin for the instrument she would be learning, so Rhys could teach her how to play. Although she sounded terrible and Jacquelle laughed at her squeaking sound, Soraya didn't let it bother her, lest she become furious again.

"If you can't learn to play the songs for the Matumi Beach Concert in time, it's perfectly alright," Ms. Katia assured Soraya, her jade green eyes glancing with empathy at her newest student. "Just do your best and have fun in this class."

The math teacher, Mr. McLee, was the most boring teacher out of all of them. He spoke slowly and with a drawl, and it didn't help that he was old, partially deaf and hobbling on a small cane, but he was good at breaking down difficult equations and clearly explaining how to solve problems.

"Aaand… cllllasss iisss disssmmissed…" he groaned, sinking into his cushioned chair. His bright brown eyes swiveled around the room and watched as all of the students eagerly exited his classroom before nodding off to sleep.

Soraya thought the old man almost looked cute as he melted into his seat and snored almost immediately.

*I don't need a nap anymore… I need answers.*

## Chapter 23: A Thousand Steps Beach

The rest of Soraya's first week of school flew by fast. She studied hard in all of her classes and avoided being near Jacquelle as much as possible. The girl became worried, however, when the gym teacher discovered the dead trees and grass she had accidentally killed. Mr. Levi even scheduled a botanist to inspect it the following week.

*They won't know it was you. There's no way they would ever know… Unless the botanist has Earth Magic and talks to the other plants that had seen everything…*

Soraya wasn't sure what to do, so she distracted herself as much as possible by studying and secretly forming a plan.

*Maybe, I can find a way of healing those plants using my Water Magic, and then the botanist won't have to come out and look at them…*

Every night, after dinner, Soraya practiced her violalin in the orchestra room with Rhys.

"If something is too difficult, slow down the tempo and use a metronome," the Shadelkin instructed like a teacher. "Understanding how to play the notes and rhythm correctly is the key. Once you have that down, then you can speed up the pace and try playing it faster."

"Okay!" Soraya nodded while looking back over her sheet music. She was determined to learn how to read it and play her parts correctly.

"Hey," Rhys interrupted. "I have a surprise for you, but we have to leave now for you to get it."

"Oh?" Soraya said, hurrying to put away her beautiful cherry red violalin and bow before following the boy curiously out of the amphitheater.

It was Astros Diem, the sixth day of the week. Soraya had a sneaking suspicion of what Rhys was planning and grinned up at him while they walked towards the front gate of Darkwood Academy.

"Are we going to Matumi Beach now?" she asked giddily, bouncing excitedly with each step forward she took. All of her fears melted away when she looked up into the Casmerahn boy's wine colored eyes.

"Jai achi null," Rhys winked.

"What do you mean, yes and no?" Soraya laughed.

"We're going to the beach, jai…" Rhys swung open a small door on the side of the wall just next to the closed gate and held it open for his friend.

"But not Matumi Beach. That one's for tourists. We're going to the best beach in town, a cove tucked away and hidden behind huge cliffs. It's also a wildlife preserve, and if we get there soon, we can see a grand sunset, dolphins jumping out of the water, and maybe even some seals."

"That sounds so amazing!" gasped Soraya. "Do the teachers need to know where we're going? Can we just leave the campus?"

"I already told them ahead of time," the boy said proudly before digging into his pocket and holding up two signed permission slips. "We just have to call and do a check in every hour and be back before midnight, or they'll hunt us down and drag us back to school. If that happens, we won't be allowed to leave again unless we have a chaperone."

"That makes sense."

It had been the first time in days since Soraya had left the school grounds. She enjoyed walking down the long tunnel of overhanging trees with Rhys and thought back to when she first saw Darkwood Academy through the car windows.

"This is so peaceful," she breathed. The two friends enjoyed the calm stillness surrounding them.

"It really is," Rhys agreed, pulling out Amraphael's diary from his pants pocket. "I brought this for you too. I worked on translating the next chapter, but I'm not a good artist and wanted you to see the strange designs sketched into here since I can't do them justice."

Soraya's heart stopped. *There are more symbols like the one I saw yesterday?*

"Th-thank you, Rhys," she said in a shaky voice. "Let's look at that while we're on the beach."

"Absolutely," Rhys nodded, his crimson eyes glowing when he timidly touched her hand. She wrapped her fingers around his, and they walked hand in hand until they turned left onto a long paved street with houses built on both sides.

*I just can't say the spells aloud if I don't know what power they'll give me. I can't let Rhys get hurt or killed!*

"The entrance is on the right and is a little closed gate hidden under a lot of trees, so keep your eyes peeled," Rhys continued.

"Alright…" Soraya pushed her worries away and helped search for the entrance. She spotted it at the same time Rhys did. It was a small, white gate standing between two houses on a cliff overlooking the sea. As they approached, the girl noticed how far below them the Vatic Ocean was.

Rhys opened the gate and held it for her, and Soraya took a small step forward and looked down. There were many stone steps leading into the canopy of palm trees below, and she couldn't see the bottom of the stairs.

"This is why it's called a Thousand Steps," Rhys stated. "There are actually two hundred and fifty-three steps on this stairway, Ujuu and I counted."

"This is amazing," the girl breathed while taking in their surroundings. The sun was beginning to sink lower into the golden pink sky, and she wanted to be standing on the shore with Rhys while watching it disappear into the horizon.

"Vadamus!" Soraya exclaimed, starting forward and descending the many stone steps. They didn't go too fast in case they slipped and fell, but they both felt the pressure of making it to the beach in time increase with each step they took. They were now racing the setting sun and wanted to beat it.

*Don't get too competitive… It's okay if we miss the beach sunset, Rhys getting hurt isn't worth it.*

At long last, after several minutes of listening to the clacking of their shoes beneath them and their steady breathing, their feet finally hit the uneven surface of the shore. Soraya immediately took off her shoes and white stockings and placed them next to the stairs, so she could feel the soft warmth of the sand trickle over her feet and through her toes. Rhys laughed and joined her by also becoming bare foot. He carefully placed the book next to their belongings to keep it from getting wet.

"We have the entire beach to ourselves," the Shadelkin boy gave a smug smile and spread out his arms. Soraya looked around and realized the entire cove formed a crescent shape like the moon. A cave jutted out from the steep stone cliff, and carved into both the sides and top of the entrance of the gaping maw were the three Azakuin Gods.

A small building with restrooms built inside lay near the stone stairway, with a large golden clock resting over the entrance. To its left was a tall lit lamppost looming over a faded blue telephone booth.

Rhys rolled up his pants legs, ran towards the glimmering ocean, and stood ankle deep in the salt water. "Venoi!" he called over to Soraya. "Come on!" he repeated in Azakuin.

The girl blushed and ran over to him, the soft sand sloshing beneath her. When her feet sank beneath the shallow water, it was cool and calming to her skin. She held up the edges of her skirt to keep it from getting soaked and joined Rhys. Together, they watched the water recede back into the sea before curling over itself to form a small wave. It came roaring back at them, the top rolling down and crashing into the ground, creating a large sea of foam as it flowed around their legs with a steady strength.

"It's amazing!" Soraya exclaimed. "This is so wonderful!"

Adoration and amusement danced in the Casmerahn boy's wine colored eyes. "I knew you'd love the beach," he said, then turned his attention to the blazing sun ahead of them. "Check it out."

Both friends watched in silence while the massive ball of light sank into the Valtic Ocean. The vibrant pinks and oranges were pushed down beneath the horizon as rich blues and purples took over. The full moon, bright stars, and planets shined through the darkness and lit up the night sky.

"I can't even believe how beautiful this all is," Soraya whispered.

"I've seen the sun set so many times, but it never ceases to amaze me," Rhys looked over at Soraya. "Was it everything you hoped for?"

"Yes, it really was."

The boy pointed at something far off in the water, a fin rising from the depths. Within seconds, it broke through the surface, and Soraya saw a sleek, gray creature with a long, bottle-like nose and pitch black eyes fly into the air for two seconds before diving back into the ocean and disappearing from view.

"Was that a dolphin?"

"Jai."

Soraya ecstatically twirled in the water. "I actually saw one in real life! Yes!" she triumphantly pumped her fist into the air.

"Alright, I don't see any seals swimming about, so do you want to go read the book with me now?"

Soraya hesitated for a moment, but knew she couldn't stall forever. "Okay, let's do it."

* * *

*A thin membrane divides our worlds, and it takes a lot of energy from both ends to keep continuous contact. Many demons are blind and deaf, but not all. They mainly communicate with Etherians through connecting with our minds, seeing through our eyes, hearing through our ears, and feeling through our touch. That is why many Etherians who have written on paranormal experiences talk of seeing visions and apparitions, especially at night. The moon affects the barrier between our worlds, similar to how it controls the tides of the ocean. (See page 33.)*

*The vast differences in communication are yet another reason why learning Apollryük was simultaneously fascinating and difficult. While Etherians communicate through reading, writing, verbal languages, and social cues, demons fuse with another's soul and share memories, emotions and experiences. However, they cannot fuse with a soul that is not within their own world.*

Beneath the paragraphs was a sketch of a symbol similar to the one Soraya had seen earlier in the week.

"Fusing with another's soul?" Rhys murmured. "I can't tell

if the author is being serious, or if he's taking illegal substances while writing this."

He held the book with one hand and Soraya's hand with the other while the girl studied the symbol. It was already unraveling before her eyes and weaving itself into an Azakuin word. Every fiber in her being wanted to pull away and shut out the image, but something deep inside kept her eyes open. It wanted her to say the word aloud, it willed her to. Despite everything that had happened earlier that week, her mouth and tongue moved without her consent.

"Slevautza."

Soraya's hand turned translucent, her ability to stay on the sand became impossible as her body faded away. She fell into Rhys, and kept falling. There was no landing, no smacking into the ground. Instead, a blinding light expanded between the two of them before a loud crack like a whip echoed through the air.

"What just happened?" Rhys gasped, though Soraya's mouth moved.

"I… I don't know," she lied.

"*Yes you do!*" Rhys' panic-stricken voice was loud and clear inside her head. "*Why else would you feel guilty… Wait, I'm feeling guilty too…*"

They lifted their right hand and both looked down. Their skin was the same color as Rhys', but the features didn't look quite right. They looked simultaneously both masculine and feminine.

"Soraya…" their mouth moved again. "What is going on?"

Even as the question escaped from their lips, they both knew the demonic spell had worked.

"*We're a fusion, aren't we?*" they thought at the same time, their voices sounding as one.

They stood up and looked down at themselves. Even their clothes were now a strange hybrid, neither masculine nor feminine. They ran to the restroom. Rhys hesitated to enter into the women's side, but Soraya pulled them both in, so they could look in the mirror.

"Look at us."

Their eyes were different colors; their left was Rhys' deep crimson red, while their right was Soraya's sky blue. Their hair was still long and tied into a braid like Rhys', but it was a strawberry blond, like Soraya's. Their black, cat-like ears twitched and lowered while they stared at the strange hybrid before them.

"Impossible…" Rhys whispered, but he knew they were looking at themselves. They both did. Soraya nervously tapped their fingers on the porcelain sink.

"I'm so sorry, Rhys…" she said sadly.

"How is this even happening?" he said slowly, his voice full of shock.

Soraya knew she couldn't hide anything from him anymore and opened up her memories to him. He took in everything; her father losing his memories and almost murdering her by accident, then him giving her the rest of his Air and Water Magic. She shared what she remembered about her mother, and even the race earlier in the week with her stealing the souls of the plants and how they healed her completely.

*"I understand if you're scared of me… I'm really sorry. I didn't mean for all of this to happen."*

Rhys' voice went quiet, scaring Soraya even more.

*"Rhys? Please don't hate me."*

"I know you didn't mean to do this," their lips moved again with Rhys taking the helm. "I forgive you."

A sigh of relief escaped from their lips when Soraya realized he meant it.

Rhys looked down at the palms of their hands and saw the Water Magic symbol on their right, and the air magic on their left.

*"Funny enough, your magic would get us into more trouble than us*

*being a fusion. There are plenty of Etherians who have different colored eyes, and it's seen as having a Gods like quality in Azakua…"*

The boy frowned and he ran their fingers over each tattoo. *"It's illegal to possess magic without a license… We could be in big trouble if anyone finds out. We have to figure out how to heal those plants with Water Magic, but maybe…"*

Another thought popped up. Rhys tried shoving it down, but Soraya still heard it despite it being low and quiet, like a breeze gently rustling through the fallen leaves on the ground.

*"Maybe… we could use Air Magic all up together… then you won't be caught in possession of it, and we could have some fun."*

*"I would love to use Air Magic with you!"*

With their heart pounding loudly in their chest, they ran outside, back onto the beach, and looked at the time. They had to call the school and check in around eight o'clock, and it was seven fifty-five.

"Let's just get it over with now," suggested Rhys while reaching to pick up the receiver. He punched in the school's office number, and they waited patiently for a clerk to answer.

"Darkwood Academy, this is Runolio speaking, how can I direct your call?

"Hey, it's Rhys Leyo and Soraya Thenayu checking in. We're still at a Thousand Steps Beach."

There was a slight pause before the man spoke again. "Perfect, call again around nine o'clock, please. You kids be safe."

Rhys quickly hung up the phone and grinned widely. *"Okay, let's use Air magic!"*

Soraya watched the water crash on the shore and had a fun idea. Rhys heard it and agreed. The girl lifted their left pointer and middle fingers and sprinted towards the ocean, the sand sinking slightly beneath them with each step they took. She then kicked them off the ground, so they were airborne, and they glided towards a wave that was just beginning to curl over.

They flew straight through the tunnel of water and ran their fingers over and through the cool, smooth, glassy surface as they did. Both seaweed and fish rode inside the bright blue wave above, below and next to them.

The circular exit ahead grew smaller and smaller as the wave toppled over itself, but Soraya and Rhys beckoned the wind to thrust them forward, and they shot out of the watery tunnel seconds before the wave crashed and settled back down onto the shore.

They climbed higher and higher into the sky, the wind brushing past their face and sweeping through their hair. They hid in a light mist rolling in and soared towards the heavens.

"This is incredible!" yelled Rhys. He looked all around and saw nothing but pillow soft clouds below and the starry night sky above stretching out in all directions. "How have you been able to restrain yourself for so long on having this much fun?"

"I guess I'm just responsible," Soraya laughed, then dove their body down, then up, and arched themselves, so they did a complete upside down loop.

"You're so cute," chuckled Rhys.

When the words escaped from his lips, they both felt it, a drift forming between them. It started in the pit of their stomach and rippled out across their entire body.

*"I think... we're separating!"*

Soraya's body tumbled away from her friend. Although she spun in circles while flying backwards, the girl still remained in the air. Rhys, on the other hand, dropped like a stone down into the mist below, his cries for help fading while he continued his rapid descent.

Soraya immediately righted herself and dove for him, propelling the wind from behind to thrust her forward faster.

*"For future reference, whenever you fly, whatever you're carrying with you also becomes lighter. You can fly with your backpack on, or even with another*

*person, like we did the other day."*

She remembered her father's words as she reached out and grabbed her friend's arm. The second she wrapped her fingers around his wrist, he became weightless, like her. She then flew them back up above the clouds, holding tightly onto him.

"We're not dead!" Rhys laughed. "We're still flying!"

Soraya positioned herself, so they were facing each other, and threw her other arm around him in a loving embrace. "I would never let you die! Never ever!"

Rhys hugged her back. "I know."

They stayed floating in the air, holding one another, both enjoying that moment in time, wishing it could last forever.

*How much Air Magic do I have left?*

Soraya checked her left hand and saw the tattoo was even more faded than before, the yellow almost blending in with her skin. "It's time to go back."

Together, with their arms still wrapped around one another, they floated back down into the mist with Rhys swaying them back and forth, as if they were dancing to music.

"Want to go to the library when we get back to school?" the boy asked. "I bet we can figure out how to heal those plants and keep your secret safe."

"Yes, we really should do that," Soraya paused. "Should we tell Ujuu and Moiya about… well, what I can do?"

Rhys frowned. "I adore my brother. I also know he might accidentally let this slip out if he becomes excited enough. As for Moiya, well, I'm not entirely sure how she would react to something this huge… Maybe it's best to wait for now, but we should tell them at some point."

"Alright," Soraya agreed. Although she wasn't entirely on board with the prospect, she also knew it was a lot of information to digest.

Their feet finally landed back onto the soft, white sand of a Thousand Steps Beach. They both looked at the cave entrance and stared at the stone statues carved around the gaping, jagged maw.

"I'm not sure if your fusion ability is entirely demonic," Rhys said. "The Azakuin Gods and goddess all have the power to fuse with one another, and you can do that too," he looked over at her in wonder. "I think… you can wield the power of the Gods."

"That sounds so blasphemous, Rhys," Soraya whispered fearfully. "I'm not worthy of being compared to our deities!"

"Think about it," he paced in a circle on the sand. "Our fusion self matched them, with each eye being a different color," he put a hand to his chin and stroked it. "Maybe, that other realm isn't purely demonic. Maybe, there are angels and demons, Gods and goddesses…"

He looked back over at his friend with his beautiful, wine colored eyes. "You could be a hybrid of more than an Etherian and a Demon, you know. It's just a theory I have based upon what I now know."

"It's a shame I can't ask Amraphael Zinvi, since he's dead…" as the words left her mouth, she thought back to the demon she had spoken with before. "Rhys, I didn't tell you about this, but a demon visited me in my sleep last weekend."

She avoided looking into his eyes as she continued to relay how he wanted her to kill Yaho, and how her arm had moved on its own.

"Whatever you do, don't give him any information," Rhys said solemnly, his crimson eyes burning furiously. He flipped open the book to the very last page and held it up. "Is this what he showed you when he asked where you are?"

"Yes." Soraya bit her lower lip. It was the same map she had seen pop up in her head.

"The X's show the most haunted locations in the world,

and I know Matumi has one over it," his ears perked up. "Where did you grow up, Soraya?"

She pointed at the Averlore Mountains, and noticed there were no X's anywhere near Rivinsdeep or Rivingale Falls, where she had spent time with her mother before the incident. They both had the same thought, but Rhys spoke first.

"I think the Demons can only talk to you when you're in a haunted location."

"Rhys, let's look at Zinvi's explanation of the moon affecting communication between our worlds."

The boy rapidly flipped through the book's pages and opened it to thirty-three, where there were two different illustrations with a small paragraph underneath.

"The only time Etherians and Demons can communicate is when the moon is half full, both during the first quarter and last quarter," Rhys read, his crimson eyes sparkling in the starlight. "Tonight, the moon is completely full. That means last weekend, Astros had a half moon."

"And that means, the demon will be able to control me again next Solis Diem…" Soraya's face turned as pale as the moon above.

# Chapter 24: Hymn of Healing

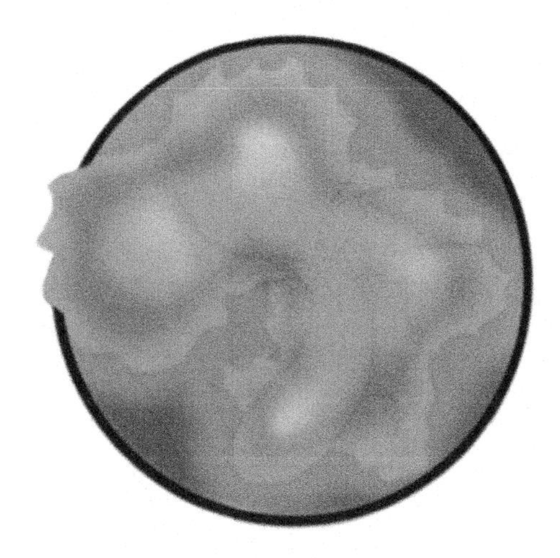

The huge, silver faced clock hanging above the roaring fireplace in Darkwood Academy's library ticked forward in a steady march.

Tick… tock… tick.. tock…

Soraya and Rhys sat across from each other at a wooden table, both bent forward, browsing through several open books, desperately searching for any information on techniques for healing plants with Water Magic.

"We're no closer to finding answers now than we were last weekend," Rhys sighed and closed yet another book in defeat. It was Aquas Diem, the fourth day of the week. The botanist was scheduled to arrive the next day to inspect the plants Soraya had accidentally killed.

"Are you absolutely sure there's no Apollryük healing spell in Zinvi's diary?" Soraya asked nervously.

"Yeah, I scoured through the whole thing for that," her dearest friend murmured. He spun around to make sure everyone else was out of ear shot before speaking again. "You can only take other souls to heal yourself, not the other way around."

"That doesn't sound very Godslike to me," the girl frowned.

*Perhaps, I am more of a demon than an angel... or goddess?*

She shook her head to rid her mind of the thoughts and opened her mouth to ask Rhys about the other symbols he had seen while reading ahead, but caught herself. *It's best to wait and read them while at the beach. I don't want any more incidents to happen at school.*

"Maybe I should just try to wing it for healing the plants?" she suggested.

"Wing it?" Rhys' wine-colored eyes widened in surprise. "They would remember you casting Water Magic, and what if you kill more by accident?"

"We have to try something before tomorrow..." she whispered so faintly, Rhys strained to hear her. "We could fuse again to hide our identity and try using Water Magic together."

The Casmerahn boy looked up at the clock. It was the twentieth hour and fourteen minutes in. Bedtime wasn't until twenty-two o'clock. They were still allowed to leave the main building and roam about the campus grounds.

"Okay, let's do it."

The two friends made their way out the front doors of the school. Both kept glancing over their shoulders to make sure they weren't being followed by anyone.

Ujuu and Moiya, thinking they were going on more dates together, were giving them time alone. Soraya felt pangs of guilt for staying out late all week and not seeing Yabo as much, but Moiya was thankfully babysitting him and giving her pet the pats and kisses he craved.

After entering the Orchestra room and making sure they were completely alone within the building, Soraya held Rhys' hands in her own.

"Slevautza."

She turned translucent and fell into him once more, slipping into his body like a glove. Transforming into their hybrid self felt much more natural for the both of them the second time around.

*"We should make our hair look different too, just in case."*

They reached down and untied the white ribbon from their ponytail.

*"Let's make two braids, so we look nothing like our normal selves."*

Soraya let Rhys take over their hands, so he could twist and weave their hair into two ponytails on both sides of their head. After tying both ends with ribbons, they walked to the boy's restroom and looked at themselves. Standing before them, in the mirror, was someone who looked like a new student they had never met before.

"Perfect," they agreed in unison.

The dirt road used for the timed mile run was dimly lit by the stars above and the waning moon looming overhead.

*"In three days, the demon will visit again."*

Despite being a fusion, Rhys moved their left hand to gently hold onto their right.

*"Let's focus on fixing this problem first."*

There were no lampposts anywhere in sight, which helped them blend in with the shadows. All they could hear were the crunching of leaves and small rocks beneath their feet and crickets chirping faintly from the tall grass.

*"There it is."*

They cautiously approached the circle of dead, wilted grass and the two skeletal trees. The broken, dead limbs and branches were scattered about on the lawn, already decomposing and being swallowed back up by the earth.

Sadness overwhelmed the girl as she stared at the destruction she had caused.

*"This is all my fault."*

Rhys squeezed their right hand.

*"It was an honest mistake, you don't need to keep beating yourself up for it."*

They knelt down, brushing the dead grass beneath their fingers. Soraya winced when a few blades turned to dust from her light touch. Despite never having used Water Magic before, the tattoo on their right hand warmed up, as if it knew the plants needed help.

*"Do you feel that too?"*

*"Jai."*

They shifted their thumb under their hand, so four fingers were raised.

*"Heal them, please,"* the girl pleaded to the Gods. Instinctively, she squeezed their thumb into their hand, and they both watched as sparkling, clear water flowed out of their palm and into the grass. It stretched and spread itself out, forming a small lake encompassing every dull and gray blade and every dead and rotting root from the two decaying trees.

"Sing a hymn…"

Soraya and Rhys froze. A faint voice, barely above a whisper, had breathed in their right ear. Rhys hadn't heard it at first through his left ear and had almost mistaken it for the light breeze rustling through the surrounding leaves.

"I haven't prayed or sung to the Gods in a long time," Rhys said sadly. "I've been calling myself agnostic for years, always wondering what the truth is since I grew up being taught two different religions."

A memory of Rhys' flashed into their mind. The boy was crouching down behind a stairway, peeking nervously in between the bars. A woman with golden hair and blue eyes, who Soraya recognized as his mother from Ujuu's photograph in his locker, was arguing with two older, more weathered looking adults.

"My husband and children are wonderful and beautiful souls!" Rhys and Ujuu's mother shouted. "Just get to know them! They are your own family, your own flesh and blood for Gods' sake!"

"Ayla," the older man frowned, the wrinkles around his lips deepening. "You should never have married a Shadelkin, and especially one who is Casmerahn. You know it's against our religion to marry anyone with a different faith."

"Our religion doesn't teach that at all! You're ripping those passages out of context!" Rhys' mother cried out in exasperation. "Myrl is a good man! Why do you refuse to acknowledge all the hard work he's done for our sons and I?"

"Daughter," the older woman stepped forward, her yellowing teeth tightly clenched together. "Those *things* you live with are not our family, and never will be. Either you move back in with us, and we'll find you a proper Azakuin man, or you will never see us again."

"Fine…" Ayla pointed to the front entrance. "Goodbye," her voice shook, but she stood and watched her parents storm out, slamming the door behind them. Only after her parents left did Ayla bury her face in her hands. Rhys wanted to go hug his mother, but hesitated to move forward. Instead, he stayed frozen in place, horrified at what had just transpired.

"How long have you been standing there, Rhys?" his mother asked without turning to face him. "How much did you hear, my love?"

Soraya's eyes filled with tears as she felt her heart sink along with her friend's.

"I do have a hymn in mind, if that's okay with you," Rhys spoke up again, his voice wavering. Soraya could see the lyrics before their eyes and hear the melody playing on an organ in their head, another memory from his childhood.

*"Of course."*

The boy possessed their mouth, and sang in a sweet and soft voice.

"Blessings flow from Gods above, mercies show their everlasting love…"

Their tears flowed down their face, dripping into the pool and rippling the glassy surface.

"They cast our sins to the depths of Sheol, and remember them not forevermore…"

The water beneath their fingers glowed a bright blue, creating a ball of light. Like a fish with flowing, fan-like fins, it swam and spread out over the dead grass and trees, leaving in its wake a trail of dancing, changing colors, like the aurora lights Soraya had seen in the night sky back in the Averlore Mountains.

"I'm one with them, and they with me, praise our saviors for eternity. Kyrie eleison, kyrie eleison, kyrie eleison."

They watched the glowing pool of water lower and seep into the soil. The once wilted, gray grass now stood tall and green. The two dead trees sprung back to life before their eyes. They creaked, groaned and shook violently as new limbs shot out and grew to replace the ones that had fallen off.

"Thank you…" the same voice whispered in Soraya's ear again, stronger this time. "Your secrets are safe with us…"

"Incredible," breathed the friends together. Everything looked vibrant and alive, even more so than before. It wasn't just the patch of dead grass and two trees that had healed, all the surrounding foliage looked brighter, sturdier, and healthier.

Soraya and Rhys noticed the pit forming in her stomach again, and the girl tumbled backwards out of her friend and hit the ground with a light thud.

"We did it!" she laughed and hopped back to her feet. "I can't believe it!"

"Shhhh…" Rhys held a finger to his lips. "We didn't do

anything," he winked, his ruby eyes glowing in the pale moonlight.

"Oh, okay," she grinned.

"How much magic do you have left?" The boy asked.

The outlines for both water and air magic tattoos were barely visible. "Very little," Soraya replied. "I don't even have to wear gloves anymore."

"That's good. Now you don't have to worry about getting in trouble with the law," the Casmerahn boy held out his hand, and the girl wrapped her fingers around his. "Venoi, let's go rest. We have another problem to solve before Solis Diem."

* * *

"Well, what do you think, Ms. Mathaius?" Mr. Levi asked curiously, his dark, purple eyes wide with shock.

"Everything looks healthy."

"But, how did it all heal so quickly? I don't understand how that happened," the gym teacher said, placing a hand on his chin and stroking his beard in thought.

The grass, gray and wilted just the day before, now looked green, lush and long. The two trees, also previously dead, were now full of colorful leaves.

"Maybe, you could use Earth Magic to ask them what happened?"

Soraya and Rhys glanced nervously at each other and held their breaths. They were hovering close by so they could listen in on their conversation. In fact, all the students were supposed to be stretching their limbs, but were quiet to hear what was going on.

"Alright," the botanist agreed, her long, black hair and white coat blowing in the light breeze. The tall, slender woman touched her right hand to one of the healed trees and closed her eyes. A bright green light flowed from her mahogany fingertips and sank into the dark red bark. "They're singing hymns of praise to the Gods, saying an angel healed them, and their prayers were answered."

"They're singing?" the gym teacher repeated in disbelief.

Ms. Mathaius nodded, her golden eyes glinting in the sunlight. "Hymns are just prayers in the form of a song," she paused and pressed her ear to the tree's trunk. "They're saying this is now a holy place. It's been blessed, purified."

"A holy place?" Mr. Levi laughed. "It's in the middle of our track field! There's nothing special about this spot at all!"

"So it would seem…" She took her ear and hand away from the bark and inspected the grooves in the wood. "Take a look here."

Mr. Levi, along with all the other students, leaned in to see.

"There's a triangle with a circle running around it. That's one of the symbols associated with the Gods."

"Well, I'll be!" exclaimed the gym teacher in surprise.

The botanist placed her hands together and bowed respectfully to the teacher. "I'm glad everything sorted itself out fine. I will make a note of this, it's quite fascinating," she said, then turned and faced the students, who were all trying to get a better look at the tree. Soraya and Rhys tried not to look guilty when her eyes hovered over them.

"Have a lovely day," she told the class before walking briskly back to her parked car near the entrance of the school.

Mr. Levi shook his head in wonder. "I'm glad everything is fine, but wow, that is strange," he looked at his students, then down at his watch. "Okay kids, let's head back to the field and play kickball."

All the students whispered to each other while following their teacher.

"Holy place? What was she talking about?"

"I wish I could be an Arcanologist someday and have magic too…"

*It's been purified…* An idea hit Soraya like a ton of bricks. *What if I were to stay in that holy spot when the demon tries contacting me again? Would that protect me?*

Before Soraya could tell Rhys, Ujuu and Moiya approached them like cats stalking their prey, both wearing large grins on their faces.

"So, have you both kissed yet?" the green-eyed Azakuin asked, her emerald gems shining.

"Kissed?"

The thought hadn't even crossed Soraya's mind.

"Geez, Moiya!" Rhys exclaimed, his face flushed red.

"Aww, is that a no?" Moiya shook her head in disappointment.

"Bro, come on, really?" Ujuu rolled his candy apple eyes to the sky. "Why do you think we've been giving you both so much alone time together?"

While the twins argued with one another, Soraya turned to Moiya.

"Say, are you seeing anyone?" the girl asked. "We're all in relationships but you, I was wondering why?"

Moiya's gaze fell to the ground. "Well, I'm happy being single."

"Oh?" Soraya leaned in closer.

"My older sister, Naviah, was pressured by our parents to get married young. She had four kids before she turned twenty-two..." Moiya frowned. "I've noticed how bitter and sad she's become from feeling like she never has time to do anything she wants to do. Naviah lived most of her life trying to please our parents. Now, she's regretting not taking charge of her own life."

She looked up at Soraya. "I think kids are wonderful, and I love my nieces and nephews dearly and have helped with raising them ever since they were born, but I don't want to end up like my sister. I just want to see the world and find out what I want to do before committing my life to someone else."

Soraya furrowed her eyebrows together. "Yeah, that makes sense. I'm sure your parents mean well, but you are your own person, and they should respect that."

Moiya smiled. "If I do date in the future, I want to be with someone like you, or Rhys, or Ujuu. You are all so lovely."

"You are too," Soraya assured her. A pang of guilt shot up the girl's chest. *I really should tell her about my abilities…*

"Rhys, are you okay?"

Soraya snapped her attention back to the twins. Ujuu was staring in concern at his brother, who had stopped walking.

"No," Rhys glared at the ground. "I don't want to force Soraya into the same position as our mom. She doesn't deserve to deal with that kind of pressure."

*Rhys...* Soraya immediately understood what he was referring to.

"Igo no frater, paenite," Ujuu pulled his brother into a side hug. "Tutum est. Felixeritis."

Neither Soraya nor Moiya were sure what Ujuu had said, but the older twin closed his eyes and nodded.

"Rhys, my mama-" Soraya stopped herself. "My step-mother was Casmerahn, remember?"

"I do remember," Rhys nodded. "But I'm not worried about your father giving you a hard time. It's society in general."

Soraya threw her arms around Rhys and hugged him. "It'll be okay. You're worth fighting for."

He relaxed and hugged her back. "You are too."

# Chapter 25: Mülock

It was the very end of Solis Diem, the first day of the week, and the sun was setting over the horizon. Soraya stood on the balcony outside the girl's dormitory, watching the blazing ball before her dip into the murky depths of the Valtic Ocean. Her long, strawberry blond hair blew gently in the cool breeze, and an extra gust of wind caused her to shiver.

*Tonight, I have to be in the holy place when the demon arrives.*

The girl's grip on the steel railing tightened as the last bit of light was swallowed up by the dark blue sea.

*I can use the rest of my Air Magic to fly down and back up to this spot, but I doubt I'll have any left for next time. I'll have to figure out a new way to sneak out of the school undetected.*

She and Rhys hadn't had time to properly strategize. Instead, they were pulled into extra orchestra practice for the upcoming Matumi Beach Concert. Much to Soraya's surprise, her fingers had memorized various violalin melodies much faster than she had originally anticipated.

*I wonder if I'm absorbing Rhys' ability to play every time I fuse with him. I don't want to steal his talent.*

Thankfully, Rhys' instrument still sang gracefully under his dancing fingertips. She silently prayed to the Gods to let him keep his hard-earned abilities before peeking at the palms of her hands, where her Air and Water Magic tattoos shimmered faintly on her skin.

*I really need to wash my gloves.*

The moon, half full and half shadow, cast its dim light onto the world below. Soraya spotted an ominous mist forming over the ocean, growing larger and darker with each passing second. She narrowed her eyes and stared as the black fog devoured everything in its path. The horizon was no longer visible. The sea and trees beneath it were enveloped by its hazy outline as it approached the school, as it marched steadily towards her.

*He'll be here soon.*

The girl's mind wandered to Jacquelle, who had been distant for the past week. The blond hadn't teased her for a few days, not even when she had stumbled while playing a new part in the song the day before. That bothered Soraya more than she cared to admit.

*What are you planning now?*

The steadily approaching fog was now outside the yellow brick wall surrounding Darkwood Academy. Soraya could see the black, ominous clouds oozing over the top of the enclosure like a slow moving waterfall.

"Soraya!"

The girl turned and looked at the neighboring tower on the other end of the roof. Rhys was rapidly waving his arms in the air to grab her attention.

"Are you okay?" he called over to her. His voice was faint, but she could easily understand him.

*My hearing and eyesight are better too. Is that also because of fusing with Rhys?*

"Yes!" she called over to him.

The balconies resided on the same level as the bedrooms. None of the boys were allowed to enter the upper part of the girl's dormitory and vice versa. Although it made perfect sense, Soraya was sad that Rhys couldn't be next to her. She wanted more than anything to fly over to him, but he had insisted she only use her Air Magic for her mission. They both knew she would have to do it alone this time.

"Hey, are you coming to bed?"

Moiya stood in the doorway with her arms crossed, dressed in a long white pajama gown, her long, flowing hair free in the wind. Yabo sat at her heels, purring while rubbing his body against her leg.

She smirked as she glanced between Soraya and Rhys on the other side of the roof. "We have cooking class in the morning, remember? Everyone else is already going to sleep."

"Yeah, let's go." Soraya agreed. "Goodnight!" she called over to Rhys one last time before entering the dormitory with Moiya and Yabo. She gently closed the glass door behind her, leaving it unlocked.

*The demon visited me sometime early in the morning last time.* Soraya sighed inwardly, wishing she had paid attention to the alarm clock after the demonic attack. *I'll just wait for everyone to fall asleep before flying down to the field.*

The girl lay on the bunk above Moiya and stared at the dome shaped ceiling above. She was careful to stay on top of her blankets, so she would make less noise while sneaking out later that night. Yabo had settled himself next to her hand, purring while rubbing his face into her fingers.

"I love you," Soraya murmured to her pandacoon. "Sorry I haven't seen you so much lately. I do miss you."

"Mow," he cooed in reply.

*I wonder if Papa felt this way, always being so busy with work and not being able to spend a lot of time with me.*

After a couple of minutes ticked by, Soraya moved her head and glanced at the alarm clock near Jacquelle's bed.

*Twenty-one forty-seven. It's still too early to leave.*

The girl was too anxious to fall asleep. All she could imagine was the demon taking control of her arm again and the damage it could potentially do to Yabo and her friends if he succeeded.

*What if he forces me to use my demonic powers? Can he possess my mouth and make me say the Apollryük spells?*

She couldn't afford to mess up. There was too much at stake.

At twenty-three thirty, Soraya decided it was safe to get up. Slowly, she inched her way to the ladder near her feet, all the while being careful not to move Yabo. His little black paws twitched and kicked slightly in his sleep, and the girl couldn't help but smile at how cute he looked.

Stepping down the wooden ladder without making a sound took forever, but Soraya's feet finally touched the cold wooden floor. With caution, she spun around the room, looking to see if her movements had disturbed anyone else, but she was only met with soft breathing and gentle snores.

Soraya slipped into the stone stairwell, making her way towards the locker room. She made sure to grab a coat for herself before walking towards one of the wide windows overlooking the track and field below. The balcony was connected to the bedroom, but she didn't want to open the door and risk waking everyone up while sneaking out. She would only use it upon her return.

*I won't let you control me again.*

The girl unlatched the lock on the window and pushed the wooden frame up. She could just make out the ground far below through the thick mist. If she ran out of Air Magic while descending, she would be in major trouble.

*I won't let you hurt my family and friends.*

She swung her legs out over the windowsill and let them dangle in the air. The girl then held out her pointer and middle fingers and took a deep breath in.

*I need answers, and you're going to give them to me.*

Soraya jumped.

For about three seconds, the world all around her rose rapidly, but a large gust of wind caught her from beneath, slowing her fall. She willed for the air to carry her towards the track and field where the purified ground lay, but she landed softly on the soil in the middle of a clearing as quickly as possible.

*I have to save the rest of my magic for the return trip. The fog will help hide me.*

As she made her way towards the holy spot, she couldn't help but feel as if she was being watched. Surrounding her on all sides were faded trees, barely visible and jutting out in severed, disjointed pieces through the thick fog.

"*Hello again, my child.*"

Soraya's throat tightened in fear. She could hear the low rumbles of several voices creeping up in the back of her head. She quickened her pace and ran as fast as she could towards the purified oasis in the sea of blood stained soil.

"*Where are you running to? You can't hide from me.*"

Soraya glanced behind her and spotted a black silhouette standing in the middle of the field, watching her with six rainbow-colored eyes; four on its face, and two on its chest. A shadow of a clawed hand stretched out from the ground beneath. It reached out to grab her, the darkness engulfing everything that lay in its path as it slithered across the dirt road.

The healed grass and trees lay ahead, just a few footsteps away. Soraya pushed herself to run even faster.

The clawed hand was closing in on her own shadow. Its long, thin fingers unsheathed as they thrust forward to strike her.

Soraya slammed into the tree with the symbol of the Gods carved into it and hugged it with all her might. She kept her eyes shut and prayed to the Gods to protect her.

"*What's this?*" the demonic voices asked curiously. Its snake-like hand halted, and the demon lifted a single bony finger and lightly tapped at the grass. A bright blue light immediately appeared from thin air, and a piece of its shadow burnt off. The voices hissed in pain from the back of the girl's head.

"*A holy place? How curious that you're not burning in agony…*"

Soraya slowly opened her eyes and glanced at the silhouette. It stood perfectly still at the far end of the track. Within seconds, without moving a muscle, the body shot forward and stood at the edge of the purified land, its rainbow-colored eyes burrowing themselves into her skull.

Soraya quelled the rising fear within her. *Do you know what I am?* she asked within her mind.

"*You are my child, yet you are not. You are many things…*" the voices mulled over the information thoughtfully. "*Zinvi went too far…*" the demon laughed, its many voices out of sync.

"*You found a way around being possessed. Congratulations, Soraya Thenayu. You are indeed safe within that space, but I can still speak to you within your mind, and make you see things that aren't actually there…*"

A large, looming shadow of a hand formed on the ground, the fingers opened wide, curling around where Soraya stood like the jaws of a snake. It formed a crescent shape around the purified grass and trees, the outlines of the long nails hanging down like fangs.

"What's your name?" Soraya asked. "You know mine, but I don't know yours."

"*Mülock!*" the voices thundered within her head.

"So, you can only see what I see and hear what I hear right

now, correct?" Soraya questioned him, realizing how little power he had over her.

"*Yes...*" the six eyes on the silhouette before her narrowed. "*You are much more intelligent than I initially thought, child, but I'm sure you didn't figure out how to escape possession from me on your own... Tell me, who helped you? I would love to see their faces and hear their names, so I can thank them later...*"

Soraya refused to answer him. Instead, she pulled up the cover of Amraphael Zinvi's diary in her mind.

"Do you know this author?"

"*Yes...*" they sounded amused. "*That cover almost captures my image, though it's missing my collection of eye colors. Those faces you see on me are souls I've kept within myself over the years.*"

The silhouette before her shivered as several faces burst through the skin in its arms and chest. Their unseeing eyes gazed at Soraya in agony, and she could hear muffled screams crying out for help far in the back of her mind. An overwhelming amount of pity built up within the girl.

*Those poor souls.*

"*I would love to add you to my collection, my dear,*" the silhouette's mouth dropped open, revealing two rows of razor sharp fangs below his lips. "*Would you like to be fused with us for eternity?*"

The very thought of being stuck with the demon revolted the girl. Her stomach churned with disgust while she ignored the shadowy figure that was staring hungrily at her from outside the purified domain.

"*You don't like that idea?*" the demon scoffed. "*Not even after I gave you a gift?*"

"What gift?"

"*The stealing souls spell, my child,*" growled the low rumbling voices in unison. "*I planted that into your head. I can sense that you used it. Shame you didn't grab a hold of your beloved pet after saying it... The other one*

*I gave the spell to murdered his family by accident... So, so tragic,*" it mocked.

"Other one? Who are you talking about?" Soraya demanded.

"*I'll answer that, but only after…*" the map of Etheria flashed once more before the girl's eyes. "*You tell me where you are residing,*" the demon's tone turned serious in a flash. "*I must know!*"

"I'll never tell you!" Soraya retorted. "Never!"

The voices hissed and spat furiously like a bubbling, overflowing pot of boiling water. "*You get one more chance. When I visit again, you will tell me where you are. You will pledge your allegiance to me and me alone, or I will possess the other one. He will hunt you down and make your life a living Hell!*"

Soraya glared into the silhouette's six rainbow-colored eyes. "You will never control me again. Go away!"

Just like the time before, the demonic entity faded from her mind, the voices becoming quieter and quieter with each passing second. Soraya looked at the ground and saw the shadowy hand curled around where she stood was also disappearing, turning more and more transparent, until it was gone.

The girl collapsed in a heap on the grass and smiled to herself. "I can hardly wait to tell Rhys what happened. We did it," she dragged her hand across the plants, like she would with Yabo's fur, and exhaled. "Thank you."

With that, she stood up and brushed the dew off her nightgown and coat. It was time to sleep. She would only get less than four hours of rest before the entire dorm had to wake up at five for cooking class, but at least she had outsmarted her foe, meaning everyone she loved was safe for now.

Soraya crept back through the mist towards the main campus and cautiously looked around. No other souls were in sight. Thunder boomed from overhead, startling the girl in her steps. After a few seconds, thin drops of rain fell from the sky.

Soraya held out her middle and pointer fingers and gazed up at the balcony of the girl's dorm before running and leaping into the air. The wind caught and carried her all the way up to her destination. Just as she was descending onto the balcony, the gust completely left, causing her to fall rather ungracefully onto the wooden surface with a loud thud.

"Soraya?"

The girl froze and spun around. Moiya cautiously moved away from behind a stone pillar, her emerald green eyes wide as dinner plates. "How did you, what were you…" she sputtered in disbelief. "What is going on?"

Her voice was quivering, both with fear and fury. "Yabo woke me up. He only ever goes to me when you're not around. I thought you were sneaking off to see Rhys, but this…" she gestured angrily at the balcony. "Explain yourself!"

## Chapter 26: News from Abroad

Moiya tapped her foot impatiently, her eyebrows knit together in frustration. Soraya had never seen her friend look so hurt before. Guilt rose within her chest at the realization that she was the one who had caused the pain.

*I knew I should have confided in her sooner.*

"I-I'm sorry for not telling you that I had magic," the girl whispered. She was still fully aware of the other sleeping students inside the dormitory and didn't want anyone else waking up and overhearing their conversation.

Lightning rippled across the black clouds, followed by a thunder clap echoing across the heavens. Soraya winced at the loud noise, but her friend ignored the weather. Although the rain was pelting down in thicker drops, the girls were kept dry from an overhanging wall sheltering the balcony.

"It's illegal for you to have that!" Moiya cried in exasperation. "You could go to prison!"

"I know," Soraya lowered her voice even more.

"You have to turn yourself in," Moiya continued, her tone

flat. "You'll get a lighter sentence if you do."

"What!" Soraya gasped. "M-Moiya! I can't do that!"

"Then get rid of it!" her friend hissed. "I'll be in trouble too if I don't report you, and I don't want to be expelled!"

Soraya's mouth fell open. "Please, just let me explain what's happening," she pleaded. "Will you at least listen to me?"

Moiya frowned and tapped her foot. "Okay, I'm listening,"

Soraya took a deep breath in, and extended her arm. "Can you hold my hand?"

Moiya lifted a brow. "If it means that much to you, then yes…" She clasped her fingers firmly around her friend's.

"I'm going to show you a lot of things, and you're going to feel everything I've felt. Is that okay?"

Even though she was still upset, Moiya managed to laugh. "Are you a psychic or something? What are you even talking about?"

"Do you give me permission?" Soraya asked again. "I need to know."

Moiya glanced suspiciously between their hands and the girl's face. "Okay… sure."

Soraya closed her eyes and gently squeezed Moiya's palm. "Slevautza."

Moiya gasped when her friend turned translucent and sank into her body. There was a bright light, followed by a loud crack like a whip, before silence took over. Their transformation was masked by another rumble of thunder from overhead.

"What the!" Moiya exclaimed and looked down at herself. She saw her dark skin, but there were now patches of lighter skin sprinkled on her fingertips. Her limbs no longer looked or felt like her own. Instead, her gloved fingers were slightly longer, and the tips were more calloused from additional violalin practice. "What is going on?"

"*I'm sorry you had to find out this way*," Moiya heard Soraya say inside her head. *"But you'll understand why in a few minutes, I promise."*

True to her word, Soraya poured her memories into Moiya's mind and didn't leave out any details. Their body shivered together when they thought about Mülock, tears formed behind their blue and green eyes at Tishva's violent episode and Adonia's death, and their heart sank at Rhys' childhood memories. When Soraya showed Moiya her beach date with Rhys, they became filled with joy.

"Oh my gosh, you had the best date with Rhys ever!" Moiya squealed ecstatically. Soraya brought a finger to their lips, and Moiya lowered their voice. "Alright, I understand where you're coming from, and I'm sorry for yelling at you."

"Your anger is justified. I'm sorry too."

They couldn't hug as a fusion, so they held their hands together instead.

"How long are we going to be like this?" Moiya asked curiously.

Soraya shrugged their shoulders. "I don't even know, to be honest, but it doesn't seem to last too terribly long. I wish I knew how to control it better."

"We should set a timer," Moiya mused. "I'm curious to find out what your average length is."

Soraya grinned. "You and Rhys are both so practical."

Their face glowed. "Thanks, Soraya. I appreciate that."

Another thought popped into their head, one they cooked up at the same time. *"We need to tell Ujuu about everything. He shouldn't be left out."*

At that moment, a pit formed in the center of their stomach. Soraya fell away from Moiya and landed on the deck of the balcony with a soft thud.

"Alright!" Soraya laughed. "Now we can go to bed."

"We should work on pushing you to your limits," Moiya whispered, her green eyes glowing. "If you're part demon or angel, that means you're using a different magic system. The more you know, the better in control you'll be of yourself."

Her face hardened as she folded her arms over her chest. "We can't let Mülock control you. You're right to be afraid of him, he could use you to hurt everyone."

"Exactly," Soraya agreed. "And I need to find a new way to sneak out of the school undetected," She and Moiya both looked out over the fog together. "That holy place is the only sanctuary I have from him."

Moiya placed a hand firmly on her friend's shoulder. "We'll figure something out. Four heads working together is better than two. Now, let's rest."

* * *

"Geez, all three of you look so exhausted."

Moiya, Soraya and Rhys were slumped in their seats at their workstation. They all had drooping, dark bags under their eyes. Whenever one yawned, the other two followed suit.

"Sorry," Soraya struggled to speak. "Didn't sleep well."

"I can see that," Ujuu smirked. "My bro here kept wandering to the balcony throughout the night. He was quiet, but I still heard him slip out several times," He lightly shoved his twin's shoulder. "What are you three up to?"

Soraya glanced over at Moiya and Rhys before speaking. "We'll tell you, but we have to be somewhere private to say."

Rhys' eyes widened for a split second as he looked at both girls in surprise. Moiya gave him a tiny nod of her head, and he replied in the same manner.

*Good. They both know that the other knows.*

"I have something to tell all three of you too, actually, so that works out perfectly."

The frying pan hissed when Ujuu gently lay several pieces of thick, apple smoked bacon into it. "I got Zaruna's letter last week…"

The boy's voice was barely audible over the sizzling strips of meat. Soraya picked up on that and realized the Shadelkin was using the loud noise as a cover-up.

"She told me about some happenings outside of our country, news we're not privy to in Azakua…" Ujuu paused when Mr. Trog slowly passed by them, then continued again after their teacher was out of ear shot. "I'll tell you more on our forty-five-minute break."

Soraya blinked in surprise at the unexpected information. Both Rhys and Moiya perked up and straightened themselves in their seats, their eyes more awake and alert than before.

"Sounds like a plan," the girl said nonchalantly.

Ujuu nodded and turned back towards the stovetop, whistling while flipping the bacon over with a pair of silver tongs.

Breakfast came and went, along with the first two classes of the day. Despite having a burning curiosity for hearing Ujuu's news, Soraya was struggling to keep her eyes open. It didn't help that the most private place they could all speak with one another was at the very top of a tall spire.

"So, what's this… news… you wanted… to share?" Rhys asked between deep breaths once the door was closed behind him. All four friends were heavily panting and winded from their long trek up to Darkwood Academy's radio room.

Rather than answering immediately, Ujuu checked the volumes for all the microphones and made sure they were muted. He then dug out Zaruna's letter from his pants pocket and carefully unfolded it.

"Chemi viata dragoste," he read aloud wistfully, his cheeks turning the same color as his eyes.

Moiya giggled as Rhys and Soraya stared at him in confusion. "It means, love of my life, in Rosinkin," she clarified for them.

Soraya awed aloud while Rhys rolled his eyes. "You dragged us all the way up here for that?"

Ujuu's blush faded. "I wish," his eyes scanned down the letter before he turned the parchment over so his friends and brother could see what he was pointing at.

"She made a word puzzle for me in Azakuin. It took me a few days to solve the message, but once I decoded it, I understood why she was being so careful," the younger twin cleared his throat before reading the deciphered portion aloud.

"Missing native girls isn't new, nor is it only happening in Azakua. It started about thirty years ago in the southern provinces of Casmerah. Native girls are starting to go missing both in Vorea and Calgreenzia, and my family fears Rosinka will be next."

Chills ran down the children's spines upon hearing the message.

"I'm afraid for Zaruna," Ujuu whispered, his hands shaking. "I want to move her and her folks back to our country since they still have blue cards allowing them to work here, but I can't afford to bring them all over. Plus, they don't have enough Lari to move right now."

Soraya's heart sank within her chest. Ujuu feeling helpless made her think about her father and how she couldn't help him with his memory loss.

"No wonder she coded that," Rhys murmured. "The Azakuin government picks what information is leaked out to the public. If everyone was aware of this, then it would throw off the election. Stefawn Zabok's strongest anti-immigration argument ties in with native Azakuin girls going missing. If it's happening all over the world, then it undermines his entire campaign."

His ruby eyes grew wide in shock. "It could mean that those in higher positions may have a hand in what's happening."

Rhys turned to face his brother. "Ujuu, do you remember what Dad had said? About why he immigrated here from Casmerah?"

"Jai," Ujuu placed a hand on his hips and stared at the floor. "He said someone had warned everyone in his village to leave, that they had to go before the Casmerahn army arrived. Anyone who stayed behind would be killed."

"That's what I remember father saying as well," Rhys stared at the younger twin. "Do you think that's somehow related to the Casmerahn girls going missing?"

"It sounds like it could be," Moiya chimed in shakily. "I didn't realize that was happening everywhere, even from where my parents came from…"

While her friends whispered with one another, Soraya couldn't stop thinking about Zaruna and her parents being stuck in Rosinka.

*They need more Lari to move, and they need to live in a place that's affordable…*

"Ujuu?" Soraya interjected. "Rivinsdeep is where I spent a good part of my childhood. It's a lovely community, and it's cheaper to live in than the bigger cities," a grin spread across her face as an idea popped into her head. "I can help pay for Zaruna and her parents to come over. Papa has a lot of Lari saved up. I can ask him if we can chip in."

The mouths of all three of her friends dropped open in surprise.

"Wow. That's very generous," Ujuu gaped. "I understand if your father says no. Moving countries is not cheap."

"Well, what's the point of having Lari if you can't use it to help others?"

Rhys smiled, his eyes glowing with adoration for her. "If only more Etherians thought that way."

"I'll call Papa today!" Soraya continued with pure

enthusiasm in her voice. "I'm sure he'll agree to it. And there are plenty of neighbors who would be willing to give Zaruna and her family a place to stay. I always worked on their farms in exchange for food and supplies, and there's lots of businesses that would hire them too."

The girl could hardly contain her excitement and started bouncing in place. "Maybe, Zaruna could be here for the Matumi Beach Concert!"

Ujuu's face lit up at the thought of seeing his girlfriend again so soon. "That all sounds wonderful!"

"Don't forget, we have something to tell Ujuu as well," Moiya reminded Soraya gently. "We only have a few more minutes before we have to get going to Biology."

"Oh yeah!" the girl gasped.

"What's up?" Ujuu grinned.

"Well, er, um…" Soraya faltered. *I probably shouldn't fuse with him since we don't have a lot of time left, but will he even believe me?*

"It's about something I can do…"

"Are you part Shadelkin like Rhys and I?" Ujuu guessed, the edges of his candy apple eyes crinkling with amusement.

"No, I'm part of something else entirely…" Soraya took a deep breath in and ignored Ujuu's inquisitive stare. "I have demonic powers."

Ujuu laughed aloud, but quickly stopped when he saw how serious his brother and friends were.

"Soraya told me this morning," Moiya spoke up. "And we all decided you needed to know, too."

"Wait, for reals?" Ujuu sounded confused. "What?"

"It's true, bro," Rhys patted his twin's shoulder. "I actually fused with Soraya twice, and I think I have a photographic memory like hers now."

"Qua?" Ujuu's eyes grew wide in shock. "Num est ka?"

"Jai, num est," Soraya nodded. "Really. We're not lying, I promise. I'll show you this weekend. We can all go to a Thousand Steps Beach altogether."

Before the younger twin could reply, all four kids froze in place. They heard it at the same time; a small scream erupting from the corner of the room.

Ujuu whipped his head around and stared at a small, black box sitting on the desk. It had a long, silver antennae sitting on the top and had several black dials and switches jutting from its front. He cautiously approached the school's scanner and carefully turned up the volume.

"Ra aris lucrurile acelea?" a woman's voice cried in horror.

"Gaiketsi! Ar gacherde!" a man screamed.

"What are they saying?" Soraya whispered fearfully, her heart pounding loudly in her chest.

"What are those things? Run. Don't stop," Moiya translated.

Rhys, Ujuu and Soraya turned to face their friend, whose face had turned as white as a blank sheet of paper.

"I think…" she gulped. "The kidnappings in Rosinka have begun."

# Chapter 27: Missing Family

"Papa? Papa, please answer!" Soraya cried desperately into the receiver. For the fifth time in a row, she was greeted by a high-pitched ringing sound, then silence.

*Where are you? Please be okay!*

She could faintly hear Ujuu's voice on the other end of the room.

*At least he got a hold of Zaruna.*

She thanked the Gods silently for that, then hung up in defeat before joining her friends. Rhys and Moiya were standing silently next to the younger twin, both leaning forward to listen in on the conversation.

"I'm so glad you can make it to the Matumi Beach Concert and stay for a few weeks," Ujuu breathed, his words brimming with gratitude.

"Yes, me too. Ve're packed, and ve're leaving for Azakua zis afternoon."

Zaruna's voice sounded faint from where Soraya was standing, but she could hear a thick foreign accent.

"My parents already agreed to let you and your family stay with them," Ujuu replied calmly, though his ears twitched anxiously. "You have their address and phone number, so call them when the ship has docked, and they'll pick you all up."

"I vill, I promise."

"Please keep me posted when you can," Ujuu paced the floor, wrapping the long, spiral cord around his fingers. "I love you dearly."

"I love you too. I have ta go now, see you in ah few days."

With shaky hands, Ujuu hung up the receiver.

Soraya was about to ask why they hadn't discussed the kidnappings, but stopped herself. *Anyone could be listening in through the phones, they have to act like they don't know anything.*

"No luck reaching your dad or his friend?" Rhys asked Soraya, his face full of worry.

"Yeah, I don't know where he is or what's going on," Soraya sighed, then thought back to Dr. Athan promising to help her father while she was at school and frowned. *Isn't Yosef supposed to be with him? I hope he's okay too…*

"Hey," Rhys placed his hand on Soraya's shoulder. "Don't panic. Maybe they're out running errands or visiting others and can't hear the phone right now."

"I haven't received any letters from Papa either," Soraya said, dropping her gaze to the floor. "He should have responded by now. Something's wrong."

"Do you have any backup numbers to call?" Moiya asked. "Do you know anyone else's contact information from Rivinsdeep?"

Soraya closed her eyes and thought back to when she worked at Delphi's Diner. Although she had never used the phone there, the girl recalled skimming through the contact information for the restaurant years ago.

"I could try phoning the restaurant…" she murmured.

"Maybe someone there would know something…" Soraya dialed the number from her memory and held her breath.

"Thank you for calling Delphi's Diner," Kalisha's voice sprung cheerfully through the receiver. "Is this for dine in or carry out?"

"Kalisha!" Soraya exclaimed.

"Um, hello? Who is this?" the young woman on the other end asked nervously.

"It's me, Soraya!"

"Oh!" Kalisha laughed. "Hey there! How's school going for you?"

"Oh good, it's great," Soraya couldn't help but feel relieved at hearing her friend's bubbly voice once more. "I hope everything's well in Rivinsdeep?"

"Yes, everything is just as you've left it," the girl could hear the smile on Kalisha's lips.

"Have you seen my Papa or Yosef lately, by chance?"

"No, actually…" there was a slight pause. "I think the last time I saw them was a few days after you left for school."

Soraya's heart thumped loudly in her chest. "I can't get a hold of Papa, and I know Yosef was staying with him the last time we spoke… would it be possible for someone to go to my house and check on them?"

A twinge of guilt shot through her the second the request came out of her mouth. It was an hour-long trek to her home in the Averlore mountains from Rivinsdeep, so asking for a wellness check was no small task.

"Oh yes, absolutely," Kalisha said with confidence. "I'll gather some friends, and we'll all go together in the next hour at the latest. We'll bring medicine and other supplies too, just in case something is wrong."

"Thank you so much!" Soraya cried. "I just want to make

sure he and Yosef are alright. I can't go myself, otherwise I would. The door should be unlocked, but there's a spare key on top of the birdhouse hanging from the porch if you can't get in."

"It's not a problem. Give me Darkwood Academy's number, so I can call you back once I have news."

Soraya gave Kalisha the information before bidding her farewell and hanging up.

"Okay, let's go to Biology now," Rhys suggested gently. "If we hurry, we'll only be a few minutes late."

* * *

The four students were met with Mr. Yung's orange, piercing gaze upon entering the Biology classroom.

"You're all tardy today," he stated gruffly. "That is quite unusual. Please sit down and write out your explanations for why."

Soraya's cheeks stung as she shuffled over to her desk and silently plopped herself into her seat. This was the only teacher who didn't ever seem to crack a smile or tell a joke while teaching.

"The whole class will wait until you have turned your papers in."

Jacquelle sniggered from behind. Soraya did her best to ignore the blond as she scribbled about her father's failing memory and how she couldn't get ahold of him.

*I should add that I asked Rhys, Ujuu and Moiya to stay and help me. I'm the reason why they're late.*

Soraya got up, dropped the note into the wooden box of Mr. Yung's desk, and hurriedly scampered back to her desk. She watched her three friends do the same.

"I want all of you to write an essay on Slow vs. Rapid Evolution," the teacher continued once all the students were seated. "Write the pros and cons for each side. This is a closed book assignment, so I don't expect exact quotes or references, though you may refer to outside sources if you wish."

The teacher glanced at the Shadelkin twins. "Rhys and Ujuu, for example, are prime examples of rapid evolution. We still do not fully understand how Shadelkins came to be."

Rhys' ears flattened as everyone stared at him. Ujuu, on the other hand, lay back in his seat, soaking in the attention.

"It's perfectly fine to reference the mythologies of their ancestors that explain how Zodia Tigress blessed their followers by giving them animalistic features to help them survive their harsh climates," Mr. Yung circled the classroom, his eyes flitting around to each and every student as he continued speaking.

"Just make sure to include the different *scientific* arguments, since that's what we've been studying for the past few weeks."

Mr. Yung paused by Soraya's desk. "Remember to write it in your own words. I'm not impressed with regurgitated information. What matters is that you understand the reasoning behind the two theories and can explain them."

*He's referring to my work...* Soraya sank even lower into her seat and stared at the blank paper in front of her.

*I'll do my best.*

The rest of the class period was spent writing the essay. Before Soraya had time to pen the last word, the bell rang.

"Time's up. Turn in what you've got."

As Soraya attempted to slink away, Mr. Yung beckoned for her by curling his pointer finger. "I need to speak to you and your friends briefly before you all head to your next class."

Rhys, Ujuu, Moiya and Soraya all glanced at each other nervously. Only when the other students had left the room did Mr. Yung clear his throat.

"I had slightly different answers from each of you for why you were tardy, but you were all consistent with Soraya's father not doing well and possibly going missing," he furrowed his thick eyebrows together in concern. "I'm sorry about your situation. Is there any updated news on his whereabouts?"

It was the first time any of them had seen the biology teacher's face soften. Mr. Yung was still frowning, but the sags around his lips were lighter, and the fire behind his orange eyes had been dulled to a warmer, more comforting light.

"Not yet, sir," Soraya sighed, her lip quivering. She hadn't had time to process her grief, but now, tears were building up behind her eyes.

"I can't promise that everything will be alright," the teacher began in a soft tone. "But I can promise that you *won't* be alone dealing with this. You have good friends who care about you, and you always have me and your other teachers to talk to in addition with the school counselors."

He took out a light blue, pre-made note from his desk. After ticking several boxes and signing his name at the bottom, he handed it to the girl. "If you need a day off from school, turn this into the front office, and you won't get penalties for missing any of your classes."

Soraya could hardly believe the note she was holding in her hands, it was as if she had been given gold.

"Don't lose it, I don't give these out very often," Mr. Yung half smiled for a brief moment before his face turned rigid and inscrutable once more.

"Thank you, sir," Soraya bowed lowly to her teacher. Her friends also bowed and murmured their thanks.

The hint of a smile played once more on Mr. Yung's lips. "Of course. None of you will be marked tardy for today. Now, hurry along. If any of you are late for any reason to your next class, tell your teachers to speak with me."

The second the four friends were in the hallway, Ujuu started laughing. "There *is* a way to escape Mr. Trog's class after all!"

"That is really nice to have," Moiya awed while pointing at

Soraya's note. "Keep it somewhere safe, like your locker. Other students would try to steal it if they knew you had it."

The green-eyed Azakuin waved goodbye before rounding a corner and heading off towards her Rosinkin class.

Soraya carefully tucked the note into her dress pocket, which ran deep enough so it wouldn't fall out, and hurried to Ms. Evi's Casmerahn class with Rhys and Ujuu.

*I can now keep up with them*, the girl grinned while staying at the twins' pace with ease. *I wonder if I'll learn Casmerahn faster by fusing with them more often, or if there's a specific spell for absorbing another's language…*

Another pang of guilt shot through her chest as she thought about Kalisha hiking the mountains towards her home. *Gods, please let Papa and Yosef be okay!*

* * *

Although the rest of Soraya's school day was uneventful, she anxiously paced the floor of the girl's bathroom above the dormitory as night took over the sky.

*Why haven't you called me back yet, Kalisha?*

Soraya decided to distract herself by finally washing her gloves in the sink of the girl's bathroom and hanging them to dry on an empty towel rack.

"Are you going to join us for dinner?" Moiya called to her from the stairwell.

"Mow?" Yabo chirped from her shoulder.

"Yes, eventually," Soraya sighed. "Go ahead, I'll catch up soon."

"Okay, if you're sure."

A few minutes after Moiya's light footsteps had disappeared, Soraya could hear another pair of feet ascending the stone stairs, heading her way. Just from how dainty and quiet they were, the girl already knew who it was without having to turn her head.

"Oh? You took off your purity gloves?" Jacquelle's snide voice echoed off the walls behind her. "Does that mean you and Rhys are officially a thing?" she laughed cruelly. "I did hear Moiya last night say you two went on a date. How pathetic that you hooked up with a Casmerahn."

Soraya paused and looked into the blond's sneering face. "You heard us talking last night?" she asked in a calm tone, though her skin crawled with unease.

"There was a loud noise on the balcony that woke me up. I didn't care to look because we had cooking class and I wanted to sleep, but I did hear Moiya's voice…" Jacquelle's grin grew wider, as if she was holding back on something. "I also heard a teacher say something about your father going missing…?"

Soraya's heart skipped a beat. "Do you know something?"

Jacquelle didn't immediately reply. Instead, her expression grew dark as she glared ferociously into Soraya's sky-blue eyes. "He called my father and spoke with him… you must have told him… And that's why…" she stopped herself, as if she were too upset to continue her thoughts.

"What are you even talking about?" Soraya cautiously took a step towards her rival. "When did Papa call your dad?"

Jacquelle forced a sweet smile on her face, causing Soraya to feel ill. "I don't have to tell you that."

"Yes, you do!" Soraya's temper flared from deep within her soul. "My father is missing, and so is his best friend. Any information on when they were last seen or heard would be helpful in finding them!"

The blond simply laughed. "They deserve whatever happens to them."

"This isn't a game!" Soraya's hand flew to Jacquelle's wrist, her fingers wrapping around her arm. "When did my Papa call your father? What day?"

"Don't touch me!" Jacquelle snarled, then tried wriggling her arm away, but Soraya's grip remained tight and unmoving.

"Tell me now, Jacquelle!" Soraya commanded. "I need to know if they're even alive!"

Her words hung in the air. For a brief second, Soraya was hopeful that it would be enough to make Jacquelle see the severity of the situation, but the blond instead slapped her face as hard as she could with her free hand.

"I said, don't touch me!"

Soraya saw red. With her cheek engulfed in flames, the fumes from her internal rage boiling over, and Jacquelle dismissing her father and Yosef's lives, Soraya had had enough.

"Slevautza!" she roared, digging her fingers into Jacquelle's wrist.

A look of horror crossed the blond's face when Soraya sank into her body. A blinding light engulfed their vision, followed by a loud crack, like a firework going off in the sky.

"*You will tell me everything, Jacquelle!*" Soraya hissed within their mind. "*When did Papa call your father? Why are you such a brat? Why are you so evil?*"

Their body flooded with fear, their knees buckled, and they fell to the floor. Jacquelle tried screaming, but Soraya held their mouth shut, her rage overpowering any involuntary movement.

"*What is happening? What did you do? Why can I hear you in my head?*" Jacquelle whimpered.

Soraya ignored her pleas and focused instead on pulling up the blond's memories. "*I don't want my father or his friend to die, Jacquelle! Tell me what you know!*"

"*No!*"

Flashes of a large, roaring fireplace entered their mind. A tall, thin silhouette of a man stood in front of it, his back turned towards them. Jacquelle tried to think of something else, so the memory would disappear, but Soraya clamped onto it.

*"Tell me!"*

"So, I got a phone call from a student's parent. He said you've been reading the files of other students," the man's voice rumbled disapprovingly. "Spreading rumors about them? Ruling the school as a tyrant? I'm very disappointed in you, Jacquelle. You should know better than to do that."

*"Soraya, please stop…"*

The man turned around and glared at Jacquelle with dark and mysterious blue eyes. "Your mother put you up to it, didn't she?"

Anger rose within Jacquelle and Soraya's chest.

"You shouldn't be granting scholarships to foreigners, Dad!" Jacquelle's voice spat from within the memory. "Mother says we should be taking care of our own first!"

"She's wrong, Jacquelle, and so are you."

"I don't have to listen to you! You abandoned me and chose *her* instead!"

Her father's eyes softened for a brief second. "I couldn't take you both in the divorce, and your mother refused to take care of your sister, Jacquelle. I had to choose her, so she wouldn't end up abandoned somewhere…"

"But those foreigners kidnapped her! It's all your fault!" Jacquelle screamed. "You brought them over, and now she's gone!"

Her father went quiet.

"I hate you!" Jacquelle roared. "You never loved me, and you still don't even though I'm the only daughter you have left!"

Her father glared down into her eyes. "You're right, I don't love you. It should have been *you* instead of her."

Soraya and Jacquelle's heart sank within them. A sharp pain rose in their stomach, as though they had been stabbed with a knife.

*"Please stop, Soraya…"* the blond whimpered while

attempting to shove the memory away. "I gave you what you wanted, that was last week on Ignis Diem. Let me go…"

Her voice faded under a wave of memories. There were so many swirling around their head that Soraya feared she'd drown in them.

"Don't disappoint mommy again, dearie."

A tall and thin woman with thick, curly blond hair and dark blue eyes floated into view. "Even though I wanted you rather than your special needs sister, I feel like I'm the one who got the short end of the stick."

*"Mother…"*

The swirling of memories stopped. Only one remained within their head. Instinctively, their hand went to their back, and Soraya felt the healed scars on her thin fingers, and shivered.

*"Please, don't make me relive this!"* Jacquelle cried. *"Please, I'll do anything!"*

Soraya's curiosity was enticed despite the mental agony Jacquelle was in. Part of her was tempted to listen, to leave the memory be, to leave the girl to wallow in her misery, but another thought entered into their head.

*"I can't help you if I don't know what's wrong."*

*"Help me?"* Jacquelle scoffed, yet she couldn't deny the pity and empathy building up within Soraya. *"You actually feel sorry for me? After everything I've done to you and everyone else? Why?"*

*"I'm not going to abandon you like your parents have."*

Their jaw dropped open in shock. Soraya gently grasped onto their other hand.

*"Please, be my friend."*

Jacquelle could no longer deny Soraya's sincerity.

*"Okay… I need help."*

Sorrow and empathy bubbled up within Soraya. *"I am truly sorry that I found out about your situation this way. I didn't mean for this to happen.*"

With all her might, Soraya tried separating their souls, until finally a pit formed in the center of their gut.

Both girls tumbled away from each other. Soraya landed on her stomach, while Jacquelle lay sprawled out on her back.

Soraya immediately hopped to her feet and offered the blond a hand up, but the girl decided to stay seated on the bathroom floor.

"I do need help," Jacquelle said, her voice trembling, her eyes reddening as tears flowed down her cheeks. "I don't know how you read my mind, or how I felt how you were feeling, but I know you really are sorry," she choked, then looked up into Soraya's face. "I'm also sorry. For everything."

Soraya sat down in front of Jacquelle, her eyes filling with tears. "It's alright, I forgive you. And I really meant it, about us being friends."

Jacquelle wiped her eyes using her sleeves. "O-okay…"

"You don't have to tell me about that memory if you don't want to either. I understand. And again, I'm really sorry-"

"Stop apologizing already!" the blond snapped. "It's fine, really," Jacquelle paused and studied Soraya's concerned expression, then let out a long sigh. "I know all about your situation. I might as well tell you about what happened to me…"

## Chapter 28: Mother Knows Best

*Jacquelle gazed out over Matumi, sliding one hand slowly down the cool glass surface of her bedroom window. The sun kissed cobblestone streets below were filled with Azakuins bustling about their day. Shopkeepers stood outside their businesses with carts full of steaming hot food fresh from their ovens, beckoning tourists to sample their stuffed pastries and buttery scones.*

*Even from the third floor of her mother's house, Jacquelle could smell the cinnamon and various berries baked into their flaky breads. Her mouth watered as she stared enviously at a group of children who had been handed small slivers to taste. The blond licked her cracked lips when the children eagerly shoved the portions into their mouths. Jacquelle frowned at being reminded of her parched throat and empty, aching belly.*

*"When is mother coming home tonight?" she wondered, glancing at the circular clock hanging above the door. Her stomach growled, reminding her that she hadn't eaten since noon.*

*Her private tutor, Ms. Gwendal Makos, came in the morning just before her mother left for work and looked after her until fifteen o'clock in the afternoon. She was a short, portly woman who seemed to only like silence and repetitive routines. She kept Jacquelle's weekly schedule consistent with reading books, writing, eating lunch, swimming laps in their indoor pool, and sewing. The only escape the blond had to this never ending cycle was in playing music.*

*The girl looked over at her pristine, lavender wooded cello. It stood proudly on a stand next to her bed, polished and poised. The more melodies she memorized, the more Ms. Demarko would take her around town to show off her skills to other adults. Jacquelle would play at fancy restaurants every weekend and use her cello case as a tip jar. Her mother eagerly emptied out the contents onto the kitchen table and hungrily counted every last cent after each show.*

*"You're going to make mommy rich," she would squeal in delight while pocketing the cash and coins. "Just keep practicing, my little prodigy, and we'll be set to travel the world together."*

*The second Ms. Makos left, Jacquelle swiftly picked up her beloved instrument and practice for hours to eat away at the long afternoons, so her mother would seemingly come home sooner. However, Ms. Demarko usually entered the house well past the girl's bedtime, accompanied by strangers.*

*"Mom, can you play with me?" Jacquelle would ask even though she already knew what the answer was.*

*"Not right now," Ms. Demarko would say. "I have to entertain my friends. Stay out of our hair, or I'll lock you in your room."*

*Jacquelle was tired of being alone. She often felt like a princess trapped in a tall tower and wished for someone to come in and whisk her away. After her empty stomach growled in protest once more, the girl walked out into the hallway, past a closed door.*

*Krista...*

*Despite knowing she wouldn't be caught, her hand hovered timidly over the golden handle. Her twin's room was now extra storage space for whatever her mother bought on her shopping sprees. Yet, a small bit of hope of seeing Krista again still lived within her, even if it was buried under the grim reality of her father and sister moving away just a year prior.*

*Jacquelle flinched away from the doorknob and pushed all thoughts of her twin aside. Instead, the girl made her way towards the kitchen. After running down two flights of stairs, she eagerly flung open the refrigerator only to find an empty jug of milk and a half-eaten red apple inside.*

*Sighing in disappointment, she plucked nature's candy and devoured it. Jacquelle tried imagining stuffing her face with a pastry like those kids were outside her house, but the crisp crunches of the apple being torn to shreds by her teeth was a reminder of how her pathetic snack was nothing like the soft baked goodies down the street.*

*Maybe, I can go outside and have samples like they were having…*

*Jacquelle stiffened up at her own thought. Her mother would have her head if she stepped foot off their property without adult supervision. And yet, her stomach whined loudly, begging her for more food.*

*She won't be home anytime soon. Surely, I can go and come back without her ever noticing.*

*After shoving on her black shoes and grabbing a spare house key, Jacquelle slipped out onto the porch and locked the front door.*

*I won't be gone long.*

*Jacquelle started down the sloping street towards the bakery a few buildings down, her face and arms warmed by the sun's blazing heat. Her home stood atop a rolling hill in the very heart of Matumi, a prized and coveted location since everything they could ever want or need was within walking distance.*

*A light breeze slid through Jacquelle's hair, the salty air tickling the girl's dry throat with each breath she took. Her eyes flitted towards the sun hovering over the sparkling, bright blue Valtic Ocean in the horizon, then back towards her destination.*

*As she approached the empty bakery cart, she paused and watched the shopkeeper struggle to pull it back into his shop.*

*"Excuse me," Jacquelle piped up timidly. "Can I have a sample?"*

*The man's blood-red eyes gazed down at her with sympathy.*

*"Null plus," he said sadly while shaking his head. "Sorry, puella. More soon, I make," he added in broken Azakuin.*

*Jacquelle slowly sank into an empty chair in front of the bakery. She placed both hands on her belly and bent over in her seat, hoping to muffle the low gurgling noises arising from her.*

*"You hungry?"*

*A boy with darker skin and midnight hair approached her, his vermilion eyes burning with curiosity.*

*"Yes, very," Jacquelle pouted pitifully. "I haven't had anything in hours."*

*"Hold on," he smiled before disappearing into the bakery. Within seconds, he brought back a buttered blueberry scone and handed it to her. "This will fill you up."*

*"Will I get in trouble for eating this?" Jacquelle asked suspiciously, her golden eyebrows raised in apprehension.*

*"No, my pater owns the shop. You asked for a sample, but from the sounds of it, I think you need more than that."*

*"Okay then…" the girl didn't waste any time tucking in. She took a bite into the soft, creamy bread and moaned with pleasure. "Thank you," she managed to mumble between inhaling pieces and swallowing.*

*"Of course," the boy beamed. "What's your name?"*

*"Jacquelle Demarko," she waited for the morsel to melt in her mouth before adding, "what's yours?"*

*"Akoni Pan."*

"Did you love him?" Soraya asked, interrupting Jacquelle's narration.

"Well…" The blond's face flushed for a second. "He used to walk me home and visit me every afternoon, bringing me pastries and baked goods, and he'd chuck rocks at the window late at night, so we could talk while my Mother was busy entertaining her guests…"

Jacquelle's blood ran cold at the thought of her mother, and she squashed the tiny, fluttery feelings that had escaped from her heart.

"She caught us."

*"Jacquelle!" her mother's sharp cry cut through the girl's cello playing. "Why did you bring garbage into my house?"*

*Akoni and Jacquelle spun around in alarm. Ms. Demarko stood in the doorway towering over them, glaring with venomous hatred at the boy.*

*"Y-you're early, mother," Jacquelle whispered in fright.*

*Ms. Demarko scooped up one of her daughter's pearly pink purses, opened it wide, and poured the contents of Jacquelle's jewelry box inside. "Why did you invite a thief into our home?" she snapped while forcefully thrusting the bag into the boy's arms.*

*Akoni's beautiful red eyes widened in shock, and he immediately dropped the purse onto the floor and slowly inched backwards towards the window. Jacquelle knew there was nowhere for him to run.*

*"H-he's not garbage, or a thief," Jacquelle stuttered, fighting to steady her shaking voice. "He's m-my friend."*

*A crooked, insane smile spread across her mother's face, a murderous flame igniting behind her dark blue eyes. She drew a whip out of her purse and handed it to her daughter. "Hit him with this."*

*"N-no." Jacquelle shrank away from her mother and the weapon.*

*"Excuse me?" Ms. Demarko cracked the whip loudly over their heads. Jacquelle turned away, shielding her face, but a sharp sting fell across her lower back, causing her to cry aloud in pain.*

*"You shouldn't be around demon eyed freaks, they're beneath you," her mother grinned, her teeth glistening with a menacing glow under her shadowed face. "Either you get punished, or that piece of garbage does. What will it be?" she asked, placing the leather cord into Jacquelle's shaking hands.*

"I- I whipped him," the blond admitted to Soraya, tears forming in her eyes. "He bled so much…"

She watched the orange-haired girl shiver at the revelation.

*Jacquelle stared at the faded red pools on her carpet near the window. His blood had seeped deep into her floor. No matter how hard she had scrubbed away at them, she knew those stains would be there forever.*

*"Are you going to sit and waste time staring, or are you going to practice your cello?" Ms. Demarko barked from behind, startling her. "I paid a lot of money for you to learn that instrument."*

*"I practiced enough today," Jacquelle replied stiffly.*

*"Don't talk back to me," Ms. Demarko hissed. "And stop feeling sorry for that Casmerahn, he got what he deserved."*

*"But, did he really deserve that?" Jacquelle dared to wonder aloud. Her mother clicked her tongue, her eyes burning into her daughter's skull.*

*"There aren't many blue-eyed Etherians left in our country," Ms. Demarko placed her slender fingers upon Jacquelle's golden locks, making her child cringe in fear. "You are special, too special to be meddling with red eyed foreigners."*

*"But why?"*

*"Because they're the reason blue eyes are going extinct. Don't mingle with them, don't associate with them, you are better than them, do you understand?"*

*"Yes, but-"*

*"I brought you into this world," her mother whispered into her daughter's ear. "And I can take you out of it. You may be rare, but I can always replace you if I have to, so don't disappoint me."*

*Jacquelle's voice trembled. "Y-yes m-mother."*

*"If that demon eyed freak ever comes back, report him for breaking in and attempting to steal your jewelry," Ms. Demarko's dark blue eyes twitched in irritation when her daughter hesitated to reply.*

*"Got it?" she barked, causing her daughter to jump.*

*"Y-yes ma'am!"*

*"Very good, now play. I want to hear your cello fill this house with music."*

*Under the piercing gaze of her mother, Jacquelle reached for her instrument, her arms weak and shaky while she unsteadily drew her bow across the strings. Ms. Demarko, satisfied, left her daughter to practice.*

* * *

"Wow…" Soraya said when Jacquelle went silent. "Your mother is really horrible. I'm so sorry you had to go through that."

The blond remained quiet, but her hand went to her lower

back once more, her fingertips brushing over the once flayed skin.

Soraya noticed and furrowed her eyebrows in concern. "You should live with Papa and I instead," she suggested.

Jacquelle laughed, but for once, it wasn't full of sarcasm. "The law doesn't work that way. I can't just leave them, I'm not an adult yet."

"Well, maybe if you tell one of the teachers about her, then-"

"No!" Jacquelle cried, cutting her off. "My Mom will make life worse for me if I tell on her. If you're really sorry, then you won't say anything."

Soraya frowned, but nodded. "I won't tell, I promise."

Jacquelle's face softened. "Good."

Soraya was about to say something else, but her stomach let out a small gurgle. "We need to go downstairs before everyone starts wondering where we are," she suggested while standing up and brushing off her dress. "Let's go eat."

"Okay," Jacquelle agreed. "But we're not sitting together at dinner."

"Fine by me," Soraya smiled, then offered Jacquelle her hand.

The blond hesitated, but decided to take it. Soraya hoisted her back onto her feet.

"It would be weird to everyone else if we were suddenly best friends," Soraya added.

"But… we are friends now… right?"

"Of course we are!" Soraya exclaimed and looked passionately into her midnight blue eyes. "I'm not abandoning you. Ever."

Jacquelle suddenly threw her arms around Soraya, pulling her into a tight hug. "You mean it?"

Soraya was slightly surprised by her former foe's actions,

but she relaxed her shoulders and squeezed her new friend back. "I promise."

After hugging for a few seconds, the blond awkwardly let go and shuffled away, her face beet red in embarrassment.

"Um, don't forget your stupid purity gloves," Jacquelle said while pointing at them, her face still glowing, her eyes shifting to the floor. "They should be dry by now."

"Oh yeah, thank you." Soraya smiled. She couldn't help but stare at the blond in wonder. This once confident and rude girl was now attempting to be nice.

"You're cute when you're kind," Soraya beamed.

"What?" Jacquelle's dark blue eyes widened in shock.

"I like this new you."

"Shut up!" Jacquelle retorted, but regret immediately crossed her face.

Soraya just laughed. "Come on, let's go."

# Chapter 29: New Friend, New Foes

"Are you okay?"

Soraya was met with Moiya's emerald gems staring intently into her eyes.

"Yes, sorry I was late, I got caught up in a conversation with Jacquelle."

Rhys's ruby gaze swiftly locked onto the blond haired student. She was sitting in her usual dinner spot, occasionally stealing small glances towards their group.

"Did she bully you?" he asked calmly, his knuckles cracking loudly beneath the table.

"No, she told me that Papa called her father last week on Ignis Diem."

Rhys went silent for a moment as he mulled over the news. "There's no way she gave that information to you willingly. What did she ask from you in return?"

"Um..." Soraya didn't want to lie. "She wants to be my friend."

Six bulging eyeballs stared at her in shock.

"I'm sorry, did I hear you correctly?" Ujuu asked, stunned by the unexpected news.

"It's clearly a trap," Rhys growled.

"Surely she's lying!" Moiya gasped.

"No, I mean it," Soraya shifted her stance. "I know about her past now, and she's sorry for what she's done."

Rhys and Moiya quickly exchanged concerned looks before drilling into her with their worried stares.

"You didn't… did you?" the Casmerahn boy asked, his fingers nervously drumming against his tall glass of apple cider.

"I did…" Soraya winced when Rhys' face fell.

"Why?" hissed Moiya. "What if she tries to blackmail you?"

"She won't," Soraya stated adamantly. "I'm confident she won't tell anyone."

"You do realize who you're talking about, right?" Ujuu piped up in a gentle tone. "The mean, rude, snobby rich kid over there who's been giving us all a hard time?"

"I know it sounds odd, but she wants to be my friend."

Rhys bent forward and covered his forehead with one hand. Moiya closed her eyes and shook her head, and Ujuu exhaled slowly as his legs jittered unevenly against the wooden floor.

"I really hope you're right," Rhys whispered between his fingers. "I'm not sure what to do if she tries anything, but we might be able to think of a backup plan."

"Ms. Thenayu?"

All four friends swiveled their heads simultaneously. Runolio, the pale, red haired receptionist, was standing behind them. "There's a phone call for you from Kalisha. Please come with me."

Soraya's chest tightened. *Did she find my father and Yosef?*

* * *

"Hey, it's Soraya."

"Hi…"

Soraya could tell from Kalisha's quivering voice that her friend had unpleasant news to share.

"We looked everywhere for them, but it's as if they

vanished."

*Oh no… no no no…*

"We searched both of their houses, so that's why it took so long to get back to you. The good news is, there are no signs that a struggle took place. There were some missing food supplies, however, so maybe they're traveling together."

Soraya's jaw ached from gritting her teeth together so tightly. "They should have said something to somebody, or left a note!" her voice raised in exasperation. "What if they're in trouble, and we can't help them because we don't know where they are?"

"I feel the same way," Kalisha sounded as if her heart was breaking. "We're going to keep looking and alert neighboring towns to keep an eye out for them. I'm not sure what more we can do. I'm so sorry…"

"It's not your fault," Soraya reassured her friend despite her stomach sloshing around unsteadily. "Thanks for everything. Hopefully, they'll come back soon."

"I'm going to give Yosef a good scolding when I see him next," Kalisha laughed shakily. "He should know better…" her voice faded, and Soraya assumed she was drifting into her own thoughts.

"Papa called the principal of the school on Ignis last week," the girl said to fill the growing gap of silence. "I hope that information helps in some way."

"It's something to work with. We'll keep looking, and I'll call you if we have any updates, okay?"

"Thank you."

Soraya's three friends and pet stood silently by, each of their faces contorted with concern at the news.

"Mow?" Yabo cooed loudly from Moiya's shoulder.

"Yes, they're missing alright," Soraya hung her head and stared at the floor, "I will find them," she vowed under her breath. "You're right, let's just think through everything and form a plan first," Rhys suggested in a calm, matter of fact tone. "There's a chance they left to meet up with someone privately."

He took Soraya's hands within his own, patting them with his fingers. "Think about your powers, and how special they are. This could be a secret meeting to discuss that."

"I don't think Papa realizes what I can do," Soraya whispered. "Why else would he send me here, where Mülock can contact and possess me every half moon? He wouldn't purposefully do that to me… I don't think so, at least…"

"We also need to test your limits before you do anything else," Moiya interjected. "And it'll be safest if you stay until the end of the school year. If your father and Yosef aren't back by then, I'll ask my parents about you living with us."

"Moiya, that's so sweet," Soraya smiled weakly. Rhys suddenly pulled her protectively into his arms.

"I'll ask my parents too, just in case," the boy said before whispering into her ear. "There's no way you're going through all of this without me."

Soraya threw her arms around him and squeezed tightly back. "You're the best."

"Um, I hate to remind you, but Zaruna and her parents are already staying with our parents…" Ujuu laughed nervously. "We don't have enough room for everyone."

"We'll figure it out." Rhys said before firmly planting a kiss on top of Soraya's forehead. Both Ujuu and Moiya awed aloud as the girl's cheeks lit up like a flame dancing on a candle.

"Took you long enough," Ujuu smirked. "And I'm really excited to see what those abilities are. Astros can't arrive soon enough," his smile faded as his candy apple eyes drifted towards the phone hanging on the wall. "And I hope I hear from Zaruna soon."

"Us too," Moiya agreed in a solemn tone. "Let's make sure Soraya eats dinner before we go to bed."

Soraya looked at her three friends in adoration. "I'm grateful for all of you."

"Same with you," Rhys hugged her one more time, and they headed off altogether towards the Dining Hall.

* * *

"Babella, tis true, the wretched queen twas using thee all along."

"Why wouldst thou save me, Annabelle?" Jacquelle's lips trembled. "After all the pain I have wrought…"

"Please, speaketh no more of it," Soraya continued to read passionately. "Anon, thou art free from her tyranny. I trust thee shall be a valorous ruler over thy kingdom."

"May the Gods above bless and be with thee forevermore."

"And also with thee," Soraya looked down into the book and realized there was only one word left to read aloud. "Fin."

She was met with loud claps from her friends and the other students in her Azakuin Literature class. Jacquelle smiled and gracefully curtsied at the applause.

"Bow with me," she beckoned Soraya to follow suit and lightly pulled the girl closer to herself.

"And that was the last chapter of *Taming of the Tempest.* You both nailed your parts," Mrs. Sworvski exclaimed joyfully. "Go ahead and sit back in your seats."

The teacher waited patiently for the two girls to sit in their respective areas before continuing on with her lecture. "Do you see how much more fun reading is when you act out stories and slip into character?"

The bell rang, and the students immediately sprang to their feet.

"Study the new vocabulary we learned, there will be a test next Lunas!" Mrs. Sworvski yelled over the rustling of papers and books being shoved into unzipping backpacks. "Enjoy your weekend!" she called after her students while they swiftly left the room and dashed to their next classes.

"I didn't expect that story to have a happy ending," Ujuu said thoughtfully. "The plays we usually read are much more tragic and depressing than that."

"It was a nice switch of pace," Rhys agreed before turning his attention over to Soraya. "I noticed Jacquelle acting nicer towards you. I truly hope you're right about her, just don't let your guard down."

"Right, I understand," She thought back to all the times the blond had been mean to the Leyo twins and Moiya. *If she's truly sorry, she'll be kind towards my friends too…*

"So far this week, Jacquelle hasn't really been mean to anyone," Moiya chimed in. "What did you do to her, exactly?" she asked while shoving her shoulder playfully.

"I promised not to say anything," Soraya replied.

Moiya looked hurt, but allowed the topic to fade from her lips.

The rest of Auras sped by without any incidents, until Soraya arrived in the Orchestra room later that afternoon.

"Class, I have some good and bad news," Ms. Katia paced in front of her students, her hands behind her back. "The Matumi Beach Concert is being moved to a different day. We are now expected to perform on Mazula 5th."

The entire orchestra murmured among themselves.

"That's too soon," Soraya overheard Emrose whisper to Vamera despite them sitting on the opposite side of the room. "None of the other sections can play through their parts perfectly."

Vamera's violet eyes rested sadly on the girl. "She could use that extra month of practicing, she's almost there. Jacquelle said so yesterday."

Emrose's dark brown eyes widened in surprise. "I didn't

expect her to ever compliment Soraya. Do you think they're becoming friends?"

"I hope so, because I can hardly stand being around Jacquelle anymore," Vamera's voice was barely audible, but Soraya could hear it thanks to her acquired Shadelkin hearing. She eyed Rhys and Ujuu, who both had also picked up on the conversation. Rhys kept his expression unreadable, but Ujuu looked genuinely surprised.

"I understand that takes away four extra weeks of preparation," Ms. Katia continued sadly. "But I believe we can do it. Our class has improved greatly on our finale song overall."

"Oh no!" Ujuu exclaimed while tugging at his ears. "I just realized I have to make *another* commercial promoting the correct date!" he slumped down into his seat and loudly blew his bangs out of his face.

"Can you play on air again?" he pleaded with Rhys. "You need to do something cool sounding to grab everyone's attention."

Soraya noticed her former rival listening in on their conversation and had an idea. "Can Jacquelle and Rhys play their duet on the radio?" she asked excitedly.

"Yeah, good luck getting her to do that," Ujuu rolled his eyes to the ceiling.

"Hey, don't speak for me!" the blond snapped from her seat, startling the three of them. "Of course I'll play the stupid duet over the radio if it means salvaging our concert!" She swished her blond curls over her shoulder and raised her bow into the air, as if wielding a sword. "Just tell me what time and day, and I'll be in that radio room, ready to play."

The younger twin scrunched up his face in thought. "Early tomorrow afternoon, thirteen o'clock sharp. Will that work for you?"

"Yes. I'll be there," Jacquelle huffed. "Rhys, you'd better be ready," She pointed her bow at him. "Because we're going to rock."

Soraya wanted to laugh at how ridiculously over the top the

blond was behaving, but held it in. *She's trying so hard to be friendly, don't make her feel stupid and self-conscious.*

"Why, Ms. Demarko, thank you for offering to do that," Ms. Katia said, the corners of her jade eyes crinkling.

"Well, duh, of course," Jacquelle placed a hand on her hip and pursed her lips together. "Everyone will come out if they hear the duet on the radio."

Without warning, Rhys raised his hand.

"Yes, Mr. Leyo?" the teacher called upon him.

"Why is the date being changed, if you don't mind me asking?"

"Some of Magicorp's leaders are attending and offered to fund it. That was the only day that worked for them."

Rhys maintained his calm composure, but the air turned cold around them. "Did they give any other reason for why they're coming out?" he asked.

"Yes, actually. They're interested in investigating the purified patch of land in the middle of our track and field," their teacher mused. "They also wish to do a demonstration of magic and encourage more students to become Arcanologists."

Soraya's body seized up as several horrid thoughts crossed her mind. *Does this have anything to do with why Papa and Yosef are missing? Do they suspect me?*

"Thank you for that information," Rhys replied in a steady voice, but his copper skin turned pale when he glanced back at Soraya and Ujuu. "We don't have a lot of time left before they arrive," he whispered. "We need to step up our planning."

"Tomorrow, let's get through the rest of Zinvi's book," Soraya suggested, her hands quivering on her lap. The boys both gave her a thumbs up.

*I have to learn how to control myself and figure out what my limitations are… I have to get rid of the rest of my Water Magic tomorrow too!*

## Chapter 30: New Spells

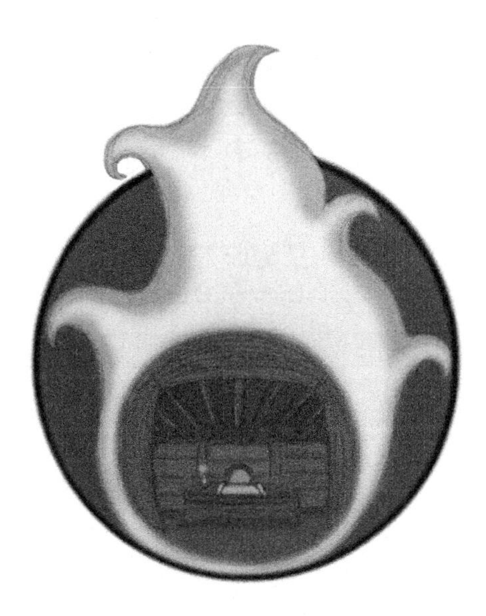

It was Yunula first, 3095, the beginning of the new year. The blazing ball of heat was slowly plummeting into the murky depths of the Valtic Ocean, its dimming rays illuminating the twilight sky in brilliant oranges, pinks and purples.

Five figures descended a long trail of steps built into the steep, rocky cliffs overlooking the hidden crescent moon cove below. The clacking of their shoes across the smooth stones were muffled under the loud echoes from the crashing waves against the sand below.

"Hey, how did the new radio commercial go?" Soraya asked the twins between breaths. "Did Jacquelle actually play the duet?"

Moiya trailed behind with Yabo sitting on her shoulder, but she cocked her head and leaned forward to better listen in on the conversation.

"She did," Rhys quickly stated. "She did well."

"No fights or drama, surprisingly, but she did want to hang out with all of us," Ujuu added while exhaling. "We told her today wouldn't work out…" his eyelids twitched when his older brother shot him a glare.

"But he said next weekend would," Rhys muttered.

"I had to buy us some time!" Ujuu gasped. "I felt a little bad. She's been nicer lately, still pushy, but trying. Maybe, we should give her a chance."

"You didn't have to give her a specific timeframe."

"I panicked, okay?" Ujuu cried out in exasperation. "I never thought in a million years she'd ask to hang out with us, give me a break!"

"It's obvious Jacquelle just wants to hang with Soraya," Moiya piped up. "Especially with Vamera and Emrose distancing themselves, Jacquelle doesn't have anyone else who would want to be friends with her."

"Exactly," Rhys turned his head and gave a brief nod towards her. "Soraya needs to figure out the Apollryük spells before some of the most powerful Etherians in our country pay our school a visit. Every second now counts. They could arrive well before then and start observing us students, disguised as talent scouts or other officials, for all we know."

The four students and pandacoon finally reached the sandy shore and basked in the warmth of the star's light. They stood at the edge of where their world ended and the life of the sea began.

"I read through the rest of the book," Rhys said while facing the cliffs so the sun shone on the pages he was holding. "There are only two spells left for Soraya to learn," his red eyes glowed through his shadowed features, his long braid flowing in the light breeze. "Mülock gave her one that wasn't in here, which means there's probably even more than what Zinvi wrote down."

Moiya clapped her hands with a loud smack and held them together. "I've been waiting all week to see this!" she exclaimed, her lush ponytails tossing and tumbling about like strings on a wind chime.

"Me too!" Ujuu grinned while bouncing in place on the soft sandy shore. "I'm tired of being left out of all the fun."

Yabo sniffed at a shell and nearly fell backwards when it started moving on its own. Seeing the new creature as prey, the pandacoon crouched down, his ears back, and silently followed behind the tiny creature scuttling across the sand. Just as the sand crab started burrowing itself into the ground, Yabo pounced.

"Mow?" he chirped aloud, lifting his inky black paws and seeing nothing beneath them.

Soraya smirked at her pandacoon's cuteness, but reeled herself back into focusing on Rhys. "Before you show me anything, tell me what the spell is supposed to do first," she said, her voice filled with unease. "I don't want to hurt anyone."

"I understand," the Shadelkin boy flashed her a half smile before his face turned serious once more. "I figured we could start with this one because it translates to shadow walk. If it's what I think, then you might be able to turn into a shadow. That would help you with sneaking out every half moon."

"Turn into a shadow?" Ujuu's toothy grin spread even wider. "That sounds so cool!" He and Moiya stood a few feet away and watched in anticipation, their eyes reflecting the setting sun.

"Ready?" Rhys asked, his ears twitching.

The girl nodded, her eyebrows furrowed together, her vision focused on the depiction of Mülock etched into the book's cover. "Show me the spell."

Rhys flipped the novel around, and Soraya's eyes locked onto the new Apollryük symbol. Just like the previous two spells, it transformed itself into Azakuin in her mind's eye.

"Shygerü," she read. The second the word leapt off her tongue, a great pressure formed on top of her head, as if something invisible was pushing her down. Her body sank into the sand like a rock cast into a lake.

"Did it work?" Soraya tried to say, except her mouth had disappeared. The girl found herself floating on her back, facing the twilight sky. It was as if she were underwater, weightless and free. Instantly, all three of her friends rushed over and came into view, each one staring down at her with jaws hanging open in awe.

"Gods! It worked!" Ujuu gasped.

"You're actually a shadow!" Moiya exclaimed.

"Are you okay…?" Rhys asked, his voice full of concern.

Soraya tried once more to speak, but after a few seconds of silence, she settled on giving a thumbs up in reply. Where her lungs should've been blossomed a burning sensation, a pain similar to holding one's breath.

"Mow?" Yabo leapt on top of her silhouette, desperately digging away at the sand to try and reach his guardian.

Soraya didn't feel his sharp claws, nor did she feel his weight upon her stomach. She wanted to tell him she was alright, but still couldn't talk, so she reached for her pandacoon's shadow. As her flattened fingertips wrapped around it, she noted his shadow was velvety, like the petals of a flower. When she gently lifted her pandacoon's silhouette off of herself, he suddenly lifted into the air, held up by her invisible arms.

"Merow!" Yabo cried aloud in fear, his beady black eyes widening in shock.

"Whoa!" Ujuu's eyes bulged from his sockets. "That is so creepy and cool!"

Soraya put down Yabo's shadow. Her poor pet, confused and terrified, skittered off the sand and clambered up Moiya's dress.

"It's okay," she comforted him with kisses on his fuzzy forehead once he reached her shoulder. "Soraya would never hurt you, she's just testing her powers."

"Hey, grab onto me please," Rhys said and held out his

hand towards his girlfriend's silhouette. "I want to see something."

Soraya obliged and gingerly clasped onto his hand's shadow.

"Fascinating," he mused. "My fingers feel cold, like it was dipped in ice water, similar to those stories where others claim to have been touched by ghosts."

He looked back down at Soraya's silhouetted form in wonder. "Go towards the stairs. I wonder if you can climb them in that form."

The burning sensation in Soraya's chest slowly inched its way across her entire body, but the girl ignored it. Instead, she tried taking a step forward, but ended up gliding across the ground like water flowing down an inclined stream.

*How do I control myself like this?* Soraya thought as she smoothly skidded up the stairs, like a backwards slide. *I slip off everything like oil, it's so weird.*

She turned off the stone steps and barreled across the cliff wall, much to the surprise of her friends. *It's almost like sledding in the snow, except I can go anywhere I want.*

A smile would have appeared on her face if she still had lips as the girl headed towards the cave entrance near the end of the crescent moon cove. *What happens if I go into the dark?*

The second she slipped inside, her consciousness expanded across the entirety of the rocky cavern. For a brief moment, she was aware of every crack and crevice and could picture the interior inside her head like a map. There was a pool glowing from multicolored algae in the very back of the cave, but other than that, she was completely alone.

The flame eating up her form finally hit the edges of her fingertips and toes, causing her to shake violently. Another pressure formed on the top of her head, pulling her up by her hair. A raging headache sprung from her forehead as she expanded out of her shadowy, two-dimensional form and lay face up on the soft, cold sand.

"Where are you?" Rhys called from the cave's entrance. His voice sounded calm, but his ears were fluttering around like crazy on his head.

"I'm here!" she managed to gasp. "I'm alright!"

Soraya lifted herself off her back and cradled her head in her hands, lifting her knees for extra support. "That was fun, but now I'm seeing stars."

"Yo, that was incredible!" laughed Ujuu, his voice echoing around the cave walls. "Okay, I believe all of you now, not that I didn't before, but this confirms it, one hundred percent!"

Yabo landed on the floor with a soft thud next to his owner, chirping loudly as he desperately rubbed his face into her side.

"Sorry for scaring you," the girl pulled her pet into her arms.

"You lasted like that for almost five minutes," Moiya grinned. "Did you want to wait on trying the last spell?" she asked while kneeling down beside her friend. "We don't want you to hurt or tire yourself out."

"I need another minute, but I must do it today," Soraya managed to look up at her friends. "I've noticed that after I try them once, I have better control of when I want to use it again next time,"

She glanced down at her hands. "Rhys, you're right, becoming a shadow means I can slip out to the purified land unnoticed."

"True, but if Magicorp elites are coming out to investigate, we have to be prepared for the worst case scenarios," Rhys frowned. "They might take away those plants to further study them, or worse, threaten to burn them unless they give information on who healed them…"

The four of them went silent as they pondered over his

words.

"What if the symbol of the Gods can protect you?" Moiya murmured thoughtfully. "You were touching the tree when Mülock was speaking to you, right?"

"Yes, but not the whole time…" Soraya said while stroking her pet's fur.

"That relic is easy to buy," Moiya mused. "They're sold at every church and can be worn as a ring or necklace. Maybe the local priest could bless one for you."

"It's worth a try," Soraya shrugged her shoulders. "I can buy one tomorrow at the church Mr. Thuron attends. He said it was close to the school campus."

"That's perfect!" Moiya cooed. "And we can hear him sing in the choir too."

"You should hear Rhys sing, his voice is so lovely," Soraya gazed up at her boyfriend in adoration.

"Th-this is not a competition," Rhys stuttered, his cheeks flushed as he looked away. Ujuu rolled his eyes at his older brother acting self-conscious.

A sudden thought struck Soraya, one she couldn't help but blurt out. "I can fuse with other Etherians, what about plants and animals?"

She thought about the purified patch of land. *Could I keep some grass in a pot and bring it into the girl's dormitory? Would fusing with it be enough to fight back against the demon?*

Rhys stroked his chin and paced in circles around her. "Maybe, I honestly don't know what your limits are."

"Would you try it on Yabo?" Moiya asked, her teeth biting her lower lip.

"And would it hurt him?" Ujuu chimed in, equally concerned.

"I don't know if I'd ever try it on Yabo, but he should be

fine…" Soraya looked up at the younger twin and remembered he hadn't seen or experienced fusing souls like her other friends had.

"What if we did the Slevautza spell with all four of us first?" Moiya suggested. "We should see how that goes. I think it would be more difficult to fuse with plants and animals since they're genetic makeup is different from ours."

Rhys listened silently as he turned the pages of the book. "What do you want to do? Fuse with all of us at the same time, or try the last spell?"

Soraya pondered her options for a moment while standing up. "Let's fuse altogether first. Ujuu should be filled in on everything too."

Rhys put the book down and held onto Soraya's right hand. Moiya placed Yabo on the ground a few feet away before holding onto Soraya's left hand. Ujuu held onto his brother.

"Slevautza."

A bright light glowed from Soraya's heart as she turned transparent and sank into Rhys. The light expanded, swallowing all four of them before a loud crack, like a clap of thunder, pierced the air and echoed around the cave.

"Did it work?" their mouth moved, and four voices spoke in unison. Soraya looked down at their hands, which were much larger and darker toned, and unsheathed their long, thin claws.

"Cool!" Ujuu's voice slipped out.

"Merow!" Yabo rubbed himself against their leg, purring loudly, and they quickly retracted their nails.

"He knows it's us," laughed Moiya as they gently pat his back. "I assumed he'd be scared of how we look."

Soraya filled Ujuu in on everything that had transpired through her memories. He took it all in, including Rhys and Moiya's perspectives.

"Holy Gods," Ujuu exclaimed. "Mülock is evil! There has to

be a way of hacking his brain and seeing what he sees!"

"The last spell has to do with telepathically communicating to others," Rhys chimed in. "I'm not sure what's going to happen since the book was so vague on details for how the spell works, but it has to be tried as well."

Rhys, Ujuu and Moiya felt Soraya's consciousness slip away from their mind. She focused her energy on creating a hole within their stomach. An empty, nauseous wave bubbled up inside them. Only when it felt like bursting out of their mouths did they fall apart and roll backwards from one another.

"You're getting better at controlling the fusions," Rhys beamed at her after brushing the sand off of himself. Only after noticing her expression did his teeth disappear. "What's wrong?"

"If this last spell has to do with communicating to others through their mind, then I need to be alone when trying it," Soraya stated adamantly, a fierce determination glowing in her eyes. "I can't risk Mülock knowing who any of you are, he'd surely hunt you all down."

"Understood," Rhys handed her the folded book by placing her fingers on the page she needed to read. "Don't look at it until we're out of the cave," he said, then kissed her cheek, causing butterflies to flutter around her stomach.

Soraya watched her three friends exit out into the starlit sky. Her headache was gone, but her whole body ached as if she had been running a marathon. The purging souls spell came to mind, but she quickly dismissed that thought. She didn't want to hurt anything else to rejuvenate her energy.

*Here we go, the last spell in the book…* Soraya's night vision had greatly improved from fusing with the twins, so she was able to read the last Apollryük spell with ease.

"Telpathia."

The vision in her left eye became pitch black, while her

right eye continued to see the surrounding cave. Startled by the sudden change in perception, Soraya swiveled her head around, and spotted a bright blue flame of two different hues hovering in the darkness of her left eye.

She cautiously approached to get a better look. Within the floating fire was an orb, like a crystal ball. The girl cupped her hands around it without touching the crackling flames. In her left eye, it levitated above her open palms. In her right eye, her hands were empty.

"So many errands to run, so little time."

A male voice as calm as the open sea arose from the orb. Curious, Soraya leaned her head in to better hear what was going on.

"Please, let me go…" another voice arose, this one sniveling in fear. The girl could just make out a room with windows facing the ocean within the floating sphere, though whether it was the Valtic or another, she couldn't tell.

"And let you kidnap more kids? Yeah right," scoffed the first. "I know what you've done, I'm never letting you leave."

"Then p-please k-kill me, I don't want to live like this!" the second pleaded.

"You're useful for spare parts," the first laughed. "If I lose an eye, I take yours, if I lose a limb, you replace mine. If someone manages to kill me, only then will I release you from my body, so you can take the death blow."

*He can fuse with others too?* Soraya thought in shock. *Is he part demon like me?* Carefully, she brought her face closer to the floating sphere to better see the room.

"I can feel you creeping up in the back of my mind, whoever you are," the first said coldly.

Soraya nearly gasped as she shrank back in fear.

"No need to be afraid of me yet. My name is Jonathan Marlot, but you can call me Jon, no one ever calls me by my full name," the first introduced himself calmly. "Please tell me who you are. If you're not going to be honest, then don't bother, I don't have time for more mind games from other demons."

"Um… well…" she hesitated. The room before her disappeared, then reappeared into view.

*Oh, that was him blinking,* the girl realized. *This must be how Mülock saw through my eyes.*

"Well?" Jon said, his voice slightly irritated. "Who are you?"

"I'm Soraya," she whispered into the orb.

"Ah."

The girl could hear the smile on his lips.

"You're the one Mülock wants me to kill."

## Chapter 31: Jonathan Marlot

"Y-you've spoken with Mülock?" Soraya asked, her heart stopping for a moment within her chest.

"Unfortunately, yes," Jon almost sounded bored. "His ego is astounding. I'd love to kill him, but he's in a different dimension, out of my reach."

"Yours isn't any better!" the second voice interjected.

Within the orb, Soraya saw the perspective change. Jon was now looking down towards the floor. Two light blue eyeballs were jutting out, like blisters, from the palm of his left hand, and a long, thin slit ran from his ring finger all the way down to his wrist. As the flap of skin raised and lowered, the girl spotted six yellow, bloody teeth poking out from the makeshift lips.

Without replying, Jon's thumb came down hard on one of the eyes until it popped like a blueberry. The flap of skin on his hand screamed while blood mixed with the white from the cracked eye dripped down like the runny yolk from an egg.

"There goes one spare eyeball," Marlot clicked his tongue. "Would you like to lose the other one, or are you going to shut up?"

"I-I'll stay quiet, I swear!" it whimpered.

"Good," Jon placed a black glove over his hand. "Sorry for that rude interruption. Continue, Soraya."

"Um…" the girl could hardly believe what she had just seen and her stomach curdled in disgust. "Well, Mülock told me you killed your own family by accident… is that true?"

The man was silent for a moment. "Have you ever seen the life drained out of someone else before?"

Flashes of two dead bodies filled Soraya's vision, and her blood ran cold at the sight of the memory. Their pale skin was wrinkled like dried fruit, their bones jutting out and ripping through paper thin flesh. Four shrunken, unseeing eyes stared at her through two misshapen skulls.

"Atohi and Che Marlot were their names," Jon said with a hint of sadness in his voice. "It was truly an accident that I killed my own parents, this is true, but I also have an incurable bloodlust. It turns out I'm part demon, and you being able to contact me in this way proves you are as well, though your voice and aura seem much gentler in nature than Mülock's."

"I know them!" Soraya exclaimed in shock. "Mama called them my aunt and uncle!"

"Yes, and your father is Tishva Thenayu," Jon continued. "He wrote a letter to my parents before that incident. He asked if they were also having memory loss issues, and they were…" he paused and let the weight of his words settle in the still air. "I'll tell you more of what I know, but in exchange, you have to tell me about yourself. Deal?"

Soraya bit her lip and pondered his offer. "Well, um, are you going to kill me because Mülock told you to?"

"I don't want to, but I can't guarantee that I won't change my mind."

Soraya stiffened. "Why?"

Jon let out an audible sigh. "Are you aware of the demonic hierarchy?"

The girl thought back to various passages from, *The Path,* and nodded her head.

"I can't see non-verbal cues. Yes or no?" his voice rumbled.

"Oh, yes!" Soraya laughed nervously. "Sorry, I forgot you can't see me."

Marlot sounded amused as he prattled on. "Mülock wants you dead because you're very high up in the ranks. The fact that you can even contact me must mean you're his equal, or are even higher than him, and he's threatened by that."

*How is this even possible?*

Soraya could barely believe what she was hearing. "What about you?" the girl asked with a shaky voice.

"Because we're not related, I'm a little beneath you, but not by much since I can also cast the purging souls spell. Demons in lower ranks cannot do this," his tone grew dark like a stormy sea as he growled. "I hate that Mülock can possess me and make me do things I don't like, which is why I want him dead."

He held a finger towards himself, so Soraya could see it pointing directly at her. "If you try a stunt like that on me, I'll make sure to kill you too, got it?"

"Y-yes sir," Soraya gulped. "I don't want to control anyone."

"I can tell," Marlot's tone softened. "That's why I can't guarantee whether we'll be friends or not. As long as Mülock is alive, he can control me. I'm sorry in advance if I end up taking your life, but it won't be on purpose."

Sadness crept up into the girl's heart. "He can control me too, actually, but it seems to just be my right arm."

"Interesting," Jon murmured. "I'm sure that has to do with how many bodies he has fused with himself. He has to use a lot of energy already to speak across dimensions, even more so to possess us."

"I guess that makes sense. I fused with some of my friends, and I felt so much stronger and more alive when I did, that I had to focus hard on separating our souls to keep testing new spells."

The girl couldn't see the grin appearing on the man's face. "Getting comfortable now, are we?" he teased. "I've started stocking up on souls in the hopes of not being possessed during the next half moon. I figure the more Etherian blood I have within me, the less control he'll have. I guess I'll find out if it works or not soon."

When Soraya didn't reply, the man chuckled darkly.

"Don't worry, it's only those who deserve it, like Orchal here," Jon pulled off the glove and glanced down once more at the miserable, bloody face bursting from his skin. "I'm just torturing him for fun at this point. Stealing children from their beds and selling them for profit…"

Without warning, he punched the face hard with his free hand, and Soraya could hear more of Orchal's pitiful shrieks erupt into the air.

"Too many girls have been going missing lately, and I'm determined to get to the bottom of it," Jon mused. "Mülock, thankfully, wants me to stop it, though he won't tell me why. That just makes me even more suspicious of what's being done to those poor kids."

"Say, um, do you have any more news about my father?" Soraya asked, hoping she had shared enough information to satisfy his offer.

"He and Yosef were going to meet with me, but I'm not sure what happened to them. They vanished."

"When were you going to see them?" Soraya asked, her heartbeat quickening. "He called the school last week on Ignis, and no one has seen him since."

"Soraya," Jon said quietly.

"Yes?" the girl asked, hope growing within her heart.

"Your poker face is atrocious. When dealing with strangers, you need to hide your emotions better," he snorted. "Gods, you wear them on your sleeve, practically painted a glowing bullseye around them, and I can't even see what you look like."

"Oh..." Soraya's cheeks glowed as shame flooded through her veins.

Jon chuckled at her embarrassment. "I'm only saying this because you're in a precarious situation. It's best if you don't trust any adults right now."

The view within the sphere shifted as Marlot waltzed over to the window overlooking the sea. "Tishva and Yosef would have met up with me last weekend, so they've obviously been abducted."

*I thought so...* Soraya wanted to cry, but kept the wall to the floodgates sealed shut. "Why did you want to meet up with them?"

"I'll tell you, but first, I want to know about that purified patch of grass in your school's track and field. I'm sure you caused it, I just want to know how."

Soraya's skin prickled. "You heard about that?"

"Word gets around Azakua a lot faster than you realize," Marlot laughed. "I'm assuming you used Etherian magic for that trick, right? If I can also purify land, then maybe I won't be possessed by Mülock, and then I won't be forced to kill you."

"I fused with my friend, and we used Water Magic to create a pool around some dead grass and trees..."

"Don't hold back on information," Jon said in a stern voice. "If you do, I will too."

"I-I used the purging souls spell on accident, that's how those plants wound up dead in the first place," Soraya breathed slowly to calm down. "While we used Water Magic, we sang a hymn because the plants asked us to, and we cried into the pool too."

"The plants spoke to you even though you don't have Earth Magic?" Marlot's voice raised in suspicion. "Fascinating."

There was a pregnant pause between them.

"You do realize you just gave me your location, right? Mülock has been trying so hard to know exactly where you're residing, and now I know."

Soraya's heart stopped. *Oh no… He's right! What have I done?*

"You're not very good with negotiating. You're too honest."

Soraya didn't know what to say, but her brain mentally tortured herself for falling so easily into his trap.

Jon was quiet for a few seconds before speaking again. "I wanted to meet with Tishva and Yosef to find out more information on my real parents. Atohi and Che were not my blood relatives, though they did raise me the best they could, considering I don't have a conscience and a strange lust for blood. They accidentally let that slip during one of their many moments of not remembering who I was."

Soraya leaned forward even more towards the floating, fiery sphere.

"My real mother's last name was Triparagen."

A memory stirred within Soraya's mind. *Wait! That sounds similar to-*

"And your mother's last name was Litrigen," interrupted Marlot. "You must know enough Casmerahn to understand what that means, don't you?"

"Jai," Soraya responded, though the temptation to slap her forehead was strong. *How did I miss this? How could I have been so ignorant to overlook the meaning of my mother's last name?*

"Li means one, tri means three, and gen means…" Soraya's spine shivered. "Generation."

"Correct," Marlot slowly clapped his hands together. "Your mother was the first of the third generation, and my mother was the third of the second generation."

"Generations of what we are, correct?" Soraya's head pounded as flashes of her mother came into view in her mind's eye.

*Were you like me all along?*

"Jai," Marlot stepped closer to the window, his reflection cast back at them through the glass. He was dressed in a long, black coat and had a large gun slung over one shoulder. His skin was ghost-like with a pale golden goatee flowing from his chin, and a large pair of blood-red shades that obscured his eyes. A round, black hat covered his head, and a pair of golden goggles sat upon it, giving him a look of having four eyes.

"Your mother was a very high ranking demon hybrid, as was mine," Jon said thoughtfully. "I want to know how and why this is even possible. I hoped that your father would know something. He and my parents all share the same issue of memory loss. I believe that was done partially to protect them, and partially to hide the knowledge of how hybrids are created."

Jonathan's lips parted into a fanged grin. "Why else would you and I be hidden in plain sight from the rest of the world, growing up without ever knowing how to tap into our abilities? And in such strategically placed locations away from haunted land?"

"My father got a letter from someone…" Soraya breathed, despite herself. "It said, don't look for your history. If we talk, you will get hurt. Be happy you don't remember," the girl paused. "Did you write that to him?

"No, that was not me." Marlot's lips became a thin line. "It sounds like whoever wrote that may be our only lead. What language was it written in?"

"Casmerahn."

"Figures. Was there a name attached to the letter?"

"No."

"Of course not," Marlot stated, his voice steady, yet

dripping in sarcasm. "Can't have the answers be too convenient now, can we?"

Another abrupt silence filled the air between them.

"Thank you for being honest with me," the man said calmly. "I do appreciate it, truly. Because you're just a kid, and I sense no malice from you whatsoever, I'll try my best to keep my distance from you during half moons."

*I might as well gain as much information as I can since I blew my cover.*

"Mr. Marlot, sir? MagiCorp elites are visiting the school in three months," the girl said in a low voice. "I'm sure they already suspect me of using magic."

"Oh, they'll show up even sooner than that," Jon warned. "Be careful and on guard. I guarantee your father missing and these MagiCorp elites visiting your school are not coincidences."

Goosebumps crawled up Soraya's arms.

"I suggest you stop practicing magic entirely, both Etherian and Apollryük for the time being and focus on blending in as a regular student as much as possible. And…" Marlot's voice sounded jovial. "Contact me again after the next half moon. If I manage to find a way around being possessed, I'll let you know. The Gods know that I've tried so many things already."

Soraya thought back to her conversation with her friends just a few minutes prior. "Have you ever fused with plants or animals?"

"I have…" the reflection of Marlot half smiled into the window. "And it was disastrous."

He took off his right glove to show her his hand. It was greenish in hue with veins that looked like vines from a bush. "I know what you're thinking, and fusing with the grass and trees is a bad idea. Don't do it, how they think and operate are vastly different from us, and that's not including what they're made of. Don't try fusing with animals either, you might accidentally kill them in the process."

Soraya grit her teeth together as she stared into the floating orb in consternation. *That could've been me a few minutes ago…*

"It's been a pleasure meeting someone else like myself," Marlot grinned into the window, so Soraya could see yellowing fangs glistening in the reflection. "I must admit, you make a great first impression, Soraya Thenayu. We have a common enemy, and it would be a shame to dispose of you too early," he waved his hand so Soraya could see. "Take care, kid. Watch your back."

The girl pulled herself away from the floating, fiery blue orb and turned towards the entrance of the cave, where a cluster of three floating spheres lay. As she ran to the opening and drew closer, she realized they were her three friends. Ujuu and Rhys' orbs were surrounded in brilliant red flames, while Moiya's was enveloped in an emerald fire.

"I-I contacted someone named Jonathan Marlot, and he's a demon like me!" Soraya blurted as she ran up to them. "He knows where I am, and Mülock can possess him…"

Soraya's shaky knees sank into the cool sand beneath her. "We might be allies since he doesn't like Mülock either, but I don't know. I think we're in trouble…"

Rhys pulled her into a tight embrace. "Not yet, we're not," he whispered, taking Soraya's quivering hands into his own. "I hate to do this to you, but use up the rest of your Water Magic, so we can go back to school."

"But I let him trick me! He has the upper hand-"

"Breathe, it's okay," Rhys assured her while patting her head and running his fingers through her hair. "Everything will be alright. You did great. None of this is your fault."

*It is, though… it really is…*

## Chapter 32: Good Shepherds' Church

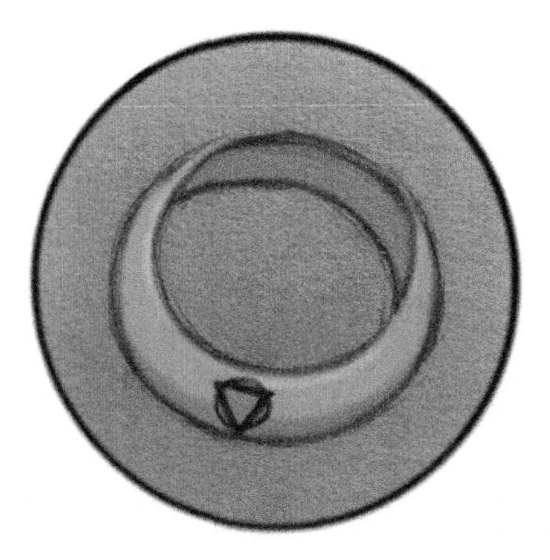

"May the Gods El, Naveah, Emmanuel, and Kyrios be with you all."

"And also with you," Soraya spoke in unison with her three friends and the congregation.

"Depart in peace, your sins are forgiven," Pastor Vern said, folding his hands together and bowing towards the Etherians who had gathered together for the service that morning.

As the Priest walked down the aisle in long strides, his navy blue robes flowing in the air with each confident step he took, the organ and choir in the balconies above burst into a beautiful melody. The congregation below belted into song.

"Blessings flow from Gods above, mercies show their everlasting love…"

*It's the hymn Rhys sang when we healed the plants,* Soraya gently nudged her boyfriend's hand with her own, and they intertwined their fingers. *His voice is gorgeous.*

The girl sang quietly, so she could better hear him. The lyrics flowed from his mouth like golden honey poured from a jar.

Ujuu and Moiya sat in the same pew as them, the younger twin singing sweetly like birds welcoming the rising sun, while Moiya's voice was pure and flute-like. Their harmonies, in addition with their history teacher's singing from the balcony, filled the musty air with life and beauty.

*Everyone I know is so talented,* Soraya smiled to herself.

When the last note of the hymn was finished, the air was filled with tiny snaps of books closing and the rustling of churchgoers gathering their belongings before forming a single file line down the aisle. It was customary to either shake the hand of the priest or bow to show appreciation after the service.

As the four friends inched their way closer to Pastor Vern, Soraya spotted a table within the Narthex. An elderly woman was in the process of laying out several religious relics in the form of jewelry and house decor.

*I'll buy a ring,* the girl thought as she noted a few thin, silver bands with the symbol of the Gods carved into them. *A necklace could snap off more easily.*

"Pastor Vern, are those relics blessed?" Soraya asked the priest.

"Why yes, they are," he beamed, his right blue and left golden eyes warm and inviting like a grove of lemon trees under a sunny sky.

"Could you maybe double bless the ring I want to buy? I know that sounds odd, but it would make me feel better if you did."

"Double bless?" the older man chuckled, the corners of his face crinkling in amusement. "I will do that for you after I finish greeting everyone here."

"Perfect!" the girl beamed. "Thank you!"

The man nodded politely in response before turning his attention towards her friends who were trailing close behind her. "Gods' Peace," he said to each of them after shaking their hands. Rhys, Ujuu and Moiya each responded in the same manner.

"You're buying a ring?" Moiya asked as they all approached the table.

"Yes, I think this one will do." Soraya picked up the silver band she had been studying while in line and looked it over. It was simple and shiny, the symbol with a circle running through each corner of a triangle was etched deeply into the silver. "It's the same design as the one carved into the tree, so I have to get it."

"That'll be fifteen Lari," the elderly woman behind the table stated aloud.

Soraya dug out her Dragulji card from her dress pocket and was about to hand it to her, but looked over at her friends instead. "Did you all want anything?"

"Thanks, but you don't have to do that," Rhys replied sheepishly.

"Let her buy us something if she wants," Ujuu lightly shoved his twin, then winked at Soraya. "We'll spoil you back later."

"But, you three always spoil me," Soraya smiled. "Please, let me return the favor," she glanced down at the four golden rings. "Would you, Rhys, Moiya and Zaruna like those?"

"That's super sweet of you, but I should be the one to buy a gift for my girl," Ujuu laughed.

"But I want to get her something too!" Soraya insisted.

As Ujuu's hands slowly reached over towards the rings to inspect them, the elderly lady's gaze grew cold. "Filthy animals shouldn't touch holy relics," she muttered under her breath, causing all four friends to freeze in place.

"W-why would you say that?" Soraya gasped. "That's so horrible!"

"Shadelkins have a different religion," the elderly woman growled. "Especially ones from Casmerah," she glared at the twins with her icy blue gaze. "You insult our Gods with your presence, you shouldn't be here."

Rhys' expression went rigid, while Ujuu gaped at her.

"I thought the Gods created everyone, and we all come

from the same lineage," Moiya stated through gritted teeth. "What happened to loving thy neighbor as thyself?"

"There are exceptions to every rule," the woman spat.

"Prunella, what is going on?" Pastor Vern asked as he suddenly appeared next to the table.

"We're apparently not welcome here," Rhys said while grabbing his brother's wrist. "We filthy animals were asked to leave."

The priest's eyes narrowed, and he glared furiously at the elderly woman. "I believe you owe these two an apology," he said while folding his arms across his chest. His skin was a deep, rich brown like a bear's fur. Although he towered over all of them, he remained calm and composed.

"I said no such thing," Prunella replied in a defensive tone. "They were about to steal these rings here, so I told them to leave."

Soraya's blood boiled at the blatant lie. "I asked them to pick out something because I wanted to buy gifts," she said while holding up her Dragulji card before glaring at Prunella. "Ma'am, you're evil for lying about my friends."

Before the elderly woman could reply, the priest chimed in. "Prunella, you've been wreaking havoc for quite awhile, but this is the final straw. You need to leave," Pastor Vern lifted a hand and pointed at the front door of the church. "You have sinned grievously against these two young men, and you continue to dig in and act as if you haven't, and within the house of the Gods no less."

The surrounding chatter quieted as everyone turned their attention towards the table.

"You can't treat me like this!" Prunella snapped. "I've been a member of this church for twenty years!"

"You haven't been paying attention to how the Gods want us to love and serve our neighbors for that long?" scoffed the pastor. "Your sins are *not* forgiven. I bind them onto you," he added in a low rumble as he pointed a finger at her. "May the Gods have mercy on your soul, because our congregation won't any longer."

The elderly woman's eyes flitted around the room, searching for an ounce of empathy towards her, but all she received back were hardened stares.

"I knew you were all deviating from the words of our Lords!" she cackled maniacally. "I noticed it when this imposter took over two years ago!"

She pointed a crooked, bony finger at the priest. "You're twisting the words of The Path to fit the crazy politics running a muck in Azakua. You voted for that traitor Starlene Inos, didn't you?" she roared, spit flying from her sagging lips. "You want more filth from overseas taking over our country, don't you? Blue eyes will die out, and pure blooded native Azakuins will be no more because of Etherians like you letting animals like these in!"

"If you don't leave now, I will call the police and have them escort you off the property," Pastor Vern said sternly. Soraya turned her head as she heard a loud creak and saw their history teacher, Mr. Thuron, holding the front door open.

"Goodbye, Prunella," he said in an irritated tone.

The elderly woman held her head high and hobbled out onto the front lawn.

"And good riddance," Mr. Thuron added when he let go of the heavy wooden door. It swung shut with a loud bang.

"I am so sorry you had to endure that," the pastor gazed in sorrow at the Shadelkin twins. "Are you both alright?"

"We'll be fine, thank you," Rhys said in a nonchalant tone, his ears twitching occasionally. Ujuu was glaring at the floor, his ears lowered on both sides of his head.

*Rhys is so good at suppressing his anger…too good.* Soraya hugged both of the twins. Moiya came over and pat Ujuu's shoulder.

"Don't worry about paying for anything. Choose whatever you want, I'll cover it," the priest said while pulling out his own bank card. "And I'll double bless them all too," he added with a wink.

* * *

*It was awfully nice of him to do that for us.*

All four students looked down at their rings. At the insistence of Pastor Vern, Ujuu had picked an additional one out for Zaruna, and Soraya had done the same for Jacquelle.

"I apologize again for that happening to you boys," Mr. Thuron sighed from the front seat of his van. "Some individuals are too set in their ways, and it's sad to see."

The twins said nothing as they both stared out at the world rolling by their windows. Soraya and Moiya were also silent, though they kept glancing at each other and the twins in concern.

When their history teacher realized the students didn't want to speak, he turned on the radio. Several jingles for local shops in Matumi played before the voice of a male newscaster came on.

"Hello and welcome back to Matumi News Network. I'm your host, Shawn Pen."

"And I'm your hostess, Marie Bunion."

Soraya's ears perked up at the familiar last name. *I wonder if that's one of Mrs. Bunion's kids.*

"The votes for the next President of Azakua have finally been tallied up."

All four students fixed their focus onto the small, rectangular box. Even Mr. Thuron shifted his grayish blue eyes down at the radio before looking back at the road.

"As we wait to hear who the winner candidate is, we will be replaying the most memorable clips from their speeches," Marie Bunion continued. "Here's a segment from the Independent Party's candidate, Stefawn Zabok.

"It is a disgrace and embarrassment to our nation that we cannot protect our own children from being abducted by criminals," a man's voice, deep and powerful, rang through the van's speakers.

"Our country didn't have this problem when we cut ourselves off from the rest of the world for two hundred years. Now, when we start allowing immigrants to live in our country, our daughters are suddenly being kidnapped from their own beds! Isn't it obvious by now who's doing this? We need to shut our borders down for good!"

Eruptions of applause rose in the background, filling the van with the loud chanting of, "shut out the world and save Azakuin Girls." All four students turned pale, as did their history teacher.

"Our next clip is from Starlene Inos, the candidate of the United Party. Remember that she is deaf and speaks in sign language. Her interpreter and speaker is Wren Carson, who is running for Vice President with Starlene Inos."

"What is happening in Azakua is indeed horrific and has to be stopped," a bold, fierce female voice blasted through the speakers. "Cutting ourselves off from the rest of the world will only ensure our demise. We are not the only ones suffering from having our daughters kidnapped, it is a worldwide phenomenon that started about thirty years ago in the Kingdom of Casmerah."

There was a hushed silence from the crowd within the recording.

"Our borders have been open far longer than when these kidnappings started. We've had immigrant families living here for many, many generations, and they are just as much Azakuin as all of us here."

*That sounds like what my father and Yosef were saying at Delphi's Diner.* Soraya's heart sank, and she said a silent prayer for them to be found and brought home.

"We must keep our borders open to fellow Etherians if we want answers for why this is happening to all of us. It's time to end the government's charade of cherry-picking information and hiding what's important from the public. We all have a right to know what is actually happening across the globe. Knowledge is power. Stay connected."

Darkwood Academy came into view from the front window. Although Mr. Thuron parked the car, all five of them stayed seated.

"And we have just received the final vote count for Azakua's next president!" Shawn's voice boomed, shaking the van slightly on its wheels.

"The winning candidate is…" began Marie.

Soraya held her breath. Rhys and Ujuu both leaned forward while Moiya closed her eyes. Mr. Thuron's shoulders tensed up as he dug his fingers into the steering wheel.

"Starlene Inos!"

"No way!" gasped Ujuu, his face lighting up.

Mr. Thuron turned to look at his students, his grayish blue eyes twinkling in merriment. "That is the best news I've heard all day."

"Wow!" Soraya hugged Rhys tightly. "She did it!"

"Starlene Inos and Wren Carson will both be sworn into office on the sixth of Mazula-" Maria Bunion was cut off as a relieved Mr. Thuron took his keys out of the ignition and slid out of the driver's seat.

Rhys relaxed slightly in Soraya's embrace. "I wonder how she did it…" he murmured thoughtfully. His wine colored eyes lit up, as if a flame had been created behind them. "Of course."

"What?" Soraya asked while hopping out of the van.

"I'll tell you in a minute," Rhys smiled while the five of them walked towards the front entrance of the school. Only after Mr. Thuron had bid them a good day and left did Rhys speak again.

"The radio room. Remember what we heard?"

"Yes," Soraya shivered when she thought back to the terrified screams they had heard on the air.

"I was wondering who leaked that audio. Starlene Inos won,

so I have a feeling she somehow had a hand in that."

Moiya laughed. "That's brilliant, no one likes being lied to."

"I'm so relieved she won. That gives me some hope," Ujuu grinned. "And you have to admit, everyone rallied against Prunella at the church, so maybe Stefawn Zabok's party is dwindling down more than we realize."

"Do you all want to study together?" Soraya asked.

"That sounds really nice," Rhys smiled. Moiya nodded her head in agreement, and Ujuu gave a thumbs up.

"Moiya, let's go get our books from the dorm and get Yabo," Soraya suggested. Together, she and her friend ran up the stairs.

"You're almost keeping up with me!" Soraya called back to her friend, who was staying on her heels.

"Yeah!" Moiya exclaimed joyfully. "I've never been this athletic before."

They rounded the corner at the top of the stairs and burst through the door of the Blue House. Soraya was met with a sight she hadn't expected. Jacquelle was crouching down on her knees and petting Yabo, who was sleeping in a sunbeam on the floor. Startled by the loud noise, she quickly snapped her head towards them.

"Uh…" the blond said as she glanced between them and the sleeping pandacoon. "I wasn't… it's not what it looks like…"

"It's fine, he loves pats and gentle scratches," Soraya grinned. "Especially behind the ears."

Jacquelle quickly stood up, her face beet red. "Whatever," she snorted.

"I have something for you," Soraya handed her the spare ring from her dress pocket. "I know you're not religious, but I wanted to give you a present."

"Oh…" Jacquelle hesitantly took it. "Thanks," she slipped the ring onto her right hand and briefly smiled down at it.

"We're going to go study," Moiya added. "Wanna join us?"

"Really?" Jacquelle's golden eyebrows arched in shock. "Are you sure?"

"Yeah, come on."

After the three girls had gathered their books and supplies, they gently woke up Yabo from his nap. He yawned, stretched his limbs, and chirped loudly at Jacquelle.

"He wants you to hold him," Soraya laughed.

"Oh..." Jacquelle awkwardly picked him up from the ground and held him away from her.

"Mow?" Yabo cocked his head and stared at Jacquelle.

"Bring him to your shoulder," Moiya giggled. "He likes sitting there."

"Like this?" the blond asked while bringing the pandacoon closer to her chest. Yabo scrambled up her arm and brushed his face into her cheek.

"Yes, good!" Soraya turned the doorknob and thrust open the door. She was about to head out but stopped. A tall woman was standing in the hall, staring at her through icy blue eyes, like a shark staring at a fresh piece of meat.

"Hello, are you Ms. Thenayu?" she asked, her grin growing ever wider on her pale face.

"Um... who are you?" Soraya asked, her legs rooting her to the spot.

"Why, I'm Norma Whispers," she glided forward on tall heels and towered over the girls. She wore a large, black circular hat with netting covering part of her face. Her outfit was a black suit over a long, tight skirt that hugged her thin hips and legs.

"Is that really your name?" Soraya couldn't help but ask. *It sounds fake.*

The woman bent forward, so her face was closer to Soraya's, her ruby painted lips pursued together into a slight frown.

"Yes it is." she whispered. "I'm your new therapist, kiddo."

"I-I don't need a therapist," Soraya stammered. *Are you from MagiCorp?*

"Oh, I believe you do," Ms. Whispers smirked. "The school made sure to hire a professional like myself because your father and his friend are missing, and that's obviously taking a toll on your mental health, isn't it?"

Jacquelle shifted her eyes between Soraya, Moiya, and Ms. Whispers, her porcelain expression unwavering. "We need to go study for exams," she huffed while attempting to move past the tall woman. "So if you'll excuse us-"

"Hold up," Ms. Whispers stepped in front of Jacquelle and placed her long arms onto her hips. "I'm not done with you kids yet. You're her friends, right? You do care about Soraya's mental health, don't you?"

"She's going to be more stressed if she flunks a test because *someone* wasted her time," Jacquelle replied in a snide tone before grabbing onto Soraya's wrist and forcefully pushing her way around the tall woman. Moiya followed closely behind her friends, and all three of them ran towards the stairs.

Soraya glanced back for a brief moment. Ms. Whispers was watching them through narrowed slits, her slender fingers rapidly tapping against her hips.

"I'm going to talk to my father about her," Jacquelle growled once they were out of ear shot. "A Professional? Yeah right! She reminds me of my mother…"

"Thanks Jacquelle," Soraya and Moiya both sighed in relief. The blond was still muttering to herself and didn't appear to hear either of them.

Soraya looked down at her wrist. "You can let go now."

"Oh. Right," Jacquelle said and instantly released her.

*We can tell her about everything… she's definitely our friend.*

## Chapter 33: Zinvi

Tishva's eyelids fluttered open. A bright, hazy ceiling light stared coldly down at him, its pale yellow beams illuminating the dark stone walls surrounding where he lay.

*Where's Yosef?*

As he lifted his head, a sharp pain shot through his skull. Groaning, Tisvha laid back down onto the cool, smooth surface beneath him. His whole body ached as if he had been slammed into by a rock. He gingerly flexed his fingers.

*Not broken… All intact.*

He carefully moved his arms next, causing the thick chains on his cuffed wrists to clack against the cold table he was sprawled out on.

"Oh good. You're finally awake," a silver tongued voice slithered into the air.

"Who are you, and what do you want?" Tishva managed to say despite his head wanting to split in half.

"You like getting to the point of things, don't you?" A tall, thin man leaned into view, obscuring the light above. All Tishva could see was a dark silhouette looming over him. "I finally found you, Tishva Thenayu. Or should I say, Favis Mortlock? Vin Torvil?"

The other names sounded vaguely familiar to Tishva. A ghost of a memory appeared in the back of his head, but no matter how hard he tried to grasp onto it, the details eluded him.

"You've had many undercover names for various missions, making it very difficult to pinpoint you."

Tishva chuckled darkly. "I can't remember much of anything anymore, so if you captured me for information, there's not much I can give you."

"I'm well aware of that conundrum," the voice replied. Glistening pearls emerged from the dark figure. "Your friend there started doing research and asking questions, alerting me of your existence. I followed the breadcrumbs and made some links…"

"Let Yosef go!" Tishva growled. "He's done nothing wrong."

"Only if you cooperate."

The longer Tishva stared at the tall figure, the more clear his vision became. The man's skin was unusually pale. He had long, silvery hair flowing down on both sides of his face, and his gleaming silver eyes pierced into the depths of his soul.

"Amraphael?" Tishva breathed.

The man's stare hardened. "No. I'm not him," he spat before pacing in circles around the table Tishva was bound to. "Just call me Zinvi."

"What do you want?" Mr. Thenayu sighed.

*Does he know about Jonathan Marlot contacting me?* He thought back to the letter he had received from Atohi and Che's son and frowned. The young man seemed desperate to meet with him and had shared the disturbing news of both his parents suffering from memory loss.

*Why would they have the same mental illness as I? Is it more common than I thought, or is something else at play here?*

Zinvi didn't respond. Instead, he stopped at Tishva's feet and glared at the man. "My army is dying. You were connected with Amraphael and his research, so I believe you can figure out how he did it…"

"Did what?" the world spun around Tishva. All he could do was close his eyes and hope the brewing nausea in his stomach wouldn't rise to his throat.

"Create the perfect hybrid between Etherians and Demoni."

Gagging, Tishva turned his head slightly and vomited. Yellow bile mixed with blood flew from his mouth, some of it dripped down the edges of his lips and onto his cheek. "Impossible…" he shuddered weakly, his throat in flames.

"On the contrary," Zinvi looked at the wall behind Tishva and snapped his slender, bony fingers together. "Grawljok!" he barked.

"Yes, my Lord?" a low, raspy voice replied.

"Come here," Zinvi curled his finger, beckoning his minion forward. "I want Tishva to get a good look at you."

A tall, gaunt man came into view. His skin was pasty white, as if he had never seen the sunlight before, and his unnaturally wide eyes were different colored. One was a dark, murky blue, and one was brown like charred wood in a fireplace. His messy hair was long, jet black and greasy. He wore nothing more than a long, white nightgown, making him look more like a sick patient at a hospital than a soldier in an army.

"Show him," Zinvi commanded, his voice echoing around the empty room.

Grawljok's body shook violently, his eyeballs rolling backwards, replaced with red veins growing over the whites like vines reaching for the heavens. Tishva's shoulders tensed as the skin on the man's face stretched unnaturally, tearing and breaking into long slits like soft dough when rolled too thin. Several clicks and pops filled the still air before blood spurt and poured out from the torn open flesh, cascading down the man's ghost-like body, staining his white nightgown and bathing the tiled floor in red.

Tishva wanted to close his eyes, but was too mesmerized by the horrific scene playing out before him. Just before he was about to throw up once more, the man's skin stitched itself back together, revealing a completely new face.

"I have the last batch of older Demoni Hybrids in my possession," Zinvi stated with a hint of pride. "They can fuse with Etherians, holding their bodies within themselves for as long as they wish, and can even take on the features of those trapped souls."

His silver eyes glanced once more at Tishva. "Demoni Hybrids are incredible shape shifters, but they leave behind a mess, as you can see. Amraphael created one that could do this in a much cleaner, more efficient way. Only he knew the perfect combination between Etherian and Demoni blood. Although he carried that knowledge to his grave, I believe it can be recreated."

Tishva grit his teeth together. *He wants me to figure that out. If I don't, he'll probably kill Yosef, or have me experiment on him…* "Why is your army dying?" he asked in a calm tone.

"I want you to figure that out as well," Zinvi's icy stare drilled into Tishva's skull. "I'm assuming it's because they have a limit for how much they can shape shift. None of them have ever made it past ten when reconstructing their features, for example."

Tishva closed his eyes and stared into the darkness. *Judging from how painful the shape shifting looks and how much blood loss there is, that makes perfect sense.*

"Grawljok, go back to your cell," Zinvi ordered with a swish of his hand. The hybrid bowed and left them as quickly as he had arrived, the only evidence of his presence was the pool of blood left in his wake.

"The hybrids obey my every command because of this," Zinvi pulled out a syringe from his coat pocket and held it in the air. Inside swished a thick, reddish black liquid. He then rolled up his long white sleeve and thrust the needle into his left arm.

"There's always a price to pay for power," he grunted while injecting the concoction into himself. "My blood type is not the same as this one, so it's rather painful for me to take it, but it's the only way to keep them under my thumb, and to keep them from killing me."

Tishva's eyes widened in surprise. *Why are you telling me your weaknesses? I'm your hostage, surely you must know you can't fully trust me.*

"I want you to find a way to fix that too," Zinvi winced and took the needle out before applying pressure with a cloth over the open wound.

"What makes you so sure that I can do all of that?" Tishva asked.

"Simple. I'll make sure your daughter lives."

Tishva's blood ran cold. "You would kill a child?"

"Oh please," Zinvi snorted. "She's thirteen, almost a legal Azakuin adult in three years," his face lit up, as if an idea had struck him. "Oh, you don't know what's happening to her, do you?"

"What do you mean?" Tishva felt the blood drain from his face.

"MagiCorp is investigating Soraya."

"W-what?" Tishva choked. "Why? What has she done?"

"They can't prove it yet, but they believe she purified a patch of land at Darkwood Academy, which means she broke the law by illegally using magic."

Tishva laughed despite feeling ill. "That takes twelve Etherians casting Water Magic all at the same time. They have to fast and pray together for three days, and sing a hymn while performing the ceremony."

He coughed up more blood as he continued chuckling. "If

anyone screws up or falls out of sync, they have to start all over. Why would they suspect her of purifying land by herself?"

"We all want to know if she did it, and if so, how," Zinvi said quietly. "I have spies within MagiCorp keeping me informed on the situation. The plants claim an angel healed them, which can't be true, and Soraya is the only student with an Arcanologist parent, making her the obvious first choice."

"Plants don't lie," Tishva reminded him. "Did anyone use Earth Magic to see what they remember looking at?"

"Yes, and it was a student no one has ever seen on campus grounds," Zinvi's lips tightened. "MagiCorp is still searching for that kid. Oddly enough, the hair color is similar to your daughter's, but that's about the only feature in common they share."

"And what about Yosef?" Tishva tried to keep his voice from trembling as he asked. "Will you let him go if I do as you ask?"

"Of course. We can wipe away his memories of this place in addition to your conversations with him, so he won't come looking for you ever again."

"You can manipulate memories?" Tishva's temple throbbed at the thought.

"The blood I inject into myself comes from the most powerful Demoni Hybrid we have," Zinvi smiled. "Only the top Demoni in the hierarchy can take away memories."

*Is that what happened to me?* Tishva couldn't help but think back to the empty grave in his backyard. *Adonia… would you know who did that? Are you somehow connected to all of this?*

"What'll it be, Tishva?" Zinvi dangled the silver key to his cuffs in front of him. "Will you join me, or will you let Yosef and your daughter die?"

* * *

Yosef was pacing the floor of his small cell when Tishva entered. Although the doctor's blue eyes lit up when he saw his friend again, he was careful not to express any emotions.

"What's the news?" he asked as Grawljok closed the caged door behind Tishva, locking both men inside.

"I made a deal," Tishva began. "You're not going to like it."

Yosef's black eyebrows raised, but he stayed silent.

"I'm going to work for Zinvi in exchange for you and Soraya's safety."

Yosef clicked his tongue. "That isn't going to end well, and you know it. Let's think of something else-"

"No."

Tishva shook his head. "I already lost one love of my life, I'm not losing the other," he looked into Yosef's eyes. "If you or Soraya die because of me, there will be no point in living any longer. At least this way, I know you'll both still be alive."

"Tishva..." Yosef pulled his friend into a hug and whispered into his ear. "Please don't do this. There has to be another way."

"You're worth fighting for," Tishva breathed. "You deserve to be free and live your life," his voice cracked. "This is all my fault, I brought this on myself."

"No, it's mine," Yosef's arms tightened around Tishva's waist. "I shouldn't have gotten too nosey, I am so sorry for snooping around, trying to find a way to make MagiCorp care about your well-being. I-I shouldn't have gotten involved."

A tear escaped from Tishva's eye. "You can't blame yourself for being a good friend. Thanks for always looking out for me. It's my turn now to do the same."

He gently pushed Yosef away and looked down the hall, where he knew Zinvi was listening and waiting on him. The drugs the silver haired man had given him were beginning to work. His headache was now gone, though he still shook and had to lean against the bars for support.

"Zinvi," Mr. Thenayu called. "I'm ready."

"Tishva," Yosef placed his hand upon his shoulder. "Be careful, brother."

"No guarantees," Tishva smiled weakly as the door was opened once more by the Demon Hybrid.

"Come on," Grawljok rumbled, his voice echoing like thunder.

Tishva placed his hand over Yosef's, gave it a light squeeze, and let go before following the hybrid. He winced when the cage door slammed shut and automatically locked behind them. Tishva could feel Yosef's eyes watching him until they turned a corner at the end of the hall. He snuck one last glance at his friend before Yosef disappeared from view.

*You'll be free soon. I promise.*

The entire walk was a zigzag through dimly lit hallways that all looked the same. How many minutes had passed, Tishva didn't know, but it seemed like an eternity.

*We must be underground.* Tishva noted the lack of windows and the uneven tiling on the ceiling. There were a few small chinks in the wall where dark brown soil showed through, confirming his theory. Grawljok finally stopped at a white door, which looked the exact same as all the other ones they had passed by.

"Go on," Grawljok spoke once more. Tishva turned the silver door knob and pushed his way inside.

Zinvi stood in the middle of the tiled floor, grinning from ear to ear. It was a larger room than Tishva had expected. A desk covered with laboratory equipment; syringes, vials, gloves, various bottles filled with Gods only knew what, lay against the wall. In the far corner was a bed, where a malnourished girl with short, curly blond hair slept.

Tishva's heart sank. *She must be drugged.*

"If you can turn this kid into a successful hybrid, then I'll allow Yosef to go home," Zinvi said as he sauntered by Tishva. "Here's her information," he thrust a clipboard into Tishva's hands.

Mr. Thenayu looked down at the name and age and grimaced.

*Krista Demarko. Age 13. She's the same age as Soraya…*

"If she dies, I'll just get another one," Zinvi smirked, causing a knot to form in Tishva's stomach. "I suggest reading all of Amraphael's notes before starting anything."

The silver eyed man gestured towards the small bookshelf in the opposite corner. "I've read through them all myself. There are some theories he obsessed over, such as different phases of the moon connecting our world to different dimensions. This one is true, I've tested it myself by contacting the demonic realm on a half moon."

Tishva blinked and stared at Zinvi, waiting for him to continue.

"Their head demon is named Mülock, and he tried possessing my own army to have them kill me. It didn't work, thankfully, but that's why we have to keep this land purified after every failed experiment…"

Tishva clenched his fist tightly around the clipboard. *Maybe, this demon isn't so bad if he also wants Zinvi dead.*

"Amraphael also believed the Zodia Relics are hidden on that floating island in space, the Never Tree Island. He theorized there was a way to travel there, but we can explore that idea later."

He pointed a slender finger at the sleeping girl once more. "This is your first task," Zinvi's silver eyes bore into Tishva's. "You have one month to figure this out. I suggest starting now."

Another wave of nausea washed over him when Zinvi locked the door. He glanced over at the child once more and held back the tears welling behind his eyes.

*I won't let you die,* Tishva vowed. *I'll find a way to save you too.*

## Chapter 34: Unlocking Secrets

"So… does that all make sense?"

Soraya waited for Jacquelle to respond, her fingers tapping the music stand in rapid succession. Ujuu and Moiya were also waiting to hear her thoughts. They had all fled to the Orchestra Room to escape from Norma Whispers. Since no other souls were around, Rhys had volunteered to look out and play his violalin by the front door. If the music stopped, it meant someone else was entering and for them to switch topics.

"Kind of…" Jacquelle's cheeks flushed pink. "Though, it does help explain how you looked into my memories."

Yabo sat on top of the blond's cello case and purred loudly up at her, his bushy tail swishing back and forth like a pendulum. Jacquelle hovered her hand over his furry body and gently stroked his back. "Next Lunas night is when you have to be in the purified land, correct?"

"Yes," Soraya nodded. "I'll contact Jonathan Marlot

afterwards and see if his plan worked."

She shivered and tried not to think about the eyeball and bloody teeth poking out of the man's hand. Instead, she thought back to her first encounter with Mülock and the strange comment he had said before departing from her.

*"You have too much Etherian blood in you. I will have to fix that…"*

*I hope the extra Etherian souls help Jon from being possessed by him.*

Rhys' violalin playing came to a grinding halt. In a flash, all four students flipped open their Biology books and buried their noses into them as if they had been studying the whole time. Loud clacking from Norma Whispers' high heels filled the air as she steadily approached the amphitheater with Rhys' softer footsteps following behind.

"There you are!" the woman exclaimed, her ruby lips grimacing. "Ms. Thenayu, I've been searching everywhere for you. Didn't your parents ever teach you any manners?"

"They taught me to be wary of strangers, ma'am," Soraya replied politely. Her friends all stifled their laughter at the unexpected response.

"But I'm not, I already introduced myself as your new therapist." Ms. Whispers towered over them, her arms folded over her chest. "You are to meet with me every Solis Diem starting at thirteen o'clock."

"By whose authority?" Jacquelle butted in. "My father is the head of this school, and I don't remember ever hearing anything about you working here." The blond stood up and glared into the woman's icy blue eyes.

"Would you feel better if you spoke with your father?" Ms. Whispers asked, her shiny teeth scraping loudly past one other with each syllable she spat out.

"Yes, we all would feel *much better* if we heard that from him rather than you," Jacquelle retorted.

"One can't be too wary of strangers these days, especially *Native Azakuin* girls," Rhys added, pulling Soraya closer to himself with his free hand.

Ms. Whispers' icy eyes narrowed into slits. "I'm not a kidnapper. You are incredibly rude to accuse me of being one."

"I never did," Rhys retorted, then stood protectively between Soraya and the therapist. Jacquelle, Ujuu, and Moiya joined him, all of them staring at Ms. Whispers with distrust. Even Yabo lowered his velvety ears and snarled at the woman.

"Alright, fine, go see Principal Demarko and talk to him," Norma growled in irritation. "But after he clears everything up, I expect to see Soraya next Solis Diem in my office at thirteen o'clock sharp!"

The woman turned on her heels and walked away, fuming and muttering under her breath.

"Persistent, isn't she?" Ujuu observed once the door slammed behind her.

"I believe she's from MagiCorp," Rhys murmured under his breath.

"I think so too," Moiya agreed.

"I'll try to get her fired," Jacquelle grinned, a mischievous glow in her eyes. "Her conduct was extremely unprofessional."

"Can we even talk to your father today?" Soraya asked. "It's the weekend, isn't he taking the day off like the teachers?"

"Nah, he should still be in his office," Jacquelle stated in a matter-of-fact tone. "Come on, I'll show you all where to go."

* * *

"I'm sorry, but Ms. Whispers is an overly qualified therapist."

"But father, she was rude and intimidating towards my friends!"

Mr. Demarko's dark blue eyes hovered over each student,

his lips parting into a slight smile as he noticed the Shadelkin twins and Moiya. "They're your friends now?"

"Of course they are, Dad," Jacquelle said, then tilted her head down and fluttered her eyelashes. Her golden locks bouncing as she tried her best to make herself look both pitiful and adorable. "Please fire Ms. Whispers?"

"That doesn't work on me," Mr. Demarko sighed while pushing his glasses up from the edge of his pointed nose. "She's already had a background check and the whole nine yards done. She is a professional therapist with a PhD in psychology. I'm sorry, but we hired the best our school could afford for Ms. Thenayu."

"That doesn't change the fact that she was awful towards us all today," Jacquelle pouted.

"If Soraya doesn't trust her, then how will Ms. Whispers be an effective therapist?" Rhys pointed out.

Mr. Demarko grimaced. "I'll speak to her privately, and if her attitude doesn't improve, then we'll see what we can do about replacing her. Is that a deal?"

"Okay…"

As the kids trudged out of Mr. Demarko's office, an unexpected voice greeted them from down the hallway.

"Ujuu!"

The younger Casmerahn twin gazed down the corridor and blinked.

"Is that…" his ears perked up, and his candy apple eyes glowed brilliantly as he lurched forward and dashed towards the voice.

"Zaruna!" he called, his voice echoing around the hall. "It *is* you!"

Ujuu wrapped his arms around the girl and lifted her into the air. Zaruna's cotton candy curls and sunshine yellow dress flowed gracefully as they spun together in a circle before Ujuu brought her back down and nudged his forehead gently into hers.

"When did you get here? How was your ride over? How are you and your parents?"

"Alvays so many questions, my love!" Zaruna laughed as she cupped her palms around Ujuu's face and brought her nose to his. "Vi arrived today, the ship ride vas long but beautiful, and vi are grateful to be here. How ah you?" she shyly flashed her sparkling pearls at him.

"I'm so happy you're safe!" Ujuu hugged her for a few seconds, then let go and spun around as everyone else gathered around them. "Zaruna, this is Soraya, Moiya and Jacquelle," he beamed while gesturing towards each one with a wave of his hands. When he reached his twin, he laughed. "You already know Rhys."

Soraya couldn't help but stare fondly into Zaruna's magenta eyes. *They're so beautiful, like tourmaline gemstones.*

"My parents ah vaiting outside for me to return," the Rosinkin girl added cheerfully as she took Ujuu's hand. "I begged them to let me see you before ve go to yah parent's house."

"I'm so glad they let you!" Ujuu kissed her cheek and took the blessed ring from his pocket. "For you, chemi no dragoste."

Zaruna giggled, her voice as sweet as sun kissed strawberries. "Chemi viata dragoste," she corrected him as she slid the ring onto her right hand. "You mixed Rosinkin with Casmerahn."

"Eh, close enough."

"Millis gratias, igo no amore," Zaruna winked while kissing Ujuu's cheek. Then, turning towards the rest of the group, she held out her hand dramatically, her rose colored eyes bright and welcoming. "Come say hi to my parents before ve go to Rhys and Ujuu's home."

She and Ujuu turned and chatted away while walking together arm in arm. Soraya's adoration for the pair soared as she noted how happy they were.

Moiya winked while nudging the older twin's shoulder. "You need to step it up with your girlfriend. Ujuu is so adorable and romantic. Don't let him out do you."

Rhys sighed, his cheeks turning the same color as his eyes. "It won't mean as much if I force things, especially if it's out of competition with my brother."

Moiya simply shook her head in disappointment.

Soraya glanced behind her and noticed Jacquelle falling behind the group. The blond was biting her lower lip and staring past Zaruna and Ujuu towards the front door of the school.

"You okay?" Soraya asked.

"I think I'll go back to the dorm."

"You can come with us," Soraya held out her hand to the girl, but Jacquelle froze in her tracks.

"I'm not sure what to say to Zaruna's parents, so I shouldn't bother meeting them," she grazed her fingers over the scars on her back and scrunched up her face.

Soraya's heart ached for her new friend. "I understand. I don't know what to say to them either," she said, then offered her hand one more time. "We can be clueless together."

Outside, on the campus grounds, was a bright blue taxi cab. Within it sat Mr. and Mrs. Markies. Soraya watched Zaruna, Rhys and Ujuu go right up to the windows and strike up a conversation with the couple. She, Moiya and Jacquelle, however, waved awkwardly from a few feet back.

Soraya leaned closer to her friends. "Do you know when the banks are open?"

"Yes, from Lunas to Astros, and they're closed every Solis," Jacquelle answered promptly.

"Are you still thinking of giving Zaruna's family Lari?" Moiya queried.

"Of course. They had to leave almost everything behind to

move here."

Moiya gave a sympathetic look at her friend. "You're so incredibly kind."

"Thanks, Moiya," Soraya replied while tightening her fists, a fierce determination rising in her eyes. "Next Astros, let's all travel into town together. We can do a bank run and treat ourselves to lunch. We'll invite Zaruna too, and I can tell her all about Rivinsdeep and give her Lari."

Moiya's emerald gems lit up at the idea. "That sounds fantastic-" her eyes suddenly bulged as a small gasp escaped from her lips. "I just realized, if Ms. Whispers is a spy from MagiCorp, then she'll want to know everywhere you've been while at school."

She lowered her voice even more, so it was barely audible. "What if they find out about you going to a Thousand Steps Beach? What if they start inquiring the wildlife there about what you've been doing?"

Soraya groaned. "Those permission slips for traveling off campus that Rhys filled out… Maybe I can sneak into the office and change the location to a different spot, like Matumi Beach, to throw her off?"

"That would work," Jacquelle started to say, then procured a key from her dress pocket. "As long as you have this."

Both Moiya and Soraya stared in surprise at the silver skeleton key dangling from Jacquelle's hand.

"Is that how you've been able to look at everyone's records?" Soraya asked.

"Duh. This can open everything in Darkwood Academy," Jacquelle added with a smirk. "My father has the copy I paid to have made. This is the original, and he doesn't even know."

The blond placed the key carefully back into her pocket. "There are some secret rooms and halls in our school too. All the coat closets in our dorms, for example, have hidden stairs leading to the roof. You just have to push on the wall near the floor, and a small cut out will open."

"That is so neat!" Soraya gasped.

"And helpful!" Moiya chimed in.

"I can easily change those records for you," Jacquelle folded her arms across her chest and grinned. "I've done it before, so I know I won't get caught."

"I'm slightly disturbed that you have experience in that area," Moiya laughed nervously. "But could you do that tonight for Soraya?"

"Oh absolutely," Jacquelle placed her thumb into the center of her chest. "You can count on me."

"Thank you!" Soraya spun around with glee. "You're a great friend."

Jacquelle's face flushed as she muttered something incoherent and gazed down at the grass beneath her feet.

"Hey ladies."

The Casmerahn twins suddenly appeared next to them. Soraya caught a quick glimpse of the taxi disappearing down the tunnel of trees looming over the driveway.

"What'd we miss?" Rhys asked, noting Jacquelle's strange behavior.

"Oh, we have a lot to fill you both in on," Moiya chuckled. "A lot."

## Chapter 35: Errands in Matumi

"This is so magical."

Soraya spun in a circle, taking in as much of her surroundings as possible. Her windswept hair flapped in the breeze like their school's flags just beneath where she and her friends stood.

"And cold," Moiya shivered and hugged herself. "I'll have to remember to wear a jacket next time."

"Who could've predicted our new hang out spot would be on the roof?" Ujuu's ears lowered to not get caught in the wind.

"This is perfect," Rhys' crimson eyes scanned over the wooden panels they had removed to access the top of their school. "Now we can meet up at night undetected."

"You're welcome," Jacquelle nodded curtly, her hands on her hips. She turned her attention towards the younger twin. "Is Zaruna still on for going into town today?"

A wide, toothy grin appeared on Ujuu at the mention of his girlfriend. "Yes. She can hang with us until sixteen o'clock today since she's working at our Mom's restaurant in the evening."

Soraya's hand inched its way into her pocket. She had her Dragulji credit card safely stashed inside, along with her birth certificate and the note her Biology teacher had written granting her permission for missing one day of school.

*Maybe I should use it for next Ignis, so I don't have to go to Mr. Trog's class after fighting with Mülock…* Soraya looked over at Rhys and smiled at him. *It'd be great if I could sneak him out of cooking at five in the morning too.*

"Which shop is your mother's?" Jacquelle asked, her eyebrows raised. "I've played my cello at every restaurant in town, so I'm sure I've been there before."

"Yohai Steakhouse."

"But the owner is Azakuin…" Jacquelle's voice faltered as a light went on in her head. "Wait, Ayla is your mother?"

"Yup," Rhys joined in. "Mom has blue eyes, and dad has red eyes."

"I didn't know that you were both half Azakuin!" Jacquelle stared wide-eyed at the twins, as if seeing them for the first time.

"You can be a descendant of a nationality and not exhibit the key characteristics most Etherians associate it with," Rhys replied. "That's why it's best not to judge by outward appearances."

"I… I'm…" Jacquelle floundered for a few seconds before spitting out, "I-I'm sorry! For all those times I was mean to you two," her gaze flitted over to Moiya. "And I'm sorry for spreading that rumor about you as well."

"I forgive you," Rhys offered her his hand.

"Me too," Ujuu grinned at her. Moiya nodded in agreement.

Jacquelle placed her hand timidly into the Casmerahn boy's and shook it.

Soraya watched in adoration. *I'm so glad they're all friends.*

* * *

"So, where to first?" Rhys asked Soraya while stroking her hand with his fingers.

Soraya used her free arm to point down the bustling street

in a commanding way. "To Dragulji Bank!"

"Well, it's the other way," Jacquelle corrected her and gestured in the exact opposite direction.

"Oh," Soraya laughed at herself. "I don't know where anything is, I've never been in town before." *Though, this looks similar to Jacquelle's memories.*

"We know," Rhys winked at her before kissing her cheek. "I'll find us a map to memorize in case we get separated."

"Merow?" Yabo cooed up at the older twin from Soraya's shoulder.

"Okay, you too," Rhys gave the pandacoon a quick peck on the forehead, causing him to purr like a motorcar.

The six friends started down the sidewalk, with Jacquelle and Moiya in the lead, followed closely behind by Soraya and Rhys. Ujuu and Zaruna stayed in the back and were chatting away together, both lost in their own little world.

"Do you really have a photographic memory like me now?" Soraya asked as she stared up into Rhys' crimson eyes.

"Yes, and it's incredibly helpful," he replied. The way he smiled melted Soraya's heart. "My scores are improving in school because of it, so thank you for that."

"No problem," she said, squeezing his hand lightly. "Did you notice how much faster Moiya is in gym class? That's all thanks to you and Ujuu."

Jacquelle, who was listening in on their conversation, joined in. "My ability to recall information has improved too, actually," she murmured just loud enough for them to hear. "I can see things in my head, like I'm looking at a picture."

"Then you have a photographic memory too!" Soraya gasped. "I didn't realize I shared that with you," an idea popped into her mind, and she blurted it out without thinking. "I wonder if I can play the cello as well as you now."

"Hey!" Jacquelle snapped, causing Soraya's chest to clench up. "I've worked hard at that instrument, don't you dare one-up me in that!"

"I-I didn't mean it like that!" Soraya gulped.

The blond frowned, but didn't respond.

"I-I'm so sor-"

"We're here," Jacquelle huffed, cutting her off.

Soraya turned her attention towards the towering building in front of them. *This Dragulji Bank looks exactly the same as the one in Rivinsdeep.*

"I-I'll be right back," Soraya stuttered before disappearing inside with Rhys in tow. *I didn't mean to make her mad! What have I done?*

Sensing Soraya's plight, Rhys pulled her into a hug while they waited in the back of a short line. "She knows you didn't mean it, just give her a few minutes to calm down," he whispered into her ear.

"I should've thought of that before I spoke," Soraya sighed. "I don't have any excuses."

"Next?" the teller at the desk called, startling the two students.

"Yes, um, hi," Soraya stuttered, then approached the young woman wearing a golden tag with the name Daria printed on it in large letters. "I'd like to take out Lari from this account."

The girl slid her Dragulji Card across the marble counter. "Here's my birth certificate as proof of my identification," she added, thrusting the folded paper into the teller's outstretched hands.

"And how much would you like to take out?" the woman asked politely.

"How much do I have in there?"

"I'll check, hold on one moment," after a few minutes, the woman came back with a receipt in her hand. "You have ₾35,957.84 total in this account."

Soraya assumed it was a lot, because Rhys' eyes almost popped out of his head.

"Can I take out ₵10,000?"

Daria looked amused. "You actually have a limit of ₵500 in one day because you're a minor, ma'am."

"Okay, ₵500 it is."

Several minutes later, Soraya, Rhys and Yabo exited the bank together and rejoined their group, who had been waiting patiently on the sidewalk. Jacquelle's arms were folded over her chest as she stared impatiently at the cars driving by.

"Zaruna, I want you to have this," Soraya beamed, holding out the white envelope towards the Rosinkin girl.

"Oh, Soraya, tank you, but you don't have ta give me Lari," the girl said, her pink eyebrows scrunching together as she stared at the gift.

"Please, take it, it's for you and your parents," Soraya insisted, the excitement in her voice spilling out. "I want you to have it, please."

Zaruna's face turned pale when she opened it and saw the amount. "Oh Gods, voah!" she gaped at Soraya in shock. "A-ah you sure?"

"Yes, absolutely."

"I cannot possibly pay you back anytime soon-"

"No," Soraya interjected. "It's a gift. No paying back. No owing me anything."

Zaruna choked, tears welling in her magenta eyes. "Can I hug you?"

Soraya accepted, and Yabo licked away Zaruna's tears. The twins gave each other fist bumps while Moiya awed loudly. Jacquelle turned her head and stared at the girls, her expression softening.

"Can we eat at your mom's restaurant?" Soraya asked the twins after letting go of Zaruna. "I wanna meet her."

"Heck yes! Vadamus!" Ujuu exclaimed before taking Zaruna's arm into his once more. "Mom needs to meet you, especially since you're Rhys' girlfriend."

Rhys blushed and shrugged his shoulders. "He's right, it's long overdue."

Yohai Steakhouse was located near the middle of the Matumi Beach pier. Soraya breathed in the fresh sea salt air, enjoying the creaking of wooden planks beneath their feet mixed with the loud thunder of rolling waves crashing against the sandy shore. On either side of them were fishermen chatting amongst themselves while waiting for fish to bite the bait on their lines.

"Soraya, look," Rhys pointed down at a large, circular slab of polished stone in the center of the crowded beach. "That's where the Matumi Beach Concert will be held," he said, then glanced at Jacquelle, who was still ahead of them and acting standoffish. "I think our duet will sound incredible."

"Of course it will," the blond retorted. "Because I've been practicing it for so long-" she corrected herself. "I mean, *we've* been practicing it for so long."

Moiya came to a sudden halt, causing Soraya and Rhys to bump into her from behind, which in turn caused Ujuu and Zaruna to collide into them.

"Oh-" Soraya began, but Moiya brought her finger to her lips and pointed ahead. Norma Whispers was standing outside the steakhouse restaurant, speaking to a weathered looking woman with long, dirty blond hair tied back into a ponytail.

"Mom?" Ujuu whispered, the blood draining from his face. "Why is Norma talking with her?"

"I think I know why…" Rhys walked over to a lamppost and pointed at a wanted flier taped onto it. "Who does that look like to you?"

Soraya's jaw dropped open. *That's a sketch of Rhys and I as a fusion!*

Her eyes flew to the bounty placed under the drawing. *A ₡50,000 reward for illegally using magic?*

"There aren't many other Shadelkins in this community," Rhys breathed, his hands shaking. "It makes sense that MagiCorp would start suspecting us since cat ears aren't that common."

Zaruna placed a hand on her chin. "I'll start vork early today..." she kissed Ujuu's lips. "I vill talk vith Ayla and see if I can get any information on that so called terapist."

The Rosinkin girl was careful to go around the other side of the restaurant and appear behind Mrs. Leyo and Ms. Whispers, forcing both women to turn their attention completely away from the group.

*She's distracting them, so we can get away unnoticed,* Soraya thought before they all turned on their heels and made their escape off the pier. Only after they had rounded several corners, so the beach was completely out of view, did they dare to speak again.

"Sorry about your date ending so soon," Moiya said to Ujuu in a sympathetic tone.

"It's okay, that was a good catch you made," Ujuu smiled weakly at her. "And thank Gods for Zaruna thinking fast on her feet. If Norma had spotted us, that could've been super awkward."

"Norma is definitely a spy," Rhys growled, his fists shaking. "I hope mom confides in Zaruna about whatever it was Ms. Whispers was saying to her. We need to know what that was all about."

"Oh no..." Jacquelle stopped in her steps and stared at the building just ahead of them. "I didn't mean for us to come this way."

It was the bakery from the blond's past. Through the wide window Soraya could see Akoni Pan ringing up orders and serving hungry customers, his vermilion eyes shining brightly from the overhanging lamps inside the shop.

"I… I wish I could apologize," Jacquelle whispered, tears forming in her eyes. "I never meant to do that to him…" Her hand shot to her back, her fingers stroking her scars. "He probably never wants to see me again."

The front door of the shop burst open with a loud bang, causing all the kids to jump. Akoni's father stood in the doorway, glaring ferociously down at Jacquelle.

"You…" he hissed. "You dare set foot on my property?"

The blond stayed in place, petrified to the spot, frozen in fear.

"Leave now, or I call cops!" he bellowed, branding his broom like a sword. "Ten! Nine!" Mr. Pan took two steps closer.

"Let's go," Soraya breathed, grabbing her friend and pulling on her arm, but the blond wouldn't budge.

"He's right to be angry," Jacquelle said flatly.

"Eight! Seven!"

The blond hung her head. "I should be punished."

"Six! Five!"

"Wait!" Rhys and Ujuu both approached Mr. Pan, their hands up in the air to show him they meant no harm.

"Sir, she's changed," Rhys said in a calm tone. "Her mother made her do that, blame Mrs. Demarko, not Jacquelle."

"Lies!" the father roared. "My son… igo no filius…" The man shook his balding head in sorrow. "So much blood lost, he hurt for months after!" he yelled, pointing a thick finger at Rhys. "She'll do the same to you too! Watch your back!"

Soraya noticed several customers gathering at the window to see what all the commotion was about. Akoni, who was just as curious, joined the crowd. Upon spotting Jacquelle, however, his demeanor changed into pure terror. Soraya's heart fell when she remembered the memory Jacquelle had recounted to her.

*I don't think he'll ever recover from that.*

"We need to leave," Moiya whispered, then gently took Jacquelle's hands into her own and tugged.

The blond's body shuddered, as if she were snapping out of a trance, and she finally budged. The five friends fled from the bakery and ran uphill past a row of houses, one of which Soraya recalled was Jacquelle's home.

"I-I'm sorry for everything!" the blond wept while slowing her pace. "I'm sorry!" she screamed, her voice echoing down the busy street.

"We're your friends," Moiya reminded her, grasping onto her hand.

"We forgive you," Ujuu added.

"But they won't ever forgive me," Jacquelle sniffed. "They never will."

"You don't know that for certain," Soraya pulled Jacquelle into a side hug.

"You're not the same person you once were," Rhys added. "Maybe they'll want to meet the new you in time. Don't despair, just keep working on yourself."

"Th-thank you all," Jacquelle cried, her sobs growing louder. Yabo clambered up onto the blond's shoulder and nuzzled himself into her cheek.

As they all headed back to Darkwood Academy, the five friends failed to notice Mrs. Demarko peering down at them from the third floor of her home, but Soraya did notice the air growing colder, as if someone was glaring intensely into her skull.

## Chapter 36: Dealing with Demons

"Aren't you going to answer any of my questions?"

Soraya kept her expression blank and unreadable, like Rhys had taught her. It was imperative that the girl hide what she was thinking, especially with Ms. Whispers snooping around and gathering information on her and her friends.

Norma tapped the top of the desk with her slender fingers, her icy, blue stare boring into the girl's eyes. "Well?"

"I already did," the girl said without emotion.

"Care to expand on your explanations?"

"No."

Soraya's eyes flitted to the clock on the wall. Thirteen twenty-seven. *Just three more minutes until I'm free…*

The past twenty-seven minutes had been excruciating for the girl. Norma had attempted various methods of getting her to open up and talk about herself and her friends. She had tried being nice and befriending Soraya for about ten minutes before losing patience and handing her a list of questions to fill out. Soraya had dawdled by doodling on the pages and giving one word answers, which only made Ms. Whispers even more irate.

Norma followed the girl's gaze and frowned at the time.

"I'll ask Mr. Demarko to double our sessions to an hour starting next Solis."

"And I'll ask the principal to find me a new therapist!" Soraya blurted aloud, much to her dismay. *I wonder if I've picked up Jacquelle's attitude by fusing with her…*

Ms. Whispers stood up, her slender figure towering over the desk. "That's it! I've had it with you!" she hissed. "You wouldn't want anything happening to your Shadelkin friends now, would you?"

Soraya blinked. "Pardon?"

"You heard me!" the therapist's ruby painted lips stretched into a sharp fanged grin. "I know one of them must have used magic, but I don't know which. They're the only two kids who have cat ears in Matumi, and I want that ₾50,000."

The image of the wanted poster Soraya had seen in Matumi flashed in her mind's eye. *Is she actually a spy from MagiCorp, or is she only interested in Lari?*

"I'm confident you know which one did it," Norma's clacking heels echoed around them as she approached the girl like a predator hunting its prey, her pupils dilated so wide they looked like tunnels leading straight into the pits of Hell.

"But they didn't do anything!" Soraya cried, beads of sweat building up on her forehead, but she didn't dare wipe them off for fear of looking guilty under Norma's scrutinizing gaze. "And they don't even have magic! Where would they get it from?"

"I'll find out," Norma's eyes narrowed into snake-like slits. "They could have dyed their hair or worn a wig, and maybe gotten a hold of different colored contacts, which is also illegal."

She pointed a bony finger at Soraya's face. "If you tell Mr. Demarko or anyone else what I said, I will hurt your friends. Got it?"

*I won't let you!* Soraya clenched her fists as she glared at the woman before her. *I could stop her here and now, but what would the consequences be for using Apollryük spells?*

Another thought popped into her head. *Jon! I can ask him for help tomorrow night, after I deal with Mülock again.*

"Time's up," Norma's sudden sweet smile sent shivers down the girl's spine. "Give me actual information to work with next weekend, or something rather unfortunate will befall one of your friends," she said, then strutted over to the office door and held it open. "I always keep my promises. See you next Solis, Ms. Thenayu."

Norma watched in silence as Soraya walked down the long hall in long strides. When the girl rounded the corner, something sharp brushed against the sides of her white leggings. When she looked down, the girl gasped. Her nails were long, like Rhys' whenever he unsheathed his claws.

*I hope she didn't see that!*

Soraya relaxed her hands, and the nails retracted back into her fingers. *This is bad… don't panic, Norma might not have noticed… or did she? I don't know!*

* * *

"Ms. Whispers is evil."

It was the middle of the night on Lunas. The half moon hovering above Darkwood Academy was shrouded by dark, billowing clouds heavy with rain.

The rest of Solis had been a peaceful, uneventful day, despite Norma's threat. Zaruna had also gotten back to Ujuu and filled him in on Ayla's conversation with the therapist.

"I know," Rhys frowned. "Now it makes sense why she interrogated mom. Ujuu and I are the only Shadelkin kids in this community, and we don't have any relatives that remotely look close to the poster drawing other than our dad, but he's too old to fit the descriptions."

Although everyone wore a jacket over their pajamas, they still shivered in the icy wind.

"How do we get her to go away?" Soraya asked. "I'm

powerful enough to protect us, but what happens if I use my powers and others find out what I can do?"

Rhys bit his lower lip. "We'll think of a plan, but let's focus on keeping Mülock from possessing you tonight first," the Shadelkin boy said, pulling her into a tight embrace. "Maybe your idea of asking Jon for advice would work, but don't worry about that right now. One disaster at a time."

Soraya melted in her boyfriend's arms. He smelled like cloudberry tea, and it soothed her anxious soul. "Alright, you're right, as usual," she said and stood up on her tiptoes, pecking Rhys' cheek with her lips. "I'll be back soon."

"We'll be here waiting," Moiya said while patting Soraya's shoulder. "Don't listen to Mülock, no matter what he says."

"Demons lie," Ujuu added. "He's a jerk who just wants to take advantage of you."

"Right," Soraya stared down at the courtyard below, digging her hands into her pockets for additional warmth. *It's weather like this that makes me miss having Water and Air Magic.*

She thought back to their last visit at a Thousand Steps Beach, when she decided to attempt breathing underwater to finish off the last bit of Water Magic she had in her possession. It had worked for ten minutes, which she found incredible, before she had to swim up for air.

"Soraya?"

The girl turned to meet Jacquelle's worried gaze. The blond was fidgeting with her ring. "Be careful, okay?"

"I will," Soraya flashed a smile, then closed her eyes and summoned the Apollryük spell for turning into a shadow. "Shygerü."

The girl's body sank into the shingles of the roof, her perspective shifting from the courtyard below to the sky above in her two-dimensional form. *I don't have to stay like this too long, I just need to get down to the ground. I don't want another headache.*

Though the forest of trees lay far below, the girl slid down the wall with ease. She felt a burning within her chest slowly spreading out across her body like the previous time. After landing on the grass, Soraya attempted to inhale air despite not having a mouth. After several failed attempts, she sucked through where her teeth would be as powerfully as she could muster, and her body finally rose from the ground, resuming her normal self.

*Ha! I figured out how to better control it!*

The girl gazed up at the roof and spotted the silhouettes of her friend's heads peering over the side.

"Telpathia," Soraya breathed. The vision in her left eye became pitch black like the time before, while her right continued taking in her surroundings like normal. When she stared up at her friends, her left eye saw orbs encased in flames. She reached out her hand for one engulfed in crimson fire, and it flew towards her outstretched palm, hovering just above her fingertips.

"Rhys, can you hear me?" she whispered into it.

"Jai," Rhys was staring down at her, so she waved at him. The girl in the orb moved her hand at the same time.

"It's like looking into a weird mirror," Soraya mused loud enough for Rhys to hear her.

"Is it possible to see Mülock with that spell?" Rhys asked. "Maybe that could help you know when he's coming."

Soraya spun herself around in a circle, scanning everywhere for him. "I can see Jon's soul, though it's a bit far away and hovering beyond the stone wall of the school," she replied, focusing her attention onto the orb with blue, red, and green fire and beckoning it to fly towards her.

It hardly moved at all.

*I might have to get closer to reach him, like when I was at the beach.*

"Don't stray too far," Rhys warned. "I know we're all wearing our blessed rings and the purified land is close by, but you still need to be careful."

"Right. I'll head over to the grass and wait there to be safe," Soraya was about to walk away from the orb, when she turned back and added, "I love you."

"Love you too."

Soraya heard muffled giggles and awes from the roof, despite standing on the ground far below her friends. She walked into the mist covered forest with a huge grin on her face, confident Rhys had turned the same color as his eyes.

As she trekked deeper into the thick fog, the girl spun around, looking in every direction possible as she inched closer to her sanctuary, but Mülock was still nowhere to be seen.

*Is he coming tonight? It would be nice if he didn't, but I can't risk falling asleep until later in the morning, just in case.*

Soraya glanced once more at the orb over the wall and stopped in her tracks. A huge, raging, multicolored fire in the shape of a man was speeding towards Jonathan Marlot's small, fiery sphere.

*That must be Mülock!*

Soraya stopped at the healed grass and trees, her thoughts racing as she wondered how Jon was going to fight back against the demon.

*How can I help him?* the girl thought, holding out her hand once more, focusing her full attention on Jonathan's soul. *Come on, fly over to me! I need to know if you're okay!*

The orb budged slightly, hovering a few feet towards her, but stopped again.

*I need to get closer.*

Soraya sprinted to the brick wall surrounding the school, the grass rustling beneath her with each step she took.

"Shygerü!"

She sank into the ground, gliding up and over the obstacle, then breathed in, rising back to her feet once more, and continued running. Darkwood Academy sat on the top of a large, steep hill overlooking the Valtic Ocean. Soraya reached the edge of the cliff and looked out over the dark, brooding sea. Hovering in the air above was Jonathan's fiery sphere, completely surrounded by Mülock's harvested souls.

"Jon!" Soraya shouted, reaching out her arm to grab a hold of the orb hanging just a few feet away from her. The fiery sphere, as if on command, floated into the palm of her hand.

"*You must kill her!*" Mülock's multiple voices roared like thunder inside the orb.

"Go to Hell!" Jonathan shouted back, sounding more irritated than anything else. From what Soraya could see, Marlot was standing on a wooden deck surrounded by clouds. Far below was a city glowing from lit lampposts and lights from various windows.

*Is he on a sky ship?*

"*Soraya can possess you like me, don't you want to get rid of her?*" Mülock asked, rage seething through his double layered fangs. Before Jon stood the six eyed demon she had seen during her last encounter. Several grotesque, bloody faces covered in thick blue veins poked out of the demon's inky black skin, their jaws wide with silent screams.

"Of course not! She's just a sweet kid for Gods' sake!"

"Jon?" Soraya whispered.

"Hey," Marlot laughed in surprise. "We were just talking about you. Welcome to the party."

"*She can contact you?*" Mülock growled, his eyeballs twitching.

"Yes, and she's probably far more powerful than you," Jon taunted.

Mülock threw his head back and roared, his beastly howls piercing through the air, causing both Soraya and Jon's ears to ring.

"*Shut up!*" Marlot barked.

With lightning speed, Jon decked the demon full in the face, his gloved fist smashing into Mülock's forehead with a loud smack, blue flames bursting from the impact and disappearing within seconds. Soraya let out a small gasp as Mülock recoiled from the punch, his six eyes rolling around, blinking in bewilderment.

"*You're going to regret that, pathetic half-breed!*"

"Oh, I'll cherish that moment forever," Soraya could hear the grin in Jonathan's voice. "Along with this one."

Marlot's leg shot through the air, kicking Mülock square in the chest. Several skulls covering the demon's upper body cracked and squished under Jon's boot as the impact sent the demon flying to the other side of the ship. Soraya expected a loud crash to follow, but Mülock's body disappeared into the floorboards instead.

"It turns out you can hurt demons if you wear blessed objects," Jon looked down so the girl could see the various rings decorating his gloved hands. "I thought I'd give your idea a try, and, well, you saw the outcome of that."

Soraya glanced down at the ring on her finger. "That's really good to know."

"Being fused with several other souls has also kept him from possessing me, which really ticked him off," Jon added while unsheathing a long, thin sword. "I had this blessed by a priest, so I'm wondering if it'll slice through him."

Both waited with bated breath for Mülock to reappear, but he didn't.

"Kid, can you see where he's at?" Jon asked, his voice calm like the cold wind blowing through the sails of the ship he was on.

The rainbow-colored flames encased around a dark silhouetted figure had completely vanished from Soraya's sight in her left eye.

"I don't see him anymore," Soraya frowned.

"He's probably left to go find you," Jon breathed. "You'd better run to that safe spot of yours, he really wants you dead."

As Soraya pulled her face away from Jon's orb, she heard a

faint call of her name. "Yes?" she asked, leaning into the fiery sphere again.

"I'll meet up with you soon. Let's chat over tea, make a plan for finding Tishva and Yosef, and destroying this stupid demon once and for all."

"I have more update news for you-" Soraya began, but Jon interrupted.

"Save it for when we meet up. Focus on surviving tonight, don't let Mülock murder you, I'd be rather upset if that happened."

Soraya ran back to the outer wall of Darkwood Academy, her heart pounding in her ears as she kept glancing over her shoulders to make sure Mülock wasn't sneaking up behind her.

*I got this, I just need to stay in the purified patch of grass, and he can't hurt me.*

Soraya turned into a shadow once more, sliding her way up and over the wall, back to the school grounds below.

*Almost there.*

Her left eye was focusing on her surroundings again, like her right. Her vision was a little blurry, but Mülock was still nowhere to be found.

"Stupid plants!"

Soraya paused and cocked her head. Someone was cursing under their breath a few feet away.

*Who is that?* she thought, tip toeing her way across the dew covered grass, careful not to make any loud or sudden noises. She peeked behind a tall oak tree and spotted Ms. Whispers kneeling down in the purified grass, her hand glowing green with Earth Magic.

"Why won't you tell me more information on that brat?" the woman hissed under her breath. "It wasn't an angel, it was a student, and I want to know who!"

Soraya cupped one hand over her mouth and slunk back into the shadows, praying to the Gods that the woman wouldn't discover her.

"*Hello, child…*"

The skin running up Soraya's spine prickled in fear as the voice crept up in the back of her head. Not only had Mülock found her, but Norma Whispers was interrogating the healed grass, blocking her only sanctuary from the demon.

"*My, what a predicament you're in.*"

Soraya could see Mülock's glistening fangs widening. His silhouetted figure stood on the dirt road just a few feet behind the therapist, who was completely oblivious to his presence.

*Do I run back to my friends for safety, or do I deal with Norma?*

## Chapter 37: A Deal with the Devil

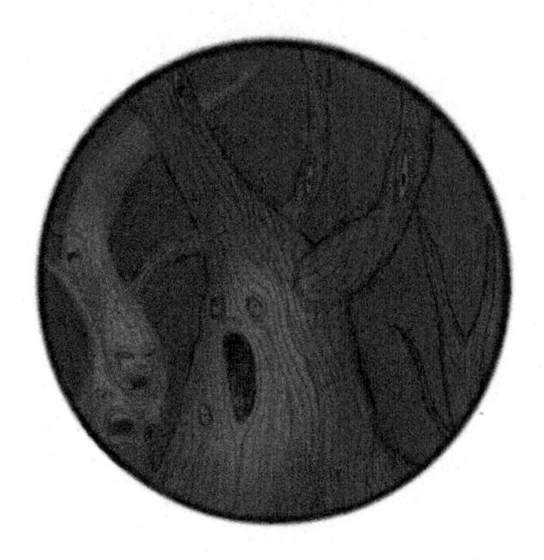

Soraya knew she was running out of time. Even if she made it to where her friends were, she would have to fuse with them to keep from being possessed, giving away their identities to Mülock. If she stayed and dealt with Norma Whispers, however… She tightened her shaking fists, thinking back to her session with the therapist.

*Norma threatened to hurt Rhys and Ujuu! I need to protect them!*

The girl whispered an Apollryük spell and turned into a shadow. She then slid across the grass until she was next to the therapist and safely inside the perimeter of the purified land.

"*Clever…*" Mülock hissed from the back of her mind. "*What other neat tricks can you perform, my child?*"

Soraya ignored him, focusing instead on taking care of Norma. *I shouldn't fuse with her in case Mülock reveals my identity.*

"*I absolutely would do that,*" the demon growled from the back of her mind.

From the ground, Soraya saw the therapist's expression change from one of impatience to disbelief.

"What do you mean there are *demons* here?"

Terror crept into Norma's voice as the plants warned her of the impending danger lurking nearby. "Th-that's impossible!"

Soraya, on cue, waved her shadowy figure across the woman's fingers.

Ms. Whispers let out a shrill squeak at the icy touch, flinching her hands away from the grass. "Who's there?" she demanded, swiveling her head around with wide, frightened eyes.

*Maybe I can scare her away…* Soraya would have smiled if her mouth was still attached. She reached for Ms. Whisper's shadow in her two-dimensional form, lifting it in the air.

"*Oh my Gods!*" Norma screamed as her body was thrust above the ground, suspended on arms she couldn't see. She thrashed and flailed around like a fish out of water, clawing with desperation at the surrounding foliage in an attempt to bring herself back down to the earth below.

*She weighs next to nothing when I'm like this.*

Soraya chucked the woman with all her might, sending Ms. Whispers flying. The woman landed on her back a few feet away, the wind knocked completely from her lungs.

*And don't come back!* Soraya would have yelled if she could speak.

"*Fascinating…*" Mülock observed. "*Within such a short amount of time, you've learned how to control so many demonic spells.*"

Norma Whispers shuddered, choking while fighting to gulp down air. A twinge of guilt tugged at Soraya's chest when she heard the woman struggle to breathe.

"*It's such a shame I have to kill you…*" Mülock's voices interrupted her thoughts.

The therapist rolled herself onto her knees, stood up on wobbly legs, and staggered away as fast as she could, sputtering and coughing as she did. Only when Soraya was sure Norma was gone did she rise from the ground, transforming back into her normal self.

"But why?" she asked, being careful to stay within her sanctuary.

Mülock stepped closer to the purified grass, his six rainbow colored eyes boring into Soraya's flesh. "*Because if I don't, Zinvi will use you against me.*"

"Zinvi?" Soraya repeated. "I thought Amraphael was dead."

"*His offspring,*" Mülock rumbled from the back of her mind. "*He wishes to reopen the portal connecting our worlds. That is why so many Etherian children have gone missing. It requires many blood sacrifices.*" In a flash, the demon was standing in front of Soraya, just inches away from her body.

"*Sacrifices of pure souls.*"

Soraya flinched in surprise, both at the news and Mülock's sudden teleportation.

"*This is why I want Zinvi gone. He cannot reopen the portal his father sealed shut, so he is attempting to make a new door. If he succeeds…*" Mülock went quiet, as if he didn't dare finish the thought.

"If he succeeds…?" Soraya dared to ask.

"*It could very well mean the end of all things.*"

Soraya bit her lower lip. "What does that mean, exactly?"

Mülock's multi-voiced cackles filled the still night air around them. "*The more blood is spilled on Etherian soil, the sooner the Titans will be awoken from their slumber. They will bring about the end of days for both our worlds if most of Etheria's land is cursed.*"

Soraya shivered, pulling her jacket tighter around herself.

"*The Gods purposefully leveraged mortal sins against Etheria's sustainability. Etherians will bring destruction upon their own heads should they continue to needlessly kill one another…*"

Before Soraya could interject, Mülock spoke again. "*You and Jonathan are abominations of nature, half-breeds created with the sole purpose of being controlled by the one who has the blood of the highest ranking demon! I'm sure the Gods would thank me for blotting you both out from history.*"

"Then why did you give us the purging souls spell?" Soraya asked, her blood boiling.

*"To see how high in the demonic hierarchy you both are. Very few can perform it, only the ones near the top can."*

Soraya stamped her foot into the soil. "It still seems counterintuitive for you to have done that!"

Mülock grinned. *"That spell only takes enough energy to completely heal yourself. I have far more souls fused with me than you do, so consuming you and Jonathan whole would be a cinch if we were in the same dimension."*

The girl frowned, pondering the demon's words. "Couldn't you help Jon and I defeat Zinvi instead of trying to murder us?"

*"Zinvi has one who can rival even my power,"* thundered Mülock. *"I've already thought along those lines, but I doubt you two could possibly resist being possessed by that one…"*

"We've already figured out how to defend ourselves against you," Soraya pointed out, hoping her tone didn't sound too snarky. "Give us all the information you have on Zinvi. Jon and I both want to save those kidnapped girls, and we all have a common goal of stopping Zinvi from linking our worlds."

The girl's very next thought to blurt from her mouth sounded strange, even as it rolled off her tongue, but she believed it was the best solution given the circumstances. "We could save both our dimensions if we work together."

Mülock's mocking laughter shook Soraya to the core, but she didn't let it show on her face.

*"You want to make a deal with me?"*

"Yes," the girl stated while glaring into the demon's six eyes. "Help Jon and I defeat Zinvi, so he can't open another portal, then leave us alone forever."

Mülock's eyes narrowed into glowing slits. *"You both have to kill the one who rivals my power, along with Zinvi and his entire demonic hybrid army. If you and Jon succeed, then I will indeed allow you both to live out your days,"* He laughed once more. *"Though you may beg me to die someday…"*

"What does that mean?" Soraya asked, but the demon

refused to answer. Instead, his six, rainbow-colored eyes moved up and down her petite figure.

"*Alright, you have a deal. Here's what I know of Zinvi's army...*"

Soraya's inner eye was clouded with a horrifying sight, one that made her knees quake in fear. A labyrinth of wine colored trees twisting and contorting over one another filled her mind, their fleshy limbs pulsing altogether, as if each contained their own heart. Several sagging faces decorated the exterior tendons of the trees, their black, oozing eyeballs forever rolling around with desperation, their mouths unnaturally elongated into silent screams.

*That's a lot of Blood Oaks!*

"*There's a lab hidden somewhere in that forest,*" Mülock said, his voices growing fainter.

Four figures appeared in the girl's mind. There were two men, one was as pale as a ghost, while the other had darker skin, like the rich, sleek coat of a horse. The other two were women, both with vitiligo skin.

"*Grawljok, Chamos, Vavrina, and Elva can perform successful fusions, perfectly mimicking the features of the souls trapped within themselves. There are many more, but they were all I was able to see at that moment. Good luck finding and destroying them...*" The demon standing before her faded completely from view, his voice no longer audible.

* * *

Soraya awoke with a start in her bed. She sat up, blinking. Yellow beams of light from the morning sun poured in through the cracks of the draped dormitory windows. Yabo was sprawled on his back between her legs, snoozing away without a care in the world.

*It feels so late in the day...*

The girl sank back into her pillow when a thought struck her. *Oh no! I'm late for my classes!*

The girl untangled herself from around her pet, hopped down to the floor and rushed upstairs towards the changing room.

Just as she found her locker, however, she stopped to read the note taped onto the front.

*We turned in your permission slip to miss classes today since we couldn't wake you up. Rest and feel better.*

There were two hearts sketched underneath. One had Moiya Marlune's initials written into the center, while the other had Jacquelle Demarko's. Beneath them, scrawled in Moiya's thick, loopy handwriting, read:

*P.S. Expect Rhys to be jealous of you skipping cooking class.*

"Poor Rhys!" Soraya laughed. She re-read the note one more time before taking it down and placing it in her pajama pocket. "I have amazing friends."

She paced the room in circles while thinking back to the previous night, her fingers twitching with each step.

*Did I actually make a deal with Mülock?* Soraya pulled up the images of the four Demoni Hybrids in her mind's eye, studying each one with care. *I haven't met any of them yet. I wonder if Jon knows who they are.*

"Telpathia," she said, expecting Jon's soul to be floating somewhere by the cliffs overlooking the Valtic Ocean like the night before, but instead, it was just outside the bedroom, hovering over the balcony. She hurried over, unlocked the door leading to the outer railing, and threw it open.

"Hello."

Soraya froze and looked up. Jonathan Marlot was sitting on the roof above, peering down at her through thick red sunglasses. His long, black trench coat swayed in the wind as the awkward silence between them grew.

"H-hi," the girl stuttered, clutching her chest.

The man leapt down gracefully onto the balcony with a light thud, then rose to his full height.

"We have a lot to discuss, Ms. Soraya."

## Chapter 38: Another Ally

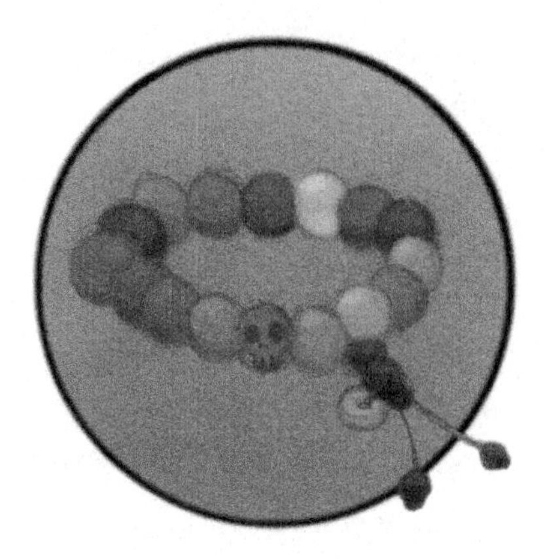

Soraya stared at the man before her. He was wearing the same cloak, hat, goggles, and glasses she had seen during their first conversation. She also noticed a lavender jacket over a faded yellow, collared shirt, but one feature in particular stuck out the most to her.

*He's only slightly taller than me?*

"I know what you're thinking," Jon's voice was like the sea, calm with an undercurrent of power. "You thought I'd be taller, didn't you?"

"Yes…"

Jon looked amused, his grin growing wider with each passing second. "When Mülock first mentioned you, I thought you'd be older," he looked her over with his hands tucked into his deep coat pockets. "What are you, ten?"

"I'm thirteen."

"You have the voice of a ten-year-old," he teased.

"*Hey!*" Soraya stomped her foot on the wooden boards beneath them.

Marlot smirked at her outburst. "I take it back… a *nine*-year-old."

Soraya pouted, folding her arms over her chest. "I promise I'm thirteen…"

Jon chuckled. "Okay, young lady, I suggest *properly dressing* like one."

The girl looked down. Because she was still using her telepathy spell, the vision in her left eye was pitch black, but through her right eye, she could see she was still in her pajamas.

"I'll be… right back…" her face turned red, like a bed of roses, while she held open the door leading into the dormitory. "Um, can you just wait on the roof for me?"

He raised a faded golden brow.

"I can join you there shortly. I don't want you to be seen by anyone else."

"Ah. Understood."

Before Soraya could slip behind the door, Yabo waltzed between Soraya's legs and meowed up at Jon.

"Hello there. What's your name?" Marlot murmured. He crouched down, holding out a gloved hand towards the pandacoon.

"That's Yabo, my pet," Soraya said, eyeing Jon warily. "Please, don't hurt him…"

Jon paused, sliding his red sunglasses down onto the tip of his nose, so his eyes were staring into Soraya's. They were sky blue, like hers, but mixed with red and green hues from the other souls he held trapped within himself.

"I only hunt for survival, and he's your family, not food."

Yabo rubbed his face into the man's fingers, chirping as he did.

"Your guardian loves you very much," Jon whispered to the pandacoon while stroking his furry back. "You both have a similar aura, very sweet and caring."

He glanced up at Soraya with a half turned smile. "I suggest getting ready for the day, I was serious about taking you out for tea."

"Oh, um…" Soraya stammered. "I don't know if I should leave school…"

"With a stranger?" Jon winked. "We don't have to do that today or at all if you're not comfortable with it. Speaking on the roof is fine."

He scratched behind Yabo's ears, and the pandacoon closed his beady eyes, purring his little heart out. "Just remember I can't contact you with that Telpathia spell, and it's best not to use the phone or letters to discuss our plans. We can always meet up outside of school with your friends accompanying you if that makes you feel safer."

"Alright…" Soraya watched Jon and Yabo for a few more seconds before beckoning for her pet to come back. When the pandacoon ignored her, she darted inside the dorm, changing into her day clothes as quickly as possible while glancing at the clock hanging in the locker room.

*Eight forty? Wow, I did sleep in a lot!*

The first break in the school schedule started at ten, so she assumed her friends would visit her around then. Through her left eye, she could spot her friend's souls clustered altogether.

*They should all be in Azakuin Literature class right now,* a pang of guilt strummed at her heart strings. *I told them about Norma Whispers and what I did to her, but I still have to tell them about the deal I made with Mülock…*

Soraya had been afraid to fill them in on everything that had transpired. Her friends would be even more worried and paranoid than they already were. The girl also feared they would be disappointed in her decision to join forces with the demon.

*I have to fill them and Jon in on everything… Today…*

Soraya went back to the balcony and found Marlot gone. Yabo was inside the dormitory with her, pawing at the glass to go back out. She knelt down and scooped up her pet.

"He left a good impression on you, didn't he?" Soraya mused, kissing Yabo's nose before sneaking to the coat closet. She pressed on a small, inconspicuous cut out in the wall. It flapped open, like a door, and she crawled through to the other side, where the spiral staircase leading to the roof lay hidden. After closing the small panel shut behind her and clambering up in the dark, she made it to the ceiling and pressed on the top, lifting it open.

Jon stood up straight, looking out over the expanse of the great blue Valtic Ocean with his hands behind his back, his long, black coat flapping dramatically in the wind.

"How did last night go for you?" he asked without turning his head.

"I… well…" Soraya swallowed. "I made a deal with Mülock…"

Jon half turned, so his crimson sunglasses glinted in the sun overhead. "I had a feeling you would be the one to convince him to take it."

"You already know?"

"Sort of-"

"Mow?"

Yabo interjected, leaping onto the ground to rub himself against Jon's legs. The man gently scooped up the pet, placing him onto his shoulder.

"He wanted me to stop the kidnappings, since he was able to possess me at the time. But then, he found out about you," a wry smile formed on his thin lips. "And you resisted him. Not only that, but you contacted me, giving me some ideas for fighting back. So now, Mülock has no choice but to work with us rather than trying to have me murder you."

He paused to pet Yabo, then turned to fully face her. "He didn't tell me everything for why the kidnappings must stop. He sees me as beneath him, a pawn to be used and discarded. He fears you more than I, ironically enough, given that you're a nine-year-old."

Soraya opened her mouth to protest, but restrained herself.

Jon noticed and smiled for a brief moment before his face hardened once more.

"I'm aware of how powerful you are. You can perform Apollryük spells that I cannot," Jon lowered his sunglasses, his multicolored eyes boring into Soraya's. "Please, fill me in on that deal," he folded his hands together and bowed low to the ground. "I promise to protect you as best I can. You have my word."

She could hear the sincerity in his voice. Between that and Yabo doting on him, she decided to believe him. "Thank you, sir," Soraya bowed back. "I'll tell you everything."

* * *

When Soraya finished explaining the previous night's events, Jon stroked his golden goatee in thought.

"Zinvi has a demonic army, and he wants to sacrifice girls to link our world with the demonic realm, which may result in the end of all things."

He lifted one finger at a time as he listed off their goals. "We must save the kids, kill off Zinvi and the other hybrids, and find the lair hidden somewhere in a forest of Blood Oaks."

"Yes, that's right." Soraya nodded.

"See how I condensed all that information down?" Marlot smirked. "You could have just said that instead of giving me a long, drawn out play-by-play of last night."

"Oh…" Soraya blushed and hung her head. "Sorry."

Jon laughed heartily. "You are very entertaining when telling stories. Sometimes, it's better to get straight to the point, is all I'm saying," he glanced at Yabo, who chirped and nuzzled into his cheek.

"I'm sure even if we succeed in doing all of that, Mülock will try to possess us again," Jon pat the pandacoon with his gloved hand while staring at Soraya. "You're a threat to him, and he doesn't like competition."

"That's true…" the girl grimaced. "If only I could purify

more land, so we don't have to worry about him being able to contact us again..."

"That would take a lot of Water Magic," Jon mused. "We could always try infiltrating one of the MagiCorp headquarters and stealing magic. We'll need lots of fire for burning the Blood Oaks anyway, might as well take as much as we can."

"That's a good point," Soraya recalled the Blood Oak forest and grit her teeth together. "But could we actually get away with stealing from MagiCorp?"

"Only one way to find out," Jon flashed her a grin. "I think it's best to wait until the school year ends before we set off on our journey. With your father and Yosef missing, we should probably add me as an emergency contact to your paperwork, so the school releases you without asking too many questions."

*Papa... Yosef...*

Jon noticed Soraya's crestfallen face, and his eyebrows knitted together in empathy. "It's alright, they're still alive, and we're going to find them."

"Okay..." Soraya sniffed.

"I must warn you, part of preparing for rescuing your dad and his friend means switching up your tactics..." he folded his arms across his chest. "I'm giving you a G for how you handled Norma Whispers."

"What? A G?" Soraya blinked in surprise. "Th-that's an average grade!"

"You did well not to run back to your friends. Mülock would've used you to murder them all, so that's why I'm not giving you a failing grade of a D or E..."

Soraya stared glumly at her friend's souls through her left eye.

"However, I'm not giving you an A or B simply because you let Norma live," Jon shrugged his shoulders. "She's going to cause even more problems now that she believes demons are afoot on school grounds."

Soraya grimaced. *I don't want her dead…*

Jonathan adjusted his sunglasses, so they covered his eyes once more. "You were smart to not possess her while Mülock was there, but you should have hunted her down afterwards, or tried harder to knock her completely out, so she couldn't run away at all, though," Jon chuckled. "It sounds like she deserved a good scare."

"Well, it was pretty fun to do," Soraya rubbed the back of her neck. "But even so, she doesn't know it was me. Plus, Mülock should leave us alone for a while."

Jon scoffed. "You can't trust him. I'm sure he'll make it look like he's keeping his end, but don't expect it to last. He'll say something along the lines of," Jon made air quotes with his fingers. "*Time's up*, even though that was never specified."

"Do you think… making a deal with him was foolish?" Soraya asked, her lip quivering.

Jon shook his head. "No, especially since you pointed out our common goals. If anything, you bought us more time before we actually have to deal with the demon, and you gained more information for us to work off of," he gave her an encouraging smile. "You did your best to manage a tough situation, and you did well."

Yabo leapt down from Jon's shoulders, waltzing back over to Soraya with a jump in his step.

"I was thinking of fusing with Norma, actually," Marlot said thoughtfully. "Adding her to my collection, gleaning information from her. It would be useful to know what side she's on, steal her Earth Magic, and…" He cracked a wide grin. "I could pretend to be her during your therapy sessions. I promise I won't interrogate you like she does."

"Can you mimic the features of the souls you have trapped

inside you as well?" Soraya asked, her blood turning cold at the very thought.

"I can..." Jon placed his thumb and pointer finger on his chin. "I store them in my body mainly for spare parts, and for transferring pain I endure in battle to them. Mimicking features for longer than twelve hours is difficult, however."

He took off his glove, revealing the hand Soraya had seen the other day. Much to her surprise, it looked completely normal. There was no mouth or eyeball in sight.

"I cast Orchal out of my body already. That worthless twit is a puddle of skin and veins somewhere in the ocean, probably shark food by now."

Soraya shuddered at the gross picture popping into her head.

"I know it's weird, but if we're going to take on other demonic hybrids, you have to use your powers to their fullest extent, do you understand?"

"Yes... I know, but..." Soraya hugged herself. "My fusions don't work that way."

"Maybe today they don't, but I think in time, you can learn to do many things," Jon held out his hand for her to shake. "Would you like to fuse with me?"

"Oh," Soraya glanced between his hand and his face, which appeared calm and stoic. "I don't know about doing that quite yet..."

*Why am I turning him down?*

Guilt crept into her blood as her hand faltered in the air.

Jon simply lowered his arm, placed his glove back on, and took a step back. "I'm not going to make you do something you don't want to do. I understand your hesitations. We're both demonic hybrids with slightly different abilities, so I'm actually not sure what'll happen either if we try it."

"You're... alright with me saying no right now?

Jon gave her two thumbs up and a sincere smile in reply. "Absolutely."

"Thank you," Soraya let out a small sigh. "And sorry."

"Don't apologize," Jon waved his hand dismissively in the air. "You've done nothing wrong."

Soraya found herself enjoying the man's company. *He respects me, it would be much nicer to have him be my therapist than Norma…*

"Are you actually going to fuse with Ms. Whispers?" the girl asked, her wide eyes brimming with curiosity.

"I think it's a good idea. How about you?"

His question hung in the air for a few moments as Soraya's brain studied multiple possibilities from several angles, like how her boyfriend's brain would assess a situation.

*So many outcomes… no wonder Rhys is quiet all the time, he mulls over every little detail!*

"It makes the most sense to do," the girl said while paced in small circles on the roof. "But what happens if she's part of something bigger than herself, like MagiCorp, and she has to report to someone constantly? You can't keep up her appearance for longer than twelve hours, and my features always come out mixed when I fuse with someone else, so neither of us could pull off living her life and ours at the same time."

"Good point."

Marlot stood still, but Soraya knew his eyes followed her movements.

"I can visit her in the night, fusing with her while she's sleeping," the man suggested. "I should be able to pick her brain and steal her Earth Magic. If she's a member of MagiCorp or some other organization, I'll let her live, convincing her she had a horrid nightmare, but if she's not tied to anything…"

Jon didn't finish his sentence, but his grin stretched unnaturally long from both corners of his face. A pungent odor of iron and ashes overpowered Soraya's nose, causing it to twitch.

*This smell, this overwhelming feeling of dread...*

Soraya's heart pounded in her ears. She took a step backwards, nausea rising from her stomach. Even Yabo's fur spiked up in terror at the sudden change in atmosphere. The smell immediately faded when the man hid his teeth under thin lips.

"Sorry, I didn't mean to scare you both like that," Jon took out a bracelet made of large, circular beads from his coat pocket and studied them, his thumb lightly tracing over each one as he did.

"What are you doing?" Soraya managed to ask once she felt more stable.

The man paused and glanced up at her. "I'm thinking of mantras and prayers. My parents taught me to do this whenever I feel the urge to rip someone apart."

"Does it work...?"

"Mostly," he chuckled, placing the beads back. "It's just a nice distraction for curbing my addiction," his demeanor relaxed as he added, "I'm glad to see you don't have to deal with bloodlust like I do. Maybe, you're not as demonic as Mülock thinks. You seem to have a holier aura surrounding you."

Soraya looked down at her feet. "I'm not sure what I am..."

"It doesn't matter. You're you, and you're a good kid."

Before the girl could reply, Jon swung his legs over the edge of the roof. "I'd best be off. We'll meet again soon," he promised, waving his gloved hand. "Contact me tomorrow, I'm off to hunt down that therapist, and hopefully satisfy my craving..."

Soraya's stomach churned at the thought.

"Remember, she threatened the safety of your friends. She's not going to play fair, and we shouldn't either," Jon added, his tone serious as he studied her torn expression.

"You're right," the girl nodded her head slowly.

"Stay safe, both of you."

"You too, sir." Soraya watched him clamber down nimbly.

*How is he going to clear the wall surrounding the school?*

The girl received her answer, however, when he turned into a shadow and slid his way down to the ground, slithered across the grass, and disappeared out the front gate.

*He can use that spell too…*

Soraya took in the grand view of the sparkling Valtic Ocean one more time before heading back with Yabo. She couldn't help but think about Norma Whispers and the fate that awaited her, and shivered.

*He's right though… she's a threat…*

The girl climbed back through the closet, shutting the small panel shut behind her, and entered into the dormitory. All was quiet, there were no other souls in sight. Soraya placed her precious pet on the bed and kissed his face before grabbing her school supplies.

*I got enough rest in, I should head to class and fill in my friends on everything during the break.*

## Chapter 39: The School Assembly

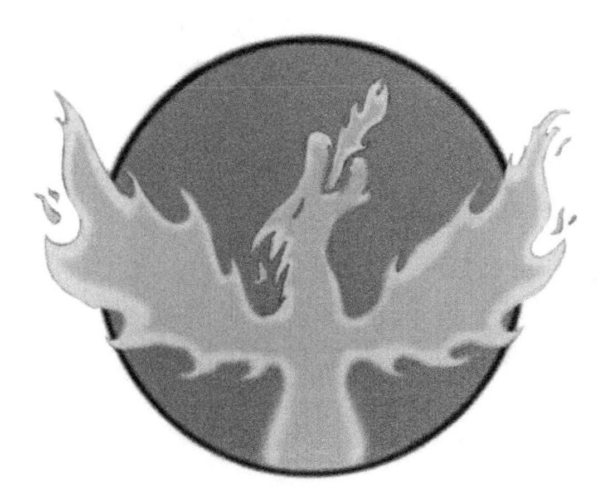

"You made a deal with Mülock *and* met with Jon?"

"Yeah…"

Rhys, Ujuu, Moiya and Jacquelle were all dumbfounded, each of their jaws dropping open in shock.

"Why do these things always happen when we leave you alone for a few minutes?" Rhys sighed, his eyes closed, his index finger and thumb pinched to his furrowed forehead.

"I think you should all meet Jon…" Soraya added timidly. "He's quite nice."

"Yes, let's meet the man who craves blood, what could possibly go wrong?" snorted Jacquelle. "Should we all hang out in a dark alleyway while we're at it?"

"I mean it," Soraya replied, thinking about how much her pet snuggled up to Marlot. "Yabo seems to like him a lot."

"Oh wow," Ujuu declared. "That *is* a good sign."

"What?" Jacquelle scoffed. "Are you serious?"

"He's right," Moiya spoke up. "Yabo's pretty good at detecting one's character. He doesn't like Ms. Whispers," the girl paused and glanced at the blond. "He only took to you recently… Remember how he didn't like you when you first met him?"

"Yabo *always* liked me!" Jacquelle huffed, folding her arms across her puffed out chest. "No need to be mean, Moiya."

Soraya stifled the laughter rising into her throat.

*That's quite ironic…*

"We should meet up with Jon in a public place this weekend," Rhys finally said. "He did offer to take care of Norma, let's see if he follows through on that."

Jacquelle shot the Shadelkin boy a glare. "I thought you out of all of us would be the reasonable one and put your foot down. We can't let him hurt Soraya!"

"If he had wanted to do that, he would've already."

Jacquelle clenched her jaw, her tightened fists shaking.

"He's extremely powerful," Rhys continued. "He could've easily kidnapped her or done us all in if that was his intention."

"Exactly, and he did no such thing," Soraya nodded in agreement. "I trust him."

She glanced at Jacquelle. "Could you add him to my paperwork as my uncle? Make him an emergency contact, so he can pick me up once the school year ends?"

"No!" Jacquelle cried, startling Soraya. "I'm not losing you!"

"But-"

The blond swiftly turned on her heels and disappeared out of the Radio Room before Soraya had a chance to continue, the clacking of her shoes fading from ear shot as she descended the winding staircase.

"Wait!"

Soraya started chasing after her, but Rhys gently caught her gloved hand. "Give Jacquelle some space," he breathed. "We're all worried about that plan."

"But Jon's going to help me find my father and Yosef!" Soraya exclaimed. "I know he can be trusted, you'll see!"

"Okay, we'll meet with him this weekend," Rhys said, his

eyebrows knitted together. "He said to contact him tomorrow, right?"

"Yes, and I will," Soraya nodded. "We'll all go out for tea."

Fast footsteps approached from the stairwell. Soraya, Rhys, Ujuu and Moiya turned their heads and saw Jacquelle panting in the doorway.

"We all have to go to a school assembly right now!" she gasped, her voice full of terror. "MagiCorp is here!"

* * *

"Greetings, students," a tall, thin man with pale skin spoke from the center of the orchestra room amphitheater, his long, dark blue cloak rippling like water with each movement he made. "My name is Alizon Doorfeather. I'm a Mage from the company, MagiCorp, and so are my companions who are here with me today." He turned, gesturing towards his comrades with a stretched out arm, his ocean blue eyes sparkling under the lamps overhead.

"Tildama Lewandow!"

A woman with skin as dark as ebony took a bold step forward, her slender figure encased in a violet, velvet cloak. Her eyes and hair color matched her clothing.

"Venara Cristo!"

Another woman lined up next to Tildama. She was slightly shorter with magenta colored hair, bright rose colored eyes, and skin mixed with mahogany and marble. Her robe was a dark pink mixed with dark reds at the sleeves and rims.

"And Finn Duraiko!"

A large, bulkier built man stepped up to join the other two women. His aqua colored hair was flecked with silver, his grass green robes outlining the muscles on his arms.

Soraya and her friends sat in the center rows of the audience, each carefully studying the Mages before them.

*Were they involved in kidnapping Papa and Yosef?*

"We are here to perform a demonstration of magic and offer the top scoring students the opportunity to join our ranks with fully paid scholarships," Alizon announced with a hint of pride.

A wave of excited murmurs rippled out from the stands.

"Imagine becoming a Mage!" Vamera whispered to Emrose while shaking her shoulder. "We can do it!"

"My scores aren't good enough, there's no way I'll be chosen," Olive sighed from a few seats away.

"What's the catch?" Rhys muttered under his breath.

The four Mages lowered their heads, then whipped out long thin pieces of wood from their sleeves in unison.

"*Fire!*" Alizon proclaimed in a dramatic voice. All four Mages raised their wands, flicking their wrists simultaneously. Instantly, bright flames shot out from the ends of their weapons, joining together into a massive fireball floating above their heads. The intense heat caused all the students to squirm in their seats.

Soraya wiped away beads of sweat from her face as the Mages split into two teams beneath the hungry flames. Alizon and Tildama danced together, spinning their wands at the same time while Venara and Finn worked on crafting the other half.

The yellow ball twisted and curled in the air, forming a dragon before everyone's eyes. The flaming beast opened its jaws, and another beam of flames erupted into the air, almost touching the ceiling of the amphitheater.

Soraya couldn't help but admire the deadly art before her.

"That's so beautiful," she breathed.

"*Water!*"

The four mages spread their legs apart into fighting stances before twirling their bodies in fluid motions. Jets of water shot out from their wands. Loud hissing filled the air as the flaming dragon was extinguished, both water and fire dissolving into puffs of smoke. Within seconds there was nothing left but a light mist hovering above the ground.

"*Air!*"

All four Mages ran and jumped, their bodies rising into the center of the mist. The cloud shrouding them moved clockwise around them, spinning faster and faster, creating a miniature tornado.

Everyone's hair and clothing in the amphitheater lifted into the air, tugging at their person to move towards the center stage.

Soraya clung to her seat's armrests with a death-like grip. *It's like we're being sucked in!*

"*Earth!*"

The floor beneath everyone rumbled and shook as the center of the stage rose to meet the whirlwind. Rock and mud stretched around it, encasing the cyclone along with the four mages.

Soraya relaxed slightly when she no longer felt the vacuum of air drawing her towards the stage.

The circular rock formation, still attached to the earth below, lowered, smoothing itself out and recreating the stage, before crumbling apart and revealing the four Mages inside. They were completely unharmed, and the tornado was gone as if it had never existed.

Clapping and whistles erupted from all sides of the amphitheater as students rose from their seats, marveling at the spectacular sights they had just witnessed. Even Soraya and her friends couldn't help but join in the cheering.

The four Mages bowed, soaking in the applause and attention, before Alizon rose and motioned with his hands for the audience to quiet themselves down.

"For the next few months, we will be meeting with each one of you, weeding out those who show promise for joining our ranks," he paused, then lifted his wand once more. "We also need your help with finding this Etherian."

Stacks of papers took to the sky, each hovering above a

student, so they could pluck it from the air with ease. Soraya and Rhys snuck a nervous glance at each other as they studied the copies of the wanted posters they had seen at Matumi Beach the other day in their trembling hands.

"If you happen to see this kid at all, please report to us immediately. He, she or they illegally used magic to purify that patch of grass that now resides in your track and field. We only have this sketch of them thanks to the plants that witnessed the event."

The silence that ensued was deafening. No one dared to make a noise as they stared at the ridiculously high reward Lari for finding the child.

As Soraya glanced around the room at all of her fellow student's faces, she realized she was the only one with strawberry blond hair in the entire school, and no one else had cat-like ears like the Shadelkin twins. She looked back at the four Mages and noticed Alizon's dark blue eyes had settled upon the three of them, his pale face expressionless.

*Oh Gods, I hope they don't suspect me or Rhys or Ujuu!*

"Thank you for your time," Alizon bowed, the three other Mages copying him. "Expect to see our talent scouts roaming about Darkwood Academy until the end of the school year. Good luck to all of you."

All the students stood and filed out of the rows, the room filled with multiple chatters from various conversations. Soraya and her friends, however, dared not speak to each other at that moment. The girl was well aware of Alizon's eyes following her every movement until she exited out the front door.

## Chapter 40: Tea with Marlot

"So, MagiCorp finally showed up."

The vision within Jonathan Marlot's orb was partially obscured by the smoke billowing from his pipe.

"Yes," Soraya leaned closer into the fiery blue, red and green soul floating above the palm of her hands. "Did you fuse with Norma?"

Cackles filled the space between them. "Oh, I most certainly did."

Soraya's eyelid twitched.

"Norma Whispers is an alias with fake PhD credentials. This woman's real name is Josephine Macklin, a bounty hunter bent on kidnapping the Shadelkin twins. She would have too if we hadn't acted when we did."

Soraya exhaled, her insides queasy. "Is she… still alive…?"

"Of course. Josephine's trapped within me, making all sorts of plea bargains and empty promises in the hopes that I'll let her go," Jon took off his glove to show Soraya the Earth Magic tattoo on his skin. "This woman has murdered countless Etherians in all sorts of horrific ways. Don't feel bad for her, she's not sorry at all."

"So, you're going to pretend to be Norma during my therapy sessions, right?"

"Yup."

"And, we're meeting up at The Dancing Dragon on Astros at fifteen o'clock, right?"

"Correct."

"Alright, I'll see you then," Soraya whispered into the orb. "Have a good night, sir."

"You too, kid."

* * *

The Dancing Dragon was a two-story beach house with the perfect ocean view on Matumi's shore. A quarter mile of white sand stretched out before it, acting as a buffer between the shop and the Valtic Ocean. A wooden sign hung from the building, depicting a dragon made of smoke rising from a tea cup.

"This looks quaint," Soraya commented as she and her friends approached the building.

Rhys gently squeezed her fingers with his own. "It does," he agreed, glancing over his shoulder.

One of Magicorp's men had been following the group around Matumi, hovering just a few feet away at all times. He was a tall, muscular man with dark brown eyes, hair and tanned skin. He wore russet colored pants, black shoes, and a white collared shirt with the sleeves rolled up to his elbows.

Soraya held the front door of the tea shop open for her friends, making sure all of them safely entered before going inside herself. She refused to make eye contact with the spy, but knowing he was watching them from the sidewalk they had just crossed over unsettled her.

Ever since MagiCorp's employees had arrived at Darkwood Academy, their talent scouts had roamed freely about the campus in addition to creating a schedule for culling through students, starting in alphabetical order.

Every day, during breaks, they would interview one student at a time, going over their test scores, asking them if they knew anything about the purified patch of land, and if they had seen the wanted kid on the poster. Jacquelle Demarko would be the first in their group to be interrogated, and she was scheduled for the following week on Ignis.

The room inside the Dancing Dragon was large and spacious, with booths lining both sides of the walls. In the furthest corner away from the front of the store sat Norma Whispers, sipping on tea while reading a newspaper through Marlot's red sunglasses.

The five friends approached the woman's table, being careful to appear as casual as possible in how they carried themselves.

"Is that you, Jon?" Soraya asked once she stood by the woman.

"Yes," Marlot extended Norma's arm, gesturing for the kids to sit. "How I look is a poor reflection of who I really am."

*That's Jon alright.*

"As your therapist, I respectfully ask that you call me Norma," Jon tilted his head down to look over the rims of his sunglasses as the talent scout stalker entered the tea shop and settled into a seat just two tables over. "I'm glad that you're finally warming up to me, Ms. Thenayu."

"Yes, and I'm sorry we got off on the wrong foot," Soraya played along, understanding she had to be careful with everything she said. "Thanks for meeting with me, Ms. Whispers, I really do appreciate your help."

"Of course," Jon enunciated loud enough for the talent scout to hear. "But before we can continue our conversation, I must ask a certain someone to leave, as I'm bound by my oath of upholding client confidentiality."

He shot a glare at the MagiCorp employee and rose from his seat. "Sir, did Ms. Thenayu invite you to be a part of this therapy session?"

The man, startled, nearly dropped the drink menu he was hiding behind.

"Did she?" Marlot, now the same height as Norma Whispers, towered over the sitting man.

"N-no."

"Then why are you eavesdropping?"

"Ma'am, there must be some misunderstanding," the talent scout laughed with a hint of nervousness in his voice. "I'm chaperoning these students."

"That's funny, I thought I was the one doing that."

Jon whipped out signed permission slips from Darkwood Academy and shoved them in the man's face. "I have proof for what I'm saying, where are your documents?"

"Oh…"

"If you don't possess signed paperwork from the school for chaperoning, and you're following these children around without their consent, then what are your real intentions?"

Soraya could hardly believe what she was seeing and suppressed her giggles. Ujuu bit his lower lip to keep from laughing, Moiya's emerald gems widened in surprise, Jacquelle looked smug with her arms folded over her chest, and Rhys kept his hands folded on his lap while observing through expressionless, crimson eyes.

The man's skin flushed a beet red. He suddenly hopped up from his seat. "I work for MagiCorp," he spat. "One of the largest companies in all of Etheria! You don't get to disrespect me like this!"

"Ms. Thenayu, does this man intimidate you in any way?" Jon asked in Norma's sickeningly sweet voice.

"Yes, he does."

"There you have it," Jon smirked when the man's mouth gaped open in shock. "I'm a therapist, I protect my clients, now leave."

The talent scout looked as if he were about to say something, but closed his mouth and stormed off instead, slamming the door of the tea shop behind him with a loud bang.

"Can we sit upstairs?" Jon asked one of the startled waitresses. "It would be greatly appreciated if we could enjoy our beverages in a more private setting."

* * *

"This is much better."

The six of them sat around a table on the roof, the salty ocean breeze ruffling their clothes and the jade green tablecloth, the roaring waves crashing against the sandy shore filled the air.

"Thanks for doing that," Ujuu said, his tarragon soda resting between his palms. "He's been following us around all day."

"No problem," Marlot replied, his fingers tracing the lip of his teacup. "MagiCorp will have to deal with Norma Whispers until the end of the school year."

"Are you actually planning on finding Tishva and Yosef with Soraya once school is out?" Rhys inquired as he leaned forward in his seat and took a sip of his cloudberry tea.

Marlot's teeth poked through his painted red lips. "I know you don't trust me, so does anything I say or promise even matter?"

"Just answer the question!" Jacquelle snapped, slamming her fist down on the table.

Jon seemed amused by the blond's outburst. "Yes, that is my plan. Are you going to add me as Soraya's uncle to her paperwork so that can happen without suspicions being aroused?"

"I don't know yet," huffed Jacquelle, her eyes narrowing. "It's too early to know if you're actually our friend or not."

"Fair enough."

"Can we come with you?" Rhys asked, his eyes studying Marlot.

"If your parents give you permission, I don't see why not."

"Wait, what?" Moiya gaped, her eyebrows raised. "Really?"

"Starlene Inos is implementing a new law on Mazula sixth, the day she becomes President," Marlot sprawled the newspaper out over the table and pointed at an article. "All criminals who have committed severe, atrocious crimes against other Etherians are to be fixed, like animals, so they can't breed."

"Whoa!" Ujuu gasped. "That's bold!"

"It's to help decrease the amount of kidnappings happening in our country, but it'll obviously deter some individuals from committing other horrid crimes…" Marlot spun his empty tea cup on the table, watching it twirl until it toppled over and stopped.

"I'm not interested in being seen as a kidnapper, so if your parents give you all written permission to travel with Soraya and I, then you can join us. Just be warned that I expect you all to pull your weight aboard my ship and train for combat."

"Your ship?" Ujuu asked, his eyes sparkling with excitement.

"Aye, my sky ship," Jon grinned. "Well, technically not mine, but one of the souls I have within me owns it."

Everyone's faces fell at being reminded of Jon's demonic powers.

"It was a ship used for carting and selling kidnapped children, and now it's not. You're welcome."

After a few moments of silence, Jacquelle spoke up.

"Aren't you afraid of being caught for all the awful things you've done?" the blond asked, her finger pointing at Jon's chest.

"No. I don't commit crimes in my real form."

Jacquelle blinked, her hand faltering in the air.

Marlot's eyes flitted over to Soraya. "She's seen what I actually look like, and we could easily be mistaken for an uncle and niece. I doubt we're actually blood related, but who knows."

Jon's smile widened across Norma's face. "My offer stands. If your parents allow you to travel with me, then I'll take you. If not, then you can't join us."

"Alright, that's fair," Rhys agreed, his hand resting on his chin. "My parents would be more easily swayed if we could convince them that you and Soraya are related, but what would the purpose of our traveling be? We can't say we're looking for missing adults, there's no way that would go over well."

"Good question," Soraya frowned, her fingers drumming across the table's smooth surface.

"We could say we're forming a band."

Everyone spun around to look at Moiya.

"Well, we all play instruments and know several songs together, so why can't we say we're performing at different restaurants for extra cash this summer?"

Ujuu flashed the Calgreneze girl a grin. "That's a great cover up story!"

Soraya beamed at Moiya's cleverness, but noticed Rhys' face hardening.

"Bro, you should probably stay behind," the older Shadelkin twin said, his head resting on folded hands.

"Mom and Dad would be suspicious of you joining a band. Plus, Zaruna's here. It wouldn't be fair to her if we dragged her into danger, especially when she just fled from her own country in search of safety."

Ujuu's eyebrows furrowed together as he stared at his brother in shock. "I get what you're saying, but I'm not abandoning you, we're kin!"

"Exactly," Rhys sighed, his expression softening. "All the

more reason you should stay here in Matumi. Someone has to protect our parents, Zaruna, and her family if things go sour."

The younger twin pondered his brother's words while toying with his tarragon soda. The bright green, fizzy drink sloshed inside the glass bottle as his wavering hand rocked it back and forth.

"Certe estka?" Ujuu asked, his candy apple eyes boring into his brother's gaze.

"Jai. Certe est."

Rhys extended his arm and pat his brother's back. "Bonubu."

*Are you certain? Yes, I'm certain. It's all good.* Soraya translated in her head. She kept her thoughts of being sad about Ujuu staying behind to herself, but was proud of herself for understanding their conversation.

"You kids should all train, regardless of who comes along and who stays."

Jon pulled out paperwork from a bag he had slung over his shoulder and placed it on the table. "I'm writing down Matumi Beach for where you kids all meet up while outside of school, but we need a secret location for you all to learn how to fight and defend yourselves," he clicked his pen open. "Any suggestions?"

Soraya and Rhys shared a silent glance and nodded in agreement.

"A Thousand Steps Beach."

## Chapter 41: Beach Brawl

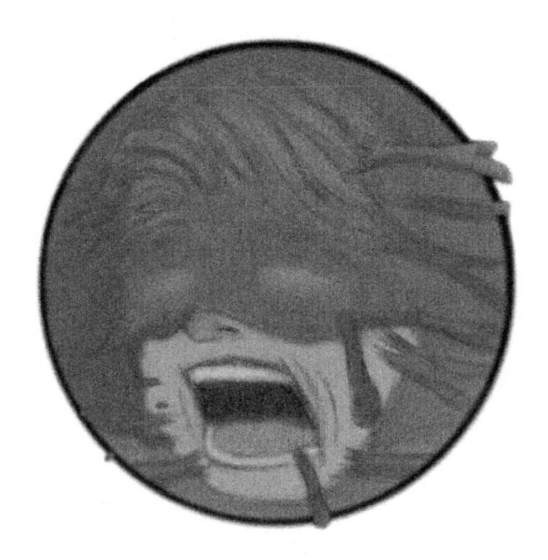

"A band?"

Ayla Leyo placed a hand on her hips, the creases of her blue eyes crinkled as she gazed down at the booth where Soraya and her friends sat.

"Jai mama," Rhys' crimson eyes glowed while flashing his mother a small smile. "Musica no utai est."

Soraya gripped the napkin in her lap, wringing it into a knot. The smell of spicy, sizzling meats and vegetables filled the air of Yohai Steakhouse, causing the girl's mouth to water.

"Venokoto yi pokimas? Quaeso?" Rhys asked, his ears perking up.

"Vos va bilisimo est," laughed Ayla. "Your father and I have to meet with Soraya's uncle before we can let you boys go, alright?"

Rhys and Ujuu gave their mom a thumbs up in reply.

"And Soraya…"

The girl froze at Mrs. Leyo speaking to her.

"I trust my son's judgement on character, you must be special if he likes you," she smiled. "And no need to be intimidated by me."

"O-okay," Soraya stuttered, blushing profusely while Ayla walked back to the kitchen.

Rhys took Soraya's hand into his own and stroked it with his thumb. "You're fine," he whispered, kissing her cheek.

Jacquelle rolled her eyes. "My dad would like you too..." she muttered under her breath in such a quiet voice that Soraya wasn't sure if she heard the blond properly.

"Salutem!"

Zaruna sped over to their table, giggling when Ujuu formed the shape of a heart with his fingers and pointed at her.

"Love you too," she winked. "Did your muzzer ahvedy take everyvon's orders?"

"She did indeed," Ujuu confirmed.

"I heard someting about a band?" Zaruna cocked her head, her magenta ponytail swishing across her white apron. "I can sing and play ze lyre, you know..."

"Jai! You should absolutely join us!" Ujuu's candy apple eyes sparkled as he gazed with adoration at his girlfriend. "We would sound so good with you-"

"It depends on how much room Soraya's uncle has on his ship," Rhys cut in, frowning at his brother. "We'll ask him if you can come along, but there are no guarantees."

"But adding harmonies would make us sound much better, plus, more hands on deck makes sense," Ujuu pushed back, much to everyone's surprise. "We all need to be prepared for what lies ahead."

Zaruna noticed the tension rising between the twins and grimaced. "I do not vant to cause trouble... I vill be back vith your food and drinks shortly..."

When the Rosinkin girl disappeared around the corner, Rhys shot Ujuu a glare.

"Bro, what gives?"

"I'm serious about her joining us, or at least giving her the option to," Ujuu rapped his fingers against the table. "If she knew what was happening, she wouldn't ever be taken by surprise if things did go wrong. I'd rather have Zaruna as a teammate than a damsel in distress we'd have to save…"

Ujuu reached a hand across the table towards his brother. "Zaruna would be upset if we kept her out of the loop. You and I both know how much it sucks to be an outsider, why turn around and do that to her?"

Rhys mulled over his brother's words before clasping onto his brother's palm. "You're right, igo no fratello. Zaruna is trustworthy."

"Let's invite her to the beach with us," Moiya suggested in a hushed voice.

"We'll fill her in on everything," Soraya added while giving Rhys' hand a gentle squeeze. "The more, the merrier."

Jacquelle pouted, folding her arms over her chest. "Fine, I guess…"

* * *

The night sky was filled with fog, the moon obscured by large, billowing clouds overhead. The sand beneath Soraya's toes was cold, and the ocean waves crashing onto the shore were taller and louder than normal.

Jonathan Marlot had turned into a shadow and circled the perimeter of the beach to make sure they were completely alone. Both he and Soraya couldn't risk being caught using their demonic powers or else MagiCorp, Azakua, and every other country within Etheria would be after them.

Although Soraya was waiting for him to return with an all clear before fusing with Zaruna, she and her friends had explained the situation to her.

Despite Soraya's story sounding absurd, even to herself at times, the Rosinkin girl remained calm and serious, treating the information presented to her as facts.

"So, you ah perhaps both an angel and demon?" Zaruna queried, studying Soraya over with her tourmaline gems.

"I could be, but I'm not entirely sure."

Jon's dark silhouetted form rose from the ground before them, his blood-red sunglasses glowing despite the lack of light.

"Not another soul in sight, but I have a request for you, Soraya," he pointed at her left eye. "Use your spell to make sure there aren't any demons lurking nearby. I didn't detect anything, but we can't be too careful right now."

"Will do," Soraya took a deep breath in. "Telpathia."

The vision in her left eye turned pitch black, just like the previous times. She could see Jonathan's multicolored soul along with Rhys and Ujuu's flaming red orbs, Jacquelle's dark blue one, and Moiya's emerald green sphere.

"It's just us," Soraya reported. "But I can't see Zaruna's soul for some reason."

"Interesting..." Jon and Rhys murmured in unison. They glanced at each other, the Casmerahn boy frowning while Marlot looked entertained.

"Maybe, it's because you haven't fused with Zaruna yet?" offered Moiya, her hand on her chin. "It's the only reason I can think of."

"That makes sense, since your fusions don't seem to be perfect," Rhys joined in. "All of us have shared abilities because of you, so perhaps part of your soul is now inside each of us?"

A horrid thought hit Soraya like a ton of bricks. "Doesn't that mean Mülock can see you all too?"

Everyone's faces fell except for Jon, who chuckled.

"If Mülock could see your friends, he would've already attacked them," Jon circled Soraya, his eyes hidden behind his sunglasses. "I think you're tapping into a holier power with your fusions, they are nothing like mine…"

"What does yours look like?" Soraya couldn't help but wonder as she stared at Jon through wide eyes.

"You'll see when we start training…" Jon's fanged smile stretched to both sides of his mouth.

Soraya turned to Zaruna and offered her a hand. "Would you like to fuse with me?"

Within the peripheral vision of her right eye, she could see Jacquelle glaring at the ground while kicking up a small dust cloud of sand.

*Please don't be jealous…*

"Yes," Zaruna wrapped her finger's around Soraya's. "I vould be honored."

"Slevautza!"

A bright light exploded from their hands, enveloping both girls. A loud crack, like thunder, struck the air, echoing off the rocky cliffs surrounding them before the roaring of crashing waves drowned it out.

Soraya and Zaruna looked down at their dark skin and smiled. Soraya hoped their hair would be pink, but to her disappointment, it remained strawberry blond.

*"Dang it!"*

Zaruna's giggles escaped from their lips.

*"Yuh hair color is beautiful too, igo no amicus."*

Soraya shared her memories and experiences with Zaruna. Although time seemed to slow down to hours for the two girls, only a few seconds had actually passed by. Soraya then split her and Zaruna's souls apart so they fell away from each other and resumed their normal forms. Within Soraya's left eye, she could now see Zaruna's sphere encased in magenta flames.

"Are you kids ready to train?" Jonathan asked, his black coat flapping in a strong gust of wind.

"Ready!" all the students shouted in unison, each splitting their legs apart into fighting stances and holding up their tightened fists.

"There is only one objective…" Jon took off his coat, gloves and sunglasses before placing them onto a rock. "Make me say, *mercy.*"

Marlot wore a simple white, short sleeved, buttoned up shirt with his black pants. "You are all on the same team…" He raised a hand and brought it down in front of him.

"Go!"

Rhys and Ujuu shared a glance, nodded and sped forward, unsheathing their long, thin claws while flanking Marlot from both sides.

Jon didn't even flinch when the boys pounced, flew through the air, and were mere breaths away from his face.

*Oh no…*

Soraya's gut twisted into knots as she wondered whether or not the man would use demonic spells to fight back.

"Slevautza!"

Jon's skin rippled and shook as if thousands of insects were scuttling beneath it. His torso, shoulders, and arms stretched and bulged, the cracking of bones and popped tendons filled the air while the buttons on his shirt burst open one by one, revealing a waterfall of blood cascading down his chest.

Rhys and Ujuu lowered their ears when they both landed on the sand, jumping backwards to avoid Jon's long, thin arms from touching them.

Jacquelle, Moiya, and Zaruna were horrified by the sight, their gazes transfixed on the blood flowing down Jon's arms and legs, watching as it pooled around him, seeping into the soft sand surrounding them. Everyone's hands rose to cover their noses when the overwhelming stench of iron filled the air.

"Help me!"

Soraya halted when she heard Norma's scream. She could see the outline of the therapist's head pressing against the skin on Jon's chest, her nose, lips and teeth breaking through his bloody flesh.

"Get me out of here!" she cried, her sobs turning Soraya's blood cold.

"If I touch your skin, you'll end up like her," Jon growled at the twins, his blue, red, and green colored eyes dancing like a lit fireplace. "You might want to rethink your strategy, children…"

*If only we had magic…*

Soraya paused and glanced at Jon's elongated, red stained hand, where the Earth Magic tattoo was still etched into his skin.

*Of course!*

Soraya memorized the pattern and inched her way closer to Jon, who was swinging his arms at the twins. Judging by how slow his movements were, the girl could tell he was holding back on his full speed and strength.

"Everyone!" Soraya yelled, catching the attention of all five of her friends. "Fuse with me!"

The twins regrouped with the girls, and they clasped onto each other's hands.

"Slevautza!"

A beautiful, multicolored light, shot from Soraya's heart, surrounded the kids and absorbed them all into herself.

*"I need to teach you all how to harvest magic."*

They lifted their hand, which was as black as midnight, and held it up, so the palm faced Jon. Soraya pulled up the image of the Earth Magic tattoo into their minds.

*"Imagine this wrapping itself around our arm."*

Together, they took the Earth Magic from Marlot, the design lifting and vanishing before reappearing on their wrist.

*"Voah, vhat I've read abbout how magic vorks... all lies!"* Zaruna's surprised thoughts rang within their head. *"I never knew ve could carry it on ah skin, I thought it only vorked vile on inanimate objects!"*

"Jai," Ujuu said through their mouth. "MagiCorp doesn't want everyone knowing the real methods."

"Let's try it out," Jacquelle grinned, curiosity welling up inside.

"Well done!" cackled the demon hybrid, interrupting the fusion's conversation. His body snapped, crackled, and twisted as he shrank back down to his normal size.

"We shouldn't waste that Earth Magic since we'll probably need it for later, so..." Jon bowed, tipping the edge of his black hat with blood stained fingers. "Mercy."

Soraya split their six souls up, and the children tumbled away from each other, each of them carrying faded Earth Magic tattoos on their arms.

"Sorry, I have to take that back," apologized Jon as he held out his bloodied palm. Each tattoo lifted off the students and reformed on the back of his hand. "Can't have MagiCorp seeing that or we'll all have bounties on our heads."

"Aww!" pouted Jacquelle. "I was really looking forward to using that..."

"Soon," Jon promised. "Just not tonight. If we ruin the landscape, our training spot will be discovered. I'll bring a different elemental magic for us to start with for our next session."

"You went easy on us, didn't you?" Rhys said, eyeing the man with suspicion.

"Of course, it's only the first class, I simply wanted to give you all a taste of what it'll be like battling demon hybrids."

Marlot put his red sunglasses back on. "It's important we stock up on magic and weapons that work from a longer range. One simple touch of skin could very well mean the end of your life, or the beginning of a never ending nightmare."

"I wasn't useful at all!" Jacquelle huffed, stomping her foot into the sand with all her might. "I didn't know what to do!"

"I feel the same way," Moiya sighed, patting the blond's back. Zaruna nodded in agreement and hung her head.

"Don't beat yourselves up over that," Jonathan gazed at the three of them over the rims of his sunglasses. "You were all powerful together, and I'll bet this was the first time any of you saw something that disgusting and scary in real life, right?"

"If it makes you all feel any better, my brother and I couldn't do much even though we have built in claws," Ujuu laughed sheepishly.

"These aren't normal circumstances," Rhys added. "We're dealing with another magic system from an alternate dimension in addition to Etherian magic. You can't be hard on yourselves, it isn't fair."

"This is precisely why we'll be training as often as possible, to prepare for the worst case scenarios," Jon put back on his cloak and gloves. "You'll all do better next session and continue to improve, you'll see."

His skin shivered again and his hair grew longer, his skull and jawbone creaked and groaned as they took the form of Ms. Whisper's facial features.

Norma's high-pitched voice replaced Jon's calm and mellow tone. "Time to escort you children back to school from," Jon made air quotes with his fingers, "*Matumi Beach.*"

Soraya's insides were squeamish at the reminder of the therapist's soul residing within the demonic hybrid, but she was grateful that Jon was protecting them, even if he did use horrifying methods.

## Chapter 42: Turning of the Tides

"Again."

Soraya and her friends thrust their blade forward. Marlot blocked the blow with the expertise of a highly skilled soldier, but let out a grunt of discomfort.

As a fusion, Soraya, Rhys, Ujuu, Moiya, Jacquelle and Zaruna had combined strength and speed. Together, they were faster at swinging their sword, their aim more precise with each lesson, their hits stronger and deadlier.

Even as individuals, their muscles remembered how to block, parry, and jab. Their agility, hearing and vision were all as good as the Shadelkin twins, their photographic memories as accurate as Soraya's, and their musical abilities now equal with one another.

"Again," Jonathan repeated, his blessed rapier raised.

The students circled him, searching for an opening.

Marlot swiveled on his feet, following their movements.

"*We could turn into a shadow,*" Soraya suggested, an image of them throwing Marlot popping into their head.

"*Or, blind him with Air Magic,*" Ujuu chimed in, the thought of creating a whirlwind of sand and blowing it into Marlot's eyes filling their mind.

*"Wait,"* Rhys scolded them internally. *"No cheating, he said no more demonic spells this fight, and we don't have a lot of Air Magic left, we need to save it for when we really need it-"*

*"I wanna win!"* Jacquelle interrupted, adrenaline pumping through their veins. *"Let's go already!"*

They lunged at the man, despite Rhys and Moiya disagreeing with the blond's judgement call. With their mind out of sync, the fusion moved slower than normal. Marlot crashed his sword down onto theirs, pinning it close to the ground before twisting his body and kicking them in the stomach.

The fusion gasped when the wind was knocked from their lungs. They flew backwards, crashing into the soft sand and landing on their back, their sword no longer in their grasp.

In a flash, Marlot appeared above them, pointing both his rapier and their weapon at their throat.

Just as quick, the fusion unsheathed their claws, smacked the swords away, and hopped back onto their feet, backing away from Marlot's steadfast approach.

"Don't hold back!" Jon taunted while dual wielding the two blades. "Those claws are sharp, use them!"

Both Rhys and Ujuu pulled up the same memory of their father within the fusion's mind. Myrl Leyo's rose-colored eyes and mahogany skin glowed in the sunlit sky, his long, midnight colored ponytail and neatly shaven beard rustling in the breeze.

"I know you boys are struggling with being bullied," he said while leading them outside. "So I've set up a training studio to teach you both self-defense."

Rhys gaped in awe while Ujuu sprinted forward, laughing and pointing at the punching bags, boards, weights, and pull up bars his father had installed around their fenced in backyard.

Myrl unsheathed his long claws and smiled at his sons.

"Only use yours when you absolutely need to. You could easily hurt or kill someone else if you're not careful."

The fusion gazed down at their hands.

*"We absolutely need to go all out!"*

Jon swung with both swords, and the fusion blocked with one hand while slashing back at the man with the other. Marlot dodged just in time to avoid being sliced to ribbons.

*"We have to be faster!"*

The fusion sprinted forward, lifting their pointer and middle finger, and swirled their body in a circle, picking up the sand using their Air Magic and creating the whirlwind Ujuu had thought of.

Marlot pulled up his shirt to cover his nose and mouth and pulled down his goggles just as the cyclone of sand enveloped him.

Taking advantage of the distraction, the fusion lifted their whirlwind off the ground, sucking Jon into the air.

*"We got him!"* Jacquelle shouted internally with glee. They shot their claws out in rapid punches at the levitating man.

Even while spinning out of control, Jon managed to block most of them, but the kids swept aside both swords with one clawed hand and pierced the man's stomach with the other.

Marlot's multicolored eyes grew wide with surprise when his blood and guts seeped through the deep gash in his shirt.

The kids froze, shock coursing through their veins at the devastating amount of damage they had caused their friend.

*"We did that… Oh Gods, he's hurt badly!"*

They stopped the cyclone and focused on gently floating the wounded man back down to the ground.

"This would've killed a regular Etherian," Jon chuckled, both swords dropping from his hands the second his legs touched the sand. "But I'm far from normal."

Out of his wound poured forth a juicy puddle of skin with

two green eyeballs and veins. The bloody mess plopped onto the sand, jiggling in place while it pulsated.

The fusion covered their mouth to keep from vomiting as the pungent smell of death and decay filled the air.

Marlot grinned, his stomach completely healed. "Under normal circumstances that would've been a victory for you lot."

"W-who was that?" Moiya asked, their multicolored eyes wide with horror.

"Oh, one of Orchal's kidnapping buddies," Marlot cackled. "Time for a swimming lesson," he added before punting the disfigured mesh into the ocean. He glanced at them, and Soraya noticed the greenish hue from his eyes was now gone.

"I'm so glad you ah our ally…" Zaruna whispered, their skin shuddering as the water splashed and turn red before the waves receded back into the ocean, taking the pile of flesh with it.

"That's enough practice for tonight."

Jon sheathed his sword while Soraya split her and her friend's souls apart, so they could resume their normal forms.

"Can we use Air Magic again next time?" Moiya asked, the excitement in her voice shining through.

Soraya knew all her friends loved being weightless and free in the wind, just like she did. Teaching them how to use it had been simple as a fusion, and everyone, including herself, craved the experience of flying, even if it was just hovering above the ground. They couldn't risk rising too high and possibly being spotted.

"Perhaps," Marlot's lips turned into a thin line. "The shipment I ordered is arriving much later than I initially thought. MagiCorp is keeping careful track of which licensed citizens are given magic and how much…"

"Wait, you're not just stealing it?" Ujuu asked, his eyebrow raised.

"You kids!" Marlot laughed. "I don't always commit crimes

to get things I need, *sometimes* I abide by the rules," his voice turned serious. "Especially when I order magic under my own name."

Soraya frowned. "Won't that cause suspicion?"

Marlot shook his head. "There's a Mage guild I joined when I first arrived in Matumi, a bunch of rich folk who like using magic to impress others," He rolled his multicolored eyes towards the night sky. "The theme for the next three months is Air Magic. I got my order from last month, but no one in the group who bought it recently has received it, including myself, meaning I haven't been singled out."

He glanced at the ocean, the light of the waning moonlight dancing in the rolling waves. "I'm a simple country man who moved to the big city and earned his mage license using his inheritance from his deceased parents. Although my record is clean, I have to keep up appearances every once in a while so no one suspects me living a double or triple life…"

Marlot glanced at Soraya. "We'll make time to push you further in your Apollryük spells," his eyes flicked to each individual. "Soraya and I might not always be able to save you with our powers. Remember, your life depends on you and your abilities alone."

Soraya glanced up at the shimmering stars in the night sky and grimaced. "The half moon will be next Ignis," She looked at Jacquelle. "The same day MagiCorp will be interrogating you at school."

"Those stupid jerks won't get any information from me!" the blond exclaimed, her nose held high.

"Prepare for Mülock to arrive just in case," Jon frowned. "I'll go back to my ship and sail far away for that night. I doubt the demon will show up because of the deal Soraya made, but we can't let our guard down."

"Zis is so stressful," Zaruna cradled her forehead in her hands. "Ujuu, I don't know if I should join in ze search zis summer, but I don't vant to separate you from yah brother either…"

"I'm staying with you no matter what," Ujuu pulled the Rosinkin girl into his arms. "I completely understand, don't feel guilty for not wanting to go. I'm just glad you know what's really going on."

"I vill keep training, I vant to be helpful, even if ve do have tah protect ah families…" her lips quivered, her eyes welling up with tears.

"You're doing so well," Ujuu smiled, kissing her forehead. "Look at how much you've learned in such a short period of time, be proud of yourself."

"Zaruna, I would feel much better if you and Ujuu stayed behind," Rhys added, his crimson eyes glowing in the starlit sky. "Thank you for training so hard," he smiled and added, "heck, you can run just as fast as us now, think about how much more you'll be able to do once the school year ends."

Soraya admired how much Rhys and Ujuu doted on Zaruna. *I wish I could've been childhood friends with them too, like her…*

A tiny seed of jealousy sprouted within the girl, but she squashed it with a shake of her head. *Envy comes from insecurities about oneself. I know Rhys loves me, there's nothing to worry about.*

Her eyes flitted between Jacquelle, who was acting aloof, and Moiya, who was beaming at the three close friends while cupping her cheeks with both hands.

*Their attitudes are night and day, but I understand why Jacquelle has issues…* she thought back to the girls' memories of Mrs. Demarko and shivered.

*That woman is evil. Jacquelle was never given a proper chance at learning how to be decent, but she's trying so hard to change despite that. She's so strong, she just doesn't realize it yet.*

Jon gazed into Zaruna's tear stained eyes. "Staying behind to protect your parents is a great idea. No one would be upset or think any less of you and Ujuu if you did that, alright?"

"Okay…" Zaruna sniffed.

"If you all need a safe place to hide, I'd recommend Rivinsdeep or Rivingale Falls," Soraya blurted out. "Maybe, you all could take a trip together this summer to check them out."

"Yeah, we totally should," Ujuu gently squeezed Zaruna's waist. "How does that sound?"

"Jai, zat vould be vise," she placed her head on Ujuu's chest. "Zanks, everyvon."

* * *

Ignis came and went without any incidents. Jacquelle was interrogated by MagiCorp and let go to resume her classes.

"It was difficult to read their reactions to my answers," the blond told the group the second she reunited with them. "But I don't think they suspect me of doing anything. Still, we have to act normal and blend in."

Despite the children staying awake and on alert for the demon, Mülock never arrived to bother Soraya or Jon.

*I should be relieved, but I'm actually even more paranoid than before.*

Two weeks later, the Shadelkin twins were cross-examined by MagiCorp separately, both careful not to reveal anything. Rhys stayed calm and collected, while Ujuu purposefully became so annoying by talking over the MagiCorp officials that his interview ended early.

"You should have seen their faces!" Ujuu laughed, giving Rhys a fist bump after rejoining the group. "They couldn't wait for me to leave!"

A few days later, Marlot finally received his order of Air Magic.

"So far, no one suspects anything," Jon said while having the kids practice harvesting magic from the wands MagiCorp sent. "The faster you are at transferring magic from inanimate objects to your hands, the better chance of survival you'll have."

Weeks turned into months. MagiCorp also grilled Moiya for answers, but she remained steadfast and didn't give away any secrets.

"Soraya, you're the last of us to be investigated by MagiCorp," she said upon returning. "You'll do fine when it's your turn, just don't panic."

Two more half moons passed by where Mülock left them all alone. Jon, Soraya and her friends continued training in secret at a Thousand Steps Beach without getting caught, and the kid's test scores exponentially grew from all their shared abilities.

"Maybe, we should sabotage our answers a bit," Rhys suggested while grimacing at how high his grades were on his report card. "We're going to all stick out if we keep doing too well in our classes."

"I do want a free scholarship for becoming a mage, but…" Jacquelle crumpled up her report card before tossing it in the bin near the library's restroom. "Protecting Soraya is worth lowering my scores for."

Both Ujuu and Moiya nodded in agreement.

Soraya gazed in adoration at each one of them while stroking Yabo's back.

*I have the greatest friends in the world.*

* * *

It was finally Astros, Mazula fifth, the sixth day of the week. Darkwood Academy was abuzz with orchestra students preparing to perform one of the longest and most difficult songs they had ever learned in front of their family, friends, half of Matumi's population, and the elites within MagiCorp.

"Rhys, are you excited to perform the duet with Jacquelle tonight?" Soraya asked her boyfriend as she twirled in her black and white performance dress. They were both waiting for the others in the hallway outside the Blue Girl's Dormitory.

The Casmerahn boy adjusted his black bowtie with shaky fingers, his ears twitching. "Jai, nervosus est."

Soraya stood up on the tips of her toes and kissed Rhys' soft lips, much to his surprise, before pulling away. "How about now?"

Rhys blinked, a grin spreading across his face. "Still a bit nervous," he pulled her into a gentle embrace and pecked her lips, then her cheek. "I should be okay for tonight," he said, a bright gleam in his crimson eyes.

"Oh no," Jacquelle sighed from behind them. "I guess it's super official now."

The couple turned and gazed at the blond. She wore the same dress as Soraya. A golden braid ran from both sides of her hair, like a halo, and was tied together in the back with a white bow.

Rhys smirked. "It wasn't obvious before?"

*Oh Jacquelle…*

Soraya threw her arms around the blond and pecked her cheek. "I promised I'd never abandon you, remember?"

Jacquelle was left stunned, her face flushed a deep red. "Yeah…" she placed a hand on where Soraya kissed her. "Sorry, I don't mean to get so jealous…"

"Hey everyone!" Moiya sang, swaying as she walked so her dress and braids bounced with each step she took. Yabo rode on her shoulder and batted at her hair.

"You look lovely!" Soraya exclaimed as she reached for Rhys' hand. "We're just waiting on Ujuu now."

Seconds later, the younger Shadelkin twin came sprinting down the hallway. "Sorry, I lost track of the time. Zaruna, her family and our parents will be there to support us! Vadamus!"

They flew down the stairs, chatting excitedly amongst themselves about how exciting the concert was going to be, their laughter echoing around them. The main foyer of Darkwood

Academy was filled with the other orchestra students dressed up and ready to leave.

"All our instruments are already packed inside the bus," Rhys explained to Soraya as they joined the crowd of anxious kids. "Once everyone's been accounted for, we'll get going to Matumi Beach."

Ms. Faye, the groundskeeper, was standing in front of the large oaken doors with Ms. Katia, the orchestra teacher. Both women were calling out student's names and marking them down on clipboards for attendance. After Soraya and her friends had been marked as present, the two adults smiled with satisfaction.

"Alright, kids, let's get going!"

"*Wait!*"

Ms. Faye and Ms. Katia looked down the hall, as did the rest of the students.

Alizon Doorfeather barged his way into the room, walking with long, fast strides towards the two women. He leaned in and whispered something to the both of them, and their demeanors changed in an instant from cheerful to serious.

Even with Shadelkin hearing and vision, Soraya couldn't make out what he had said due to the many murmurs and hushed ramblings from fellow students filling the air.

After a minute, the two women bowed to the Mage. "Children, go to the bus," Ms. Faye commanded in a booming voice while holding the oaken doors open, allowing the students to pass by.

As Soraya and her friends inched forward, the girl noticed Mr. Doorfeather's eyes hovering over their group.

S*omething's about to happen…*

"Ms. Thenayu," Alizon said once the group was next to him, his voice brimming with authority. "I have some update news regarding your missing father, and I need to ask you some questions about another matter. I need you to come with me right away."

Rhys's fingers tightened protectively around Soraya's hand.

"Can my friends join me?" Soraya asked as she stared into the man's mysterious blue eyes.

"I'm afraid not, your friends must perform, especially the ones who are playing the duet."

Soraya's gut twisted into knots. *This is on purpose!*

"We'll be back soon," Rhys gave the girl's hand a gentle squeeze. "I promise."

*Don't leave...*

Rhys, Jacquelle, Moiya, Ujuu and Yabo all gave her sympathetic looks.

*They're all worried...*

Her heart sank when Rhys' grip loosened and slipped away from her hand.

"Igo va amareoum," he said quietly before they were all swept away into the throng of students heading out the front door.

*I love you too...*

Mr. Alizon towered over Soraya, his eyes ablaze with a strange fire that scared her.

"Let's go, Ms. Thenayu."

## Chapter 43: The Interrogation

The once warm and welcoming hallways were now cold and eerie as Soraya followed closely behind Alizon Doorfeather. She wanted nothing more than to run away and join her friends at the Matumi Beach Concert, but she had to hear him out.

*What news about my father does he have? Does he know where Yosef is too? Unless he's lying...* The girl knew the route they were taking and bit her lower lip. *Why are we going to Norma Whisper's office?*

Echoes of a heated conversation bounced off the stone walls as Alizon and Soraya rounded another corner. The girl's eyes widened when she spotted Tildama Lewandow, Venara Cristo, and Finn Duraiko all towering over Jonathan Marlot. Each Mage pointed their raised wands at her friend who was disguised as the therapist.

"Josephine Macklin," Tildama spoke, her voice low and menacing. "You're under arrest for impersonating a psychologist, falsifying documents, committing theft and third-degree murder."

Soraya's blood drained from her face. *Don't arrest Marlot!*

Despite the seriousness of the situation, Jon chuckled. "It's about time you all caught on to *her* evil deeds…"

Finn's eyebrow raised. "Don't you mean *your* evil deeds?"

"No," Jon held out his wrists so Tildama could handcuff him. He swiveled his head, spotted Soraya, and flashed her a wide grin. "Don't worry, kid, I'll see you soon, everything is fine."

"No, Ms. Macklin," Venara smirked. "You're never coming back to this school. I doubt you'll ever see the light of day again."

"Yes, Josephine will rot alright," Jon cackled. "But *I* won't."

Venara stared in disbelief. "How did you pull off being a therapist for so long?" she clicked her tongue. "You're clearly insane."

Soraya held her tears in as she watched the three Mages haul Marlot away. *Jon will escape… He has to!*

Marlot smiled at her before disappearing behind a wall. It reminded the girl of her father vanishing from view before she boarded the Rivingale Express.

*Please… I can't lose you too…*

Alizon, who was studying her carefully through narrowed slits, opened the office door. "Ms. Thenayu," he beckoned, curling his pointer finger. "We need to have a little chat about Ms. Whispers. I have some questions to ask you."

Soraya didn't want to go inside the room with him. It took all her willpower to fight the urge of running down the hallway and freeing Jonathan. "Sir, I don't know you that well, I just don't feel comfortable being with you alone…"

The girl took a step back. "Can we talk another day? I'm so confused and overwhelmed by what I just saw, I-I don't think I'll be much help."

Alizon's face hardened. "That woman was a criminal pretending to be a therapist. I understand that you're emotional, but I really need to ask you some questions-"

"I want a teacher or the principal to be with us!" Soraya

cried, her body shaking.

"Ms. Thenayu, this will just take a minute-"

"*No!*" Soraya yelled, then turned and ran down the hallway, her heart pounding in her ears. *I'm not letting him corner me! No way!*

The pounding beneath her feet stopped. She looked down and gasped.

*I'm airborne!*

Her body, now levitating off the floor, floated towards the Mage. No matter how much she fought and wriggled in the air, she couldn't get back to the ground.

Alizon had his wand out, a smug smile painted on his face. "I said," he growled, flinging the door open with a flick of his wrist. "I have questions to ask you."

Soraya flew into the dark room and landed on the floor with a light thud. The blue-eyed Mage slid inside behind her and locked the door.

"I call the shots around here, Ms. Thenayu," he said, his lips curled into a sneer. "I don't have to cater to a brat like you."

Soraya's sky-blue eyes darkened while glaring at the man looming over her. "You can't treat me like this," her voice shook with anger as she hopped back to her feet.

"You couldn't be more wrong," Alizon grinned while curling three fingers around his wand. He brushed his pointer finger against his middle, creating a soft sound, like a match being lit. Instantly, a yellow flame sprung from the hanging lamp above.

"Have a seat," he commanded, shifting his fingers once more to summon Air Magic from his wand. A chair leapt off the ground, lurching towards the girl before dropping just behind her.

Soraya hesitated, but sank down into the cushioned blue pillow covering the wooden seat.

"Now," Alizon paced in circles around the girl, his hand twirling the piece of polished wood. "Olive Wilder remembers you resting in a patch of dead grass a few months ago…"

Soraya's heartbeat quickened when she recalled the incident. *I wasn't resting! Jacquelle pushed me during the mile run!*

"In that same spot, one week later, the grass was healed. The symbol of the Gods appeared, marking the land as sacred," Alizon hunched down, his eyes level with Soraya's. The man's dilated pupils were hungry, like a monster ready to attack. "Tell me, Ms. Thenayu, how did you do it?"

"I didn't do anything!"

"Don't lie to me!" Alizon hissed through clenched teeth. "You and the Shadelkin twins look too similar to that angel the plants saw! We know you three were somehow involved!"

Soraya kept her expression blank. *He doesn't have a lot to go off of, but he's not giving up.*

"Shortly after that, your father and Yosef Athan, only two of the greatest Mages of all time, vanish from the face of Etheria!"

Soraya blinked. "Don't you have updates on them?"

"Tell me how you purified the grass, and I'll fill you in on what I found out."

"I already said, I didn't do anything-"

*Thud!*

Alizon's hand heavily onto the desk, startling the girl. "Stop lying," he said, his voice low and menacing. "Josephine Macklin, a thief and murderer, masquerades as your therapist and has taken you and your friends off campus during these past few months."

He inched forward, the rancid undertone in his minty breath filling the space between them. "Where have you and your friends been to with this woman? We've sent scouts all across Matumi Beach. Neither Etherians nor plants remember seeing your group anywhere along that shore."

*I shouldn't wait too long to answer… I can pull from different memories so it's not a complete fabrication of events.*

Soraya kept her voice calm and steady. "Norma Whispers was gaining our trust, taking us to tea shops," She furrowed her eyebrows, forcing herself to look into the man's searching eyes. "Looking back, it makes sense she was trying to learn about us and earn our trust. I had no idea about her criminal background-"

"I've had enough of your lies, Ms. Thenayu!" Alizon barked, cutting her off. He flicked his wand at Soraya, levitating her off the ground once more.

"I have an acquaintance who paid me handsomely to try this with you…" Alizon procured a syringe full of dark red liquid from his robes, its sharp, thin needle glinting in the pale lamplight.

"The experiment was successful with a recent Etherian, a girl your age. Although her dosage was from an inferior source to keep her in line, mine is from something far greater…"

"Wh-what are you going to do?" Soraya tried shrinking away, but she wasn't in control of how the wind spun her around like a leaf.

"I'm going to look into your mind, search through your memories and gain your abilities," the man grinned, then brought his wand down. The air around Soraya grew heavy, pinning her to the ground, so she couldn't move. "I will also wear your skin as a disguise and get answers from your friends," Alizon added, his dark blue eyes shining in the dark. "You're father and his friend are missing, and shortly, you will be too."

The Mage stuck the needle into his own arm, wincing slightly while injecting the mysterious liquid into his vein. "My acquaintance said the first transformation will be the most painful, but the power I'll have afterwards will make it all worth it…" he added before tossing the empty, hollow instrument over his shoulder.

Soraya watched in horror as his eyes receded into his skull, rotating backwards so thin, bloodshot veins filled the white spaces. He screamed, dropping his wand on the ground beside him while his whole body shook and rippled like sand crabs scuttling across the sandy shore. His hands shot to the ground as his neck bulged and stretched like a fleshy accordion.

*Is he… turning into a demon?*

The girl, terrified by his painful transformation, shifted her gaze to the wand on the floor and focused on memorizing the elemental patterns etched into it. Despite being distracted by the haunting cries and beast-like groans coming from the man, she was successful in harvesting the magic. Icy kisses of Water and Air Magic appeared on Soraya's right hand, while warm stings of Fire and Earth Magic engulfed her left hand. Alizon's wand was now nothing more than a regular stick.

"*We will… link minds…*" two layered voices escaped through Alizon's sharp fangs. The man was twitching violently on his hands and knees like a rabid dog, blood and spit dribbling down his unnaturally wide jaws and dripping onto the wooden floor.

His cape was forgotten in a bloody heap beneath him, his shirt ripped to shreds as giant bubbles of skin boiled and rose from his back before bursting forth with a giant, bleeding hand. It had long, sharp claws and one milky white eye in the palm's center.

Soraya held her pointer and middle fingers out and fought to raise her hand from the incredible pressure coming down on her.

*Get off already!*

The Air Magic lifted, allowing Soraya to roll away. The bloody hand plopped down onto the floor where her head had been seconds before.

"*Hold… still…*" Alizon's double voices commanded.

An overwhelming urge to obey welled up inside Soraya, leaving her legs paralyzed.

*This feeling! It's similar to Mülock's first visit with me, and when that Casmerahn voice spoke to me from the back of my mind!*

"*Are you aware of the Demonic Hierarchy?*" Jonathan Marlot's question floated into her head.

"*Zinvi has one who can rival even my power,*" Mülock's thundering voices echoed in her brain.

Soraya put two and two together, and a lightbulb went on inside her head. *Alizon's power must be from the demon who is the most powerful, the one Zinvi has in his possession! No wonder Mülock was afraid of Jon and I being used against him!*

The Mage's layered cackling filled the room as Soraya struggled to move her limbs.

"*So... you are a demon hybrid after all! My acquaintance suspected as much!*" Alizon's voices sounded more like himself, as if he were in control again. His bloody third hand crawled on its fingers with spider-like movements and launched at the girl's face, like a venomous snake striking its prey.

Although her feet were frozen in place, Soraya could still move her fingers, arms and torso. She raised three fingers and summoned fire from her palm. Just as the hand was about to clamp its claws onto her head, a reddish orange fireball shot into the air, torching the demonic entity, engulfing it in flames.

Alizon's voices shrieked in pain while his third limb twisted and whipped itself around, desperately attempting to douse the fire licking its exposed flesh.

"*Stop moving!*" the Mage ordered in shrill, demonic screams.

Soraya's whole body turned rigid, as if she had turned to stone. Fear gripped her heart when she failed to move her muscles.

The bloody hand, partially burned from Fire Magic, clamped down onto Soraya's head, the sharp nails digging into her skin, the milky white eyeball seeping into her hair.

"*Show me everything! Fuse with me!*"

Soraya's eyes were wide with horror when her mouth moved on its own. Her lips opened to speak the Apollryük fusing spell, her tongue moved to form the sounds, her lungs exhaled, giving her the breath to say the word…

*"Stop! What are you doing?"*

Soraya swallowed the spell down her throat when the Mage's tight grip suddenly released her. She glanced up and noticed the arm was writhing in pain. A blue flame crawled up his skin, devouring and turning to dust everything it touched.

*Did my blessed ring do that?*

*Crash!*

The office door flew open from Jonathan Marlot kicking it in. Soraya knew it was him because of his coat, hat and sunglasses. His skin, though still pale, looked younger. His goatee was gone and replaced with a clean-shaven face and black hair.

*He must've let go of Josephine Macklin's soul.*

Jon looked at Soraya over the rims of his sunglasses, then Alizon's demonic form, then back at the girl. One eye was an electric blue, and the other was vermilion.

"Kid, we need to go."

Soraya tried running towards him, but her limbs were still stiff. Jon let out a small sigh, scooped her up into his arms, and bolted down the hallway.

"Plug your ears, so he can't control you," he huffed, handing her a pair of noise cancelling headphones from his trench coat pocket. "You can't obey if you don't hear or understand him."

"*Come back!*" Alizon's demonic voices screeched, his body oozing out of the office, leaving a trail of blood in his wake while he barreled towards them with an unnatural speed.

As Jon turned the corner, he and Soraya were met by the other three mages standing before the staircase entrance. A wide, stained-glass window took up the stone wall above.

"Sir, what are you doing-" Vamera began, her hands on her hips.

"Look behind us," Jon interrupted before leaping over

them and using Air Magic to keep him and Soraya airborne. He flung a powerful burst of wind forward, breaking the window and sending glass shooting everywhere. Rather than have the shards fall, Jon kept them hovering in the air and shot them backwards towards Alizon.

The Demon roared in pain, causing the three Mages to swivel their attention towards the oncoming beast.

"W-what is that?" gasped Tildama.

Soraya glanced over Marlot's shoulder and watched the demon attack the other three mages. Her body shuddered when Alizon's chest ripped open, exposing his rib cage and gory innards, his flesh expanding to wrap around Finn. The Mage dressed in green screamed while being absorbed into the beast's body.

The two women Mages whipped out their wands and did their best to battle the demon, but Jon flew up high into the air at such a fast speed that Soraya couldn't see the outcome of the fight.

Jonathan gently tapped the girl's shoulder and gestured towards her ears. She took off the headphones to hear him.

"I'm sorry to say this, but I'm pretty sure your friends and their families are in mortal danger. We can either all be on the run, or you and I can go back and hopefully defeat Alizon and the remaining Mages so word doesn't spread about us and what we can do."

Marlot grasped her hands with his gloved ones and gently lifted her out of his arms, so she was floating next to him. "Can you move again?"

Soraya flexed her limbs and fingers and found she was back to normal, and nodded.

"What do you want to do, kid? I won't judge your decision either way."

The girl closed her eyes and took a deep breath in. "All I know, is I want to protect my friends no matter what."

Jonathan gave her a reassuring smile that reminded Soraya of Rhys, and a pang of sorrow shot through her chest.

*I don't want them to be on the run! They should all be free to live a good life....*

"They're worth fighting for," the girl tightened her grip on Jonathan's gloves. "Let's go defeat Alizon."

Marlot's toothy grin stretched across his face. "I won't hold back in this fight. I might scare you with what I can do, but I promise you, I'm on your side. Remember that no matter what, alright?"

The two hybrids plugged their ears once more and flew back towards the broken stained-glass window, not knowing who or what they would find standing victorious.

## Chapter 44: Matumi Beach Concert

*You can do this.*

Jacquelle glanced at Rhys, his red eyes glowing from the sunlight reflecting off the Valtic Ocean. He tilted his body forward and bobbed his head.

She understood his signal. It was time to begin their duet.

Jacquelle shifted her bow strokes from long and elegant notes to a quick, bouncing melody. Her fingers flew across the neck of her cello, hitting each string with perfect accuracy.

*Listen to his tempo, follow the teacher's baton.*

Her blue eyes flicked towards the violalin players. Ujuu and Moiya sat side by side in the middle of their section. Although both of her friends were now better musicians thanks to their constant fusing for the past few months, they insisted on sounding mediocre to avoid drawing unnecessary attention to themselves. Jacquelle's vision moved and hovered on the empty seat behind Rhys, and her heart sank.

*Soraya's in trouble, I just know it! Stupid, flippin Alizon!*

The song emanating from her cello grew more and more intense as she poured all her anger into her playing. Jacquelle was tempted to rush, but held back.

*Soraya should be here playing at the concert with us! This isn't fair! How dare that dumb Mage take her away from me!*

Jacquelle switched her attention between Rhys and her instrument. It was the most difficult part of the song, yet her focus was divided. She wanted to throw her cello down and rush back to save Soraya, but she had to finish their musical piece.

Her fingers, dripping with sweat from the sun's scorching heat, slipped slightly, turning a note sour. The blond's skin prickled, dread building up within her stomach. She avoided looking at her mother's expressionless stare from the audience.

*No one will remember that, not unless I draw too much attention to it.*

Jacquelle clenched her teeth together and pressed on, refusing to allow one single mistake to destroy their duet. After a few more minutes of playing her hauntingly beautiful melody with Rhys' sweet and sorrowful song, they finally descended and rejoined the rest of the orchestra.

The blond's body relaxed once she slipped back into the easier rhythm the rest of her section was playing, and she glanced at the audience.

Zaruna gazed in adoration at Ujuu while sitting between her parents and Mr. and Mrs. Leyo. On the Rosinkin girl's lap was Yabo, munching on a boiled egg.

Jacquelle dared to steal a glance at her mother and noticed she was sneering at Myrl Leyo, her nose wrinkled in disgust.

*Mother... why are you so awful?*

The blond couldn't believe they were at the final stanzas of their song. She played the last few melodies with ease and held out the last note before the surrounding audience erupted into a roaring applause that complimented the crashing waves along Matumi beach's coast.

Ms. Katia, pleased with the performance from her students,

summoned them all to rise from their seats. "Give it up for our finest violalin player and cellist!" the teacher added as she pointed at Jacquelle and Rhys. The two beamed at one other before taking a bow, both students panting and melting in the blazing heat.

"Good job," mouthed Rhys to her. Although his voice was drowned out by the clapping and cheering, Jacquelle easily read his moving lips.

"Thank you," she replied, her cheeks flushed from the heat and his compliment.

Once the crowd's applause died down, the Orchestra students put their instruments into their cases and waited to load them onto the bus, which was parked in the shade a few feet away from the stage. Jacquelle, Rhys, Ujuu and Moiya all stood side by side as they shuffled forward in the line. Zaruna and Yabo came over to greet them while Ms. Faye paced in circles, twirling the key to the vehicle in her fingers.

"When can we go back to school?" Jacquelle asked the groundskeeper with a hint of impatience in her voice after tossing her cello into the trunk.

"Well…" Ms. Faye floundered for a proper explanation. "I was just given word that we need to stay out of Darkwood Academy for another hour or two…"

"What?"

"I'm not quite sure what's happening," the woman added quickly when she noticed the girl's face fall. "But the police and MagiCorp elites are on it, so I'm sure we can all go back once they've dealt with whatever the problem is."

Jacquelle's blood boiled. *Alizon… I knew I should've punched his stupid face!*

Rhys placed a hand on the blond's shoulder. "Ms. Whispers is there too," he reminded her, despite his fingers shaking. "Soraya isn't alone."

"Let's go make sure she isn't alone!" Jacquelle cried, twisting her shoulder out from under the Casmerahn boy's hand and stomping off towards the streets of Matumi.

"Young lady!" Ms. Faye called after her. "You need to stay with us!"

The blond smirked. She didn't care what the groundskeeper said, the older woman didn't have any true authority over her.

"*Jacquelle Feuétoile Demarko!*"

The girl halted, her skin shivering as her hairs stood on end.

"Y-yes, m-mother?" she stuttered, afraid to turn around. Jacquelle knew she was in trouble, but wasn't sure why or how severe the punishment would be.

"Did you and your friends need a ride back to the school?" Mrs. Demarko asked sweetly, her pearly teeth glistening in the sunlight.

*What are you planning?* Jacquelle hid her fear, making her porcelain face appear blank. "That is awfully kind of you, mother, but we really ought to wait here-"

"Oh, but you were in such a hurry to go back," Mrs. Demarko pointed out, her voice sweet as sugar, but Jacquelle detected the poison beneath it all.

"Nah, it's reckless to go back now," the blond countered. "Especially with the police and MagiCorp elites taking care of something important."

"Like, the arrest of Ms. Whispers, for instance?"

Jacquelle's jaw dropped. Rhys swiveled his head and stared up at Mrs. Demarko while Ujuu, Moiya and Zaruna's eyes grew wide with shock.

"Soraya's therapist is under arrest?" Jacquelle's skin crawled with unease. *Can that weirdo Jon even escape from MagiCorp?*

Mrs. Demarko plucked a car key from her pocket. "I'm sure Soraya is feeling so confused, she'll need you all more than ever."

Rhys narrowed his eyes. "True, but that doesn't mean we can just break the rules and wander into this serious situation unattended."

"But I'm an adult who can chaperone you all, dear boy," Mrs. Demarko laughed, her pitch loud and shrill. "My former husband is the principal of the school, so of course I'm in the know for everything that's going on."

Jacquelle and Rhys subtly exchanged looks. They didn't need to say anything out loud, they both knew leaving with the woman was a bad idea.

"It would be safest if we stayed put," Rhys said stiffly. "Can we call Soraya and see how she is?"

Mrs. Demarko's eyeball twitched, her head jerking slightly. "I will ask..." she said, her lips wavering, a bulging vein on her forehead threatening to pop.

"Pardon me, kids," a larger man with suspenders said while barging through the line of students waiting to load their instruments onto the bus. "Are you all ready to take pictures on the Matumi Beach stage?"

Mrs. Demarko rolled her eyes as the man waved his hands, beckoning for the Orchestra students to follow him and line up for a photoshoot.

"Make sure to stay hydrated," he added, pointing at a large cooler filled with chilled bottles of water, each having the name of a student printed on them.

Jacquelle and the other Orchestra students took their assigned bottle and downed them, the cool liquid quenching their parched throats. In her peripheral vision, the girl noticed her mother's smile widen once they had all finished their beverages.

*Did you do something to our drinks?*

Before the blond had time to tell Rhys and the others her suspicions, the photographer directed the kids where to stand, so they could all fit in the shot. Ms. Katia joined and stood in the center. They were all asked to hold perfectly still as the man proceeded to take pictures with his giant camera suspended on a tripod.

"Excellent," the photographer approved. "We'll take a few more for good measure. Everyone, smile!"

When the camera's light flashed brightly in the children's eyes, Jacquelle's head started spinning, her limbs turning numb.

"I don't... feel well..." she moaned, dropping to her knees.

"Jacquelle?" Rhys frowned and knelt down beside her. "What's wrong?

"What hurts?" Moiya chimed in as she held her other hand.

"Hang in there," Ujuu added while beckoning Zaruna to fetch more water.

"She's probably dehydrated from playing in the sun for so long," Mrs. Demarko said as she swiftly appeared at her daughter's side. "I'll take her straight home to rest, she should feel better soon."

"Wait-" Rhys objected, but Mrs. Demarko had already picked up the blond and was leaving just as quickly as she had arrived.

"She can't do that, can she?" the Casmerahn boy asked Ms. Katia.

"Mrs. Demarko is her mother," the Orchestra teacher pursed her lips together. "So technically she can."

"I don't wanna go home!" Jacquelle weakly protested while her eyes threatened to close and her brain turned to mush. "I wanna be here with my friends!"

"They shouldn't be your friends at all," hissed her mother quietly in her ear before dumping her into the back car seat. "You're such a disappointment, but you're still useful to me, for now..."

Jacquelle's world spun around her drooping eyelids. Her head was heavier than usual, her arms nothing more than deadweights at her sides, and even her legs refused to move.

"Are we… all… poisoned…?" the blond struggled to ask, her speech slurred.

Mrs. Demarko ignored her daugher. When the engine of the car roared to life, she drove down the street, adjusting her rearview mirror, then lifted a walkie-talkie to her lips.

"Krames, I'll meet you at the wharf in fifteen minutes. The targets are following us, over," Mrs. Demarko pressed a button near the bottom of her device and spoke again. "Doorfeather, bring the brat and reward money to the wharf in fifteen minutes, over."

Despite how hard Jacquelle struggled to stay coherent, her world turned black.

* * *

Soraya held onto Jonathan's hand as they flew back through Darkwood Academy's broken stained-glass window. The pair landed in the carpeted hallway, their eyes following the thick trail of blood leading down the stone staircase.

Jon tapped the girl's shoulder and pointed at the floor. She looked down and spotted three different wands sitting in puddles of red.

*Alizon must've won…* Soraya grimaced. She thought about the three Mages forever being stuck inside the demon's body and shuddered. *Is it even possible to save them?*

Marlot used Air Magic to suspend the three pieces of wood in the air, turning them over so they could inspect them thoroughly. To both Jon and Soraya's surprise, there were still elemental symbols carved into them.

The two demonic hybrids harvested the remaining magic from the wands, their tattoos turning even more opaque on their skin.

"Jon?" the girl asked, placing a hand gently onto his shoulder.

"Yes?" he replied, taking his earbuds out.

"I think… we should fuse…"

"Oh?" Jonathan flashed her a wry smile. "Are you absolutely sure?"

Soraya nodded. "We need to communicate quietly, and it would be easier to use our minds to talk."

"True," Jon slipped off one glove and held out his hand to her. "But I think you should be the one to say the spell. You are the more powerful of the two of us, let's try your way of fusing rather than mine."

Soraya clasped her hand around his. Before she said anything, however, a tiny blue flame erupted between them, and Jon squirmed in her grasp.

"Take off your blessed ring first," he said through gritted teeth.

Soraya immediately let go of him and pocketed her blessed jewelry. "Are you okay?" she asked, guilt welling up inside. "I'm so sorry!"

"I'm alright," Jon chuckled, staring at his reddened palm. "This is why I always wear gloves when dealing with blessed items, it slightly burns me when it touches my skin."

Jonathan flexed his fingers, and his hand healed completely. "After we're a fusion, put it back on. I'm curious to see what'll happen, since your holier powers seem to protect you despite the demonic blood running through your veins," his electric blue and vermilion red eyes locked onto hers as he put his earbuds back in and clasped onto her hand once more.

"Say it."

"Slevautza!"

Soraya turned translucent, sinking into Jonathan before a bright light enveloped them both. A loud thunderclap echoed around the stairwell as the two turned into a shadowy creature. Although they couldn't quite see what they fully looked like, their arms and legs were a deep navy blue with a strange white glow hovering over their skin. The four elemental tattoos on the backs of their hands shined brightly like stars in the night sky.

*"Please, have mercy on me!"*

Soraya heard the faint cry of the other man within Marlot before Jonathan silenced it.

"*Shut up, Jolo,*" Marlot growled internally. "*We need you for spare parts,*" his voice softened as he addressed Soraya. "*Try on the blessed ring, please.*"

Soraya slipped it onto their finger. Nothing happened.

"*Fascinating,*" Jon mused. "*I can touch holy objects without being burned when fused with you… let's fry Alizon to a crisp.*"

They reached for Jon's blessed trinkets hidden inside one of his many coat pockets and put them on the rest of their fingers.

"*My rapier is in Ms. Whisper's office hidden under a loose floorboard,*" Marlot added, planting the exact location within their mind. "*Let's get that too,*" a quieter thought entered their head. "*It's a shame I left my rifle back on the ship…*"

Minutes later, they emerged from the office, fully armed and ready to fight.

"*Remember, kid,*" Jonathan added. "*If Alizon manages to possess us, there's no telling what kind of damage we'll do to everyone else and each other…*"

The fusion pushed away thoughts of failure and instead focused on hunting down the demonic hybrid roaming the hallways of Darkwood Academy. They turned into a shadow to avoid being detected, sliding down dimly lit walls and stairwells, following the river of blood to the heart of the school.

*"Oh no!"*

They paused, hovering on the ceiling. Some of Soraya's classmates were huddled altogether in a corner, rooted to the spot in fear.

Alizon's huge, blobby form towered over them, his melting skin oozing down his skeleton, bubbling and popping like a witch's brew in a cauldron. Amidst the loud, unsettling cracking of bones, another set of bloody, skinless hands tore through his back. They unfurled, stretching unnaturally, before shooting down upon the children.

"*He doesn't have his bloodlust under control,*" scoffed Jon. "*What a coward to attack defenseless kids!*"

Soraya agreed, and they took a deep breath in. Their body sprung forth from the ceiling, becoming third dimensional once more before they flew towards Alizon with their unsheathed sword pointed at the demon.

Within seconds, Alizon's newly grown limbs were sliced off and flopping around on the ground like fish gasping for air. Blood spurted from the remaining stalks, blue flames inching their way up them, turning everything they touched to dust before dying out. The demon's layered voices roared in pain as he turned to face the fusion.

"*Get out of here!*" Soraya and Jon yelled at the kids in their triple voices. The students, quaking in fear, made a mad dash towards the front entrance of the school.

"They're going to have nightmares about this forever," Jon commented while watching the heels of the last student disappear around the corner.

"*At least we saved them,*" Soraya thought, then brought their right hand up, summoning their Air Magic to drop pressure down upon the bloody beast.

"This is what Alizon did to me earlier," the girl growled, their blood boiling from the memory of her being pinned to the floor. With their left hand, they tapped into their Fire Magic by curling their three fingers and hurling a huge ball of flames at the demon.

Despite Alizon's layered screams piercing through the air

like a howling wind, Jon's earplugs and headphones drowned out his voices. Since their focus was on frying the demon, both Jon and Soraya failed to notice the cut-off limbs joining together, their fingers rearranging to look like the hundreds of legs on a centipede.

Three eyes poked through the bloody tendons at its head; one pink, one green, and one purple, the veins beneath them snapping as long, sharp nails came down, creating fangs for its makeshift mouth. Blinking, the strange beast hoisted itself up onto its hind legs, its unusually long neck and torso leaning back, like a cobra ready to strike, before thrusting itself forward and sinking its teeth into Soraya and Jon's back.

"*Gods!*" cried Soraya and Jon, their upper back stinging as inky, black blood gushed from their wound, sticking their shirt to their skin.

The creature bit down even harder into their flesh, despite tiny sparks of blue flames erupting from the wounds and singeing the beast's face. In a flash, the monster yanked the fusion off their feet, dragging Jon and Soraya back to Alizon's writhing, burning body.

"*It's trying to make us fuse with him!*" Soraya screamed, panic rising within their tightening chest as she lost control of her movements.

Jon took over, making their nails grow long, like the Shadelkin twins. He reached behind and sliced through the monster's slimy neck, its lower half falling away while the head still hung onto their back. Grunting, Marlot ripped the fangs out of them, flinging the decapitated head away before roasting it and the rest of the body with Fire Magic. The beast squealed while curling up into a ball and shrinking, turning to ashes.

"I know this is scary, but we can't freeze up," Marlot explained, sheathing their claws while drawing upon Jolo's soul to heal and patch up their wounds. "You're smart and capable, Soraya, you got this."

Alizon's body rippled and stretched as his arms and legs snapped off. Blood shot out of cut veins, splattering the walls while his severed ligaments contorted themselves into strange positions. They grew their own demented, twisted parts to crawl along the floor and attack with.

"What the Hell!" groaned Marlot, their foot tapping impatiently. "Just die already!"

A sudden idea struck Soraya. She didn't need to say anything aloud, as Jon heard the plan in their head and agreed it was the best course of action. Together, they switched their magic element, blasting them with water before turning it all to ice. Within seconds, Alizon and the new creatures were frozen solid, their mouths ajar. Everything was petrified but their swiveling eyes.

"*Careful…*" Jonathan cautioned as they switched to Air Magic, lifting the ice covered demon and his hoard with one hand and themselves with the other. "*And off to the purified land we go.*"

The fusion floated up and out the broken stained-glass window, beckoning for the frozen demons to follow with their fingers. They drifted through the air and landed lightly in the middle of the track and field while lowering Alizon and his ligaments onto the holy ground. They watched brilliant bursts of blue flames explode into the air, melting the demonic entities in seconds, turning them all to ashes.

"I feel bad for the other three Mages," Soraya whispered. She removed her headphones while watching the last pieces of Alizon crumble to dust. "I wish we could've saved them."

"Me too," Jon sighed while pocketing his earplugs. "I could've learned so much about MagiCorp from them and stolen even more magic… and what great disguises they would've made…"

Although disturbed by his reply, Soraya couldn't help but laugh. "You're so demented," she said, shaking her head before splitting their souls apart and putting her ring away.

"Aww," Jonathan winked while pocketing his blessed jewelry with gloved hands. "Thank you."

Both demon hybrids slumped down onto the grass, their bodies sore from relying on Apollryük spells for so long.

"You did well, kid," Jonathan said, lifting his fisted hand towards her.

"Thanks," Soraya bumped it lightly with her tightened knuckles. "I couldn't have done that without you."

"Meh," Jonathan shrugged his shoulders and placed his blood-red sunglasses over his eyes. "You need to have more confidence in yourself."

"Rhys and Moiya say that too…" Soraya frowned, her friend's faces filling her mind. "I'm so bummed that I missed the Matumi Beach concert, I was looking forward to that for weeks."

"You could always check on your friends and see how they're doing," Jonathan suggested as he lay back in the grass with his arms folded behind his head.

"True," Soraya took a deep breath in and exhaled. "Telpathia."

Through her left eye, she could see her friend's fiery orbs hovering a few feet away. With a flick of her wrist, they flew over to the girl, floating just a few inches away from her face. Several seconds of silence passed as Soraya rapidly switched between gazing at Jacquelle's pitch black sphere and a battle taking place within the others.

"No way!" she gasped, jumping to her feet, adrenaline pumping through her veins once more.

Jonathan sat up and stared at her, his lazy smile replaced by a thin line and raised eyebrows.

"We need to go now!" Soraya cried, her body trembling. "They're in trouble!"

# Chapter 45: The Rescue

*There's too many of them.*

Rhys swung his unsheathed claws at another slave trader's legs and tore through his flesh. The man howled in pain, clutching his bleeding wound while falling onto the wooden planks beneath their feet, his club slipping from his blood soaked fingers and clattering onto the wooden floor.

The Shadelkin swiftly plucked the weapon from the ground and knocked the whimpering man out with it.

*Can't have him attacking me from behind.*

Rhys' head and limbs were growing heavy with sleep, yet he gritted his fangs together and fought on, pushing hard to resist the drugs Mrs. Demarko had slipped into his water. He glanced over his shoulder and saw both Moiya and Ujuu were staggering in their steps while helping Zaruna fight off another kidnapper.

The Rosinkin girl fought fiercely, valor fueling her jabs and swings with the club she had stolen. Although Zaruna hadn't had any of the drugged water, her movements were slowing due to fighting nonstop for so long. She narrowly dodged the net a man had tried throwing over her and shot the last bit of Fire Magic at him from her palm. The man screamed and writhed on the floor as his skin roasted instantly from the intense impact of heat.

"Rhys? Can you hear me?"

The Casmerahn boy heard the gentle voice creeping up in the back of his head and smiled. "Soraya, are you alright?" he whispered, keeping his voice down.

"Yes! Alizon turned into a demon, but Jon and I stopped him," Soraya's tone was concerned. "What's going on? Is something wrong with Jacquelle?"

Rhys' vision spun with each step forward he took. He was careful to avoid the bodies and puddles of blood lying around on the wooden floor.

"Jacquelle's mom poisoned her water bottle with something that knocked her out at the concert, while the rest of us were given drugs that kicked in later, so we'd have time to follow."

The boy stumbled slightly and cursed to himself. "Mrs. Demarko didn't need to kidnap all of us, she just needed to grab her own daughter. She knew we'd try to save her."

The Shadelkin glanced down the ship's hallway at a slave trader on the ground who had been skewered in the chest. "My father joined us and is scouting out ahead. He and Zaruna aren't drugged, thankfully, but the rest of us are feeling the effects kick in as we speak."

The boy knew that if it weren't for Mr. Leyo accompanying them in their rescue mission, they all would've been captured already. Rhys could hardly believe how amazing his father was in fighting off the crew with just his claws.

However, despite Myrl aiding them, everything had gone horribly wrong in a matter of minutes. Rhys filled Soraya in on how Mrs. Demarko had entered into a secluded area of Matumi Beach that was hidden behind tall wooden walls. She had been escorted by men with clubs, nets and magic while carrying her unconscious daughter.

That shady activity alone told Rhys they would be ambushed if they weren't careful, but he hadn't realized their drinks had also been spiked at the time.

Rhys glanced down at the ghost-like outlines of Water and Fire Magic on his wrist, so Soraya could see. "We all harvested magic from the crew, which helped keep us alive, but they didn't have a lot. My Dad and Zaruna can't win by themselves. Ujuu, Moiya and I are doing our best to stay awake, so we can save Jacquelle, but it won't be long before we pass out."

"Jon knows where that place is, we're on our way! Just hold on!" Soraya's pleading voice faded from Rhys' mind.

The Casmerahn boy prayed silently to the Gods for her and Jon to arrive quickly and for them all to escape together.

*I hope Mom got a hold of the police.*

Rhys knew it was a long shot to rely on them since they were probably still dealing with whatever catastrophe was going down at Darkwood Academy, but he had asked Ayla to call and inform them on the child abductions occurring in Matumi Beach.

The Casmerahn boy's thoughts were interrupted when his father, who was just a few steps ahead of him, ripped his sharp nails through another slave trader's chest.

"Son," Myrl tilted his head, indicating towards a locked door as he untangled himself from the dead man hanging from his claws. "I think Jacquelle is in there."

The group surrounded the door, waiting with bated breath as Rhys blasted it with his remaining Fire Magic. The wooden entrance burned to a crisp, and the boy showered it with the rest of his Water Magic, dousing the flames, so they could enter.

"Stop or I'll shoot!"

Everyone halted as Mrs. Demarko's shrill voice pierced

through the air. The crazed, bloodthirsty woman stood in one corner, pointing a pistol at Jacquelle, who lay unconscious in her arm. A huge cage took up the other half of the room.

The group glared at the evil woman as she pointed at Rhys and Ujuu with a slender finger and pointed towards the open cell door. "The cat freak twins must go in there. Do it or she dies!"

Mryl stood stone faced, while Zaruna and Moiya's eyes filled with terror. Rhys and Ujuu shared a silent glance, then slowly walked towards the open cage.

"Don't hurt Jacquelle," Rhys growled while standing before the entrance. "She's your own daughter, what's wrong with you?"

Mrs. Demarko dug the pistol into the back of the blond's skull. "Just get in there or else!"

Zaruna took a step forward, but Mr. Leyo gently clasped onto her hand and shook his head. Ujuu glanced over his shoulder and mouthed, "I love you," to both of them before entering into the cell with his twin.

"It'll be okay," Rhys reassured his father, Moiya and Zaruna as Mrs. Demarko, still with her gun pointing at Jacquelle, swung the door shut and locked the cell door. "The police are on their way right now."

Jacquelle's mother blinked in surprise at the boy's words. "All of you, head towards the top of the ship," she switched from pointing the gun at her unconscious daughter to Moiya.

Rhys' blood ran cold. *Come on, Soraya and Jon, please hurry!*

The Shadelkin twins watched Myrl, Zaruna, and Moiya walk out the door with Mrs. Demarko in tow, keeping her pistol pointed at the Calgreneze-Azakuin girl's back. At the last second, she dropped Jacquelle to the floor and locked the cabin door behind her.

"Poor Jacquelle…" Rhys shook his spinning head and groaned in pain.

Ujuu leaned against one of the thick metal bars and slid

down until he was sitting on the floor. "Soraya and Marlot will save us," he said, then flashed a weak smile at his brother while his body swayed back and forth. "I'm sure of it."

Rhys sighed, then bowed his head into his chest. "True, but we can't count on that. We have to make our own plan to escape…" He closed his drooping eyelids and finally surrendered to sleep.

On the deck above them, a gunshot fired.

## Chapter 46: Death of Innocence

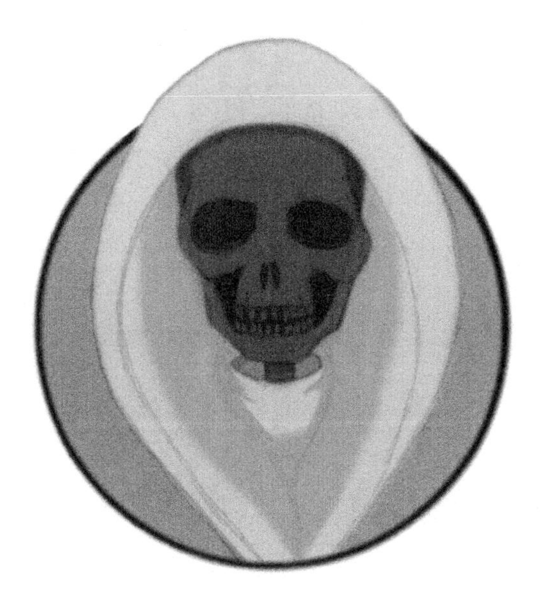

"*Damn you!*" Mrs. Demarko screeched. Yabo's fangs were dug deep into her hand, and he wasn't letting go.

Moiya fell to the ground, crying out in pain at the bullet that had shot through her shoulder.

*If Yabo hadn't attacked her, it would've hit my head!*

"Stupid animal!" the woman screamed, whacking the pandacoon's head hard against a wooden wall. A sickening crack echoed in Moiya's ears. Her eyes filled with tears as she watched Yabo go limp and fall to the ground. In the back of her mind, she could hear Soraya scream.

Myrl took the opportunity to lunge at Mrs. Demarko with his claws. Zaruna also sprinted at her with the club pointed at the woman's lungs.

A wall of flames burst into the air, separating the two from killing Mrs. Demarko. The last living crew member had intervened, a large, beefy man with a bushy beard and brown trench coat that they hadn't seen before.

"You murdered my men!" the man bellowed before addressing the woman behind him. "Liza! I thought these brats would be easy to kidnap!"

"It seems they know how to cast magic," Mrs. Demarko said while reloading her pistol. "That should be more than enough proof for MagiCorp to lock up those twins," She gestured with her head towards Moiya and Zaruna. "You can finish off the girls, we don't need them."

"And what of the man?" Krames asked, his blue eyes narrowing at Myrl.

"He'll be our scapegoat. He's the one who murdered the girls."

Mryl's claws extended another few inches as he glared at the pair before him.

"But you've already shot the girls with your gun," Krames frowned. "He has claws-"

"We'll shoot him in the head, wipe our fingerprints off the gun, make him hold it, and frame it as a suicide," Liza's eye twitched in irritation. "Must I always think of everything?"

"Vat's going to happen to Jacquelle?" Zaruna asked, her grip on the club tightening while she glared at the woman through the orange flamed wall.

Mrs. Demarko cackled, her pupils small against her wide, hungry eyes. "My dearest daughter is a disappointment, but soon she won't be…"

She grinned maniacally and raised her pistol. "My eldest daughter is the first successful hybrid of an Angel and Etherian ever created, the next evolutionary step for our kind, and Jacquelle will be the second!"

Liza shot again at Moiya. The girl bent over in shock, her hands instinctively grasping at the wound in her stomach as it filled up with blood.

"Moiya!" Zaruna cried as she sprinted toward her friend.

*Bang!*

The Rosinkin girl screamed and collapsed onto the deck, blood seeping down her wounded leg.

"Ugh, my aim is off!" Mrs. Demarko cried, wincing in pain at her bleeding hand. "That stupid thing bit down to my bone!"

Mryl ran at Liza despite the fire floating between them, but Krames moved the wall at him, forcing the Shadelkin to jump backwards to avoid being burned.

"You'll be arrested for all of this," Mrs. Demarko laughed at Mr. Leyo, who looked both furious and horrified at her cruelty. "You filthy demon eyed freak," she pointed her gun at Zaruna again, aiming for her head.

Before Mrs. Demarko fired, two shadows slithered onto the ship's deck on either side of her. In an instant, she fell to the ground, pulled down by invisible hands, her gun clattering onto the deck.

"Liza-" Krames yelled before also slamming into the ship's deck alongside her.

Myrl, taking advantage of the situation, picked up Zaruna's club from the ground and knocked Krames out over the head with the wooden weapon so he couldn't shoot more fire from his palm.

As Liza struggled to rise, both Jon and Soraya's bodies rose from the ground. Myrl took a step back out of shock.

Mrs. Demarko immediately rolled back onto her feet, but Jon kicked her back down and held is sword at her throat.

"S-Soraya... Jon..." Moiya choked.

"Stay with me!" Soraya cried and knelt down next to her friend, but the girl's emerald gems fluttered shut, her breathing growing more and more shallow with each passing second.

*"No!"*

Tears trickled down Soraya's face as she looked over at Yabo's lifeless body, then at her dearest friend, who was dying in her arms. *This shouldn't be happening! This is all Mrs. Demarko's fault!*

Zaruna banged her fist against the floor and sobbed for Moiya and Yabo while Myrl knelt down beside her, tearing off his sleeves to bandage her wounded leg with. Even Jonathan, who was busy keeping Liza down, had his eyebrows knitted together as he glanced at the dying girl.

"I'm not losing you too!"

Soraya grasped onto Moiya's cold hand, her body shaking. She wasn't sure how fast she could save her friend with Water Magic, but she knew another way of healing.

"Slevautza!"

A thunderous crack whipped through the air as Soraya and Moiya fused together. The girl now had the same wounds as her friend, their lives draining from the bullet wound in their gut, their shoulder aching and bleeding.

Their world teetered as it slowed down. Time came to a grinding halt, freezing everyone and everything around them. Even the blood from their wounds had momentarily stopped.

"Wh-what's happening?" Moiya asked, her voice full of fear. "Are we dead?"

"Mow?"

"Yabo?" Soraya and Moiya gasped together and turned their aching head in the direction of the soft sound. The pandacoon's translucent spirit was rubbing against their hand, his pink tongue floating through their fingers before he ran off to join a figure cloaked in white.

"It's not your time yet, Ms. Thenayu," a gentle voice arose from beneath the hood. Two skeletal hands as dark as ebony lifted the cloth, revealing a black skull. "But in your fusion form, I'm afraid you will also die if Ms. Marlune doesn't make it."

"I can save her!" Soraya insisted while tightening their fist.

"Yes, you can," the skeleton placed a hand on top of their

forehead. "But there's always a price to pay with relying too heavily upon demonic spells. More land will be cursed with the more lives you steal. You must learn to tap into your angelic powers and purify the land, or the Titans will destroy Etheria."

An image of a full moon hovering over the sea filled the fusion's mind.

"Half Moons connect Etheria with the demonic realm, while Full Moons connect it with the Angelic Realm," the skeleton scooped up Yabo's spirit into his arms and stroked the purring pandacoon.

"On the next full moon, contact the Angels, ask them to help guide you to the Zodia Relics. I'll look after this pure soul until you reunite with him again in the future."

"I love you, Yabo!" Soraya and Moiya cried together. They reached their hand out towards their beloved pet, tears streaming down their face.

"Merow!" Yabo cooed at them one last time.

In a flash, the skeleton and pandacoon vanished. Jonathan appeared before them, dragging a confused and frightened Mrs. Demarko over to their outreached hand. Time started again, their blood flowing once more from their deep gashes.

"Stay with us!" Marlot roared. When the fusion's fingers touched Liza's wrist, Jon bellowed, "Soraya, save Moiya!"

"Chistyrke!" the girl yelled with all her might, digging her nails into the woman's flesh. Mrs. Demarko screamed as her skin shriveled up, her soul now coursing through the fusion's veins.

The hole damaging Soraya and Moiya's vital organs closed and healed within seconds, the bullet wound in their shoulder disappeared completely. Even after the pain had left, Soraya didn't let go.

"*Soraya, I'm going to live, I'm okay now…*" Moiya thought, but the fusion's fingers still clung tightly to Liza's arm.

*"Soraya... you can let go..."*

The fusion looked up and realized they were holding a corpse. They finally released the skeletal woman.

*"I should feel sorry for her, but I don't..."*

A small sting of guilt built up within Soraya. Moiya pat their other hand. "Jacquelle is free from her now," she said through their mouth. "And so are we. If it weren't for you, I'd be dead."

Soraya nodded, then split their souls apart, her body tumbling away from her friend. To her relief, Moiya didn't have any scratches on her.

"I'll try healing you with Water Magic," Soraya said, turning to the Rosinkin girl and giving her a hug. "Thank you for protecting everyone," she looked up at Mr. Leyo. "Thank you too, for everything."

"Of course," Zaruna sank into Soraya's arms, giving her a gentle squeeze.

Myrl's rose colored gems studied Jonathan and Soraya through a guarded expression. "What exactly are you two?"

"I'll explain later," Jonathan said while stooping down over Krames, who was still passed out. "Myrl, go get your sons and Jacquelle," he said in a quiet voice.

The man nodded and disappeared in a flash. Marlot waited a few seconds, then whispered, "Slevautza."

Soraya, Zaruna and Moiya winced as Jonathan's body morphed to envelope the man into himself. After a few unsettling snaps and crackling of skin and bones stretching, Krames was no longer on the ship's deck.

"I needed to hide the evidence," Jonathan explained to the girls. "And we need to get out of here before the police arrive."

# Chapter 47: School's Out Forever

The radiant sun slowly rose above Matumi Beach's rolling waves. The salty sea air rippled through Soraya's long strawberry blond hair, making it dance along with the flag raised at the top of Marlot's sky ship.

"The Black Dog?" the girl asked curiously while gazing up at the crows nest sitting atop the wooden pole, reading the red letters in the flying black banner.

"Aye, I renamed this beauty," Jonathan patted the cherry wood helm like one would a pet. "My parents had a black Labrador for a short period of time. He was the smartest dog I've ever met."

His multicolored blue eyes seemed far away for a moment before he blinked and looked back at the girl. "Ned disappeared as quickly as he had arrived, as if he were on a mission. He helped me during a time when I was feeling depressed about dealing with my bloodlust. He comforted me when I needed it, so I named this ship after him."

Pangs of sadness plagued Soraya's heart as she thought

about Yabo. "I miss my pandacoon so much!" she sobbed, burying her face into her hands.

They had held a small funeral for her beloved pet by burying him in the purified patch of grass under the tree with the symbol of the Gods. Red ferns had grown in his burial place the next day.

Jonathan pulled Soraya into a hug, allowing the girl to cry on his shoulder. "Yabo's in Heaven, and you'll see him again someday," the man reassured her. "He knows you love him."

A few more seconds passed before Marlot pat her back and let go of her. He then dug out a tissue and handed it to the girl.

"Thanks…" Soraya blew her nose and tossed the rag into a trash bin on the deck of the ship.

Jonathan pulled out a pocket watch and grimaced at the time. "Are you sure your friends are coming?"

"I know they are!" the girl said adamantly, stomping her foot into the planks beneath her feet. "They'll be here soon, you'll see!"

Marlot chuckled at her childish outburst, causing the girl's cheeks to redden.

Only one week had passed since Alizon Doorfeather and Liza Demarko's failed kidnapping attempt had occurred.

Mr. Demarko had closed Darkwood Academy's doors for the Matumi Police to properly investigate the misconducts of MagiCorp, to look for clues in solving why Josephine Macklin was now a strange blob of skin, and for the school's staff to clean up the bloody mess Alizon had left behind. This meant all the kids had to return home early and wait to complete their schooling the following semester.

Thanks to Jacquelle forging paperwork, Jonathan was successful in persuading the principal that he was Soraya's uncle and to release the girl into his care until Tishva Thenayu was found.

Jonathan and Soraya had taken advantage of the situation by stocking up on supplies and preparing for their trip. The girl knew it was time to leave Matumi and search for her father and Yosef, along with hunting down the other demonic hybrids and saving the abducted girls.

"Hey!"

The girl's heart leapt joyfully in her chest at the sound of Rhys' voice from over the ship's railing. She flew to the side and gazed down in adoration at the older Shadelkin twin.

"We came to say goodbye…"

Rhys, Ujuu, and Zaruna stood off to the side with Mr. Leyo while Jacquelle and Moiya wore backpacks, carrying suitcases in one hand and cased instruments in the other.

"Of course!" Soraya beamed, then turned to grin at Marlot. "See? I told you so!"

Jonathan lowered the plank so the girls could walk aboard with their belongings. "Signed permission slips from your parents for traveling abroad?" he asked sternly, holding out his hand.

Both Moiya and Jacquelle gave him their paperwork and passport, which he read through and pocketed in his black coat.

"It was easy convincing my parents to let me play music to earn more Lari," Moiya winked at Soraya. "Especially since they are busy working and don't want me arriving back home early."

"My Dad was also glad that I'd be traveling and playing music," Jacquelle puffed her chest out with pride. "He's not too sad about mom mysteriously dying either, neither one of us miss her."

Soraya threw her arms around both girls, pulling them into a hug. "I'm so happy you're coming with me!" she laughed while leaning into them both. "I'm so glad you're all here!"

Rhys, Ujuu and Zaruna joined in the group hug, every one of them grateful to be together again.

Soraya thought back to the previous week when she and

Jonathan had sat down and spoken with the Leyo and Markies families. The two couples knew the group's true intentions behind their travels and had decided against allowing their three children to join.

"Papa," Rhys spoke up as he watched the girls board the ship. "Please, let me go too."

Mr. Leyo frowned. "We already decided no…"

"Just me, not Ujuu and Zaruna," the boy's wine colored eyes danced with a raging fire behind them. "The end of all things is at stake if Soraya and Jonathan lose, we would all die anyway."

Myrl closed his eyes and took a deep breath. "Rhys, please-"

"I'll run away to join them then," Rhys stated. "Just like Mom ran away from her family to be with you," he looked up at his father. "It's the same thing. Would you rather know where I am or not?"

Myrl sighed. "Always so logical," he murmured, then took out a piece of paper from his pocket and wrote out a permission form for Jonathan to keep. "We'll have to go back home and grab your belongings-"

He stopped when Rhys opened the trunk of his father's car and pulled out a backpack, along with his violalin case.

Ujuu smirked. "I wouldn't expect anything less from you, bro," He fist bumped his brother's hand, then pulled Rhys into a tight hug. "Don't die, or I'll kill you."

"Same with you," Rhys patted his brother's back and let go. "Zaruna, look after Ujuu," he winked before giving her a gentle hug.

"Of course I vill," she beamed, tears brimming in her magenta eyes.

"I love you Rhys," Myrl hugged his son for a brief moment, then let go. "I'm proud of you. You are just like your mother. There's no stopping her when she has her heart set on something."

"Love you too, Pater," Rhys bowed to his father, then took

Soraya's hand. "So, where are we off to?" he asked while boarding the ship with her.

The girl gazed into his beautiful crimson eyes as they glinted in the rising sun before placing a hand on her chin. "Well," Soraya pondered. "I think I should use Telpathia. I want to see if I can find the demon's lair so we have an idea of where to go."

"You heard the lady," Marlot said, stretching his knuckles till they popped. "But maybe let Rhys, Jacquelle or I do the negotiating if they happen to sense your presence, alright?"

"Hey!" Soraya pouted, causing the rest of the group to laugh at her.

Seconds later, Marlot stood behind the helm. Soraya was next to him, searching for other demonic souls within her left eye. Rhys held her hand, giving her a gentle squeeze.

"That cluster is really far away," Soraya commented, pointing at some floating, fiery orbs hovering just over the horizon. "That dark red one is glowing the brightest…"

"Let's look into that one then," Rhys suggested as he looked out over the Valtic Ocean despite not being able to see it. "You can call it over, right?"

"Yes, if I really focus on it while curling my fingers," the girl explained while doing the motions. The orb moved across the ocean towards them at a steady speed, then stopped several hundred feet away.

"Did you get it yet?" Moiya asked, her green gems sparkling.

"No, it's still super far from us," Soraya admitted.

"Oh come on!" Jacquelle sighed impatiently. "It'll take forever at this pace!"

"Hold on," Marlot laughed. He used Air Magic to unfurl the sails, then switched to Water Magic for hoisting up the anchor. "We'll set sail and get closer."

The Black Dog rose and took to the skies. The kids waved at Mr. Leyo, Ujuu and Zaruna on the dock below and watched the shore and land fall away from the bottom of the ship. The ground shrank in size the higher they climbed into the air.

"Almost there!" Soraya exclaimed. "Just keep going straight."

Several minutes went by before she was able to successfully summon the orb and have it float in the palm of her hand. "Everyone, quiet," she said before leaning her face into the fiery red sphere. Although the flames crackled and danced with intensity, the ball was filled with darkness.

"Hello?" Soraya called into it.

Instantly, the demon hybrid she had contacted opened its eyes.

"Igo no sorehsan, adiuva sodse!"

The girl almost fell backwards in shock.

*My older sister, save me?*

"Malik," Soraya whispered. "Igo no fratello?"

"Jai! Adonia va nos no mamasan-" the boy went silent and turned his head, listening to approaching footsteps echoing around the white room.

"Oh my, you shouldn't be awake," a slick tongued voice slithered from the orb in Casmerahn. A man with long, silvery hair and eyes of the same color came into view. "Can't have you causing trouble, little demon King."

"Kill this man!" the boy screamed in Casmerahn. "Kill Zinvi and set me free!"

The urge to obey the child's command overtook Soraya's body, but she didn't know how to carry out the order since she was miles away from her younger brother.

Rhys and Jon were careful not to speak aloud, but they inched forward and eyed the girl warily, making motions with their hands to grab her attention.

Soraya held up a hand to let them know she was alright before leaning close to the orb again.

"Who are you talking to?" Zinvi demanded as he plunged a needle into the boy's cuffed arm and drew blood from him. "Are you trying to contact someone and have them save you?"

The vision within the orb narrowed. "Your army will turn on you," Malik continued in Casmerahn. "They can't help but obey me-"

"Since you won't answer my question, back to sleep you go!" The silver eyed man laughed while injecting another needle into the kid's arm. This one was a syringe filled with a dark yellow liquid. "It's my army," Zinvi clicked his tongue. "Don't forget that."

The imagery within the orb clouded over, turning black once more when the boy fell into a deep slumber.

"The powerful one in Zinvi's possession..." Soraya told her friends in a shaky voice. "The one who Mülock wants me to kill... it's my younger brother, Malik!"

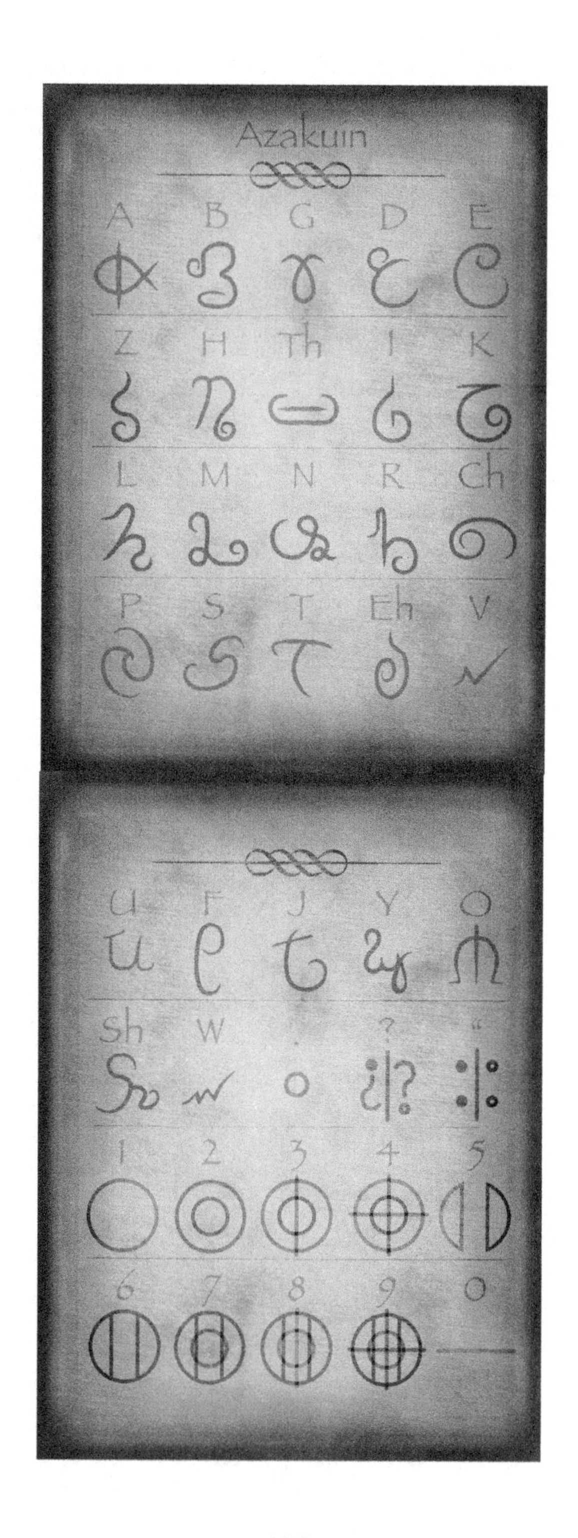
Azakuin
A B G D E
Z H Th I K
L M N R Ch
P S T Eh V
U F J Y O
Sh W . ? "
1 2 3 4 5
6 7 8 9 0

**Name Pronunciations:**

Soraya: Soar-rai-ya

Thenayu: Thin-eh-you

Tishva: Tish-va

Adonia: A-doe-n-ya

Yosef: Yo-sef

Kalisha: Ka-lee-sha

Rhys: Ree-s

Ujuu: U-ju

Leyo: Lay-o

Moiya: Moi-ya

Jacquelle: Jac-ell

Marlot: Mar-low

Myrl: Mur-l

Ayla: Eh-la

Zaruna: Za-ru-na

Markies: Mar-keys

Runolio - Ru-nol-i-o

Komoreby: Ko-mor-eh-be

Yabo: Ya-bo

Amraphael: Am-ra-fai-el

**About the Author/Illustrator:**

Christina Anne Silva was born and raised in California, has moved an ungodly amount of times across the United States, and is currently residing in North Dakota. She and her husband, Santiago, play music together in their band, Project : Constellation.
When Christina isn't driving a forklift, cake decorating, writing, drawing, or playing violin, she's spending time with her amazing family.

Thank you for reading my story!

**Special Thanks**

When I started my writing journey, I went from someone who was terrified of sharing my writings to self publishing nearly two years later.

There are so many people I would like to thank for giving me encouragement, support, feedback, and leaving positive reviews.

RowanCarver, SeanScruffy, MarieLotte, EpicsofNoche, Nefertitifenison, Tin2rh7, SuVida77, Project_velocity, AncientDoom, Apple_Brooklyn, Fayesther, AziaElga, Hn1kk0, MarjorieK64, YelenaLugin, Willvote4u, Silverlyrebird, Philipshen, JH_Foliage, Gareth92, K-J-Whitten, DaniBrull, ChloeQuinn, Hottiesoftie, Pipwusa and many more.

All of these people are incredible authors and wonderful people, please check out their stories on Wattpad and Amazon.

Thank you all for your support,
it means everything to me.

Made in the USA
Middletown, DE
10 May 2022

65492938R00272